Praise for
Dennis Danvers and
TIME AND TIME AGAIN

"*TIME AND TIME AGAIN* is a tremendous and powerful work of fiction that packs the punch and suspense of the movie *Dead Again*. Dennis Danvers is a great author. . . ."

—Harriet Klausner, *Affaire de Coeur*

"Dennis Danvers has written a unique and intriguing tale of repeating life patterns. . . ."

—Jill Smith, *Romantic Times*

"Danvers has many of the virtues of a true novelist. . . . He will go far."

—*Los Angeles Times*

"Danvers is a polished writer. . . . *TIME AND TIME AGAIN* is a love story . . . [that] says volumes about the power of love and the limits of imagination."

—Theresa Ducato, *Booklist*

"Danvers, author of the suspenseful, erotic, contemporary love story *Wilderness*, firmly establishes his place as an offbeat but exciting romance author with *TIME AND TIME AGAIN*. . . . Strong undercurrents of passion and suspense combine to produce a fast-paced, well-written, and non-formulaic romance novel."

—*Library Journal*

Books by Dennis Danvers

Wilderness
Time and Time Again

Published by Pocket Books

TIME and TIME Again

DENNIS DANVERS

POCKET BOOKS

New York   London   Toronto   Sydney   Tokyo   Singapore

This book is a work of fiction. Names, characters, places and incidents are products of the author's imagination or are used fictitiously. Any resemblance to actual events or locales or persons, living or dead, is entirely coincidental.

POCKET BOOKS, a division of Simon & Schuster Inc.
1230 Avenue of the Americas, New York, NY 10020

ISBN: 0-671-53448-3

First Pocket Books printing August 1995

10 9 8 7 6 5 4 3 2 1

POCKET and colophon are registered trademarks of Simon & Schuster Inc.

Front cover illustration by Honi Werner

Printed in the U.S.A.

For my stepgrandfather, Howard
For my stepdaughters, Ginger, Katia, and Marina
And for my stepgrandson, Jake

Jesus said, "If you bring forth what is within you,
what you bring forth will save you.
If you do not bring forth what is within you,
what you do not bring forth will destroy you."

Gospel of Thomas 45:29–33

... the novelist explores a virtual past, a past of his
own creation, and "the truth that he assumes" has
its roots in that created history.

Feeling and Form, SUZANNE LANGER

TIME and TIME Again

DUMFRIES, *November* 20, 1769.

WHEREAS my wife *Susanna Grier,* clandestinely absconded from my house in *Dumfries,* on *Monday* the 30th of *October* last, carrying with her by water some of my most valuable effects and houshold furniture, viz. two Negro children, RACHEL, a girl of 5 years old, JESS, a boy of 3, and a white boy, her son, of 14 years old, of a sickly complexion, with one dozen of silver spoons a silver ladle, one dozen of silver tea-spoons, marked R*S*G, two trunks, two tables, a little chest, some china ware, a gun, a watch, two beds, and kitchen furniture, too tedious to relate. I am informed she went for *Norfolk,* and it is suppose is gone off with one *Anthony Richards,* a convict, who came in two years ago, whom I set free, and entertained in my house as I had a good opinion of him; but he has turned out a fellow of consummate villany and ingratitude. He is about 6 feet high, 30 years of age, long faced, pock pitted, large mouth, black hair tied behind; he has had good education, and talks fluently, is as genteel in person as insinuating in address. He carried off my horse with him, and several valuable books, went off about the same time she did, and was seen going down the country towards *Norfolk.*

Any person therefore who will apprehend them, so as I shall recover my effects, shall have TEN POUNDS reward; and I hereby forewarn all persons whatever not to give her credit on my account, as I will not pay any of her debts. I likewise forewarn all masters of vessels from carrying them out of this colony

ROBERT GRIER.

I WAS SITTING IN THE READING ROOM OF THE VIRGINIA HISTORI-cal Society, where I worked, about halfway through rewinding a microfilm of the *Virginia Gazette* some patron had left in one of the readers. There was something wrong with the machine. It made a horrible whining sound when it got going too fast, so I was rewinding the film in wailing spurts, absentmindedly staring at the screen, watching the words blur and return to clarity as I stopped and started. I was reminded of the old movie cliché where a whirling news-paper comes flying toward the audience and fills up the screen with a significant headline. Nothing much exciting here though—tedious proclamations from the governor, two-century-old gossip, ads for slave auctions and land lotteries.

The machine screamed like a derailing train, and I let up on the switch. There, a little left of center, in a jumble of ads and announcements, the words *clandestinely absconded* seemed to jump out at me. This was more like it. Curious, I read the following letter:

Dumfries, Nov. 20, 1769

Whereas my wife Susanna Grier clandestinely absconded from my house in Dumfries, on Monday the 30th of October last, carrying with her by water some of my most valuable effects and household furniture, viz. two Negro children, Rachel, a girl of 5 years old, Jess, a boy of 3, and a white boy, her son, of 14 years old, of a sickly complexion, with one dozen of silver spoons, a silver ladle, and one dozen of silver teaspoons, marked RG, two trunks, two tables, a little chest, some china ware, a gun, a watch, two beds, and kitchen furniture, too tedious to relate. I am informed she went for Norfolk, and it is supposed is gone off with one Anthony Richards, a convict, who came in two years ago, whom I set free, and entertained in my house as I had a good opinion of him; but he has turned out a fellow of consummate villainy and ingratitude. He is about 6 feet high, 30 years of age, long faced, pock pitted, large mouth, black hair tied behind; he has had good education, and talks fluently, is as genteel in person as insinuating in address. He carried off my horse with him, and several valuable books, went off about the same time she did, and was seen going down the country towards Norfolk.

Any person therefore who will apprehend them, so I shall recover my effects, shall have TEN POUNDS reward; and I hereby forewarn all persons whatever not to give her credit on my account, as I will not pay any of her debts. I likewise forewarn all masters of vessels from carrying them out of this colony.

Robert Grier

I read it again, more slowly this time. I fancied I could hear Robert's voice, brittle with rage and humiliation. I fished some discarded Xeroxes out of the trash can and got one of the little pencils we keep by the card catalogue. Everyone was described but Susanna. I supposed, if I were

Robert, I wouldn't want to describe a wife who'd run off with a convict. She was pretty no doubt. I wrote her name on the paper. I saw her as a tall woman, about thirty-five, with thick red hair. A *widow,* I wrote beside her name. I liked her. She was the center of the story, the one with a choice to make, the one who forced others to choose.

Her son, Grier said. Why not *my son* or *our son?* I gave him a name. *William,* I wrote, *Susanna's son by Miles, S's 1st husband, dead 9 yrs.* He'd wanted to go. He liked this convict. I saw him driving the wagon, the convict at his side. Jess and Rachel, part of the *household furniture* to Robert, sat beside Susanna in the back. He was asleep; she stared sadly at the road behind them. I wrote down their names, wondered whom they'd left behind. *Nancy and Jesse,* I wrote, *adult slaves.* I pictured them sitting in a dark, smoky kitchen, talking. *They love one another,* I wrote.

I read the letter over again. Why did Robert wait three weeks to write it? Even in 1769, they were long past being "apprehended," after that much time. It must've been a formality, a legal loose end, but his rage got the better of him when he came to the subject of *one Anthony Richards.* I saw Anthony most clearly of all, much handsomer than Robert made him sound and every bit as charming. I wrote down his name, with as much flourish as I could manage with a three-inch pencil, and wrote: *sexy villain.* I smiled to myself—there was nothing like a sexy villain to help a plot along.

I pushed the copy button on the microfilm machine and watched the copy slide slowly into the bin. It was manna from heaven.

"Thank you, Robert," I said, and hummed along with the machine's whine as I rewound the rest of the film. I had the seeds for a new novel.

The Historical Society was my "day job"—the one that paid the bills but didn't interfere too much with my work. My true vocation (or addiction, according to my deceased husband) was writing novels—at age forty-two, six I admitted to, five unpublished. The last one—*Noah's Raven*—had been out for about a year. My editor told me it was a promising beginning for a new writer. Since then, I'd been thrashing around for a new book with three false starts, each one worse than the one before. When I came across Robert Grier's letter, I knew my search was over.

I looked over my sheet of paper and added a younger son, James, for Robert and Susanna, a son she leaves behind, the image of his father, a small-minded fool. I thought about carrying the novel on with this young son's life and perhaps his descendants. I got some more paper out of the trash can and started sketching out a plot. I was in the middle of figuring out a rough genealogy, when Andrea, my favorite co-worker, flashed the lights and teased me in a playful singsong, "Yoo-hoo, Marion, we've been closed for thirty minutes. You have to come back to earth now. The world is calling."

"Oh shit," I wailed, and jumped up from the microfilm reader, banging my knee, scooping up the pages I'd strewn on every flat surface around me.

Andrea leaned against the doorframe and watched me scurry about. "Day care just called," she said. "I think you've been naughty. What the hell you been doing, anyway? I didn't even know you were still here."

I waved the sheets of paper at her like a sheaf of hundred-dollar bills. "A new novel," I said.

Andrea shook her head. "Marion, you are too much. You need to get a life—a *real* life."

"Two kids is more than enough reality for me," I said on my way out the door.

I ran to my car and raced to Happy Grove Day Care, where a pissed-off Tiffany or Alison or Brendan—I could never keep them straight—stood waiting with my two stepdaughters, Kareth and Lorena, twelve and seven respectively.

"Where've you been?" Kareth wanted to know.

"The eighteenth century," I joked, and told them about the letter I'd found. They listened politely. They were used to their stepmother getting wacked out about some story or other.

"Can we go out for dinner?" Kareth asked, and I agreed, saying we were "celebrating my new book." They toasted me with Shirley Temples.

I STARTED READING EVERYTHING I COULD GET MY HANDS ON about eighteenth-century Virginia. I dragged the kids to Colonial Williamsburg and embarrassed them by quizzing the interpreters mercilessly. Whenever I had a free moment at work, I tried to track down more information about my characters. I found out that Anthony had come over on the *Justitia,* even found his Old Bailey number. I found out nothing much about the Griers, except that Robert left some substantial debts behind him when he died.

There were reams of genealogical records at the Historical Society I could've plowed through, but by this time the characters and their story were becoming so clear to me, the truth about them would just be a distraction, so I started writing, getting up at four every morning and working till I had to get the kids to school and me to my job. I wrote the first three chapters up to the day of Anthony and Susanna's flight in a few months. Then I was stuck, completely blocked. I couldn't figure out what was wrong. I just couldn't write it. I revised, I made outlines, I did more research, but it didn't matter.

One afternoon, after about three months of this, I took a sick day and drove through the rain to Dumfries, where Susanna's story had supposedly taken place. I looked at the tombstones, toured the little museum. I took a dozen Polaroid pictures—buildings, streets, tombstones whose inscriptions were worn away—and spread them out on my table in a diner across from William's Ordinary, an eighteenth-century tavern—one of three Colonial buildings still standing in Dumfries. It looked embarrassed there. I drank coffee and watched the building for a couple of hours but could never decide what it was being used for now. Not that it mattered. It was obvious that Robert didn't drink there anymore. It was obvious, driving down Highway 1 back to Richmond, that the Griers didn't live anywhere around here anymore—unless they'd opened a body shop or a driving range or a Taco Bell.

The problem with my novel wasn't the time or the place—it was as real to me as places I'd lived in my childhood. The problem was the people who lived there. They were keeping secrets from me, even though I'd made them up and figured I should know them inside out.

So I put an Author's Query in the *New York Times Book Review* for any information about Anthony Richards, the Griers, or their descendants. I felt silly doing it. What did the historical characters matter anyway? I was writing a novel, not a history.

A few weeks later, I was about to ditch the whole project, when I got a call from a man who introduced himself as Raymond Lord in a rich, melodious voice. He'd read my query, he said. He had quite a bit of material on the Griers, including a travel journal by their great-granddaughter that I might find particularly interesting. He lived in a restored plantation in Culpeper County. Would I care to come to dinner on Saturday?

Nothing could've kept me away.

MY DESTINATION WAS A PLANTATION NAMED GREENVILLE, EQUI-distant from D.C. and Richmond, an hour's drive northwest from Richmond, pretty much in the middle of nowhere. I was about halfway, going north on Highway 522, looking for the first turn past the Rapidan River, before I thought much about what I was doing—driving to a strange man's house in the middle of nowhere because he'd read my ad in the *Times*. I could hear my mother saying, *I don't know if that's such a good idea, dear.*

But it's for a story, I would've said back to her. Tom, my husband, used to complain that I lived in my own little world, that I thought more about what the people I made up were doing than about my own behavior. Now that Tom had been dead for four years, and I couldn't argue with him about it anymore, I had to agree he was right. The girls had been eight and three when Tom died in a rock-climbing accident at the age of forty. The rock-climbing trip had been my birthday present to him. We'd been married almost exactly a year. That seemed like a very long time ago now. Now, it seemed like it'd always been just me and the girls.

A white board sign materialized out of the darkness: *CUCKOO*. Whatever Cuckoo consisted of, I couldn't see it in the dark, but according to the directions Raymond had given me over the phone, my turn would be about twenty miles ahead. I stared hard at the road and tried to picture Raymond in my mind. He had a voice like Ronald Colman, only with an Old Virginia aristocratic accent. "River" had been "rivah." "House" was almost "hoose" but managed some diphthong in between. That accent usually intimidated me—such people often ended up asking who "my people" were and then looked quietly distressed when I told them my dad had been a traveling salesman from Texas. But I'd liked Raymond's voice—warm, familiar, and sexy. I'd liked it just fine.

It'd started to snow, a light flurry. If it was snowing back in Richmond, my girls would go crazy. Snow always shut the city down. Everyone mobbed the grocery stores, and school was always canceled. Everything stopped, while children went through three changes of ice-encrusted clothes and adults drank hot toddies. This didn't look like it was going to amount to much though.

I checked my watch. It was taking me a little longer to get to Greenville than I'd planned. I'd have to be sure to leave early. The only person I could find to stay with the girls on such short notice was their Aunt Ruth, Tom's little sister—twenty-seven and still living at home, a clone of her mother.

Kareth had rolled her eyes and stamped a foot when she got the news. "Couldn't you just chain us up in the basement or something?"

"She's your aunt," I offered lamely. "She's very fond of you."

7

"You called her a 'tight-ass little bitch' after the last time you talked to her on the phone."

"That was the time before last. The *last* time, I told her she was a sweetheart for staying with you guys. She may not be entertaining, Kareth, but you'll be safe with her."

"Safe—more like sterilized or something."

"Accept your fate, Kareth. It's not like I go out that often."

"Okay, okay," she intoned as she walked up the stairs, her hands in the air as if beseeching the gods.

About two weeks after Tom died, Ruth had come by to have some coffee, to comfort me, and to get a few things she knew Tom would've wanted her to have. She asked me as she sat with his microscope in her lap, twirling the focus and peering at nothing, "Have you found Cathy yet?"

Cathy was the girls' biological mother. She'd left on the trail of cocaine a year before I met Tom. She'd called a couple of times before I was in the picture—once from Albuquerque and once from California—asking Tom for money, but after she called from Texas and I told her Tom had remarried, she never called again. The only communication she'd had with the girls had been a birthday card for Kareth that arrived on Lorena's birthday.

"Why would I want to find Cathy?" I asked Ruth, hoping that what I thought she was thinking couldn't be right.

"To take the kids," she said, looking into the microscope again. "I mean—they *are* hers. You're still young enough to get married again. What would you want with somebody else's kids?" She looked up from the lens and smiled at me, taking a sip from her coffee, completely unaware I wanted to strangle her. "At least that's what Mom says," she added, as if I didn't already know exactly what Tom's mother had to say on any subject.

I FOUND THE TURN EASILY, A SNOW-SPRINKLED ROAD THAT RAN parallel to the river between broad fields. A neat white fence ran along the north side of the road—the horse farm

Raymond told me would be a landmark. The fence seemed to hang suspended in the darkness. I topped a low rise and my headlights caught a sign swinging from chains beside a narrow drive that turned south toward the river. I slowed to a crawl. *Greenville,* the sign said in large letters, and beneath in smaller script, *est. 1850.*

The road led to a circular drive, a huge frozen fountain in the middle. I parked behind a royal-blue Hudson, gleaming as if it were new. I guessed it to be a 1950. I pressed my face against the driver's window, cupped my hands around my eyes, and looked inside. Everything was original. Every bit of chrome gleamed. The radio looked like it could pick up *The Inner Sanctum.* The door was unlocked. The keys were even in the ignition. I just wanted to sit in it, smell that old-car smell. My father'd had a '50, not quite as upscale as this one. It'd been his favorite car, a legend in our family.

With my hand on the door handle, I looked up at the house. Four huge white columns in the front made it look as if the snow had risen into the air to form them. The house itself was a huge brick box, three floors, with a verandah off the second floor. The whole place was lit up. Lights lined the stone walk. A plaque by the front door announced it was a Virginia Historic Landmark. I told myself what I would've told my kids—that maybe it wasn't such a good idea to get inside this man's car without asking first.

I STOOD BENEATH THE COLUMNS AND LOOKED UP. THEY ROSE AT least forty feet into the air and were more than six feet across. "Subtle," I said to myself, just as the door opened, and I almost burst out laughing.

But when I saw the man who opened the door, my mirth vanished. He was the most beautiful man I'd ever seen. His eyes were large and somber, the color of burnt cork. His face, with its strong cheekbones and angular features, seemed fashioned from chiseled oak. A thin scar ran from his scalp along his nose to his chin. I wanted to know the story behind it. I wanted to touch it.

He was smiling at me as if I were an old flame and he was overjoyed to see me. I smiled back, but I couldn't say anything. I just stood there like a post. I was suddenly aware of the emptiness at my back, the snow sifting down in the lights that circled the fountain. My hand shook as I finally thought to offer it to him.

"Raymond Lord," he said, and took my hand like Charles Boyer might've done, with a slight bow, still looking into my eyes. "And you're Marion Mead, though you're much prettier than your book photo."

"You've read *Noah's Raven?*" I failed to keep the incredulity out of my voice. He'd led me into the foyer and was taking my coat.

"I read it before I answered your query. I thought of it as a way of getting to know you. I liked it a great deal. The heroine intrigued me." He laughed at himself. "I found myself wanting to step into the book and rescue her from her perils."

I laughed nervously. "She'd just invent new ones."

"She was young," he said, as if that forgave everything, as if he were speaking of someone real. "I hope you didn't have any trouble finding the place."

He stood close, studying me. There was something familiar about him, but unsettling and sexy, like a lover in an erotic dream. "No, your directions were quite clear," I said. "Once I got past Cuckoo, I couldn't miss it."

He smiled at this. "I was concerned when I saw it was snowing."

"It's nothing. Just a light flurry. It won't amount to anything."

He listened to this as if I were actually saying something significant, or it didn't matter what I was saying—he just wanted to hear the sound of my voice. I wondered if we were alone in the house. He offered his arm. "Welcome to Greenville," he said. "I'm so glad you've come."

He led me to a spiral staircase at the back of the foyer. "While we're here I wanted to show you my favorite feature

10

of the house." We leaned out to look up the sinuous helix winding up through the middle of the house. It seemed to go on and on. High above us, rococo cherubs smiled from a dazzling blue sky.

"In the original house," Raymond said, the both of us still leaning into the stairwell, "the main entrance was on the middle floor, but I couldn't resist this staircase from down here. Sometimes I go up and down it for no reason whatsoever."

"The painting on the ceiling, is that original to the house?"

"No. I had it done after a ceiling in London. I sketched it from memory and hired an art student to paint it for me. I'm too impatient to paint a ceiling myself."

"May I see it?" I asked as we righted ourselves.

"Certainly."

I took the banister and followed Raymond to the top, the smooth wood sliding through my hand. He moved gracefully, looking back over his shoulder several times as if to make sure I was still there. We stood side by side at the railing on the third floor and looked down into the circle of light that was the foyer. "Very nice," I said.

The cherubs were now only a couple of yards over my head. They were all laughing. One even had his eyes closed, lying on his back, his arms and legs thrashing with glee. Raymond kept his eyes on me as I admired them.

"I love it," I said.

He beamed. "I'm glad you like it."

A young Asian woman stepped into the foyer below us and called up the stairwell in a language I didn't recognize. Raymond answered her in the same language, then spoke to me. "Marion, this is Rachel. She wishes to know if you'd like a cocktail before dinner."

"Scotch on the rocks," I said.

"Like your heroine in *Noah's Raven.*"

He spoke to Rachel in the strange language again, then in English, saying, "Rachel, this is Miss Mead."

11

"Marion," I called down to her, and gave her a small wave. "Call me Marion."

Rachel nodded at me furiously, smiling all the while as she disappeared from view.

"She's new to this country," Raymond said. "She finds our informality a bit intimidating sometimes. We don't get too many visitors out here"—he gestured at the house around him and laughed—"except carpenters and painters and plasterers and plumbers."

"It's beautiful."

"Thank you. I thought we could have our cocktails in the library. I can show off the rest of my house later."

"I'd love it," I said. "The library's downstairs, I hope. I want the experience of descending the stairs."

"By all means," he said.

We walked down, slowly, our footsteps echoing in the stairwell.

"I love that sound," he said.

AT THE BOTTOM OF THE STAIRS, HE LED ME TO A PAIR OF DOORS, the same deep red wood as the banister. The door handles were iron sea serpents set in a bowl-shaped recess with stars above and waves below.

I stepped through the doorway, froze, and gaped. Books lined every wall—forty feet from floor to ceiling. Balconies ran around the perimeter at the second and third floors. There was a large stained-glass window on the second floor, but I couldn't see it clearly from where I stood. Shelves and balconies and doors curved seamlessly, giving the illusion that the room was round, a cylinder the size of a grain silo stuffed with books on cherrywood shelves; maple grapevines twined in profusion; a chandelier the size of my van hung from the ceiling; a circle of overstuffed leather chairs ringed the blazing fireplace.

"Jesus Christ!" I said, and Raymond laughed.

"I'm glad you like it," he said.

I looked around the room trying to make out some of the titles of the books that surrounded us, but all I could discern was that many of the bindings were incredibly old. On the ground floor, where the corners would've been in a square room, the shelves were twice interrupted by wide, shallow drawers, also curved. I guessed they probably contained maps and scrolls, perhaps even stone tablets. At the outside corner of the house was a door covered with a high-relief carving of a street scene. It looked medieval. At our feet was a cherry-and-willow compass rose maybe twelve feet from point to point. "Did you design this room?" I asked. "Surely all this can't be original."

"None of it is, actually. I gutted the three rooms that used to form this corner of the house to make the library. I suppose I should've at least done everything to period, but I wanted it varied, like the books on the shelves."

"May I look?"

"Of course."

Most of the books were old, some were new. They were in every language. Most were completely obscure to me, quite beyond my English major's provincial grasp of the history of books. I couldn't detect any principle of organization. There were clusters of languages and periods but no larger pattern. A shelf of very old-looking Arabic texts sat next to a row of English novels whose authors were unknown to me, and whose titles in gold were things like *The Rake Undone* and *The Lady Regrets*. Beside them was a squat row of old, simply bound volumes with no markings at all on the spines. There were even several shelves packed with videotapes of old cartoons. Here and there, sitting among the books, were carved animals.

"How do you find anything?" I asked.

He smiled at me again, that lover's smile I'd seen at the door. "I have a prodigious memory. I usually find what I want."

I looked away from his intense eyes, back to the room around us. "I like your library," I said. "I love stories. Any kind. My husband used to say that I preferred stories to reality, that I'd like to take up residence in one of my books."

"You are divorced?"

"I'm a widow."

"I'm sorry."

I nodded at the fire, never knowing what to say when people comforted me. I was sorry Tom was dead, but I wasn't sorry I was a widow. "And you?" I asked. "Are you married? Divorced?"

"I'm a middle-aged bachelor," he said. "Something of a dying breed."

A set of doors opened behind us, and Rachel brought in our drinks. I took mine and thanked her. She bowed and left quickly, closing the doors behind her without a sound.

"Shall we sit?" Raymond asked, gesturing toward the oxblood chairs. They wheezed as we sat in them. The leather was soft and pliable like old gloves. I imagined myself in a huge leather-clad hand.

"So tell me," he said, "how did you come to write a book about Anthony Richards and the Griers?"

I told him the story of finding the letter in the *Virginia Gazette*. He hung on my every word, asking for clarification of the smallest detail.

"So it was a complete accident. You'd never heard of these people before. If that particular microfilm hadn't been left out, you might never have come to write this book." This seemed to please him a great deal, though I wasn't sure why. "I remember reading that letter," he said. "It's really quite pathetic."

"I suppose it is. But the man has lost his wife and son."

"I believe he called him *her* son, hardly the bereaved father. And they'd fled three weeks before. He took his sweet time, don't you think?"

It was a rare treat to have someone to talk to about my characters, someone who seemed to have thought about them (or at least the people they were based on) a great deal himself. It didn't hurt that I found him so attractive. I said, "That's one of the things I try to explain in my book."

"And what else do you try to explain?"

"Why a woman would leave her husband to run off with a convict."

"Perhaps she was in love with him."

"I don't think so."

"Because he was a convict?"

"I don't know. I just don't think she was." I laughed. "At least in my book she isn't."

He smiled. "I suppose that's what matters. How far along are you?"

"I've written up to their flight—three chapters. Lately, it hasn't been going so well—Susanna's being stubborn."

"Then she's real to you?"

"In a sense. My characters are very real to me—when I'm lucky."

He nodded, seeming to give this more thought than it deserved. "Perhaps I can change your luck," he said. "What have you been able to find out about the Griers and Mr. Richards?"

"Besides the ad, nothing much of anything. I know that Anthony came over on the *Justitia*. I found his Old Bailey number."

"And what was his crime?"

"I don't know. I never pursued it. I knew I wanted to make him a counterfeiter, so there wasn't any point."

He nodded his approval. "Why did you decide on a counterfeiter?"

I shrugged. "Sometimes it's hard to remember the process exactly. I was reading a book on crime in the eighteenth century, and how counterfeiting was considered treason then—one of the few crimes punishable by being burned at the stake, like witches. It seemed like the perfect crime for Anthony. I guess it's because people put their faith in him, but he's not what he seems."

"By people, you mean Susanna and Robert?"

"And the boy, Susanna's son."

A troubled look passed over his face, and he touched the scar on his forehead lightly with the tips of his fingers.

"Are you all right?"

He smiled. "I'm fine. I was just thinking of the boy—caught up in the madness of his elders. It's a theme, I'm afraid, that strikes too close to home." He swirled his brandy and took a sip. It was then, as he looked up at me, I realized that behind his apparent pleasure in my company, he was a sad, even wounded man. "Have you been able to find anything further on Susanna or Robert?" he asked.

"Nothing on Susanna. Robert died shortly after the Revolution, leaving quite a substantial debt behind him."

"Sometimes death is the only way to settle a debt."

"I don't know. I'd rather not have to die for my Mastercard."

"Indeed," he said, laughing—a deep, resonant laugh that made me feel witty and appreciated.

There was a light rap at the door, apparently a signal from Rachel that dinner was served. He rose to his feet and offered his arm. "Let's move into the dining room, shall we?"

THE DINING ROOM WAS SURPRISINGLY SIMPLE AND UNADORNED. The flooring looked original. The sideboard, table, and chairs were boxy and primitive, all the edges worn smooth from years of use. The table was set for several courses.

"What shall I call you?" he asked as he held my chair. "Do you like Marion? Mary? Mare?"

I looked up at him. "Marion."

He looked into my eyes, towering over me. "Marion. It's pretty. It suits you."

"Thank you," I said, and lowered my eyes like some embarrassed girl.

He walked around the table and sat across from me. "Who chose it for you?"

"My father. If I'd been a boy, I would've been Robin. My dad was a great fan of Errol Flynn."

"Why wouldn't he have just named you Errol?"

"I asked him that once, and he looked at me like I was nuts. I think it was a sacred name to him—too great a burden for any child to bear."

"And what does he think of Kevin Costner?"

"I don't know. My father's dead."

"I'm sorry," he said.

I expected him to change the subject. Most people do when it comes to death. Instead he poured wine for us both and said, "But what do you imagine—If your father *were* alive, what would he think of Kevin Costner?"

I laughed. "Oh, that's easy. He'd hate him. He'd refuse to go see the movie, maybe set fire to any reviews that implied that this imposter could ever measure up to Errol. He was an Errol Flynn man all the way."

Raymond nodded his approval. "Bogart?" he asked.

"Not charming enough."

"Cary Grant?"

"My dad liked a hero to swing from things—ropes, chains, chandeliers—whatever came to hand."

"Weissmuller?"

I made a face. "Tarzan might be adorable, but he was never charming."

We both laughed at this and smiled at each other. "And what would he think of me?" he asked quietly.

His eyes that had seemed so frightening at first were full of kindness and affection, as if he were an old, familiar friend. "He'd like you," I said, "because you didn't let a little thing like death scare you away from talking about him. Thanks. I haven't gotten to talk about him much since my mom died."

"Did she like Errol Flynn?"

"She liked him okay. But she was absolutely, totally, completely crazy about my dad."

"A most fortunate man," said Raymond.

"He was crazy about her too."

"So you come from a happy family."

"I guess that makes me something of an oddity."

"Indeed."

"And what shall I call you? Raymond? Ray?"

"Well." He spread his hands in the air in a gesture of complete open-mindedness. "How do *you* see me?"

"Definitely a Raymond."

He picked up his glass, offering a toast. "Raymond and Marion it is, then."

RACHEL SERVED US AS IF SHE WERE INVISIBLE. PLATES APpeared and disappeared as if by magic. My wineglass was never empty. I suppose I should remember everything we ate, everything we talked about, but I can't. I just let myself sink into the ease of it, talking on and on about myself. He was tirelessly interested. I even told him about my first completed novel when I was eighteen, described its dreadfulness in great detail. It was about a fellow who lived in a Dumpster and called himself "Occupant" after the mail he received there.

He found even that amusing. I was lovely, I was fascinating, I was a great wit. It'd been a long time since anyone had been smitten with me, but here was this man my age, handsome, smart, sweet—even rich—who seemed totally enthralled with me. He wanted to hear the story of my life, and I wanted to tell it, though I edited shamelessly to create Marion the Romantic Artist. I didn't talk too much about Marion the Mom who spent her time taking kids to lessons and cooking tuna-noodle casserole after working all day at a tedious job.

Since Tom's death, I hadn't gone out with anyone more than twice, and usually only once. It wasn't widow's grief. I just wasn't interested. But Raymond was another matter. I was frighteningly interested. The fact was, I wanted him. By the time we finished dinner, I was thinking to myself, If this man doesn't sleep with me, I'll just die.

AFTER DINNER, WE HAD COFFEE IN THE LIBRARY IN FRONT OF THE fire, before my long drive home. I didn't want to go home, but after the third cup of coffee and several more stories from Marion's Life, my parenthood began nagging me like a chorus of wicked stepsisters, and I finally said, about two hours overdue, "I *really* have to go home now."

"But I haven't shown you the rest of the house," he objected with a smile.

"I'll have to take a rain check. The girls' aunt is none too graciously staying with them. She probably intends to murder me when I walk through the door. If I leave right now, she'll have another hour to decide on the means."

He laughed and rose to his feet. "Then I won't be an accessory. But we're almost forgetting why you came— Pearl's journal."

He led me to the carved door I'd noticed earlier. Close up I could see the carving was of a village, the street receding into the doorway. Tiny faces looked out from the windows lining the street. A sad-faced man with a donkey stood in the foreground.

"Is this medieval?" I asked him.

"The original was. It's a copy. The original was destroyed by fire." He pulled a latch concealed in the center and opened the door. "My study," he said.

It was tiny, just enough room for a secretary in the corner and two straight-back chairs. The secretary was covered with stacks of papers and journals; an old-fashioned inkwell and quill sat on the corner, a pewter mug full of pocket-knives next to that. To the right of the secretary was a small door I took to be a closet. There were no windows. The only decorations were carved animals, a shelf of them to the left of the secretary—a horse, a lion, a hippopotamus, a family of ducks. I picked up the lion. It looked like it could've come from a Rousseau painting. Its mane circled its head like a rainbow. "Did you make these?" I asked.

"Yes. I've always liked to whittle. An old man in Africa taught me all the real whittling I know. You can keep that lion if you like."

I put it back down. "I couldn't do that."

"I must have several dozen lions scattered throughout the house." He pointed at the shelf of animals. "These are the ones I've done in the last couple of months—the ducks took up some time. When the shelf gets too full, I move them out into the house. The library's full of them. I tell you what. I'll make you a lion of your own—the next time I see you."

He smiled at me and picked up a manila envelope and handed it to me. "Marion Mead" was written across the front of it in strokes I guessed had come from the quill. His handwriting was old-fashioned, romantic. The *M*'s were tall and elegant. I stared at my name as he spoke. "I only have a Xerox of the opening pages of Pearl Strickland's journal. The harsh lights really aren't good for the paper. But if you're interested in seeing the rest, you can come up anytime. On one condition."

"And what is that?" I asked, looking him in the face, clutching the envelope tightly to keep my hands from trembling.

"That I may read your novel in progress."

I broke into a smile, let out the breath I'd been holding. "I'd like that. I'd like that a lot. I could use a second opinion at this point."

He looked into my eyes. "Then we're collaborators." For a moment I thought he was going to kiss me. But then he stuck out his hand. It hovered there, motionless. I almost didn't take it, stared at it as if it were there simply for my examination. But abruptly, I released my death grip on the envelope, and my right hand shot out as if it were spring-loaded. He took it and squeezed it in both of his, holding it a moment before he let it go.

OUTSIDE, THE SNOW HAD STOPPED. EVERYTHING WAS STILL AND quiet, except for the sound of the river in the distance. The Hudson sat gleaming in the moonlight, dusted with snow. As we walked by it on the way to my van, holding hands and taking slow, leisurely steps, I couldn't believe I heard myself saying, "Would you mind if I sat in your car. My dad had one a lot like that when I was a kid."

He beamed and pulled the door open, showering our feet with snow. "Get behind the wheel," he said.

I slid across the soft, gray fabric and took a deep breath. It smelled just like my dad's car when I was a kid. Raymond came around and sat on the passenger's side. Shotgun, we used to call it. "You can drive it if you'd like," he said, holding up the keys.

I shook my head, ran my hands over the wheel, nearly as big around as the tires. The horn button was like the one I remembered from my dad's car—a plastic coat of arms with an elongated pyramid flanked by two castles above and two sailing ships below.

I pointed at the radio. "Six buttons, to spell out HUD-SON. Everybody else had five." I pushed them, watching the tuner jump from station to station. "My dad and I had this game when we were going somewhere by ourselves. We'd push each button, get a phrase from each one, and try to make up a story that made sense out of the whole thing.

"My dad was a traveling salesman. He'd take me and my mom with him in the summers to places like Waco and Beaumont and Waxahachie." I tossed my head toward the empty back seat. "I sat back there and listened to my mom and dad telling stories. Whenever he was home, I'd sneak into the garage and sit in his car and pretend I was driving, that I was out on the road."

I felt like high school kids on a date sitting in a parked car, the glass steamed over, our breath forming clouds in the air. "So how come someone like you never married?" I asked, holding the wheel, looking out over the hood.

"Someone like me?"

I looked over at him. "Handsome, wealthy, charming."

"I've been waiting for the right woman."

"Long wait," I said quietly.

He was looking at me, looking again as if he wanted to kiss me. I wanted to be kissed. He reached out and took my arm, and I let go of the wheel. He leaned toward me and kissed me, pulling me gently into his arms. I wrapped my arms around him, and we held each other close. I didn't want to let go. I didn't want to stop kissing him. His mouth was soft, familiar somehow, knowing. I gave myself over completely to this stranger's kiss, and when it was over, I wanted desperately to kiss him again, but instead I lay my cheek against his and whispered, "I'm afraid I really have to go." His arms loosened around me. I squeezed him tight and let him go, stepping out of the Hudson into the cold, before I decided to stay.

He took my hand and walked me to my van. I got in, started the engine, and rolled down the window, smiling at him, I was sure, like some moonstruck teenager. "Thank you for everything," I said. "I had a wonderful time."

He stood with his hand resting on the open window, looking at me with his dark, serious eyes. "Call me the moment you finish reading it," he said, pointing to the envelope that lay on the console beside me.

"All right."

He stepped closer. "Promise?"

I laughed. "I promise—I'll read it the minute I get home and call you in the middle of the night just to spite you."

"Nothing would delight me more," he said. He kissed my cheek and stepped back from the van.

As I drove away, I watched him in the rearview mirror, staring after me until I was out of sight.

As I drove home, courting speeding tickets all the way, I told myself this whole deal was too good to be true. I'm pretty smart, fairly pretty, but I'm nothing special. I'm just a middle-aged, single mom who writes stories so I can pretend to be someone else, or several someone elses. I'm not interesting, I'm not important. But Raymond looked at me as if I were intensely important.

If he wanted to think that, I would let him, as long as he'd kiss me like that. I sighed and remembered, a stupid smile on my face. I didn't really know him, and there was definitely something odd and brooding about him. But I didn't care. That just made him all the more intriguing and sexy. There was a flat, dull voice in my head advising me not to rush into anything, but I ignored it.

Besides, he had this journal. I glanced at the envelope on the seat beside me. It could be another dead end—a bunch of old recipes and comments on the weather—but I didn't think so, not coming from Raymond. I hadn't even asked him how he got hold of it. I'd been too busy telling him I was every bit as interesting as he seemed to think I was, too busy letting him know I was just as interested in him.

RUTH WAS ASLEEP ON THE SOFA, AND THE KIDS WERE IN BED. I didn't have to listen to Ruth's usual complaints about the kids' behavior and her analysis of just what I should do about it, because, when she saw the time, she was too pissed off to speak. It'd be a long time before I could ask Ruth to keep the kids again.

After she left, I checked on the girls. Lorena's tiny snore filled her room. Kareth called out in her sleep, "I'll do it! Give it to me!" but didn't stir.

I put on my robe and climbed up into my attic office, which is to say I laid plywood on the attic floor, stuck all my stuff up there, and called it an office. I had to step over the air-conditioning ducts to walk around, and it was an oven in the summer, but it was mine.

I turned on the lamp and sat at my desk. I pulled the stack of pages out of the envelope and laid them before me. Pearl, he'd said her name was. The crisp newness of the Xerox pages contrasted with the old-fashioned script. The old paper of her journal showed up on the copies as a pale gray, as if the words were suspended in smoke.

I hoped like hell I could use it. I wanted an excuse to call him, an excuse to go back to Greenville again as soon as possible.

Dear husband,

I don't know where to begin. Even my salutation is a bit hasty, since you are not my husband yet. I have spent hours wondering about you—who you are, what you care about. I thought perhaps you might have spent a little time wondering about me too. And I wished there was a way I could tell you—everything all at once—the things that husbands and wives know about each other that no one else knows.

This wish led me to the idea of writing those things down in this book and giving it to you when we meet in the Oregon Territory weeks hence. As you can see, this book is a feminine thing. I hope the flowers and lace don't put you off as you read it. I picked it out for myself when my mother said I should keep a devotional book and write down my thoughts and my prayers. Whenever I sat down to write in it, however, I felt foolish and stupid writing to no one.

But now I have you and a long boat ride to Panama, then another to Oregon, and I've already heard rumors, though we're barely out of sight of Charleston, that we may find ourselves waiting a good long while in Panama for the boat to Oregon. So you see, I have plenty of time to fill this book up with everything you should know so you won't be marrying a stranger. It will be my wedding present to you, if you still want to marry me after you've read it!

This morning I boarded the steamship Ohio off Charleston, going out to meet her in a small steamer whose tossing and bobbing left my fellow passengers (three gentlemen) hanging over the side with seasickness. The Ohio is really quite a splendid vessel. I am told it is called a "side-wheel steamer." I love to watch the churn of the wheels in the water. There are three decks, but I have only seen the top one where my cabin is. My cabin is splendid with lovely oak walls and cedar in the tiny closet. I have so few clothes, it is more than adequate for me. To tell you the truth, I open it just to smell the wood. My father was a cabinetmaker and taught me to love the smell of cedar, oak, and pine, scooping up handfuls of shavings and holding them to my nose when, as an adoring child, I would watch him work.

Mr. Morgan, one of the seamen, informed me that there are 250 cabins and 80 berths in steerage. I am not sure what "steerage" is, but I suppose I will learn. I paced off the dimensions of what will be my home for the next few weeks and estimate the boat to be 250 feet long and 50 feet wide. Several of the passengers, some of whom I'm afraid are already near death with seasickness, thought my striding up and down the boat in my longest stride (which is almost exactly three feet) a most peculiar sight, but I have never been on a boat of such a size and wished to know just how big this leviathan is!

The most wondrous thing about this vessel, however, is the elaborate carving which graces its prow—A Sea Monster! Its dragon head snarls at the waves and its serpent tail is at least 40 feet. It makes me think of the sailors long ago who used to imagine such creatures swallowing up their ships and yet took to the sea anyway! These men were much braver than I, who sail into the unknown with a cedar closet and a husband waiting for me.

I have studied the daguerreotype Mr. Tarrington passed on to me of you in the goldfields. You must tell me what it was like to be part of the Gold Rush! You are a very handsome man. Your hand gripping the shovel looks powerful and strong. You also look lonely and unhappy. I hope you don't mind my saying that, and I mean no fault by it, for when I've looked in the glass these last several years, it is the face I have seen on myself.

I regret that I had no likeness of myself to send you, but Mr. Tarrington said you were not particular about appearance. Well, if you are not, you will be the first man I've ever met! I do not think you will be displeased with me, however, for I have often been told I am quite pretty and confess I think myself so. I hope you won't think less of me for that, for I do know what beauty is worth by itself—less than nothing. Whether there is more to me than beauty, husband, you will have to decide for yourself.

But when you first see me, this is the creature you will behold: Tall (five feet, eight inches), with long dark hair, slender and rather long in the waist. My face is an oval with large blue eyes and high cheekbones, a mouth small but not thin-lipped, and a nose I fancy is too large but have had that opinion shouted down by everyone with whom I've ever shared it. I have good posture and (I blush to say it) a handsome figure.

As I read over the last paragraph I am tempted to strike it out, for I fear I am sounding the flirtatious coquette. But if a woman cannot flirt with her husband, then with whom may she flirt? And I have sworn myself to not crossing out a line that I say here, for I want you to know me just as I am. I want these pages to speak to you, and words said cannot be unsaid or called back from the air. If I resort to the cowardice of the bold black line through everything that gives me doubts, then how will I ever tell you all my secrets as I have sworn to do? In any event, when you read these lines you will already have seen me for yourself and reached your own conclusions.

This afternoon we saw Tybee Lighthouse through the veil of a misty shower. Now the sun is setting among the jagged piles of a broken thundercloud, and streaks of lightning like ribbons of light dart all round the horizon. This is a most wondrous thing to me who has led a landlocked life with my mother and my grandfather, never seeing the ocean until I journeyed to Charleston.

As I sit alone in my cabin, I wonder whether this book should rush to tell you everything about myself, or whether, as young girls do, it should proceed shyly. But alas, I am not so young—being twenty-five years old with hard adventures (which I will soon tell you of) that add years unseen by others and unmarked by birthdays. We, who have never seen each other, have agreed to marry! Surely the rashness is already done! What I may confess in this little book, whether it be tonight or years hence, will not quicken the current into which we have already plunged.

The storm has passed now, and the moon is rising over the water, reflecting from each wave as if the lightning had shattered and fallen into the sea. Such a time seems fitting to hold the mirror up to myself, and reflecting upon these pages, let you see—

When I think of my family, I think of my grandfather, James Grier, not because I bear him any great affection—I bear him none—but because I have been shaped by my family (I am tempted to say "whittled") and he has fashioned my family after his own image. He was raised by his father, Robert Grier, who was dead before I was born, but I fancy that the two of them were a great deal alike. His mother, Susanna, ran off with a convict named Anthony Richards, when James was but four years old. James's old slave Nancy told me the story when I was but a little girl. "Your granddaddy" (she told me by the light of the kitchen fire) "has a snake coiled round his heart just like his daddy who put it there!"

Whether his father put it there or not, I cannot attest, but that my grandfather has a serpent for a soul I can affirm with greatest surety. The effects of his venom showing most clearly in my mother, Faith, his daughter.

I never knew my grandmother, Sarah, except by way of a painting of her that hung in my grandfather's house. My mother says this painting was done before she was born, when my grandparents were first married. The only words I've ever heard spoken of my grandmother were when my grandfather would rail against my mother telling her she was a "whore" just like his mother! A "whore" just like his wife!

I do not know what my grandmother may have done to earn such approbation, but I can see her portrait in my mind's eye as if it were hanging before me in my tiny cabin (though I think she would sway a bit, for the wind that has blown away the storm seems to be stirring up the waves!). She looks out from the canvas, however, with a steady, thoughtful gaze, her hands folded in her lap. I fancy her, except that she is much prettier by far, with a strength in her that a man of sense should welcome in a helpmate. I do not think she was a harlot. Leastways, the man who looked on her and put his brush to canvas could not have thought so! Would that he had married her instead of my grandfather! Nor do I think my mother a harlot—whatever my mother's faults, harlotry was not one of them! But I shall speak of her presently.

My grandmother bore my grandfather four children—Robert, who was stillborn; James, who died in his sleep when he was but two; Daniel, who died at four while my mother, the fourth, was still a babe in arms. I think that Sarah's chief crime against my grandfather consisted of not giving him a son, for he mightily wanted a son. My mother, Faith, was small compensation in his eyes for three sons dead in the space of eight years.

You are probably saying to yourself by now—"She promises to tell me of herself, and yet prates on about her grandparents and her mother! When will she tell me something of herself?"

You are right. This is a poor meeting indeed. It is a hard thing to speak of myself, harder than I had thought. I have with me a bottle of brandy and a small tumbler, so I will share a drink with you, dear husband, and drink to our long and happy marriage.

I will be braver in the morning, and so, for now, good night.

Later the same night

Since I could not sleep, I went on deck to see the moon—marvelous and high overhead—until I was shooed indoors by a most petulant seaman who seemed to think waves would sweep me from the top deck simply because it was night! I thought to myself (before I was driven indoors) that the same moon shone on you, though it must be much lower in the sky. Good night once again. I sleep.

Wednesday, July 3, 1850

Dear husband,

I am once again in my cabin, pen in hand. It has been a day of diverse impressions. At dawn, we saw the lighthouse of St. Augustine, marking the land where the Spanish Explorers sought after gold and Fountains of Youth! I stood at the railing and watched flying fish, creatures I could never tire of watching, revealing as they do the marvelous inventiveness of Nature—fish that fly and soon a woman in the wilds of Oregon! Mr. Morgan informed me that there are fish that walk upon land, but he may have been entertaining himself with my wonder, as men will sometimes do.

The white beaches seem completely uninhabited except for an occasional tiny hut with a trim, ducklike boat lying in the offings. Beyond the beaches looms an interminable forest of live oak, mangrove and cypress. I imagined the Indians still living in those dense forests among the cypress swamps, the same people who the Spaniards fancied held riches and secrets they must possess.

My solitude was broken by a gathering of young men, dominated by one of the sort who enjoys the music of his own discourse, especially if the discords of others' opinions do not intrude. He spoke of Ponce de Leon and De Soto as if they had sailed from Olympus instead of Spain. I kept my counsel, for I have found that the slight breeze of a woman's opinion has little effect on the gale of such a young man.

He was not content with my silence, however, but sought my confirmation of his high opinion of the Spanish explorers of old. At his insistence, I advanced the opinion that the Spaniards with their muskets and armor were no more than pirates, and foolish pirates at that if they hoped to conquer time by taking a bath in what would surely be (if I judge the landscape correctly) a swamp!

This brought laughter from Mr. Morgan, who had joined us at the rail, and embarrassment to the young man whose fine oration I had discredited. His companions too joined in the laughter and teased him for being "bested by a woman" as if that were cause for great shame. I regret the young man's embarrassment, and I wish our conversation had not attracted such general attention, but I could not let pass uncontested the notion that heroism consists of armor and cannon and plunder, when better men and women have ventured into the wilderness to make a home with no more than the clothes upon their backs.

There are few women on board the Ohio, so I find myself something of a novelty. I suppose sailing for the far west is a man's enterprise, but I am set out to become

a wife—a task for which a man is ill-suited! The worst of
being one of the few women is the assumption by the
others of my gender that we must all band together and
form a female society—even though we might not have
two words to say to each other on dry land. I like my
fellow women, but I cannot abide a silly woman, and one
such has selected me (because we are about the same age)
to be her special companion on this voyage.

Her name is Mrs. Thomas Banes. She has asked me to
call her "Kitty" (I suppose her name is Catherine), and
she is the very image of a pampered lap cat. This
afternoon (I had successfully evaded her all morning) she
included me in an enterprise which has upset me greatly.
You, who have adventured unfettered to California and
the Oregon Territory, can perhaps share my feelings of
outrage at what this Kitty visited upon a fellow creature
for her entertainment.

A giant albatross from the South Seas, apparently
blown this far north by storm winds, was sailing in the air
above our vessel—following our progress in a friendly,
curious fashion—when a couple of the young sailors
suggested to Mrs. Banes that they might snare this bird
and bring it on board with a hook and line. This they
proceeded to do, prompted by her girlish encouragement
and in spite of my objections, baiting the hook with a
piece of pork. At first they sailed the magnificent bird
back and forth at the end of the line as if it were a paper
kite. Then they hauled in the hapless bird and stood it on
deck like a slave at auction as Kitty's dog (this cat keeps a
dog!) barked furiously all the while, dashing in and out
and back and forth as if someone were shaking a dust
mop. The bird looked with disdain upon his captors and
snapped his tremendous bill with a resounding clap
whenever the barking dust mop ventured too close. I
fetched Mr. Morgan, and at my entreaty, he put an end to
this cruel entertainment and reminded the sailors they
had more pressing duties than catching birds for the

amusement of ladies! I silently applauded him in my heart.

The bird was tossed into the air and it soared away south, glad to be free of the Ohio and silly women. One of the sailors informed me that the hook caused the bird no harm whatsoever. I said nothing, but thought to myself that being plucked from the sky—where he soared so beautifully—and being held prisoner for a cat and her dog was more than enough harm for any creature to endure!

Kitty, her game spoiled, went off to her husband to sulk. This worthy gentleman may be found at any time playing cards on deck with a circle of wifeless men, talking of goldfields and riches. He comforted her, I am sure, in the same mollycoddling voice I have heard him take with her before at this same roundtable of adventurers. He is a very fountain of sympathy, though his eyes never once leave the cards except to roll round in his head and thus indicate to his fellows what he actually thinks of his wife's prattle! She, her face properly buried in a handkerchief, does not witness her husband's antics. This secret manly communication provides great amusement for Mr. Thomas Banes's companions and himself.

These semaphores of condescension, I confess, make my blood boil! To be sure, if I were Kitty's husband I would tell her she is a silly little fool, which of course he does not do—her failings being too trivial to be corrected. For her part, she regards her husband as someone to whom she may air her complaints without fear of contradiction, and as a most excellent purchaser of lap dogs.

But all women are not silly women like Kitty. Men may roll their eyes at each other if they like, but for every silly woman there is a silly man to sue for her on bended knee, with two or three more waiting on the porch should their companion's suit prove unworthy!

It seems I have let my pen run away from me again! I am not sure why I am so irked by Mr. and Mrs. Thomas Banes. I think it is because I do not want us to be like them.

I have had my tumbler full of brandy now, and have calmed down considerably. This will be hard for you to believe, but I am actually a very quiet person. Words tumble around in my brain, and I carry on long conversations within myself, but I rarely share them with anyone. This pen, however, seems like a hook snaring word after word until, before I know it, I have blurted out heart's secrets I would tremble to tell face to face. I am glad of this, for I hope we will share an intimacy such as I find so easy on this page. I hope it will tutor me in sharing my secrets with my life's companion, and prompt him—you, dear husband—to share your secrets with me.

It must seem to you, reading over the incidents that I have just reported, that I have difficulty getting along in the society of others. That is, perhaps, true. My mother attributes this fault, as she does all my faults, to pride. I am too proud. But it is a silent proud, of no real harm to anyone save myself.

The truth is I am a good friend to those who seek a friend. I am a poor hand at Ungrateful Daughter or Hellbound Grandchild, a positive failure as Amusing Young Lady. But Friend is a role, though I have been asked to play it too rarely, I have given all my heart and soul. Mrs. Banes does not want a friend, however, simply a witness to her amusements.

It is Mr. Morgan who proves to be a truer friend. I learned from Mrs. Banes that he is not a member of the crew of the Ohio—that he is bound for Panama to take the helm of the Falcon and sail her up and down the California coast. My Pacific passage is booked on the Oregon, so I will not witness this worthy gentleman's skill as a sailor, but I shall miss his pleasant, good-hearted companionship.

I have spread before me the advertisement that brought us together. I still marvel at the series of coincidences that led me to this tiny square of print and the series of events, which you no doubt know, that set me on this voyage! I had been in Richmond only a short while and was looking for employment with little success. It was a hot steamy day, and I sought shelter for a moment in a hotel near the railway station. On the seat beside me was a newspaper, folded so that your advertisement was the center of the page. A circle had been drawn around it, apparently by the unknown person who had left the paper lying there. Little did this person suspect, I am sure, that she was marking the map of my destiny!

"A Southern Woman"—that is I—"Unafraid of hardship"—I have always proven myself so—"to found a home amid the rich bounty of the Oregon Territory." A "home"! The word made me dizzy! I have spent my life "borrowing" other people's homes—sometimes the lender has been kind and sometimes not—but a home of my own, I have never had.

You describe yourself as a "plain and simple man." What a cipher that is to fathom! I have imagined you a Tennessee Methodist Democrat (A Farmer—who, before he found gold—had a dog and a fishing pole to his name), a Sailor come ashore to raise a family in the mountains, a Clerk from St. Louis who caught the Gold Fever and left behind a sweetheart I am now summoned to replace. All of these are plain and simple, and yet they are not. I will know soon enough, I suppose, what sort of plain and simple you are.

By the light of morning, I confess, the prospect of setting out for Oregon to marry a complete stranger seemed most foolhardy. But whether it be curiosity or fate, I was at Mr. Tarrington's office by ten o'clock, newspaper in hand. I expected a crowd of curious young ladies, but I was the only one.

I did not care for Mr. Tarrington at all. He possesses enough arrogance for a roomful of lawyers. He informed me that he had never met you, and that all the arrangements had been made by correspondence. He explained that you wished to start a large farm, that you had already constructed a house upon a vast tract of land in the Willamette Valley (I have since learned where that is!). I listened, waiting to take my leave, when he showed me the daguerreotype of you.

I do not know why, but I knew that I must meet the man whose image I held in my hands, and straightaway I had signed the papers that have set me on this voyage.

I suppose I should tell you that I often have such intuitions. My mother once remarked to a friend of hers who was about to share some vicious gossip about a neighbor that "nothing gets by" me. I was ten when this occurred and ever since I have had cause to remember that phrase.

One example will serve. When I was about fifteen my mother and her cousin Amity conceived the notion that I and her seventeen-year-old son Jonathan should be thrown together. We were related, but not so close as to make it a sin should we decide eventually to marry. Marriage, of course, was never mentioned to me, though her motives were easy enough to guess. For years, a certain phantom of my mother's imagination—a Fine Christian Gentleman—had haunted her conversations with me.

I was invited to spend a Sunday with Amity and Jonathan, having dinner and such. Jonathan and I were set to shelling peas. I saw immediately, however, that Jonathan was not interested in me.

Cousin Amity came and looked in on us, leaning over Jonathan. She was wearing a loose-fitting cotton shift and as she stood over us, her breasts revealed, Jonathan's eyes fixed on them with delight. Amity was a lovely woman, and so were her naked breasts. I looked up at Amity and saw her gaze was fixed on Jonathan admiring her nakedness. She had a sweet and sensuous smile upon her face.

When I returned home that evening, I told my mother that she could forget about me and Jonathan because he was in love with his mother. She told me I was a hateful child from the Devil, but I noticed that she did not have to ask me what I meant or how I knew.

So you see, husband, not much is lost on me. I hope this quality will help me be a kind and sensitive wife.

It grows late, and I am weary. Until tomorrow, good night.

Thursday, July 4, 1850

I have sworn to write in this journal every night if possible. But I am too weary to hold a pen, and so, good night.

Friday, July 5, 1850

Dear husband,

We have made our way to Cuba! I have set myself up a little place on deck with a chair and table, perfect for writing. I read over my entry of last night, and I blush to confess I was a little tipsy when I wrote it, as I shall explain. Mr. Morgan suggested to the company that we hold a dance in honor of Independence Day. He said the waters were calm and that the weather would be splendid. We were in the tropics, he said, and led us all to believe that was something really quite magical!

And so it was. As Mr. Morgan predicted, the moon was near full and not a cloud in the sky. The full moon on the ocean may be a common sight to you, but to me it was as if I had been lifted into the heavens. I wished I could dive into the moonglade (Mr. Morgan taught me that word for the glowing aisle the moon lays upon the sea) and swim to the horizon—but I feared the cries of "Woman Overboard!" might distract me from my pleasure!

Before the festivities I retired to my cabin and endeavored to make myself the Beauty. While beauty's advantages are much overstated, it is most convenient at a dance—if you mean to dance (and why else attend a dance?). I have brought but one dress with me suitable for a festive evening—the one I intend to wear when first we meet, so there's no need to describe it to you—it will be sitting beside you as you read!

When I came back on deck I found it transformed into a gay ballroom. Mr. Lawrence, a plump man with a quiet manner, had made paper lanterns—dozens of them—and strung them all about. Red, white, and blue streamers (brought along for this occasion by Mr. Morgan) were wound around every available surface by Michael and Bret, the only young children on board I've seen thus far. They are fine boys, always busy. I have not been able to identify their parents with certainty since they flit about so and keep company with virtually everyone on board. Even at meals they always seem to be in motion! Some of the crew decorated the deck with flags I believe are intended to signal other vessels. And for all I know they were—"Taking on Gaiety! Sinking Fast!"

Mr. Morgan brought out a violin; and Mr. Sutton, a tailor from New York, a concertina. We danced for hours! I even took a turn with the Captain (a pompous man with great moustaches who is rumored to be a bigamist). After playing with great energy for over an hour, Mr. Morgan surrendered his violin to Mr. Banes who proved to be quite accomplished. I danced several dances with Mr. Morgan who said that though his fingers were quite tired, his feet felt quite gay.

When all were exhausted Mrs. Banes sang, a performance quite as worthy of praise as most feline sopranos I've heard. Mr. Morgan disagreed, however, and pointed out that the ship's cat was to be preferred, since she could be made to stop by tossing her a fish. I offered to fetch one from the galley, but by then Kitty had finished.

The Captain had ordered a punch brought on deck to quench our thirsts, and it was this punch that was my undoing. It was made with the exotic fruits of the region and more than a little rum.

The highlight of the evening, however, was the dancing and singing of the Mexican family who came on board in Florida. Three generations, a dozen in all, are bound for California. The grandfather, a delightful man with white hair and mahogany skin, played upon the guitar, while his son played on drums, the likes of which I have never seen. The rest of the family danced. And such dancing! They whirled and stamped and snapped their fingers in a blaze of color and excitement. It was quite the most wonderful thing I have ever witnessed! Mr. Morgan joined them with his fiddle and they played a round of Spanish tunes. Teresa, who is about eighteen, sang so beautifully I wept, though I did not understand a word! Each passion was conveyed without words in a way I find quite impossible to explain.

After her performance we lingered on the deck basking in our contentment, talking amongst ourselves. Teresa, needless to say, was sought out by many to compliment her on her beautiful singing. Two of her younger brothers stood by her as she greeted her admirers. They spoke up in Spanish, and Teresa was thus obliged to translate for them. Teresa is the only one in the family who speaks English well, and thus she speaks English for them all. I asked Mr. Morgan, who speaks Spanish, what the two boys were saying, for they seemed to be enjoying themselves in some way at their sister's expense. Mr. Morgan told me that Teresa's brothers were teasing her. They said to Teresa, while smiling at Mrs. Banes, "Tell her she sings like a pig being strangled!" and poor Teresa had to make up something she could say to the waiting Mrs. Banes. I asked Mr. Morgan if he would accompany me to pay my compliments to Teresa and whisper in my ear whatever the brothers might say to me.

As we approached, the two brothers smiled at a fresh opportunity to torture their sister. I told Teresa that she sang wonderfully, and that I would die to dance as beautifully as she. As before, the brothers stepped forward to speak some goading nonsense. The older of the two, a boy of about sixteen named Martin, smiled and said (by Mr. Morgan's account), "Tell her she looks as though she needs a man to love her!" Before Teresa could think of anything to say, I said to her, "Tell him I have found a man to love, and I am bound for Oregon to marry him!"

Teresa's eyes opened wide. "You speak Spanish?" she exclaimed.

"No," I replied, "I read minds."

She turned on her brothers like a whirlwind and told them this, and a good deal else besides, which I hardly needed Mr. Morgan to translate for me!

The transformation of the two rascals into sincere penitents was quite marvelous to behold. They withered under their sister's wrath like grass in a high wind. Mortified that they had given offense, they sought my forgiveness in a manner so sweet and humble I was quite touched, for I knew they meant no real harm to anyone. When they set out to beg the pardon of everyone present whom they had thus wronged, I begged them stay and toast the company instead, which we all did with great enthusiasm.

Then the younger brother, Pablo, who has only a few words of English, managed to convey through hand gestures and the words "I" and "dance" that he would teach me how to dance, and every bit as good as his sister! He pronounced my name as if it were "Peril"—with a marvelous rolling R! I found it quite charming and allowed him to lead me onto the dance floor.

I played the Señorita until my feet could take no more, and I confess I've never had such a marvelous time. The grandfather, Simon, asked Teresa to tell me that while my face might be from Virginia, my feet were Mexican! So you see, by the time I found my little cabin, I could not write a word.

But I must tell you the truth, some of my gaiety was simply a means to avoid this page, for I suppose I should tell you now that I have a terrible secret to confide in you. Or perhaps it will not seem a terrible secret to you. How do I know what you will think, a face in a daguerreotype? Why is it you wanted to know nothing about me except that I was free to marry, had no children, and could leave immediately? Mr. Tarrington made it clear that he wished to know nothing about me for that would take up his valuable time. He had secured someone who met his employer's qualifications, and now he could collect his fee.

Very well, I said nothing. But now I find myself on this voyage to meet a husband who knows nothing at all about me. Perhaps none of my story will matter to you for good or ill, but it matters to me. It matters to me that you know.

That's the true reason for this journal. I have something I must tell you, that I want to tell you with care. Face to face with a new husband in a new land, I would only stammer it out in a muddle. I can't trust speech to tell it well, and I fear it must be told well if at all.

For me, it begins when I was born, three months after my parents' wedding. My father, Gerald Withers, was a cabinetmaker, as I have said. He and my mother formed their attachment when he came to work on a new addition to my grandfather's house. My grandfather, who fancied himself a gentleman planter, would never have consented to their marriage if it had not been for the undeniable fact of me in my mother's belly. My mother never forgave my father for his participation in the event which revealed to my mother's father what he so consistently maintained anyway—that she was flawed, a mere human, a sinner he would call it. Sad to say, my mother would agree.

While James Grier was forced to consent to the marriage of his only daughter to a cabinetmaker, he would not allow that his daughter's husband should remain one and forced him into more suitable employment as his overseer on the plantation. An overseer has many duties, most of which my father performed with skill and efficiency, but his chief duty he could perform with only the greatest reluctance—and that was the beating of slaves. Nancy explained to me that a slave, who might earn nothing else from his labors, will oftentimes work only to avoid the lash, and without it he might take it into his head to decide for himself what he should sow and what he should reap.

I have most of this from Nancy, who would set me down beside the fire with milk and cookies and—perceiving that no one else would so much as speak of my father once he was gone—tell me stories of him and much else besides.

One incident I can recall for myself with greatest clarity occurred when I was six. We were seated at table, when one of the slaves, a boy about my age named Douglas who was my playmate and friend, stumbled and fell under the weight of a huge pitcher of milk he was carrying into the dining room. He crouched—terrified—his hands cut and bleeding—surrounded by the shards of the pitcher in a huge puddle of milk and blood.

My grandfather ordered my father to beat the child. For a long while my father said nothing. Finally he rose from the table without a word, wrapped the boy's hands in his napkin, and led him away. A few minutes later, my father returned, saying that he'd had done with beating his fellow creatures, that he was quitting this place forever, and that my mother could choose to stay or accompany him as she saw fit.

I jumped up from my chair and ran to him, saying that I would go with him wherever he might wish to go and be glad of it! We both wept mightily and clung to each other, but as often happens to children at such times, I was whisked away so that the adults might wage their war.

The result was that in the morning my father was gone,

and my mother and I remained with my grandfather. I was proud of my father for standing up to my grandfather, and resolved that I would someday do the same. Such foolishness! I was a young girl, as readily if not as viciously beaten as any slave should I prove myself worthy of such an honor. My mother, a grown woman, still quaked before her father as if before God Almighty. I soon realized I did not have the luxury of rebellion. After that, I became a timorous, mousey thing, creeping from room to room out of sight. My mother saw my father's departure as the just wages of her sin. I, being the tangible fruits of that sin, served as a constant reminder of her wickedness.

Naturally, her greatest fear as I was growing up was that I would prove to be a sinner such as she was. Like many people, her fears were sufficient testimony of their own truth, and she—and my grandfather of course—were quite convinced I had violated every Commandment save adultery and murder—those only wanting opportunity—at an age when my greatest crime was to have stolen a cookie from behind Nancy's back!

My mother began to speak to me of the Devil when she spoke to me at all. By her account, he was everywhere, lurking in every dark corner, waiting to reach out and claim me as his own. Many a night I could not sleep for fear of my mother's Devil, who only waited for me to drift into sleep so that he might carry me off to Hell! And thus I spent many a fearful year.

Then the most marvelous thing occurred! I hope you will not think me mad. I was not quite fourteen, lying in bed—whether awake or asleep I cannot say—when the Devil himself appeared in my room and sat on the foot of my bed! He was quite a handsome fellow, though not so handsome as to seem prettified, and he wore a fine suit of clothes as if dressed for a ball. His eyes were the most striking thing about him—full of intelligence and good humor. He introduced himself in the politest terms possible and told me that I shouldn't fear him, for he was actually not a bad sort of fellow at all. I did not wish to rush to judgment, but I offered that his reputation was quite otherwise.

This seemed to sadden him (though he was quite a gay fellow generally) and he allowed that many evil reports were circulated about him that had no basis in fact. Whereupon he picked up the Bible which always lay on the table beside my bed (where I knew my mother expected it to be!), opened it to the second chapter of Genesis and bid me read aloud. As you might imagine, this surprised me no end, for my mother held that the Devil was a great enemy of Scripture.

I complied with his request and read the story of Adam and Eve. When I had done, and the parents of us all were quite cast out of Paradise, the Devil inquired as to who I liked better in the tale—the ill-tempered God who jealously guarded His magic trees and blocked our return to His Garden with fiery swords, or the Serpent with the fruit in his mouth? I had to allow that I preferred the Serpent.

He then bid me read the story of Job—and it is quite the most horrible story I have ever read! That such a man should suffer for his goodness simply to support the wager of a vain old man still makes my blood boil just to think on it! Once again the Devil asked my opinion, and I did not hesitate to tell him that I thought God most wicked indeed, though I did not find his own behavior quite blameless either. Why, I demanded, had he goaded God in such a manner when he knew what He was capable of?

He confessed to shame over his conduct, but asserted that he had been driven to it by the self-satisfied arrogance of the Deity who took such pride in His hapless slaves.

I allowed that I could understand his annoyance, but that he would have been better advised, for Job's sake, to have kept his counsel.

What most angered me about the tale (I told the Devil) was that Job is never told why he has suffered so horribly.

God appears to him as a great wind, prating on about leviathans and crocodiles, and how did Job dare presume to inquire after his own suffering, all the while knowing that He himself was responsible for it all, a silly wager to satisfy His vanity! I ventured the opinion that if a man could not inquire after his own suffering, then he might as well not be allowed to inquire after anything, and the Devil quite agreed.

We read that night every mention made of the Devil in the pages of the Bible. In every case, I had to allow that he was not such a bad fellow. With Revelations, we both admitted we could make no sense of it one way or the other and resolved to tackle it another day when we were more rested.

After that I became a regular reader of the Bible, which pleased my mother mightily. Little did she know that I discussed everything I read at night in bed with the Devil. It seemed to me that more mischief had been done in the world by God, than by all the devils put together. I told the Devil I planned to cast my lot with him, but he preferred, he said, that I cast my lot with myself, and so I have done, for better or worse as you shall see when I finish my tale. For now I have quite written myself out until tomorrow.

By THE TIME I'D FINISHED READING PEARL'S JOURNAL, IT WAS two in the morning. I wanted to dance in the streets. This was a writer's dream come true. Pearl was a novel all by herself—a woman setting out for the wilderness to marry a complete stranger, a woman whose boon companion was a charming Devil. I riffled the pages, wondering how much more there was of it.

I opened up my tiny laptop computer and started a new file I titled "Pearl." I started taking notes on what I'd read, but found myself staring instead at the manila envelope with my name penned across it. I imagined Raymond's voice saying my name, whispering it.

I'll read it the minute I get home, I'd said, flirting, never thinking I would. And I'd promised to call—again, never thinking I would. I wrapped my arms around myself and swayed. *Nothing would delight me more,* he'd said.

I scooped up the phone, a cheap cordless. The "Lo Batt" light, a tiny red dot, pulsed at me. I turned it on anyway and got a dial tone overlaid with the murky static of an old AM radio. I stabbed out the number before I had a chance to change my mind.

Raymond answered on the first ring. "Hello," he said in a perfectly normal voice, as if it were two o'clock in the afternoon.

"Hi Raymond," I said. "It's Marion, honoring my promise. I just finished reading the journal."

He laughed. "You called. You actually called."

He sounded so happy, I was touched—and flattered. "I hope I didn't wake you," I said.

"I'm awake most nights."

"When do you sleep?"

"I nap in the afternoons. Besides, I was sitting up, hoping you'd call, though I didn't think you would. I was afraid I'd frightened you away."

I knew exactly what he meant, but said, "Why should I be frightened of you?"

"I thought perhaps, as they say these days, I was coming on too strong."

"You were a perfect gentleman. You didn't come on any stronger than me." I curled up in my chair, pulling my knees to my chest. "Raymond, can I ask you something? What is it you see in me? I'm an average-looking forty-two-year-old woman with two kids and a mortgage and three shoeboxes full of rejection slips. You don't even know me. I have a terrible history with men."

"You save your rejection slips?"

I laughed. "Okay, you caught me. But if I *had* saved them, I'm sure they'd fill at least three shoeboxes. I'm just saying, Raymond, that I don't understand why you seem so interested in me."

"Seems, madam? Nay, it is. I know not 'seems.'"

I smiled to myself. *"Hamlet.* You like Shakespeare?"

"I love Shakespeare."

"What else do you love?"

For a moment I didn't think he'd heard me. Then he said, in his soft, warm voice, "I'd love to see you again. That is, if you'd like that."

"I'd love to see you again too." I closed my eyes, holding the receiver with both hands, listening to the static wax and wane like some storm out on the moors. "Besides, I'm dying to read the rest of Pearl's journal."

"I'll put on another pot of coffee."

I laughed. "Not tonight, silly. I've got two kids in bed sound asleep."

"Then tomorrow, anytime."

"If you mean today, I hope to spend most of it sleeping to make up for last night. Besides, the kids have plans."

"How about Monday?"

"I have to work during the week. I used up all my sick days when the kids had the flu. I can only get away on weekends."

"Why don't you come up next weekend? I'm afraid I'll be tied up for several weeks after that with a pressing matter I can't put off."

"I doubt if I can find anybody to stay with my kids on such short notice."

"Bring your girls with you. Spend the weekend. They can ride, hike in the woods. I have a splendid collection of cartoons they can watch. You can use my library. I can read your book. And we can get to know each other."

I was stunned. I sat up straight and put my feet on the floor. "Me and my kids—for the weekend?"

"That's right. What do you say? This old place could use some life in it, don't you think? I have plenty of room. They can share a room, and you can have the room next to theirs."

I imagined scenes from an idyllic weekend full of laughing children and romantic evenings, imagined Raymond in my arms, kissing his mouth, kissing the scar on his forehead, his face in my hands. I took a deep breath and shook it off. "Raymond, it sounds wonderful, but I don't know if I can get away. I'm scheduled to work Saturday. But I might be able to persuade a friend to cover for me."

"Well, give it a try, and if I don't hear from you before Thursday, I'll be expecting the three of you Friday evening for dinner, and I won't let you leave until after lunch on Sunday."

"I'll have to think about it, talk to the kids."

"Of course," he said. "In the meantime, perhaps you could mail me some of your book, so I can get started?"

"I'll send you the first chapter."

"I look forward to seeing you again," he said softly.

"Me too." I turned off the phone and laid it on the desk, the tiny red light still blinking as if it were a bomb.

I KNEW I COULDN'T SLEEP, AND I WASN'T READY TO FACE THE decision of whether or not I was actually going to spend the weekend with a man I'd just met. I put Pearl's journal in the envelope and turned back to my computer. I loaded the first chapter of my novel. I wanted to read it over before I let Raymond read it. Even if I decided not to spend the weekend with him, I could still let him read my book. *On one condition,* he'd said. I smiled, remembering my reaction.

Susanna's Story

Chapter One

Gordon Patterson squinted at the creek with the same look Susanna had often seen men level at horses and women who'd grown lame or fat. "She's silting up, I tell you, dying like you and me. But she's dying faster. Won't be no more than would muddy your boots in a year or two."

He was talking to her husband, Robert Grier, who thought Gordon an idiot and suffered Gordon's theories with the smile one offers idiots.

Gordon, unperturbed, turned to Susanna and cocked one eyebrow. "Mehantesset says one, maybe two years, only snakes will be swimming where our flatboats now sail." He made a motion with his arm of a snake swimming.

It was one of the things she liked about Gordon, his talking with the Indians. She never had. They frightened her, though she thought her fears foolish and scoffed at the tales the men told to frighten young women. The Indians were nearly all gone off to the west in any event. Those that remained behind, she thought, must be lonely and angry.

Robert broke in, his patience gone. "You can't be serious! We should uproot an entire town on the basis of some old savage's ravings after he's smoked a pipe or two and drunk a good deal of your whiskey?"

"Not so much as you're wont to drink," said Gordon, winking at Susanna. "And we're smoking his tobacco, after all. Damn sight better than yours."

"Well, if he's so damnably smart, perhaps he could take a turn at doctoring your patients or running the store. Or perhaps the whole damn colony!" He stood with his arms folded across his back, as if offering defiance even to those behind him. Susanna hated him whenever he took that stance, hated herself because she'd married him, knowing who he was when she married him.

"A splendid idea," she said. "You already have a convict keeping your books. A savage, as you call him, performing the rest of your duties might boost the profits and give you leisure to read." She smiled at Gordon. "Robert believes gentlemen should spend all their time reading dead languages and esoteric tracts. It stimulates his mind and his thirst."

She turned and went up the hill, Robert sputtering behind her. She knew she wasn't being fair, but fair had nothing to do with it. She hated him. She'd exhausted all fairness long ago.

She turned at the door and waved to Gordon, who held up his walking stick and continued his hike along the creek. Robert stopped at the path that crossed through the apple grove to the stable and looked up at her, his arms still behind his back as if bound.

"Why do you insist on making a fool of me?" he said.

"Are you coming in?" she asked. "Or are you going to Whiskey Row?"

"Answer me!" he shouted up the hill.

"You make a fool of yourself," she said quietly, looking off now toward the creek.

Robert fought back his anger. "I have given you a fine home, taken in your son, even gone to the expense of a tutor for him. I will not be made a mockery in front of my neighbors. I do not deserve such treatment. Is that clear?"

She wanted to say that she and William already had a home, that the tutor was a convict who spent most of his time tending to Robert's affairs, and that his neighbors knew as well as she what an ass he was. But she said none of this and kept her eye on the creek, a silver line in the sun.

He turned on his heel and strode toward the stable. She entered the house, climbed the stairs to her room overlooking the dying creek, lay on her bed, and fell asleep.

Robert found Jesse sitting on a stump beside the stable, cleaning a saddle while Anthony leaned against the wall behind him talking in his melodious, soft voice. The saddle looked tiny in Jesse's hands. Anthony looked like a reed beside him.

Robert said, "Jesse, saddle Robin and be quick about it."

"Yessir, Mr. Robert," Jesse said, and went into the stable.

Robert turned to Anthony. "And what are you doing here? Have you finished with the ledgers I gave you this morning?"

"Oh yes sir, begging your pardon, sir, but I was just asking Jesse if he had seen any of young William's books. He seems to have mislaid some of them."

"Mislaid them!"

"Yes sir. Most particularly his Latin books. If I may say so, young Mr. William has a distaste for the study of languages."

"I should think it would be more accurate to say that my wife's son has more than an uncommon distaste for anything but self-indulgent melancholy!"

"Yes sir."

"If it weren't so damned expensive, I'd send him back to Scotland, in spite of what his mother might say." Robert looked back at the house. "Ever been married?" he asked Anthony.

Anthony shook his head. "Begging your pardon, sir, but marriage was never for me. The wicked life I led was not suitable for a wife."

Robert snorted out a laugh. "I suppose that's one thing to be said for a life of crime." He called into the darkness, "Dammit Jesse, where's that horse?" and then to Anthony, "Well, what books of mine did the sullen little bastard 'mislay'?"

"The *Aeneid*, sir, but Jesse found it in one of the stalls." He held up the book, which had been in his hand the whole time. "It's unharmed," he said, then smiled, "the language as beautiful as ever."

"Have you read the Dryden translation?" Robert asked.

"Oh yes sir. It's really quite fine."

"But it's not Virgil," said Robert.

Jesse appeared with Robert's mount, and helped Robert into the saddle. Robert looked down. "Perhaps we could discuss Virgil some evening," he said to Anthony.

"I would be honored and delighted," Anthony said, bowing as Robert rode away to Williams Ordinary, his favorite tavern.

Jesse shook his head and spat on the ground. "You sure have your ways, Anthony. You figure he believe that shit about William chucking his book in the stall?"

"Of course. He would believe anything evil of the young widow's son, and will add lying to his crimes when the boy tries to defend himself of the charge of tossing the blessed Virgil into a horse stall. I expect he'll beat him."

"More likely beat you. Why do you care about what Robert does with that boy anyway?"

"The loathing of others can often be advantageous, Jesse. Loathing is a great motivator. People often lack the finer emotions, but not the baser ones. Agree with another man's loathings, and he'll trust you like a brother."

"That ain't saying much if you be the brother."

Anthony laughed good-naturedly. "You are a most comical fellow, Jesse. But as I have told you, trust is unnecessary between us. We share a common loathing of enslavement. I intend to leave soon. When the time comes, if you had one of these wagons in good shape for a trip to Norfolk, you could join me."

"We ain't going nowhere."

"Perhaps, but an attentive person such as yourself must have noticed that Mr. Grier is an unhappy man. He fancies himself a victim of great misfortune, all alone in his misery. He needs a sympathetic companion he can trust."

Jesse laughed. "Trust you? He ain't that big a fool."

Anthony smiled. "He has a beautiful wife, a house and slaves. In a few years, with prudent management, he could return to his precious Glasgow a wealthy man. And yet he sees himself as fortune's wretch. He's a fool all right. I merely intend to put his foolishness to good purpose."

Susanna awoke to the sound of Jesse splitting kindling between the kitchen and the house. Jess, three, and Rachel, five, crouched a few feet away, darting in to gather the sticks that flew into the air with the thud of Jesse's ax, retreating as he raised it into the air again and brought it down with tremendous force. Rachel undertook the task with her usual somber air—quiet, efficient, distracted. Jess scurried about in a great frenzy, his eyes ablaze, snatching up the sticks in quick, lunging movements, as if they were fleeing from him. She could hear his shrieks of joy.

Her sons, William, fourteen, and James, four, sat in the doorway to the kitchen watching the slave children scoop up the sticks. William, his long, thin face painfully earnest, winced with each thud of the ax. James swung his stubby legs back and forth. He had a lap full of straw he tossed into the air with an explosive gesture in imitation of the splintering wood. Bits of straw hung from William's thick, unruly hair, but he seemed not to notice.

I have two sons, Susanna thought, and neither one looks anything like me. James was a little Robert. And William looked like Miles, her first husband, dead now for nine years, his life burned up in a sudden fever six years after they'd married and come to the colony—the happiest time in her life.

She married Robert Grier four years later, in the spring of 1764, because he asked her, because she was twenty-seven years old with a nine-year-old son, and because she hoped that the aching sadness of losing Miles would go away, that she might form a new affection for Robert, who seemed so devoted to her. Now, after five years of marriage, Robert's devotion had vanished, as well it might, for no matter how hard she tried, she couldn't feel for him as she had for Miles. Robert was not a bad man, but life to him was a burden. Susanna and William, even James, were simply part of that burden. Susanna thought it evidence of the essential injustice of the world that Miles, who'd loved life, had it taken away, while Robert, who felt life misused him at every turn, would probably die an old man back in Glasgow, a rich merchant who'd made his fortune in Virginia, getting from life everything he'd asked for.

She supposed she should have gone back to Scotland when Miles died, but there was no one there for her anymore, and she liked this place, so wild and huge, even though it had frightened her at first. She sat in front of the mirror and brushed her hair. Miles used to say it was the color of a red fox and had watched her brush it out, took it up in his hands and ran his fingers through it. Robert seemed embarrassed when she let down her hair, even now after five years, though he rarely saw it down anymore.

She put up her hair and put on a headscarf. She felt as if she'd reached the end of her life, not that she would die soon but that she might as well, for nothing was ever going to change, nothing was ever going to happen. She turned away from the mirror and went down the stairs, enjoying having the house to herself as she often did this time of day.

At the bottom of the stairs, she stood at the doorway to the parlor. It had been unseasonably warm. The windows were all open, and a breeze blew through the house. She liked her house. She only wished she lived here without Robert. The thought had crossed her mind more than once that if Robert were to die, she wouldn't go back to Scotland but stay here in this house. But she didn't figure Robert was about to die anytime soon.

She went out the back door and crossed the yard to the kitchen. It was starting to cool now, with maybe an hour of daylight left. Everyone had apparently gone into the kitchen to watch Nancy fix supper.

The sun had sunk halfway into the trees. It wouldn't be long before Robert came home. He didn't stay out after dark. In the middle of the summer he wouldn't come home till past eight. She'd walk about the place, sometimes even go for a ride. There wasn't time for that now.

She stood in the empty yard and watched a solitary crane flying overhead. How did it know which way to fly? Did it know anything at all? Or was it like her, down to dumb luck. She breathed deeply. She liked this time of year, the rich, clean smell of fall. But soon winter would be here, all of them cooped up together like prisoners. She didn't think she could bear it.

She stepped through the open doorway into the smoky warmth of the kitchen, blinking her eyes in the darkness.

William jumped to his feet and brought her a chair. "Mother," he said.

My Sweet William, she thought. He says so little to me, one word at a time, but each one kind and adoring. "Thank you," she said to him.

He looked at her with dazed gratitude.

Nancy turned from a kettle of chowder and smiled. "Evening, Miss Susanna."

"Evening, Nancy. It smells delicious."

All of a sudden, Jess charged across the room, stumbling over Rachel, who was asleep on a blanket by the fire, and launched himself into Susanna's lap. "Zanna," he said, his tiny arms held out to her.

Jesse called from the corner where he was mending a shoe, "Jess, don't be climbing all over Miss Susanna."

"He's all right," Susanna said, and wrapped her arms around Jess's tiny body and shook him like a rag doll, setting him in her lap, where he curled up in her arms. "Where's James?" she asked Nancy.

"Me and the Little Master had us something of a misunderstanding," Nancy said, laughing. "You know how he gets. Last he told me, he was going to his room."

"That's probably the best place for him when he gets like that. I trust we'll see him at dinner."

"He told me to bring him his supper on a tray."

"You'll do no such thing, Nancy."

Nancy laughed. "You got nothing to worry about, Miss Susanna. Don't expect even Mr. Robert want me to spoil Little Master that bad."

"Mr. Grier hasn't returned home, has he?"

Jesse looked down at the shoe in his hands. "No ma'am."

Susanna knew Nancy had had a husband in Maryland before she came here. At least she'd called him her husband, though slaves couldn't marry. He'd died of a great fall. She rarely spoke of him. Nancy and Jesse didn't call themselves married, but they seemed so to Susanna, more than she and Robert.

Nancy said, "The flour's wormy again, Miss Susanna. I think I should bake a nice big loaf of worm bread for the man who keep selling us this wormy flour, since he like worms so much."

Susanna laughed. "I'll suggest it to Mr. Grier."

Nancy gave her a broad grin. "I'll hide and watch."

"Worms," said Jess. "Worms, worms, worms." He wiggled his fingers in the air. Susanna snatched at them, and he squealed with laughter as he pulled them away. She looked over at William, his eyes still fixed on her, awaiting her attention with perfect and adoring patience.

"And how are you, Sweet William? I haven't seen you since breakfast."

"I've been translating Virgil, Mother. It is so beautiful."

"I have only read it in translation. I envy your learning."

"Anthony says I have a gift, that I should study Greek and perhaps Hebrew."

"That's wonderful," Susanna said.

"He's helping me with my poetry also and says he'll lay claim to an inscribed copy of my first book as his reward!"

"Where is Anthony?" Susanna asked. He rarely joined them in the kitchen, but when he did, he was a marvelous storyteller.

"He be around here someplace," Jesse said.

Nancy tossed a handful of herbs into the kettle.

"Most likely in the henhouse stealing chickens from the fox."

"What have you got against Anthony?" Susanna asked.

"Let's just say I've known me some Anthonys in my time."

Susanna noticed William's frown. "William, what do you think of Anthony?"

William blushed. "I like him. He's taught me Latin, Mother."

"He's your tutor, William. He's supposed to teach you Latin."

"He's not just my tutor, he's my friend."

Jesse tossed the shoe into the corner and rose to his feet. "I better be getting down to the stable," he said. "It's getting onto dark. Mr. Grier be home directly." He crossed the room in low hulking strides and was gone out the door.

Nancy looked after him, her face lined with concern. "He take too much on himself," she said softly. She turned to Susanna and gave a sad smile. "He worries me something awful."

Jess was now half asleep. Susanna held both his hands in one of hers. "You love Jesse, don't you?" she said.

"Yes, I do."

"Is it the same as with your husband?" Susanna blushed. "I mean, do you feel the same?"

"You don't ever love two people the same way, but I love him just as much."

Susanna rose slowly so as not to awaken Jess, and laid him beside Rachel. "I am happy for you," she said. She couldn't tell Nancy she envied her. It would be a cruel thing to say. Nancy had come to them three years ago, six months after Jess was born to Jesse's sister Annie. Robert had sold Annie, keeping her children, and bought Nancy a week later. The last three years would've been unbearable without her, Susanna thought.

She and William walked arm in arm back to the house. "Perhaps you and James would like to dine early this evening," she said. "Robert will most likely be in an ill humor."

"Yes Mother," he said.

Susanna heard Robert returning home just before dark. He was nearly blind when the light grew dim. Susanna had known this since before James was born, though Robert vehemently denied it. Jesse must also know. She imagined Jesse knew most of her husband's secrets.

This night Robert was silent throughout dinner. Susanna would've preferred he scream at her, for then she could scream back. Silence just became a stew of guilt. She excused herself and went up to her room. She heard Robert in the parlor beneath her, stirring up the fire. He would drink brandy and fall asleep.

She lay on her bed, stretching out her limbs, staring at the whiteness of the ceiling, closing her eyes, trying to imagine Miles crossing the room, sitting down on the edge of the bed, touching her. She listened for him, heard his footsteps, but her imagination failed at his voice. He would not speak to her. He would not tell her what to do. She opened her eyes and took in the dark, empty room. He was dead, and she wept for him again, but she was sick of her grief and wanted to be done with it and wished he would just die.

She fell asleep, and she wasn't sure how long she lay there before she heard voices coming from beneath her in the parlor. She couldn't make out the words, but the voices had a boisterous sound, and she couldn't imagine such a thing.

She went to the top of the stairs and listened. It was Robert and Anthony. Robert's voice had crept higher than usual, as it did when he was excited and full of himself.

Anthony's voice was melodious, a gentleman's voice. He'd been a counterfeiter, sentenced to burn at the stake, but at the last moment his sentence had been commuted to transportation to the colony. Robert had purchased him to tutor William, though he also kept the accounts Robert found so difficult to keep himself.

She'd been with Robert the day he bought Anthony. She remembered Anthony stepping out of a line of criminals and bowing. He was a handsome man, tall, his hair as black as a raven.

For months, Susanna had noticed Anthony looking at her with more than common interest, but she'd ignored his looks. There were few women and many men in the colony. She could not begrudge the men such looks. She only wished her husband would look at her in that way on occasion, or at least years ago she'd wished that.

She moved silently down the stairs and sat on the bottom step, a few feet from the doorway into the parlor. She could hear them both perfectly. They seemed to be talking about books. Robert loved to appear learned—he scorned his neighbors as ill-read louts.

Anthony was defending Dryden's translation of the *Aeneid:* "I find in it many fine things with the added pleasure of rhyme—'Thrice and four times happy those (he cried),/That under Ilian walls, before their parents, died!' I've had such thoughts since coming to this land, if I may say so, sir."

"You've committed the poem to memory?"

"I remember everything I read, sir, everything I see, as if I had it before me. I consider it a gift."

"A convenient gift for a counterfeiter, I would imagine."

"Yes sir, I'm afraid so, sir."

"No need to look penitent. You're stuck here now, tutor to an idiot. Come on, drink your brandy. Let's talk of Virgil. I don't care what you say, you'll never persuade me that English is as fine a vessel for poetry as Latin."

Susanna smiled to herself. How incredible, she thought, Robert is attempting to make a friend of Anthony, a friend he owns, how perfect for him.

Anthony spoke after the clinking of glasses. His voice had changed somewhat, a little less formal, a little less the-slave-in-the-parlor. "If I may say so, sir, I believe it's the story wants changing, not the language."

Robert laughed. "How marvelous! Change the *Aeneid*? How?"

Anthony didn't hesitate. "I think Aeneas could have learned a thing or two from Jason."

"You've read Apollonius?"

"And Euripides as well, sir."

Susanna could hear the clink of a bottle as Robert poured himself more brandy. "Well, go on, what could Aeneas have learned from Jason?"

"That he didn't have to leave Dido. He should've taken her with him, like Jason took Medea. She would've come. Any woman who will kill herself for you will surely follow you to Italy."

Robert was incredulous. "But that wasn't his destiny. He must go to Italy and marry. He would have to leave her sooner or later."

"My point exactly. Why leave a beautiful woman until you have to? He can abandon her when his destiny comes calling, as Jason did. In the meantime he can enjoy her."

Robert laughed out loud. Susanna had never heard this particular laugh before. Perhaps this was his tavern laugh. He was still laughing as he spoke: "Have some more brandy, Anthony. You are a true scoundrel."

"Perhaps. But I think Apollonius knew more than Virgil about the sort of men who found empires. Men who arrange life to their own advantage instead of the other way about. Take Aeneas. He need not marry Dido. If I were a woman, I would rather be a mistress than a wife."

"Is that what you have done with women?"

Anthony laughed. "No sir. No woman has ever loved me sufficiently to follow me past the churchyard."

Susanna stepped into the room. Robert was on his feet pouring brandy for Anthony, who sat in a chair by the fire. "I am sorry," she said. "I had no idea you were in here." Robert stared at her as he swayed a little on his feet. She looked down at the floor.

"Sit down, Sue, and join us. We were discussing Virgil. Anthony here maintains that Aeneas is altogether too noble. Let's get the woman's view on this—what do you think?"

Robert was sometimes magnanimous when he was drunk. She liked him best then. Usually her reading was a source of friction between them. After Miles's death she'd read all his books, except those in Greek and Latin. She'd read the Dryden translation. Robert had belittled it, and then her for reading it. Unlike Anthony, she'd been given no opportunity to defend Dryden or herself.

She sat down and raised her eyes to look into Anthony's. He was smiling at her as if she'd just removed her clothing. It was the same way Miles used to smile at her when he wanted her. She held his eyes.

"In what way," Susanna asked Anthony, "is Aeneas too noble?"

"In leaving Dido. I maintain he should have taken her with him. Carthage would have a new queen inside of a week, and Aeneas would have his Dido."

"I must confess," said Susanna, "that I quite agree with Anthony."

Robert laughed. "Damn you, Anthony. I notice you say nothing of Jason and Medea to *Mrs.* Grier."

Anthony bowed his head in false penance. "I confess I am something of a sophist."

Robert, who was still standing, all puffed up and enjoying himself immensely, turned to Susanna and waved his forefinger in her direction. "But what of Dido when Aeneas must marry Lavinia?"

"By then," Susanna said, "she would be so angry she wouldn't do anything so foolish as to kill herself."

Anthony winked at her and said, "Course, she might murder Lavinia, and then Destiny would be quite undone."

Robert spun around, delighted, his forefinger now in the air. "You see. It must happen just as Virgil has it! Anything else would subvert Destiny. I have you there, Anthony!"

Anthony did not even glance at Robert, who paced back and forth before the fire and explained the genius of Virgil until all the brandy was gone. Instead he smiled at Susanna with frank desire. Robert seemed not to notice that his wife and servant were not listening, that they were reaching a silent agreement to sleep together at the first opportunity.

At ten-thirty, Susanna excused herself and went up to her room.

By then Robert had slumped into his chair, rattling on. "What was it Horace said in *Ars Poetica?*"

"What lines?" said Anthony as his eyes followed Susanna out of the room.

"I can't remember what lines!" Robert blustered.

Susanna laughed softly at the top of the stairs as she heard Anthony begin to recite the *Ars Poetica* to the bleary-eyed Robert.

At eleven o'clock Anthony helped Robert upstairs and laid him on his bed. He closed the door to

Robert's room and crossed the hall to Susanna's. He stepped in, closing and bolting the door behind him.

Susanna stood in the middle of the room in a cotton shift. Her long red hair hung down her back. She didn't want to speak, didn't want him to speak. He crossed the room, and lifted her chemise over her head. He admired her body, then indicated, with a small gesture of his hand, that she should lie down on the bed.

He studied her again, smiling. Susanna was trying to remember the last time a man had seen her naked. When Robert made love to her, he never removed all her clothing. It must have been the last time Miles had made love to her. The fever had struck the next day. Exactly one week after the last time he'd lain in her arms, he was dead.

Anthony reached out, spread her hair in a fan around her head, and kissed her. He sat on the edge of the bed and removed his boots, never taking his eyes off her. He stood, undressing slowly, looking at her.

She imagined Robert breaking down the door, shooting them both with his pistols. Perhaps this will be the last time I ever lie with a man, she thought, but this didn't bother her. I would rather die this way than silt up like an old creek.

He lay down beside her and ran his hands up and down her body. All this time, he'd been smiling; then the smile vanished, and he kissed her, gently at first, and then hungrily. As they kissed, he took her thighs and slid her under him. She guided him into her and gasped as he moved, slowly, carefully, deep inside her. She closed her eyes and the world dissolved. All that mattered was her body and this man moving inside of it.

Gradually, he began to move more urgently. She opened her eyes and saw the room vibrating to his rhythm, heard the squeals and groans of the bed. She thought of Robert awakening to this racket. What would he do if he found them like this? She closed her eyes and clung to Anthony's shoulders, moving with him, frantically now, the bed squeaking and clattering, but she didn't care. She didn't care. She didn't care. She let out a long, ragged scream, moving against him as hard and as fast as she could, never wanting him to stop, wanting a pleasure so intense that it would obliterate Mrs. Grier forever.

Finally they collapsed in silence, heaving for breath. She moved her hands up and down his back, slick with sweat. She wanted him again. Even as she waited for shame to creep round her heart, she was planning when they could meet again. Neither one of them had spoken. She dreaded that in a way. What would he say to her now? What will I say to him?

"Anthony," she whispered, "do you suppose he heard us?"

He raised himself up on his arms and smiled down at her. "Listen," he said softly.

At first she couldn't hear it, but then she caught the sound through two closed doors—the unmistakable cadence of a man snoring.

"Come to me tomorrow," she said.

He grinned. "Most certainly, Mrs. Grier."

She put her hands to his face. "No. Only if you want to."

He took her hands and pinned them above her head, kissed her neck and breasts. "Not only do I wish to call on you tomorrow and the day after, Susanna. I'm not yet ready to leave you tonight."

Nancy awoke curled up against Jesse in her narrow bed by the kitchen window. It was barely light but Jesse was already awake, propped up against the wall, looking out the window.

"What you looking at, sweet man?" she said.

Jesse squeezed her shoulder but continued to look out the window. "Our master throwing up in the creek," he said. "Been down there going on a half an hour."

"Why you always worrying what everybody else doing? Worry about yourself more." She snuggled up against him. "Worry about me."

He turned from the window. "It wouldn't hurt you none to think a little more about what's going on around you. I wouldn't be bad-mouthing Anthony to Miss Susanna if I was you."

"Why you say that? The man's a snake."

"Maybe so, but she done had that snake in her bed last night till three, four in the morning."

"How you know that?"

"I heard them. Woke me up. Screaming like a couple of cats, windows wide open. Heard him crossing the yard later—whistling like a songbird."

She shook her head. "Everything wake you up."

"Man who raised me up say a man shouldn't learn to sleep too good—lion be glad to let you sleep in his belly, white man glad to put you in irons and you wake up a slave till you die."

She smiled at him and touched the deep lines on his brow. "Sweet man, there ain't no lions round here, and you already a slave. If you sleep more, you wouldn't be so tired and worrisome all the time."

He took her hand, kissed her fingers. "I ain't tired now."

"I have to get up and fix breakfast," she said, but lay back on the bed.

Jesse twisted around on top of her. "Miss Susanna be lying in her love bed all morning, and Mr. Robert, he won't want no breakfast this morning."

They made love, then lay in bed for only a few minutes before Nancy said, "I got to be getting out of this bed."

Jesse said nothing, but ran his fingers over her stomach. She was a deep, almost blue, black. He was much lighter, the color of dark honey. Watching Mr.

Grier with Rachel and Jess, he was now sure his first master had been his father. He never knew his mother and couldn't ask her, and Adam, the old blacksmith who taught him everything about metal and horses and how to get along, would say nothing about her except she'd been there and gone. But his master had always treated Jesse special. Sometimes too nice, sometimes too mean, but always different from the other slaves—the same way Mr. Grier treated Jess and Rachel.

The one Jesse couldn't figure was Susanna. She was smart, not much got by her. She had to know Jess and Rachel were her husband's slave bastards. Yet she treated them like they were her own children. Rachel appeared by the bed, her eyes still full of sleep, and spoke to Nancy. "I'm hungry," she said.

I PRINTED UP A COPY OF THE FIRST CHAPTER AND SHUT OFF MY computer. It was almost four in the morning, but I was still wide awake. I wrapped my robe around me and went down to the kitchen. One of the fluorescent bulbs over the sink was flickering. I rapped the fixture, and it stopped. I found a small snifter on a high shelf and poured myself a brandy.

She's real to you, Raymond had said of Susanna. When he reads this chapter, I thought, he'll probably think she's me, grieving for the lost love of my life. Outside, a gray cat slunk across the top of the fence in a crouch, intent on some purpose. I sipped on my brandy and watched it.

I wasn't Susanna. I had no lost love. I'd liked Tom, he was a good friend, but I never really loved him. I loved his children.

I met him when I was waiting tables at a restaurant where I was the only waitress over thirty, wondering how much longer I could keep working shit jobs so that I'd have time to write books I couldn't get published.

Tom came in with Lorena and Kareth, then two and seven, and I did all my kid tricks to boost the tip. I brought them crayons and paper, extra napkins, extra cherries in the

Shirley Temples—exactly the same number in each one. I asked the kids their names and told them mine, talked to them about their drawings. I liked them immediately, and I could tell they liked me. The next time they came in, Tom asked to be seated in my section.

The fourth time I'd waited on them in as many weeks, Lorena knocked a water glass into Kareth's lap, and I took Kareth to the bathroom to dry her off. She was soaked through, so I got a sweatshirt out of my car and put her in it. She turned in front of the mirror, as if modeling a Paris gown. She told me about her mom, using all the terms she'd learned at school—"My mother is a chronic drug abuser. She abandoned us, and now we're a single-parent family." It was the matter-of-fact tone that broke my heart, the pamphlet language she'd been given to deal with it. I knelt down and hugged her, and she said, "My daddy thinks you're pretty."

When I brought her back to the table, Tom looked at me as if I'd just plucked his daughter out of the bulrushes. I sat down at the table and talked with them, ignoring the rest of my section. When Tom wanted to know how he could return my shirt, I invited them to dinner at my apartment.

We were married three months later. I was about five years older than Susanna was when she took off with Anthony Richards.

THE SOUND OF CATS SCREAMING—FIGHTING OR MAKING LOVE—interrupted my reverie. I took my brandy upstairs and lay in bed wide awake, trying to decide whether to take Raymond up on his offer. God knows, I wanted to. I knew Raymond had been joking about making another pot of coffee, but if it hadn't been for the girls, I would've been there by now, probably in his bedroom.

Raising the girls had kept me from doing a lot of stupid things I otherwise would've done. I had them to thank for many blessings. It didn't matter how much I wanted Raymond, I wasn't going to do anything to upset my girls.

Not that they wouldn't want to go. All I'd have to do was mention horseback riding, and they'd start packing.

And they'd want me to go. They were always urging me to go out more often. Kareth especially. They thought I was lonely. They thought they wanted a stepfather.

When it came down to it, the only thing I was truly afraid of was that things would get too serious. Hell, maybe things had already gotten too serious. I saw the whole evening in my mind, staring at the ceiling, my arms wrapped around my pillow. I remembered the way he looked at me, the way he listened, the way he spoke to me, the way he kissed me. The way I kissed him. The way I felt. I had to see him again. I thought about calling in sick to work sometime during the week, dashing up there while the kids were at school, but felt ridiculous, like some kid cutting class.

No, I wanted him to meet my girls. I wanted them to meet him. I lay in bed trying to imagine this meeting, finally drifting off to sleep for a couple of hours. When I woke up, I'd made up my mind.

I got out of bed, splashed cold water on my face, and got dressed. I opened the curtains. Everything glistened with frost. I wanted to be with him. I wanted the upcoming week to vanish so that I could be back at Greenville, sitting by the fire. If I could've gone alone, I would've, but I didn't have that choice. I couldn't wait weeks before I saw him again. Besides, I told myself, remembering the manila envelope lying upstairs on my desk, I need to read the rest of Pearl's journal.

The kids will love it, I assured myself. If things don't work out, we'll just pack up and leave.

I MADE A BIG SUNDAY MORNING BREAKFAST, LOTS OF SUGAR AND fat. Kareth and Lorena half listened as I told them about Raymond—that he had a journal I needed for my work, that I could only look at it at his house in the country, an old plantation where he raised horses. Their eyes shot up at the mention of horses. I described the place to them, throwing in horses with every other breath. Then I asked them if they'd like to spend next weekend at this equine paradise.

"Are you kidding?" Kareth said. "So is this guy really rich or something? Living in a plantation."

"He seems rich, yes."

Lorena and Heather had been listening in silence. Heather was Lorena's alter ego—a battered stuffed bunny with fat cheeks and floppy ears, a fluffy, foot-high Charles Laughton. "Heather wants to know what a plantation is," Lorena said.

"A plantation," Kareth answered with her usual authority, "is a place where they have slaves."

"Used to have slaves," I corrected.

"My friend Lonnel says that slavery never ended. It's just taken on more subtle forms."

Lonnel sat next to Kareth in the band. I'd met him at PTA programs. He was a handsome young black man. His name came up often. They were both nerds. "Well, I can't argue with Lonnel, but if there were slaves at Greenville, I didn't see them."

"Lonnel says they're in Africa and South America and China, so we don't have to look at them."

"Are we going to China?" Lorena wanted to know. Kareth rolled her eyes and buried her face in her arms.

"No dear," I said. "We're going to a great big house in the country where a nice man is going to let you ride his horses."

Lorena grinned from ear to ear, and Heather hopped with glee.

Kareth watched Heather and rolled her eyes again, then grew serious. "I know he's got this journal and everything, but you kind of like him too, right?"

"Yes, I do. I like him very much."

She burst into a grin. "Way to go, Steppie!"

Lorena had been drawing bunnies on horseback galloping across her napkin, paying us no mind. At Kareth's outburst, Lorena snapped her head up. "What?" she demanded urgently. "What did she do?"

"I bet he's cute too, right?" Kareth asked me, ignoring her sister absolutely.

"Who's cute?" Lorena shrieked. "Tell me who's cute!"

"Raymond," I told her. "The man with the horses." I turned to Kareth and smiled, cocking one brow. "Actually, 'cute' is a word for puppies and little tykes. Raymond is a very handsome—and sexy—man."

Kareth dropped her eyes and turned red. The tips of her ears looked as if she'd just come in from a blizzard. Lorena looked from one to the other of us. "What?" she wailed. "I don't get it!"

MONDAY MORNING I SENT RAYMOND THE FIRST CHAPTER OF MY book, with a note saying I'd be there if I could get off from work Saturday. All I had to do was persuade Andrea to pick up Saturday for me. With horse shows and violin recitals and swim meets, I'd asked her often enough before.

Monday afternoon we were sitting at a table in the back room having coffee. Andrea, who grew up in New Jersey, was telling one of her Virginians-don't-know-how-to-drive stories. When she'd exhausted the idiocy of the particular Virginian in question, I said, "You know that novel I've been working on?"

She nodded and sipped her coffee. "Sure, I've heard of it once or twice or three times. You need to get a life, Marion."

I ignored this refrain. "I've found a manuscript—a journal by a woman in 1850. It's wonderful material. Anyway, I can only look at it on Saturdays. It's in this guy's house outside Culpeper. He says I can come up this Saturday, but I'm supposed to work . . ."

She waved her hand at the rows of newspapers, books, boxes of letters, diaries, maps that surrounded us. "I should give up my Saturday so you can look at the last piece-of-crap manuscript in Virginia that I'm not locked up with every day?"

I could see I had to change my approach, so Tuesday and Wednesday I let out details of my romantic evening at Greenville—how he looked deep into my eyes as he took my hand, fed me a gourmet meal, hung on my every word, and kissed me in a steamy, parked Hudson, and how I then drove back to Richmond in the middle of the night, called him in the wee hours, and felt a glow all over as he begged me to come to him next weekend—if only I didn't have to work on Saturday.

Andrea and I had worked together since shortly after Tom's death. Our sex talk usually consisted of her complaining about her husband, Victor. It was Andrea's oft stated opinion that I took insufficient advantage of my single condition. "If you won't screw them on the first date," she'd once observed, "and you won't go out with anybody twice—I think I'm beginning to detect an unhealthy pattern here, Marion."

On Thursday, she pulled me into the break room and sat me down, looked me in the eye like a big sister. "Marion, it sounds to me like this guy wants to fuck you. So what I want to know is, what are you going to do about it?"

"We've spent one evening together—a few hours."

"Oh come on, Marion. He's nice, he's sexy, he's rich, he's handsome. You owe this to *me,* Marion."

"Does this mean you'll work for me Saturday?"

"Sure, sure, but you got to listen to me, Marion." She leaned forward, serious, gently tapping out her points on my forearm. "Friend to friend. You could use a screaming good fuck." She straightened up. "A *screaming* good fuck. And furthermore, you should tell me all about it Monday morning." She danced her eyebrows and laughed. "I'll stick it in Victor's ear. Maybe he'll figure out what to do with it."

I PICKED UP THE KIDS AFTER SCHOOL ON FRIDAY, MY VAN LOADED up with the junk they thought they needed to take. Kareth took the very back seat. Lorena sat in the front passenger seat with Heather on her lap. At her side was her souvenir Mickey Mouse from Disney World, a smiling mouse the size of a Dalmation.

"How soon till we get there?" Lorena asked as we pulled onto the interstate.

"A little over an hour," I said.

"I'm bored."

"Maybe Heather would like to tell Mickey a story," I said. Heather frequently told stories to whoever would listen.

"What is the place called we're going, again?" Lorena asked me.

"Greenville. It's a plantation."

"I mean, what is the man's name?"

"Raymond. Raymond Lord."

"Okay," she said, and narrated in a soft voice, "Once upon a time there was a man named Raymond, and he lived in a big green house full of horses, and a very beautiful princess bunny named Heather came hopping up to his house, and he said, 'Hi Heather, would you like one of my magical horses?' and Heather did and rode and rode and rode happy ever after the end."

"Heather," I said. "How were the horses magical—what made them different from any other horses?"

She pondered this a moment. "You could ride them all you wanted for as long as you wanted and never have to go home and have dinner or anything," Heather said.

"How long till we get there?" Lorena asked.

"About an hour."

Lorena yawned and curled up into a ball with Heather at the heart of it and went to sleep.

For an hour I had a silent car to think in. Kareth lay on the far back seat as if it were a couch, a magazine with some anorexic on the cover inches from her face. Just like me when I was her age.

Traffic was heavy. I was in the slow lane—a long line of trucks barreling along at seventy. I was thinking about my book, hoping Pearl's journal would provide the clues to get me unstuck. I'd been blocked for a few weeks, even a month before, but nothing like this. Sometimes I had to throw out weeks of work, but I'd always written, ever since I was a little girl. This book was different. I'd started telling myself that if

I couldn't write it, I couldn't write, that maybe it was time to go back to school and get a master's in library science or museology—get a real job and forget this novelist crap once and for all. Of course, I knew I wouldn't really quit writing. That was just a scare story I told myself. I was too addicted to quit.

I took the exit at 522 and slowed down to fifty-five, the only car on the road as far as I could see. Everything got quieter. I looked in the rearview mirror and watched the interstate disappear over the hill. Ahead of me, two lanes wound through farmland and woods. This was my dad's kind of highway. Once when my dad came back from a long road trip, I'd asked him what he did on his trips besides be a salesman. "Think," he'd said.

Maybe Andrea was right—maybe what I needed was a screaming good fuck. But screaming good fucks usually led somewhere I didn't want to go. I used to take the first few steps—or leaps, more like it—into many a stupid affair. The few romances I had that weren't set to self-destruct from the outset would start to frighten me. I'd say to myself, This doesn't feel right, never sure what I meant, and bolt—once two weeks before I was to be married. I'd decided it just might be easier on everyone concerned if I didn't take the first few steps to begin with.

I liked my life the way it was. The kids were right—I was lonely. But that hadn't seemed like such a big deal anymore. I'd been wild from the time I hit puberty until I met Tom. In high school, I liked bad boys, and while I myself never stole any of the stolen cars I'd ridden in, while I myself had never dealt any of the drugs I consumed, my boyfriends had. Most of my high school boyfriends ended up in prisons or mental institutions. Those that hadn't, should have. It was a miracle I didn't have a record, not so much as a traffic ticket, though I'd been a passenger in six major car wrecks by the time I graduated from high school.

After that I moved on to my professors in college, other women's husbands, and other hopeless cases. All this craziness was fueled by a longing I knew none of these men could satisfy. But I went after them anyway, like Susanna with Anthony. But someone looking back at me, like I was looking back at Susanna, would know none of this about me. Officially, I was a model citizen. No one had ever advertised my sins. I'd never been arrested or tried for any of the damage I'd done. I'd never even gotten pregnant.

And then five years ago, the girls came along and saved my life. I actually became the model citizen I'd seemed to be, and I was happier than I'd ever been. It wasn't that the longing had gone away completely; it'd become a manageable background noise, like a sentimentally charged song from an old affair playing over the PA in the grocery store, a heart tug as I searched for a particular brand of cereal. I told myself that my hormonal tide was going out, and most of the time was glad of it.

Then I laid eyes on Raymond, and the longing came back in a rush, all its intensity intact. If anything, it seemed stronger for having been dammed up.

I looked down at the speedometer and saw I'd crept up to seventy-five. I took my foot off the gas and coasted back down to fifty-five. In a way, Raymond didn't seem to be my type. He was too nice, too kind, too sensitive. Maybe, I told myself, I've finally gotten some sense. Maybe, a voice deep inside of me whispered, he was the one I'd been looking for all along.

I passed the *CUCKOO* sign, and still couldn't see anything I would call a town. I passed an abandoned café I remembered from last time, a log barn, a row of willows. I'd see him again soon, spend the whole weekend with him. I felt a tingle in my chest. My hands were sweating. He's just a guy, Marion, I said to myself. He's just another guy. But I didn't believe myself.

As we turned off by the river, Kareth closed her magazine and crawled out of the far back seat and sat on the back of the console. "Can we listen to the radio?"

I turned it on. "How was your magazine?" I asked.

"I read this really dumb story." She yawned and stretched, leaned into the space between the two front seats, and squinted out at the road ahead of us. "I knew how it was going to end halfway through the first page."

I leaned over and kissed her cheek. "My little critic. Now sit back down and put on your seat belt."

I'D WORN JEANS AND A SWEATER TO MAKE IT CLEAR I WASN'T trying to impress anyone, that I was here to work, and this is what I worked in whether he liked it or not. I'd changed clothes a half-dozen times, spent an hour messing with my hair. I hadn't done so much thinking about what I was going to wear since I was a freshman in college and my closet looked like a miniature costume shop. But this time, I'd decided over the last week, if I was going to do this, I wanted to look like myself, a middle-aged woman with two kids.

We stopped in the drive and had just set the bags on the ground when Raymond walked down from the house. His baggy wool trousers were soft and worn. His sweater drooped from his body in warm, comfortable folds. He put his arm around my shoulders and smiled into my eyes.

"Good to see you," I said, smiling back, letting myself get lost in his gaze.

"Can we ride horses?" Lorena asked loudly. I cut her a look that advised her to be seen and not heard.

Rachel and a young, slender black man appeared, scooped the bags from the drive, and disappeared into the house. "They'll take your things to your rooms," Raymond said. He bent down and put out his hand to Lorena. "You must be Lorena. I'm Raymond, unless your mother thinks that all adult men should be 'Mr.'"

"First names are fine," I said.

Lorena's hand moved toward Raymond's in slow motion. How many adults had she shaken hands with? If she'd been a boy, of course, it would've been dozens by now, but this might be the first time she'd ever shaken hands with a grown man. As she took his hand, she concentrated, looking up at him to see if she'd done it right. He smiled down at her, gave her hand a pump, and let it go. Lorena stood straight as a reed.

Kareth, who'd been watching all this in silence, dropped her eyes and stuck out her hand. I thought she might collapse in a heap.

"And you must be Kareth," Raymond said. "You have your mother's beauty."

I was relieved to see Kareth take this as a compliment without pointing out that Raymond had never laid eyes on her mother. Lorena, now clinging to my waist, said, "I have it too."

Raymond roared with laughter. "And so you do! Let's ride some horses, shall we?"

He looked over their heads to me. "If that's all right with your mother."

"I'm their stepmother," I said. "They call me Marion."

"And Stepmommo," said Kareth.

"And Marion Mom," said Lorena.

"Steppie," said Kareth.

"Sweetie pie," shouted Lorena.

Kareth sneered. "That's what *Daddy* called her, you little idiot."

"I call her that sometimes too!" Lorena wailed, her fists balled up at her sides.

"Stop it!" I hissed.

The silence was absolute as they nodded their hanging heads. "Now, do you want to ride horses or go back to Richmond?"

"Ride horses," they mumbled quietly.

"Then straighten up."

I looked now at Raymond. "Pardon me while I do my wicked-stepmother routine."

"Quite all right. I'm sorry. I didn't realize you were their stepmother. The way you spoke of them. I just assumed . . ."

"That's okay. They're little jerks, but they're my little jerks." I put my arms around them, and they leaned up against me, though Kareth gave me a retaliatory nudge for calling her a little jerk, or perhaps it was for putting her in the same category, any category, with Lorena.

As we walked down the road to the stable, the girls broke loose and ran on ahead, climbing onto the fences on either side of the road, beckoning the horses to come to them.

Raymond took my hand. "It's good to see you again," he said.

"I had a wonderful time the other night talking your ear off."

"I enjoyed every minute of it." He pointed at Kareth and Lorena, who were petting a huge white mare. "It looks like your girls are already having fun."

"You have the sacred animals. As you can see, they insisted on wearing their paddock boots and riding pants to school so they could ride the minute they got here, though I told them they'd almost certainly have to wait."

"I hope you don't mind that I suggested it."

"I don't mind, if you don't mind being a hero."

He laughed. "It's a welcome change. I take it you don't share your girls' passion for riding?"

"I just never learned."

"I'd love to teach you."

I shook my head. "Not today."

"Then we can have some coffee, perhaps discuss your novel while the children ride. Thomas will take good care of them." The slim black man had somehow beaten us to the barn. He stood inside the paddock, looking to Raymond for instructions. "Thomas," Raymond said. "This is Kareth, and this is Lorena. This is their stepmother, Marion Mead." Thomas nodded at us all but didn't speak.

"I wonder if you'd take these two girls on a trail ride," Raymond said.

"Be glad to," Thomas said.

Raymond turned to me. "I need to check on one of the

mare's records while I'm down here. I may have a buyer for her. I'll be right back." He walked into the barn.

I WATCHED AS THOMAS CAUGHT THREE HORSES WITH PRACTICED ease and brought them into the yard one at a time. The girls stood on the bottom rung of the fence and pleaded with him to let them groom and tack the animals themselves. "You girls know what you doing?" he asked.

"I do," Kareth said, "and I can help Lorena when she messes up."

"I won't mess up," Lorena bristled.

He looked over Kareth's head to me for my ruling, and I nodded.

"Kareth, help your sister with a minimum of condescension, okay?"

"Okay," Kareth said, without taking her eyes off the horses.

Thomas tended to his own horse as he kept an eye on the girls. I joined him at the rail. "How're they doing?" I asked him.

"They doing fine." He looked at me. "I picked out the gentlest horses on the place."

"Oh, I'm not worried."

"They take lessons in the city?"

"That's right."

"When I was a kid in Kentucky, horses all I cared about. Got me a job mucking stalls at a racetrack." He shook his head. "The groom there taught me what he know when the boss wasn't looking. But these ain't no racetrack horses—run too hard and shot up with every damn thing." He smiled at the broad, grassy fields. "These horses be living in horse heaven."

"So you like it here?"

He didn't look back at me. "It's all right," he said.

"This is the kind of saddle I want, Marion, okay?" Kareth said over her shoulder as she tightened the girth.

"Whenever you want to buy it."

"For my birthday."

"We'll see."

"Me too," said Lorena, who pulled her saddle from the rail and staggered about with the vain hope of putting it on her horse's back.

Thomas moved quickly to her side. "Let me give you a hand with this." He didn't take it from her but clasped his own hands beside hers and helped her heave it onto the horse. "You just need a little help is all. You doing fine."

"What do you say, Lorena?"

"Thank you, Thomas," she said.

"She's just a little kid," Kareth explained to Thomas. "But she thinks she's got to do everything I do."

"Fortunately," I said to her, "when you were her age, you didn't have an older sister to make you feel inadequate all the time."

Kareth made a face but didn't push her luck.

AS THEY WERE MOUNTING UP, RAYMOND RETURNED TO MY SIDE.

"You girls want to see the river?" Thomas asked. "Have 'em back in about an hour," he said to me.

The three of them trotted out of sight down a narrow lane. "I had five brothers and sisters," I heard Thomas saying before their voices faded away.

And then I was alone with Raymond again. "I like Thomas," I said. My voice was already getting the brittle chirp it takes on whenever I get nervous or scared.

"He's a good man," he said. He took my hand. "Let's go in and sit by the fire, shall we? I've been looking forward to this."

We took the shortcut Thomas had taken, a path from the back of the house to the stable. He pointed out a low brick building behind the house. "That used to be the kitchen. Rachel's and Thomas's apartments are there now."

"They live here?"

"Yes. It's easier for them that way. There's nothing much close by."

On the back of the house were smaller columns, echoing their grand cousins out front. From the back I could see that the roof formed a huge W, that its squared-off appearance was an illusion. From back here, the oddity of the house was even more apparent. Whoever designed it had no sense of architectural fashion from any century I knew about.

We entered on the ground floor into the kitchen. It looked remarkably like the kitchen of a restaurant where I'd waited tables when I was an undergraduate, a square of stainless steel and fluorescent lights, a huge six-burner stove. It reminded me of the days when I was writing my second bad novel, long before I'd met Tom or the girls, when I did incredibly foolish things as a matter of course and called that "experiencing life."

Rachel stood at the island, chopping onions. She laughed, wiping at her tears with her shirtsleeves, nodding and smiling at me.

"Hi Rachel," I said. "It's good to see you again."

"It is pleasure see you again also, Marion." She said each word with care, as if called on in a language class.

I put out my hand, and she cocked her head. "Woman shake hands?" she asked.

"Yes," I said.

She wiped her hands on her apron. Without bending her elbow, she swung her arm slowly toward my waiting hand. I took her hand and gave it a quick squeeze. She laughed out loud, a wonderful girl's laugh, and swung her arm back to her side, smiling at me with unbridled goodwill.

I bowed to her, and Raymond spoke a few foreign words to her as we went through a swinging door into the sitting room.

There was a fire blazing, and coffee set out on a table by the window. The room was packed with things, on shelves, on tables—pipes, knives, pocket watches, knickknacks of all descriptions. The sheer number of things was intimidating.

Even the walls were covered with objects. Above the mantel were guns and knives and swords and some odd contraptions I assumed to be weapons also, all of them at least a hundred years old. A small glass case that looked like it had once displayed necklaces at a fine jewelry store was stuffed with dozens of pocketknives. What a boy he is, I thought. Perhaps that's why he's remained a bachelor. Maybe that's why I like him so much.

The mantel was covered with carved animals. Some looked like they were from Raymond's hand, but most didn't. My favorite was an ivory dragon in the middle of the display, spreading his intricate wings over the whole flock from ducks to tigers.

Raymond was pouring our coffee. "Cream, no sugar?"

I nodded, and he handed me my coffee. We sat by the fire in Colonial rockers, a small table between us.

"I love your house," I said.

He was obviously pleased. "It's been something of an obsession with me these last few years, fixing it up just how I'd imagined it. It's an extension of myself."

"A true Virginian."

He considered this. "Yes, I suppose I am—always looking to the past, not quite sure what to do in the present." He gestured at all the things around us. "That's why I keep the past so ready to hand."

He took a sip from his coffee. "I was intrigued by the chapter you sent me. That time and place, those people—they all seem very real to you."

"In a sense. My characters are my extensions of myself."

"Susanna in particular?"

"Yes, I suppose so. She's the focal point of the story. I put a lot of myself into her."

He nodded, listening carefully. "I hope you don't mind my asking, but her widow's grief—is that your own?"

"In a way," I hedged. "I know what it is to have been a grieving widow."

"Of course, but do you grieve as she does? After all those

84

years." He leaned forward in his chair ever so slightly. He spoke quietly, but his tone was urgent, insistent.

"Susanna and I are different. She's more desperate than I've ever been, has fewer choices she can make."

"Is that why she sleeps with someone who's almost a complete stranger to her, a criminal?"

"They've been in the same household for two years."

"But he would've been a mere face, a man looking at her, as she herself says, one of many men looking at her."

I laughed, trying to lighten things up a little. "Not all looks are created equal."

"And what was so special about Anthony's look?" His face was serious, intent upon my answer.

"It was dangerous," I said, looking into the fire, away from Raymond's gaze—another dangerous look, a different, more subtle danger. I felt weak in the knees. His eyes could've been Anthony's, just as I'd imagined them—dark, mysterious, penetrating. "She knew if she slept with him, it would change her life forever. She wanted her life to change. She didn't care much how."

"But she didn't love him?"

"No."

"That's sad, don't you think?"

"I do," I said. That's what drew me to her story. I thought I understood her.

"And what about you, Marion? Do you want your life to change?" His tone had softened. He might've been an old friend, asking a question he already knew the answer to.

"I'm quite content," I said, and looked him full in the face to show him my contentment.

"You still might wish to change your life," he said.

I looked about, taking stock of my contentment as if it were one of the many objects in the room. The fire glittered from the wings of the dragon.

"I suppose so," I said. "That would depend on the change." I drank from my coffee, wondering what changes Raymond had in mind for my life, wondering how he wanted me to change his.

"I'm sorry," he said. "I've been prying."

"That's okay." I laughed. "I do it all the time. It saves time." I looked up at the weapons as if I were studying them. "Tell me how you came to own Greenville."

His eyes moved around the room, taking it in, taking in the rest of the house in his mind's eye. "It had long been abandoned. It was a decaying hulk sitting out here. I didn't want to see it become a ruin. It had sentimental value to me. So I paid twice what it was worth and bought up all the land around it."

"You used to live around here?"

"Yes."

"When you were a boy?" I prompted.

He hesitated. "When I was a young man."

"Do you know the history of the place—when it was built, who built it? It's such an unusual house."

"A man named Philip Pendleton Nalle had it built in the 1850s. He'd enjoyed an upturn in his fortunes from smuggling slaves. His partner brought them up the Rappahannock from the coast, then Nalle brought them here and took them to Richmond to sell. He accumulated enough money and respectability to turn in his drunken partner to the authorities and divert all suspicion from himself. Ironically, it was the partner who drew the original plans for the house. In later years Nalle sold cattle instead of slaves. The historical record doesn't reveal how he made his first real money."

"If the records don't show how this man made his money, then how did you find out—do you have records no one else has seen?"

Raymond set his coffee on the table beside him, stood and fiddled with the fire, put another log on, though it didn't really need it. He crouched before the hearth, turning logs with the poker. They popped and sparked. The flames sprang up and cast him in a new light. He stood and faced me, took a deep breath.

"I've made a study of the man who designed this house. I

know quite a bit about him. But I'm not a real historian. I have no real documentation."

I smelled another story. "Do you have letters? A diary?"

"No."

"Then I don't understand. How do you know all this stuff?"

"I remember everything, like Anthony."

"A photographic memory?"

"Yes. May I ask how you came to give Anthony such a trait?"

"It just came to me one night. I'm not sure where it came from. To tell you the truth, I wasn't even sure such a thing was possible."

"I'm afraid it's quite possible."

"So, all those books—you remember them all?"

He laughed. "Only the ones I've read."

"Why do you keep them after you've read them? I mean, if you remember them perfectly."

"The memory of a book isn't the book itself—the experience of reading it—any more than the memory of a lover is the same as being in love."

I smiled at this. What a nice way to look at it, I thought. "But I still want to hear more about the slave smuggler— what were the sources you looked at?"

He stood before me, kissed his fingertips, and laid them on my lips. "You're trying to make a story out of my architect, aren't you?"

I kissed his fingertips. "I confess. Tom used to say I cared more about my characters than I did about the real world."

He caressed my cheek, and I closed my eyes. "I envy your characters," he said.

I reached up, held his hand against my cheek, and looked into his eyes. "You shouldn't," I said.

He sank to his knees and kissed me, his hands cradling my face. I pressed my hands against his, took them into mine. We broke the kiss and rested our foreheads together, looking down at our clasped hands. "Raymond," I whispered, "You scare me a little. My feelings scare me."

"Mine too," he said, and rose to his feet, gently pulling me to my feet. "Let me show you the rest of my house."

"I'd love to," I said. "Let's start at the top and work down."

He laughed. "See there. You're doing it too. Any excuse to climb that staircase."

THIS TIME WE WALKED UP HAND IN HAND. I LIKED THE FEEL OF being beside him, the way he moved, the way he felt. I liked him. He was the most intriguing man I'd ever met.

"What's up here?" I asked when we reached the cherubs.

"My rooms," he said. "First, I want you to see the library from up here."

The doors were inlaid with beaten metal in geometric patterns. I'd never seen anything quite like them. As we stepped into the library, I came face-to-face with the chandelier. It looked like a neoclassic flying saucer hovering motionless maybe six feet from the railing.

"Two contractors told me I couldn't put a chandelier that size in here." He laughed. "They were right of course. The original was in a room three times this size." He slipped his arm around my shoulders, pointed at the ceiling. "The roof is now reinforced with steel girders, as are the walls."

"Wouldn't it have been easier just to build a new house?"

"Much easier."

I pointed at the chandelier. "So tell me about the original."

"It was in a church in London."

"What about those doors back there?"

"They're Babylonian, from the dwelling of a priest."

I put my arm around his waist and hugged him. "You're certainly eclectic in your tastes."

"Life's more interesting that way."

Raymond's bedroom took up the back of the third story. It was simple and comfortable. Besides the carved animals that were all over the house, the only decorations were drawings hung on the wall—architectural sketches, landscapes, a few portraits. The furniture was a jumble of styles. My favorite piece was a massive sleigh bed.

"Where did you find that wonderful bed?" I asked. "I suppose it's Albanian or something."

He smiled. "Strictly American. I found it at an antique shop near Amherst."

On the bedside table were framed photographs. The one that caught my eye was a little white boy, obviously the young Raymond, squinting into the sun, standing next to a tall black man, his hair turning gray, dressed in what looked like a janitor's uniform. They were standing in front of a wooden hut with a thatched straw roof.

"Is that the man who taught you to whittle?"

"Timothy, yes. He came to live at my father's mission when I was three because all his children had died and there was no one to take care of him. My father put him in that silly outfit. Timothy called them his 'Christian clothes.'"

"You are fond of him."

"Oh yes."

"Do you have any pictures of your mother and father?"

"No," he said with a sharp edge to his voice. "We're not close. We've been estranged for some years now." He turned away and walked across the room. Mom and Dad were apparently a sore subject.

He opened the door to a bathroom the size of my bedroom, a fourth of it taken up with a hulking glass shower stall. Jets and sprays studded its walls like armaments.

"What's this? Hurricane in a box?"

He laughed, and the sound echoed loudly in the tiled room. "I like toys," he said.

"And what century is this from?"

"Strictly twentieth."

As we stepped into the library on the second floor balcony, he pointed out a door in the corner, directly above his office. "I've set up Pearl's manuscript in that office there. Your room's this way." He continued along the balcony, a step ahead of me, and I watched him move. Though he affected this relaxed, unhurried air, he was intent on something.

My room looked familiar somehow, but I couldn't place it. It was simply furnished with a wardrobe, a secretary, a four-poster bed, a bedside table. I parted the curtains and looked out over the fields to the river. "Nice view," I said cheerily, but he'd grown quiet and pensive and only nodded his assent. I guessed the mention of Mom and Dad had opened some old wound.

The girls had the other back bedroom. There was a connecting bath between us. A room with a TV, VCR, pool table, and stereo was in front of the girls' room.

We descended a back stairway that came down from his room, opened onto the girls' room on the second floor, and ended at the kitchen on the ground floor. Rachel was no longer there. On the counter where she'd been working was a row of sealed plastic containers.

I pointed to the refrigerator beside the stairs. "You mean they have their own personal stairway to the refrigerator in addition to Raymond's pool hall in the next room?"

"I'm afraid so."

"You're not trying to win them over or anything."

"Certainly not. It's Stepmommo I'm after."

"Oh God, please don't call me that."

"All right," he said quietly. "It's Marion I'm after." He put his hands on my waist and pulled me to him, put his arms around me, and kissed me. I wanted to be kissed impulsively, to be swept away, but I couldn't shake my fear.

I broke the kiss and clung to him, staring into the room behind him. I'd had an affair with the owner of that restaurant whose kitchen looked so much like this one. He'd been full of ardent intensity too. We'd made love on the stainless steel counter. He'd lifted me onto it and dropped his pants around his knees. The whole time, the phone was ringing. It was his wife and two kids and mortgage and duty and first loyalty calling—all the things he'd set aside for a couple of weeks of romantic adventure, like a sea cruise. He let me keep working there even after he quit fucking me, until he hired someone else he wanted to fuck, and I might tell her my story before he got the chance.

"Marion? Are you all right?"

Raymond was still holding me, looking at me with concern.

"I'm sorry. I'm fine, really. This kitchen—it reminds me of a place I used to work. It brought back old ghosts."

"Only me here now."

"And perhaps moving a little too fast."

He dropped his arms and I laughed, drumming my fists lightly on his chest. "Not that slow," I said, wrapping my arms around his waist and laying my head on his chest. "Just hold me," I said. "Just you, right now."

THE GIRLS RETURNED FROM THEIR RIDE OVERFLOWING WITH praise of the horses, Thomas, the river, this moment in their lives. I took a quick shower and turned the bathroom over to the kids. Kareth waited until Lorena was in the tub, and she had me to herself, to ask if Raymond and I were "serious."

I answered in my best Mom voice: "We just met, honey. We don't know each other well enough to be 'serious.'"

Kareth gave me the look I deserved and shook her head. "Maybe so. But nobody's told him that. He looks at you like you are pure sex."

"Pure sex?"

"It's just an expression."

I laughed and sat down beside her. "It certainly is that. And you're right about the look. But you know, Kareth, there's more to 'serious' than just how some guy looks at you."

She made a face. "I know that. So has he said anything?"

She sat on the edge of the bed, thirty years younger than me, asking me to confide in her.

"He likes me, honey, and I like him. Don't worry about it."

"I'm not worried. I think he's nice." She bit her lip. "You

know, I wouldn't mind if you got married again. I mean, it's not like I think you should be like 'true to Daddy's memory' or some junk like that, and Lorena doesn't even remember him. She might like to have a daddy. It's like she never had one.''

I took her hand. "So you're just looking out for your little sister?"

"No, not exactly."

"I'm glad you like Raymond."

She nodded and spoke without looking at me. "Well, don't you think you ought to go hang out with him or something while he fixes dinner?"

I laughed and gave her a hug. "Yes dear, that's just what I was about to do."

I WENT DOWN TO THE KITCHEN AND STOOD IN THE DOORWAY watching him cook. There was a pot of what I guessed from the smell to be onion soup already simmering on the stove. Beside him was a platter of sautéed veal scallops. Clad in a chef's apron, wooden spoon in hand, he was preparing a sauce, adding seasonings and wine. "I'm impressed," I said. "A true cook—you're not even using a recipe."

He turned around and broke into a smile. "I didn't know you were there. Glass of wine?"

"You don't mind if I watch?"

"Don't be ridiculous." He fetched a high stool and set it beside the island, poured me a glass of wine. "Actually, I'm a fraud. I always cook from a recipe." He tapped his forehead. "I keep them up here."

"You remember cookbooks?"

"I read my mother's cookbooks when I was a boy. It was that and the Bible around my house." He pointed at the sauce he was stirring. "Page twenty-five, 'Veal Scallops with Tarragon,' *Elegant French Cookery* by Miriam Bascham: 'Remove all but a tablespoon of fat from skillet. Add one tablespoon shallots and stir over medium heat for half a minute. Add one-quarter cup dry white vermouth, one tablespoon minced tarragon leaves, and one cup brown stock.'"

I laughed. "This talent must've come in handy in college."

"I never went to school. I'm entirely self-educated."

"You just read, and remember it all."

"That's right."

"This must be rare."

"Extremely."

"Have you been studied? By psychologists, I mean."

He gave me a rueful smile. "I have talked to my share of psychologists, I'm afraid." He removed the skillet from the heat, stirring in a cornstarch paste and cooked mushrooms, and returned it to the fire. "But what about you?" He put his fingertips to his forehead and closed his eyes, feigning clairvoyance. "You were an English major, am I right?"

I laughed and shook my head. "It's the Amazing Raymond. Okay, Amazing, what did I specialize in—what was my passion?"

He looked at me, studying me as if he were actually thinking about it. "You would love the Romantics," he said. "The nineteenth century."

"Yes, I would."

He smiled, quite pleased with himself that he'd guessed correctly. But it hadn't felt like the lucky guess of a stranger, more like an old friend filling in a missing piece of information from a store of intimacies.

I peered into his eyes. "And you would like Byron, am I right?"

"I would indeed."

"And you know it all by heart?"

He nodded.

"Give me a stanza, then. I love Byron."

He laid down the spoon, thought a moment. *"Childe Harold,* first canto, eighth stanza—

*"Yet oft-times in his maddest mirthful mood
Strange pangs would flash along Childe Harold's
     brow,*

As if the memory of some deadly feud
Or disappointed passion lurk'd below:
But this none knew, nor haply cared to know;
For his was not that open, artless soul
That feels relief by bidding sorrow flow,
Nor sought he friend to counsel or condole,
Whate'er this grief mote be, which he could not
control."

It was beautiful, the way he spoke the words, the way he looked at me with his great sad eyes as he spoke them. He was beautiful. "Bravo!" I said, applauding as he made a small bow. I reached out and tugged at his apron. "Come here," I said, pulling him toward me. "I want to kiss you."

"Because I can recite Byron?"

Perched on the stool, I was as tall as he was. I wrapped my arms around him. "No, silly. Because you recited it to me."

I'D WARNED THE GIRLS UNDER THREAT OF DEATH THAT THEY WERE to at least attempt to eat whatever was served for dinner without objection or commentary. The warning was unnecessary. They pounced on the food as if they ate veal with tarragon every day. They were impressed that Raymond had prepared the meal. They were impressed with everything about Raymond as he talked with them throughout dinner, drawing upon his seemingly limitless store of knowledge to amuse them, enlighten them, and ultimately captivate them.

As for me, I was deliriously happy, laughing and joking, equally (though more deliciously) captivated. Once, I caught the girls trading significant glances over my remarkable behavior. They smiled their approval like little Buddhas and looked at Raymond, their eyes agleam with the knowledge that he was the source of this miracle.

It was a small thing, I suppose, but I realized at that moment that this was the first time since Tom's death that the three of us had sat down at the same table and shared a meal with a man. I watched his profile as he gave his unwavering attention to some meandering story Lorena had launched into. Even Kareth's inevitable promptings to clarify or speed the tale along were delivered without the usual sneer, in a spirit of goodwill. I could get used to this, I thought.

As we were having dessert, he asked Kareth if she wanted to be a novelist like her stepmother.

"Maybe," Kareth said. "I write some now, but it's all just silly stuff. It doesn't *mean* anything or have symbols or any of that stuff." She glanced quickly over at me, then back to Raymond. "I get lots of good ideas."

"Tell me about one of them," he said.

"Well, I had one on the way up here when I was reading this really stupid story. It's this girl's birthday. And she thinks everybody's like totally forgotten her, even her boyfriend. But what's really going on is, her boyfriend's throwing her this totally huge surprise party. So she spends the whole story feeling sorry for herself and thinking her boyfriend's some kind of complete jerk, until they have the stupid party for her and everybody's all gooey happy at the end." Kareth paused and looked around as if everyone were watching her on the high board. She took a deep breath and continued. "But I thought about writing a story where everybody *does* forget her stupid birthday and she's got to like deal with it instead of whining around for twenty pages."

Raymond nodded, quite serious. "It's awful not to be remembered, don't you think? How's she going to deal with it?" There wasn't a trace of condescension in his voice.

Kareth thought hard and said, "I'm not sure. I haven't figured that part out yet. I guess if I were her I'd be pretty mad at my boyfriend for forgetting me."

"What would you do?" he asked, not like an adult drawing out a kid but like someone who really wanted to know.

She shrugged and laughed, turning red. "I don't know. I've never had a real boyfriend."

"Perhaps," Raymond suggested, "if he's forgotten her,

he's not a real boyfriend, and she should find someone who values her more."

Kareth winced at the loss of this imagined boyfriend. "But everybody forgets things sometimes. She could probably forgive him if he's really sorry, and she like really likes him a whole, whole lot."

Raymond smiled. "So you think how she feels about him is the most important thing?"

Kareth nodded. "And how he feels about her."

He looked at me, his eyes full of passion and melancholy, searching my eyes for how I felt about him, and I held his gaze. I could hear Andrea in her best I'm-leveling-with-you tone, *This guy wants to fuck you, Marion. You going for it?*

"May we be excused?" Kareth asked quietly.

"Of course," I said. "Go on upstairs and get ready for bed. I'll be up shortly." They kissed me good night and, without any prompting from me, Raymond as well, then vanished.

"The girls have taken note of our attraction," Raymond said when they'd gone. He caressed my cheek with his fingertips. I closed my eyes, and he kissed me. He was passionate but unhurried. We might've been old, comfortable lovers.

"My kids think you're wonderful," I said.

"They are the ones who are wonderful. You're a very good mom."

I shook my head. "I got into the picture kind of late actually."

"Maybe so. But they're full of you—your curiosity, your wit, your good heart, your fondness for stories."

"My heart's not so good."

"Tell those girls that, and see what they say."

"Raymond, you don't know me that well."

"You mean, I don't know that you didn't love your husband?"

He hadn't said it with any rancor. He was letting me off the hook, letting me know he'd intuited my faults and thought none the less of me. "Is it that obvious?"

"No. I've just been paying attention."

I smiled at him. "I know. I rather like it."

"But I haven't left you a moment to work. You said you have high hopes for Pearl's journal."

"I do. But maybe this is what I really need—to feel this happy. I feel so good, I could write two or three novels." I laughed. "Then I'll make you read them all, one by one."

For the briefest of moments a deep pain crossed his face, and he looked away, struggling to mount a smile, apparently hoping I hadn't noticed. "I hope Pearl's journal proves helpful," he said.

"Raymond, are you all right?"

"I'm fine, really. I . . ." He gestured in the air, searching for words, trying to keep the pain at bay. He surrendered to it and his hands fell to his lap. "Happiness is fragile," he said quietly. He turned and looked at me with a crooked smile. "That's all. I was just thinking that happiness is fragile."

I took his hands. "It doesn't have to be."

He gave a small laugh. "That's always the hard part, isn't it? Knowing what has to be and what doesn't."

I squeezed his hands. "We'll figure it out."

"I hope so," he said. He looked into my eyes for a good long while. "Marion, would you spend the night in my rooms tonight?"

Every cell in my body imagined themselves making love to Raymond, but I knew I couldn't say yes. "Raymond, I want to get an early start on that journal you're so eager for me to read."

"You may sleep if you wish," he said gently. "I just want to be with you."

I picked up his hands and kissed them. "Raymond, I think you know what I wish. But I can't. Not our first night here. The girls expect me to be in the next room. Lorena has nightmares sometimes. Kareth walks in her sleep . . ."

He smiled, and we stood up together, still holding hands. "I guess it's one of those things that doesn't have to be," he said.

"Just not tonight," I corrected him.

"What would you say about tomorrow night?"

I looked into his eyes. "I'd say tomorrow night has to be."

I'D HERDED THE CHILDREN INTO BED AND CHANGED INTO MY pajamas, when there was a knock at my door. It was Raymond. "If I can't lie with the fair Maid Marion tonight," he said, "perhaps she would grace me with the next chapter of her romance?"

"Of course. I almost forgot. I'm dying for you to read it." I pulled him into my room, and started digging through my bag for the next chapter while he sat on the corner of the bed.

"Maybe I can help you get unblocked," he said.

"I'm just having trouble. I didn't say I was blocked."

"Kareth did. She stopped by the kitchen while I was cooking. I think you were in the shower. She's really quite proud of her stepmommo. She held forth on your virtues nonstop, with only occasional lapses to complain about her sister."

I finally found the pages behind a magazine in one of the dozen side pockets and pulled them out. "She likes you," I told him, handing him the next chapter. "She told the last man I went out with that I snore and bounce checks."

"Who was the last man?" He took my hands and gently pulled me into his lap, put his arms around me, kissed me on the neck. I put my arms around his shoulders, and he held me close, rocking back and forth ever so slightly.

I kissed his temple, ran my fingers through his hair. "The last guy, if you must know, was very nice and took me to a hockey game. He bought me popcorn, and explained hockey and his ex-wife when things slowed down on the ice."

I leaned back so I could look him in the face. "But what about you? Who are the women in your life? You're rich, handsome, charming, sexy. The kind of man who's usually divorcing somebody like me to marry a twenty-three-year-old with a perfect body."

"I'm not like that."

"Apparently not. But why not? I'm not a bow-wow, but Raymond, trust me, you could do better."

"You're wrong," he said. He kissed me on the mouth, slow and sweet. Then he picked me up and laid me on the bed as if I were a child being carried in from the car late at night. I thought he might get into bed beside me. I wouldn't have stopped him. But instead he pulled the covers up to my chin, kissed my forehead, and said, "Good night."

He crossed the room in three strides. "Remember," he said from the doorway, pointing up at the ceiling with the pages of my manuscript, "I'll be reading right over your head."

I listened to his footsteps mounting the stairs, watched the ceiling, listened to him move about his rooms. What must've been his torrential shower came on, and I imagined going up the stairs and sneaking into his room, stripping and stretching out on his bed, waiting for him to discover me and make love to me, perhaps change my life forever.

But I didn't.

Susanna's Story

Chapter Two

Robert knelt on the muddy bank. His breeches were soaked through. His head throbbed. "Damn Gordon Patterson!" he exclaimed to himself, for it was to Gordon that he attributed his disagreement with Susanna, his immoderate drinking, and its humiliating result. He stood, still a little unsteady on his feet, and glared at the creek. The old fool was right. Ten years ago when Robert first came to Dumfries from Glasgow, the creek was broader and deeper than now.

The warehouse he managed was over a mile upstream from the Potomac where oceangoing vessels were loaded and unloaded from boats. But, he reasoned as he walked back to the house, if we can't load it on boats, the niggers can haul it all the way to the Potomac. He stopped at the kitchen and banged on the door. "Bring me my breakfast!" he shouted.

His head throbbed, and the gentle slope to the house seemed like a steep incline. Still, he thought, it was pleasant to converse with Anthony. He wondered what Anthony might know of philosophy. Gordon's idea of philosophy consisted of a few ill-remembered phrases from the *Orations* of Cicero. I should have stayed on at the University, he thought. What was that place in London where Anthony had said he was educated? He couldn't remember. Not Glasgow, of course, but it was remarkable the way he could remember everything.

He stopped at the back door, his hand on the knob, and looked off toward the town. It was a tiny thing, a blemish on the face of the wilderness. He missed home.

He went into the small back room where he usually took his breakfast, and sat at the table, pulling off his mud-caked boots and throwing them in the corner. He could have stayed at University, he reminded himself, if it weren't for Edward and James, his elder brothers. He grew up watching them squander their father's money. It was his father who suggested America to him. It was that or the clergy, and Robert, while firmly believing in God, did not wish to devote his life to Him.

His father secured him a position with John Glasford & Sons of Glasgow, managing their warehouse and store, importing furniture and spirits and silverware—anything the planters might buy—and exporting tobacco. He'd served an apprenticeship for five years as assistant storekeeper under an amiable man named George Campbell whose fondness for gaming and women prompted him to turn a blind eye to the deficiencies of his underlings so long as they didn't advertise his own to his superiors. When Campbell broke his neck in a fall from a horse, Robert took over his duties.

Glasford's chief factor was a man named Neil Jamieson in Norfolk, a positive dolt in Robert's opinion, but his supervisor nonetheless. When he first met him upon arriving in America, Robert joked that he had never kept books before, only read them. If Jamieson perceived his wit, he gave no sign of it but pressed on with his description of Robert's duties as a company representative in Dumfries. Fortunately, for the last two years, Robert had Anthony to take care of the books. Jamieson, who had railed at him about the books before, now (as Robert's counterpart in Quantico had reported to him) held them up as an example to the other drones in his employ. Robert smiled to himself, as he had many times in the past two years, over his good fortune in acquiring Anthony —who not only kept the books and saw to things at the store but who also pacified Susanna's insistence on a tutor for her sop of a son.

Nancy came in the back door with his breakfast. "Where's Anthony?" he said.

"He be with Mr. William this time of morning."

"Tell him to come here."

"Yes sir."

"And clean those boots."

"Yes sir."

"And this floor."

"Yes sir, which one you want me to do first?"

He narrowed his eyes. She's a pretty one just like the last one, he thought. That same saucy look in her eye, defying me all the time. "The floor," he said.

She got a bucket and brush and went down on her knees, scrubbing the boards free of the mud he'd tracked in. He watched her moving back and forth, her butt in the air.

Susanna came down the stairs in riding clothes. She saw the trail of mud, Nancy at one end of it on her hands and knees. "Good morning, Nancy," she said quietly.

"Good morning, Miss Susanna, would you like some breakfast this morning?"

"Yes please."

Robert scowled. "Finish the floor later. Take these boots and fetch my wife's breakfast."

"And Anthony, sir?"

"Yes, yes, do I have to say everything twice?"

Nancy scooped up the boots and was gone. Susanna sat down at the table. "What about Anthony?" she said.

He laughed. "I thought I would like a stimulating discussion with my breakfast. Last night has whetted my appetite for more."

Susanna smiled and looked out the window. "Oh, I'm sure Anthony has a fund of debates for you, even knows them by heart."

He put a sausage in his mouth and chewed. There was something damned odd about her this morning, he thought. She looked almost giddy. "Going riding?"

She turned back to him, a trace of the smile still on her face. "Yes, I want to try out Camilla."

"Break your fool neck on that horse. She's smart as hell. You can see it in her eyes. But she does what she damn well pleases."

"You just don't know how to treat her, Robert. You don't have a way with horses."

Robert took another furious bite from his sausage. "It would take the Devil himself to handle that horse. I mean to sell her—to the Devil, if he'll have her."

Camilla was a new mare Robert had won in a boxing match between Jesse and one of Colin Somervell's boys. Jesse had shattered his jaw in the seventeenth round. Colin said he died next morning. Colin was master of the *Justitia,* importing convicts and slaves, exporting tobacco. It was from Colin that Robert acquired Anthony, the only time Robert had bested Colin in a trade. Robert reminded himself to give Jesse some reward, a day off to go visit some wench, perhaps. He was swindled on that horse, should've known not to trust Somervell, but still, Jesse fought like a lion. It was only fair he should get something.

"Good morning, Miss Susanna, Mr. Robert." It was Anthony. He bowed slightly.

Like a Frenchman, Robert thought. "Sit down, Anthony, have some of my breakfast. Damn wench always cooks enough for three men and a nigger. We were just discussing that damn mare Somervell swindled me with. My wife means to ride her."

"Please join us," Susanna said. She gestured to the seat beside her.

"You are most kind," Anthony said as he sat down.

Robert shoved his plate toward him. "Have you finished with those books I gave you?"

"Oh yes sir, last night, after you retired."

Robert smiled. "'Passed dead away' would be a more accurate description I should think. I blame you for getting me started on Virgil."

"I accept all responsibility, sir."

Robert laughed out loud.

Susanna had never heard Robert laugh at the breakfast table. She looked over at Anthony. How does he do it? she asked herself. His eyes caught her glance and held it. She felt her heart quicken, then came back to herself and looked to Robert, who had noticed nothing, who was loading his pipe as he talked to Anthony.

"I trust everything was satisfactory in the accounts?"

She felt Anthony's hand upon her thigh. Robert continued to fiddle with his pipe. "I regret to say, sir, that I found some evidence of theft."

Robert lit his pipe, leaned back in his chair, and blew a cloud of smoke above the table. "There's always theft with niggers, Anthony. You know that by now." Anthony was slowly pulling up her skirt. She stared ahead, smiling at Robert.

"This was tobacco, sir."

Robert's chair lurched back to the floor. "Tobacco?"

"Yes sir." She felt his fingertips on her bare skin as he wrapped his hand around her thigh.

"Rum, trinkets, candles—yes, but why would a slave steal tobacco?"

"Perhaps someone has gone into business, sir. If I may say so, I do have some familiarity with businesses of this sort."

Robert's eyes narrowed. "Yes, I suppose you do. What should we do about it?"

"Lay a trap. It should be relatively easy to determine when the next theft will occur. Criminals are very predictable. That is why we're caught." His hand moved up to her crotch. He began to caress her. She closed her eyes; then he was gone.

"Fetch the books, I want to have a look at this."

With the hand that had just made love to her under the table, Anthony drew paper and pencil from his coat. "No need, sir. I remember them." He wrote numbers on the paper as he spoke. "I calculate three hogsheads of tobacco missing from our inventories, weighing approximately a thousand pounds each, probably stolen one at a time. At twenty-three shillings sixpence per hundred-weight, the estimated cash value is thirty-five pounds five shillings. I'll know more when I have a chance to verify the inventories."

"Good Lord. Well, get down there, right away, and let me know immediately what you discover."

Anthony rose and stood with his hand on the back of Susanna's chair. "There's just one other thing, sir. Did you want me to dispatch this report to Norfolk, or wait until we've cleared this matter up?"

Robert snorted. "My God, man, wait."

"Yes sir." Anthony continued to stand.

"Well, what is it?"

"There's just one other thing, sir. Mr. Jamieson will be here Monday, and I suspect he will wish to see the books."

"Good Lord, you're right." He waved his hand at Anthony's chair. "Sit down, sit down. What do you think we should do?"

Anthony remained standing. "Begging your pardon, sir, but it seems to me that we don't have time to apprehend the thief and recover the stolen goods. I should think our only recourse would be to make up for the loss, sir."

"You mean buy some tobacco with my own money."

"It would give us time to get to the bottom of this, sir, without causing undue upset to Mr. Jamieson."

"But it will need to be inspected and marked."

"If I may say so, sir, the inspector's honesty is not so sturdy that it will bear the weight of a few pounds."

Robert scowled and rubbed his chin. "Very well, take care of it."

"Begging your pardon, sir, but I will require some cash for the transaction."

"Of course, of course." Robert rose and went into the study.

Anthony bent over Susanna, took her face in his hands, and kissed her mouth. "I will see you later," he said, straightening up as Robert reentered the room with a paper in his hand. "This will authorize you to draw up to fifty pounds from the store in my name. Will that be sufficient?"

"I should think that will be most sufficient, sir."

Jesse was cleaning the last stall when Anthony walked into the stable. He leaned against his shovel. "What you want?"

"Saddle me a horse, Jesse. Which one's Camilla?"

"Saddle your own damn horse. Camilla's the black mare in the last stall."

Anthony took a halter from a hook on the wall and went to the last stall. He pulled a carrot out of his

106

pocket and fed it to Camilla. "Have you thought any more about our escape?" he asked Jesse.

Jesse spat on the floor. "Course I thought about it. But let me tell you something. Once we gone from here, you ain't Master Anthony. You got that? You saddle your own horse, you fight your own fights, you shovel your own shit." He threw the shovel into the wheelbarrow beside him. "You understand?"

Anthony slipped the halter over Camilla's head and led her out of her stall. "I think you made yourself abundantly clear, and I quite agree. While my servitude may only require me to shovel metaphorical shit, it is shit nonetheless. I had to deposit our drunken master in his bed last night, a task I didn't exactly relish." He passed the curry comb through the mare's black coat in a circular motion.

"What about his wife? Seems to me you relish that pretty good."

A smile spread across Anthony's face. "Jesse, my opinion of you has risen to new heights."

"You be rising to the height of the nearest tree if he catch you."

"Mr. Robert Grier couldn't catch me if I mounted his wife before his eyes. His stupidity is monumental, Jesse. I have made my fortune with the cooperation and assistance of the Mr. Griers of the world." He brushed Camilla vigorously as he spoke.

"Made your fortune? That what you doing here? Making your fortune?"

"That's exactly what I'm doing. I made a fool of myself over a woman, a mistake I won't make again."

"That why you messing with Miss Susanna?"

Anthony grinned and ran his hand down Camilla's left front leg, lifting up her hoof effortlessly as if by silent command. He leaned against her and picked the hoof clean. "But you see, one may play without playing the fool."

"What you getting out of it?"

Anthony laughed and lifted another hoof. "Come now, Jesse, don't you think Miss Susanna a handsome woman?"

"What I think don't matter. She the master's wife. She practically got the noose in her hands. You ain't taking that chance just for your fun."

Anthony finished the hooves and put on her saddle and bridle as he spoke. "I don't know. A willing woman is a most wonderful thing. But in this instance, I'm afraid you are right. We need someone inside the house, Jesse, someone who will gladly give me access to all her husband's private papers, including your bill of sale, with which I can create with mere words on a page (skillfully forged): Jesse—the free man."

"And Nancy."

"Of course. Have you discussed our plans with her?"

"She don't trust you. Can't say I do either."

Anthony laughed, pulling the girth tight. "Jesse, you don't have to trust me. We are escaping together. If I am caught, I will hang. If you are caught, you will be beaten, perhaps sold. You are too valuable a property to destroy. You only have to trust that I value my own life."

Jesse spat on the floor. "Maybe that's all you value."

"No. I value freedom as well. Seems to me you may have a choice to make—you can be a free man or you can stay here and shovel shit, kill men to win your fine master another horse he can't ride, sleep in the kitchen like a dog—all so you can enjoy Nancy. She's a pretty thing, I'll grant you, but I don't think she's worth it."

Jesse seized Anthony's coat, slammed him against the wall, and held him, his feet dangling above the floor. He hissed into Anthony's face, "You say nothing about Nancy, you understand me? You ain't the shit on my shoes compared to her."

Anthony was calm, a slight smile on his face. "As you wish, but you still have a decision to make. I will soon have the cash to finance this little venture. I won't hesitate to leave without you if necessary."

Jesse loosened his grip and let Anthony slide down the wall to his feet. "You just leave Nancy out of this."

"That's up to you entirely." Anthony straightened his coat and led Camilla into the yard. Jesse followed behind. "Let me know by tomorrow morning," Anthony said as he mounted. "One more thing." He held the reins in one hand and pulled back his coat sleeve to reveal a device strapped to his forearm. "As a blacksmith, this should interest you: an iron rod, sharpened to a fine point, spring-loaded. The release is my own little secret. It would have passed through even a finely muscled stomach such as your own. I didn't kill you because I found your defense of Nancy's honor affecting, but I would advise you not to touch me again." He kicked Camilla and took off at a gallop.

Jesse stood in the yard and watched him go. He wanted to break him in half like a rotten stick. He was evil through and through. But so what? he thought. What choice do I have? Me and Nancy heading out of here wouldn't make it more than a mile without his forged papers and quick words. Looking good, sounding good—more a master than the master himself. Nobody cares if he's evil, unless he do it to them, unless they see him do it. Why should I care?

He heard footsteps behind him and turned to see Susanna crossing the yard, all dressed up to ride. Why would a woman like that get mixed up with the likes of Anthony? Made no sense to him. "Good morning, Miss Susanna."

"Good morning, Jesse. I've come to try out the new mare. Is she fit to ride?"

"She be the fittest horse we got, Miss Susanna."

"Robert seems to think she has bad manners."

"She just like her head is all. Mr. Robert all up in her mouth all the time. Camilla, she don't like to trot along like some carriage nag. You'd like her just fine. Trouble is, Anthony took her not more than a minute ago, asked for her special. You want me to saddle up Robin for you?"

She stood staring in the direction Anthony had gone, her eyes squinted slightly, her lips pursed. Jesse wasn't sure she'd heard his question, but didn't know whether to repeat it. She turned back to him. "Anthony knew I was going to ride that horse. Why do you suppose he took her?"

"I don't really know, Miss Susanna. You want me to saddle up Robin instead?"

"I think I know," she said in a quiet, matter-of-fact tone. For a moment Jesse had the crazy notion that she was going to tell him she and Anthony were lovers, tell him all about it. He wouldn't know what to say.

But the moment passed, and she gave him the same tired, kind smile she always did and said, "Robin will be fine, thank you, Jesse."

From his bedroom window, William watched his mother disappear into the apple grove on her way to the stable. He was supposed to be translating the fourth book of the *Aeneid,* but he couldn't concentrate. Sometimes William thought Virgil shook out his words like tumblers full of dice. The lines were always beautiful, but he was damned if he could ferret out the sense. He stared at the grove—a few apples still clung to the high limbs—and wondered whether his mother was going to meet Anthony. He'd heard them the night before, as he lay in bed watching the moonlight —their low voices from her room, then the creaking bed, then his mother crying out. Then, it began again.

His mother didn't love his stepfather. He'd always

known that and wondered why for so long his mother seemed not to know. She knew it now. Everyone, he supposed, even little Jess must know it now. He's seen as well as I, William thought, the looks that passed between Nancy and Mother as Robert—deep in his cups—spewed out some new idiocy. What were those looks exactly? Apologies. For him. For being his wife.

He slammed his fist down on his desk. God, he hated that man. What was it Anthony called him? "A Cock with a Wig." He liked Anthony. Anthony was smart. William had watched him make a constant fool of Robert the last two years, and Robert never seemed to notice. He wished he could be as clever as Anthony, outwitting everyone who lorded it over him—everyone who thought they were so smart. But did Anthony really love his mother? Did she love him?

He didn't want Anthony to be clever with his mother. He knew men seduced women and cast them aside as Jason had done with Medea. He wanted him to love her, to carry her away from Robert, like Tristan took Iseult away from his stupid uncle.

Surely Anthony loved her. How could a man help loving his mother? She was the most beautiful woman William had ever seen. Even Anthony, who had been all over the world, must see how beautiful she was, and how kind.

He sat down at his desk and put his head in his hands. He tried to remember his father. He was five when he died. His mother knelt on the floor in front of the fire, sobbing and beating her fists on the hearth as he clung to her, digging his hands into her shawl so he wouldn't be shaken loose, calling out, "Mama, Mama, Mama." It was his only memory from that time. It had wiped out all the rest, except for one. He was in a rowboat in his father's lap. His hands were on the oars, and his father's were wrapped round his. They glided across the water like a swan.

Now he had a fear of the water, would never set foot

on a boat. He feared drowning, feared snakes. He would see his mother crying over his drowned body as she had cried over his father's. He couldn't do that to her.

William sharpened his quill and took a fresh sheet of paper. William wanted to be a writer. Anthony said he had great talent and encouraged him to write whenever the muses came. He began to write a poem he'd been composing in his head for several days—

The Progress of the Moon

Star-decked Diana hangs her bow up in the sky
Come home from hunting all the day in
    shadowed wood nearby
She wraps herself in sable against the evening
    cold
As Philomel entertains her Queen with dark
    tales of old;
She sings of Daphne fleeing the sun to become
    his laurel crown
She sings of . . . . . .

He paused to think what else Philomel might sing of, when the door opened and Robert stepped in, his riding crop in his hand. Apparently he means to beat me, William thought. He put down his quill and stood, waiting to hear his crime.

"And what is it you're doing, boy?"

"I was composing, sir."

"And is that the task to which Anthony has set you?"

"No sir. He instructed me to translate the fourth book of the *Aeneid,* but I was finding it quite difficult, and I wished to rest a bit."

"Is that why you see fit to chuck my books into a horse stall, so that you may 'rest a bit'? I shall rest this crop across your backside for your insolence."

"But sir, I never chucked any books into a horse stall. Why would I do such a thing?"

"Why indeed! Do you call Anthony a liar then, your beloved tutor, who reported your crime to me only yesterday?"

William did not know what to say. Why would Anthony say such a thing? Why would even his stepfather accuse him of such an odd crime if the idea hadn't been put into his head?

"Have you nothing to say for yourself?"

William shook his head.

"Bend over the desk then."

William obeyed, and Robert began to beat him. The tears started in William's eyes, but he refused to give in to them. With each stroke he said in his mind, "You are a fool, you are a fool. Anthony has bedded your wife and you don't even know it. You are a fool."

When Robert had done, his breathing heavy, his wig cocked to one side, he left the room as abruptly as he had entered.

William went to the window and looked out again, too sore to sit down, the tears streaming down his face. Why would Anthony say such a thing? he asked himself again. He is my friend. He says we are fellow prisoners here, and that someday perhaps we'll escape. He must have had a reason, some trick he was playing on my stepfather, our Master, the fool.

This morning, before Nancy called Anthony away, William had said to him as they were reviewing the subjunctive, "How do you bear being a bound convict, Anthony, a man such as you?"

Anthony had laid aside the book and leaned back in his chair, a smile on his face. "Well, my boy, it ain't always the greatest joy to be a prisoner, as you yourself may know. But others have had it worse than me, worse than us both put together. They become a prisoner up here." He tapped the side of his head with his forefinger. "One such was a Mister Jack, a mate of mine he was. We'd fallen into some bad business, and we were being shipped off to Port Royal to die in the sugar fields. Well, we was let up on the deck to take some air with about twenty other of us, when he says to me, 'Anthony, I've had done with thievin' and all the rest of it. When that lightning struck yester eve, it was striking out for me. I am ready to die,' he tells me. 'I have repented my sins.' There had been a fearsome storm the night before, lightning crackling round the masts, and repentance, as you may well imagine, is a common ailment among thieves about to die.

"Well, he had a wild look in his eye, he did. A look such as I've seen in the eyes of many a man about to die in a fit of foolishness. So I lay my hand on his shoulder like this and says, 'Repenting's no reason for dying, Jack. Don't tempt your fate, as they say.' But as fate would have it, the captain, a stupid fellow named Carter, spies a bird upon the bowsprit at that very moment and dances about all in a fluster shouting out he'll free any man amongst us who might tell him what sort of bird it is! Now I knew it to be a southern albatross blown into the north by the storm, but I kept my counsel, wanting to test the winds as it were, for freedom is a fine enough thing, but freedom and ten pounds, that be finer still.

"Next thing I know, Carter's seized a gun and shot the bird, and his treasure has fallen into the sea. This did little to advance the cause of his knowing what sort of bird it was, it being the same sort alive or dead. He stares at the bobbing bird for a moment, then shouts out the same offer of freedom to anyone who'll bring him that bird! While I was the only one on deck who had a knack for riddles, yet there were plenty of fellows who fancied they could swim, and over the side they went.

"Jack was the first of them, dashing across the deck and leaping over the rail as if Jesus Himself was waiting in the waves to take him in His arms. 'Twere no contest. Some dozen lads were in the water swimming for all they were worth, but Jack outswims them all, his arms going like a mill wheel, until he reaches the bird and seizes it by the neck. He holds it aloft and seems to rise out of the water with the huge bird in his grasp, when a shark, no doubt drawn by the bleeding bird, shears off Jack's arm at the shoulder and goes below with the morsel.

"But there was Jack, holding the bleeding bird in his remaining arm. And then he starts to swim!

"Now you might imagine that hardened criminals like those on every side of Jack might take the bird from him and secure their own freedom, but not a bit of it. They made a lane for him to pass back to the ship, where even the crewmen waiting to haul him back on board—as mean a bunch of strutting bastards as you might ever want to meet—cheered Jack on. You have never seen such a pitiful sight as Jack swimming with one arm, and that one burdened by the weight of the massive bird. Now it's true enough his mates didn't lift a hand to help him, and if poor Jack had died in the water, the battle for that silly fowl would probably have drowned the lot, but the fellows wanted to be fair to Jack and let him have his chance.

"Well, Jack made it to the deck and handed the captain his favorite, and instantly expired, falling at his feet like a sandbag. Can you imagine such a thing?"

William shook his head and had to allow that he could not. He raced through the story over and over in his mind. "Did you tell him?" he asked.

"Tell him?" said Anthony.

"Tell the captain what sort of bird it was."

"Of course. That's how I was able to return to England and ply my trade for another few years before my return to America aboard the *Justitia,* where no such good fortune as mysterious birds presented themselves."

"Then your friend Jack, he didn't have to leap into the ocean and die. He died because you kept your counsel."

"No, he died, my friend, because he was ignorant of sharks. And captains as well. The only reason Carter honored his bargain with me was his fear I might spread the tale of how he'd damaged valuable cargo with his folly—a fear, I confess, I suggested to him with a few insinuating remarks."

Anthony rose and patted William on the shoulder. "We both sought our freedom, lad. His way was foolish and blind." He pointed to his own eyes. "These eyes are sharp, and I am patient. Therein was the difference between us and why I am alive and he is dead. There's as many kinds of freedom, lad, as there are slavery. You must keep your eyes open and wait for the sort of freedom you want. What's freedom to other lads might be slavery to you." He snapped with his hand in imitation of a shark's jaws. "I ask you who's free, lad, Mister Jack or the shark?"

William had wanted to ask him about his mother but knew it was not yet the right time. Now, he stared at the grove, forgetting for the moment what else Philomel might sing. He touched his shoulder, thinking of Mister Jack and Anthony. He would keep his eyes open and wait.

Susanna rode until late afternoon. She had ridden to the creek and sat upon the bank in sight of the warehouse, then back toward town, hoping to cross Anthony's path, zigzagging back and forth across field and road until the sun was low in the sky.

Robin plodded toward the stable in a stumbling walk, his preferred gait. Susanna had no desire to urge him on. She had too much to think about. But as she topped a rise, she looked up from her reverie and saw that the sky was golden, that everything was golden. As often happened at such moments of joy, she thought of Miles, who most likely would have been at her side when she made such a discovery years before. She would have seized his arm and cried, "Oh, look!"

But he wasn't there any longer, so the joy turned to sadness. She had come to see Miles as the thief of all her joys. She had loved him. She loved him still. But she longed to forget her grief, forget him if she must. As she tried to forget, of course, she only thought of him more. She wished the fever had burned up the memory as well as the man.

She was surprised not to find Jesse in the barn, but assumed that Robert had set him to some task or other. She took her time storing the tack and grooming Robin. Camilla was back in her stall. Susanna liked her. She was strong, seemingly afraid of nothing. She would make a strong jumper. She ran her hands up and down her powerful shoulders. The horse nickered and tossed her head.

Susanna stood in the yard and watched the sun setting, turning the creek red. She tried to enjoy it alone but failed. She turned her back on the sun and reluctantly followed the dim light from the house up the hill. She hoped that Robert would once again drink too much, and she would take Anthony into her bed. She had spent the day wondering what was going through his mind, wondering what would happen next.

She could barely see the sandy path at her feet as she walked into the apple grove, where the shadows were deeper still. A hand appeared out of the darkness and seized her arm just above the elbow, and drew her into the shadows, where an arm wrapped round her waist and pressed her against the body she knew to be Anthony's. She clung to him and turned her face up to his, still unable to see any more than a darker shape in the general darkness, a darkness that grew as he bent to kiss her. He lifted her from the ground. She tightened her grip around his neck and wrapped her legs around him. He set her down on a low, thick limb, tore aside her clothes, and thrust himself into her. The limb swayed with his movement. She heard apples thudding to the ground. She shuddered and stifled a scream, tears streaming down her face.

She opened her eyes and saw Robert staring directly at them.

"Susanna!" he said in a loud voice. "Are you out here?"

"It's Anthony, sir."

She felt him slide out of her, whispering to her, "I mean to earn my freedom tonight. Come to me later." He turned, buttoned his breeches, and walked toward Robert, leaving her sitting on the bough.

"I believe Miss Susanna retired to her room some time ago, sir," he said.

"Anthony! I was actually looking for you. Did you take care of that matter for me?"

"Everything is quite in order now, sir."

"Splendid! Splendid! I don't know what I'd do without you. What would you say to some brandy then? I'd like to sound you out on natural philosophy and theology."

"I never say no to brandy, sir."

"What do you think of Newton?"

"A most precise fool."

"Ha! I knew I could count on you for a thoroughly outlandish opinion."

Robert's laughter and their voices gradually receded up the path to the house. A square of light flashed from the doorway and was gone. Susanna slid from the bough to her feet.

* * *

118

Jesse watched Robert and Anthony walking back to the house, laughing and talking, then a few moments later, Susanna sneaking up the path like a fox. He'd seen Anthony lurking about the orchard and followed a little ways off to see what tricks he was up to now. He saw it all—Anthony mounting Susanna right before Robert's eyes—just like he said. A man who could do that could get away with just about anything—even running to freedom. And I mean to go with him, he thought. Don't matter if he's a snake. Maybe a snake know the way.

He ran from the orchard, leapt across the creek, and hurried into the kitchen. Nancy looked up at him. The firelight flashing from her face made her so beautiful it brought him up short. She was sewing him a shirt. It lay in her lap.

"Lord, what's got into you?" she said.

"I seen Anthony and Susanna right in front of Master's eyes. Plucked her like an apple, he did. Master looking right at him—seeing nothing."

"What in the hell you talking about? And keep your voice down. These children are sleeping." Jess and Rachel were bundled up in a blanket by the fire.

Jesse spoke in the low rumble he used around sleeping children. "I'm trying to tell you." He gestured toward the orchard as if they were still there for her to see. "What part you don't understand? I tell you they was hot after it, Master squinting in the dark like he does, looking right at them. Anthony just pull up his pants and charm the master out of some more of his brandy, slick as you please. I tell you, Nancy, he can get us out of here with our freedom, and I aim to go with him."

Nancy put down the shirt and sighed. "Listen to yourself, Jesse. Man beds a lonely woman, and you want to set out with him and get yourself killed. The man's no good."

"Miss Susanna don't think so."

"Whether he good or bad don't make no difference to her. Maybe she like it he ain't no good. But you ain't no white woman he's loving up to. You a nigger. No-good white man twice as no-good to you. Tell me I'm wrong."

"I ain't telling you nothing. Wouldn't do no good." He slumped down into a chair and glowered at the fire. "The man need me to get him a wagon. He'll give us signed papers setting us free. I give him twenty wagons for that."

"They ain't yours to give."

"What that matter to me? Everything stolen from me. I ain't got no life 'less I steal it back."

Nancy laid her hand upon his arm. "You got me, sweet man. We got it good here. We could be working to death in the fields here about. Instead we here in town keeping up this little place."

"How long before one of these niggers he want me to fight kill me while white men be laughing and hollering and drinking whiskey? That last one of Somervell's, I'm telling you, Nancy, he damn near had me, fighting like a mad dog 'cause Somervell say he give him his freedom if he take me. You should've seen his eyes, like two coals—'cause he was fighting for his freedom. And what was I fighting for except what we got here in this kitchen? And what kind of life is that? We can't be married proper. We can't raise no family. Our children be sold soon as they big enough —like these two here." He pointed at Jess and Rachel and spat into the fire. "Like the bastards he sires on you sooner or later."

"I can handle him."

"You a slave, woman. He can do whatever he want with you. When he get tired of you, he get himself another to raise up his bastards to sell—just like he done with Annie. I done studied this story once. And

120

here I'll be—the biggest, strongest nigger in these parts—until some other nigger kills me for no other reason than we're both niggers."

He knelt before her chair and grasped her hands tight. "Nancy, come with me. I can't live like this no more—making like I don't know what's going to happen. Maybe I get killed running. Maybe I can't get no work. Maybe freedom ain't nothing worth having. But I won't know where it's all going every single day. Leastways I can feel like I've got a hand in it, that I can make things turn out like it should be—you and me with a family on our own place somewhere. It don't have to be much. We tough, Nancy. We get by, you'll see."

Tears were streaming down his face. Nancy brushed them away with her hands and took his head in her arms. "Oh, sweet man, I do love you so."

"Then come with me."

She kissed the top of his head. She'd lied to Susanna. She loved Jesse more than her first husband, more than anything. It wasn't right to let that go. "What about these children?" she said.

He looked at them, piled up sleeping by the fire like two pups. "We take them with us."

She closed her eyes and tilted back her head, tried to see what she should do. I can't see the life Jesse want for us, she thought. It's like the old folks' stories of life back home. Everything too perfect. Everybody nice as you please. I can't see it. But I can see Anthony, clear as day, putting a bullet through my sweet man's back. Jesse's right—Master rape me sooner or later, and Jesse might get killed in one of these dogfights he throw him into, but taking off with Anthony was like running to a hilltop to get away from the lightning.

"I'm sorry, Jesse," she said. "I feel it in my bones. It's not right to take up with that man. The man's evil. No good can come from going with no evil man. If it was just me, I might do it, but I can't take these children off with no man like that."

"You rather they be sold?"

"I ain't got no choice about that. I been sold, couple times. Now I be here with you and these children, and life's good. All I can do is love them while they're here. Children always leave you—freedom or no freedom."

"That how you aim to spend your life—loving other folks' kids till they old enough to be worth some money or a couple hogsheads of tobacco?"

"Stop it!" she screamed, and stamped her foot. "Stop it! You think I like being a slave? You think I don't know what it means? Maybe it means I got to love other folks' children and hope other folks love mine when they sold out from under me. What's wrong with that? You think that old nigger raised you didn't love you, didn't know every day that a big, strong boy like you was going to be sold for sure? You want to tell me he shouldn't have done it? I love these children and never regret it—you understand that?"

Jess and Rachel watched them from the hearth, their eyes still heavy with sleep. "You children, go on back to sleep now," Jesse said. Rachel promptly lay down, clamping her eyes shut and pulling Jess down beside her. "I'm sorry, Nancy. You know I didn't mean nothing like that. Ain't nothing wrong in you loving these children, loving me. You the lovingest woman I ever know. I just want to take you with me is all, take these children, too."

"I wish I could, Jesse, but this feeling's too strong. It ain't right."

"And this is?" He stood up, swaying back and forth, pointing to the floor beneath them. "This ain't no way," he said. "This ain't no way." He shook his huge head back and forth. "I love you, Nancy, but I got to go while I got the chance. Might never happen again."

She picked up the shirt and started setting in the sleeve. "You do what you got to do," she said.

"I come back for you," he said. "When I have enough money, I come back for you."

She looked up at him, the sweetest man she ever knew, but full of notions that would never leave him alone, eating up his insides. "Don't make no promises you can't keep," she said.

I WOKE UP BEFORE THE ALARM WENT OFF, THREW ON SOME clothes in the dark, and checked on the girls. They were sound asleep, piled together like pups. The door to the stairway was left ajar, so I figured they'd raided the refrigerator at some time in the night. Who knew when they finally conked out. Of course, there'd been no nightmares, no sleepwalking. If I'd spent the night in Raymond's room, they wouldn't have even noticed.

I thought about going down to the kitchen to get some coffee, but I was eager to get to work. It'd been a long time. Besides, I was high enough without caffeine. My writing was getting back on track, I was falling for a wonderful man, and he was falling for me. I'd never believed God was in His heaven, but certainly, this morning, all was right with the world.

I went into the bathroom and brushed my teeth. I splashed cold water on my face and toweled it hard with one of Raymond's soft towels. The shelves beside the sink were stocked with toiletries, all new and unused. Scented soaps, shampoos, body oils, bath powder. And perfumes, half a dozen of them. I picked up each bottle, smiling at the erotic names, taking a whiff of each one, wondering which Raymond would like. I chose one the color of brandy, in an antique-looking crystal bottle whose facets bore no label or marks of any kind. I smiled at myself in the mirror as I dabbed on the perfume. I'd never been around anyone so intent on pleasing me. I brushed out my hair, long and silvery gray, and felt beautiful.

I GOT MY COMPUTER AND WENT INTO THE LIBRARY, BREATHED IN the intoxicating scents of books and wood. The only light was a spotlight shining through the second-story stained-glass window directly across from where I stood. I hadn't gotten a good look at it before: Raymond had kept me more than a little distracted. I couldn't help noticing it now. It seemed placed to be viewed from precisely where I stood—

Christ stood before an open crypt, a shovel in his hand. The blade glinted like a polished sword. His other hand touched a woman's cheek. Her golden hair swept down her back, her long red cloak was slipping from her shoulders as she reached for him, her body leaning toward him, her fingertips not quite touching his lips. Flowers the color of her hair grew round their bare feet. Their eyes were fixed on one another. Their painted faces were filled with longing.

Noli me tangere, I remembered from art history class, touch me not. Mary Magdalene meets Jesus risen from the tomb and mistakes him at first for the gardener. I studied their faces and decided their longing had nothing to do with the halos round their heads. They might've been Tristan and Iseult if it weren't for the wound in his side, the color of her cloak.

Hovering above me, the underside of the chandelier glowed with swaths of gold and red. I felt a twinge of fear—I had no idea why—and shook it off. I felt like a kid afraid of the dark.

I found a rheostat beside the door and gave it a crank. A circle of floodlights beneath the third-floor balcony made a bright white ring around the middle of the library. I walked around to the corner office, running my hand along the railing, taking in the sheer number of books that filled the place. More than anyone could read in a lifetime.

The door to the office was simple, made from solid oak bowed slightly to fit into the curved wall. The knob, a silver rose, was in the center.

The office was furnished with a plain writing desk and two chairs, a state of the art desk chair upholstered in soft, black leather and a ladder-back for guests. I rested my hands on the back of the desk chair and kneaded the cushions like dough. The desk lamp was already on. Pearl's journal, a battered, mud-stained version of the "feminine" book she describes, sat in the middle of the desk. I touched a frayed flower and smiled to myself. I felt like I was meeting a lover.

I rolled out the chair and lowered myself into it. Under the arms were discreetly placed switches, one for each finger. I played with them and the chair reshaped itself, grew warm, purred. I finally settled on a configuration, deciding against warm and purring.

Beside the lamp was a pewter mug filled with pens and pencils of every color and degree of technological sophistication, even a fountain pen. Beside these was a small coffeepot, set up and ready to plug in, a note taped to the side—

> *Good Morrow, Maid Marion.*
> *Look in the drawer.*
> *Love,*
> *R.*

I didn't want to go for the drawer right away. I wanted to savor it—a surprise from my lover. I plugged in the coffeepot and it started to gurgle, filling the tiny room with the scent of coffee. A mug and a small pitcher of cream sat beside the pot. I recognized the pitcher as coming from the pottery at Colonial Williamsburg. It was still cold to the touch. I must've just missed him. I wondered where he was, what he was doing. I imagined him on horseback. I gave him a sun coming up behind him, at least an hour early.

On the wall to my left, at eye level, were two shelves of books—several dictionaries, including a rhyming dictionary, a visual dictionary, a name dictionary, and a couple of dictionaries of slang. A thesaurus, a concordance, a historical atlas . . .

I couldn't wait any longer. I rolled myself back, pulling the drawer open slowly. There was a small package, wrapped in red with a gold ribbon. Affixed to the front instead of a bow was a flower fashioned from cedar shavings. I smelled it and carefully removed it. I unfastened the paper and ribbon and set the plain box in my lap. I opened the lid and found a wood carving of a reclining female lion. One cub lay curled up beside her, the other sat behind her, holding her head in the identical vigilant pose as her mother. I turned it over in my hands, studying the care with which each muscle and contour had been made.

There was a card inside the box that read, *The lion I promised you and her two fine cubs.*

He must've made it after he'd met the girls, so the only time he could've done it was the night before, working into the wee hours, laboring over this beautiful lioness just for me. It looked like the three of us. Anyone might look at it and tell how we felt about one another, how the artist felt about us. It was the sweetest gift anyone had ever given me.

I held on to the mama lion, turning her over in my hands, until the coffee was done. I set her beneath the lamp where I could see her and fixed myself a cup of coffee.

I set up my computer beside the journal and opened the file of notes I'd already started.

I carefully opened Pearl's journal, as if it might crumble in my hands, but the paper was still strong and flexible. Her script was ornate but not delicate, slanting forward, moving across the page with the same stride she must've used to pace off the *Ohio*. I found my place, took a sheathed pen in my hand, and playfully made as if to write, following Pearl's nineteenth-century loops and swirls, imagining Pearl's hand moving across the page in her tiny cabin no bigger than this office, felt the rise and fall of the boat,

A chill went up my spine, and I plucked the pen from the page and laid it on the desk, my heart racing. It was the second time that morning I'd felt afraid for no apparent reason. But I was too happy to give it much thought. I smiled at my lioness, settled into my perfect chair, wrapped my hands around a fresh mug of coffee, and read.

The weather has turned. Sheets of rain dance upon the
water, so that all but the crew are driven indoors. I light
my lamp and speak to you. The day lies before me to
finish my story. Reading over what I have written so far, I
am sure you must think me mad or frivolous or both by
now. But I assure you, my tale is not a frivolous one, and
I have found that now I have begun it, I must see it
through until the end.

I spent my young years with Nancy, whose stories by
the fire told me where I had come from, and who I was,
and who I might wish to be. I read all the stories in the
Bible and found the company of the Devil. As yet I
had no story of my own to tell, but that was soon to
change.

When I was eighteen, Douglas came to me in the parlor
where I was reading the Bible, and told me that Nancy lay
dying. He told me to come quick, she was asking for me,
and she did not have long for this world. I hurried to her

129

tiny cabin across the stream. All the slaves were gathered around outside, singing low to help her on her way.

I was brought to her bed. She was over ninety years old. That morning she had seemed the same to me, as if she could only grow old but never die. But in the course of a day, she had become a tiny and frail creature with the life almost gone from her eyes. Her voice was husky, and I had to bend over to hear her rasping out my name. "Pearl, Pearl, fetch me Pearl."

When I came close, her eyes fastened on me and tears sprang to her eyes. She seized my cloak in her hand which I would have thought too weak to stir from the bed. "Pearl, listen to me. I know who you be. It all come clear to me now. I know you all along, know you since you was a baby."

She began to cough, and I tried to pull away, for I feared the excitement of my presence might kill her in an instant, but her grip on my cloak was unyielding.

"I am here," I told her. "You must rest. I will stay here beside you."

But nothing would mollify her, and as soon as she'd recovered her voice, she pulled me down so that she could whisper in my ear. "I know you all along. You know me too. I know you remember your Nancy. You be Susanna. I remember you, child. I know you all along."

A chill passed through me the likes of which I have never felt before or since, but I told her I did not know what she meant, for Susanna—my great-grandmother whose infamy I have already told you of—had died before I was born. I was to learn no more. Nancy's hand loosened its grip, and she died.

I clung to her and wept over her body until I had to be forcibly removed and carried from the room. Douglas led me back to the great house, for I scarcely knew where I was and could not have managed on my own. I stayed abed for two weeks, seeing no one, reading the Bible and talking with the Devil.

One day Douglas brought me my food on a tray, and I bid him sit down. I asked him if Nancy had been any relation to him. He said that no, she was not, but that she had raised him up, and she was the only mother he had ever known.

I told him that while I saw my own mother every day, the same was true for me. We both wept at this and fell to talking about Nancy for the better part of the afternoon. I asked him if he would bring me my food next day, and he pledged to do so if he could, though Mr. Winthrop, the overseer who succeeded my father, might have other notions.

My grandfather was gone to Richmond at this time on business, so that things were generally lax about the place. I knew this Mr. Winthrop, a hateful odious man, to be excessively fond of spirits and suggested to Douglas that a bottle laid across his path as a temptation in the morning might effectually keep him out of the way for the better part of the day. Douglas laughed and said he was up to such a stratagem and would have no trouble recruiting accomplices to carry it out.

The result was that he returned next day somewhat earlier than before, announcing that something of a holiday had been declared among the slaves—for the good Mr. Winthrop lay abed drunk. When we had done laughing at Mr. Winthrop's expense, I asked Douglas if he remembered my father.

He didn't answer right away. I realized later that he was deciding whether to tell me the truth. Slaves lie with great regularity, since the truth is often a petition for the lash. I was the master's granddaughter. If I took insult at anything he said or did, I could have him beaten.

But Douglas was brave and trusted me. "I remember your daddy," he said. "He left on account of me. I never forget it."

"I remember that too," I said, wanting him to go on.

He said, "No one but him and me remembers the part

I remember, for there weren't nobody there but us two. After he takes me out of the dining room, he pulls me into the pantry and kneels down beside me and takes hold of my hands. 'All hell's going to break loose,' he tells me. 'You hide in here 'til you hear Mr. James go on upstairs.' Then he kisses my cheek like I was his own little boy and goes on out. I stayed there like he told me and didn't get whipped. It was the first time I knew it was wrong to be a slave. Nancy had told me, but I was just a child, born a slave. Might as well tell me it was wrong for the sun to come up in the morning. But when Mr. Gerald kiss my cheek, I knew it in my bones for the first time."

For the second time in two days we wept together. I have tried to set down his words exactly and believe I have done so, for I can still hear them in my thoughts even now.

The next day, Douglas did not come to visit me as we had arranged. I arose from my bed, and summoned Caroline, a slave a few years younger than myself with an aptitude for gossip, to help me with my toilette. I soon learned from her that Winthrop had overheard some of the slaves laughing about Douglas putting one over on the overseer with a certain bottle of spirits. The result was that Douglas had been severely beaten and set to digging up stumps and rocks in preparation for planting a field far distant from the house. This was several days work for several healthy men, but Mr. Winthrop had promised a stroke of the lash for each stone and stump unturned when he came to fetch Douglas in the morning.

With scarcely a word to anyone, I went to the kitchen and made off with a ham, a loaf of bread, ointment and bandages. In the stable I struck the pose of a princess and called for Bucephalus—Grandfather's strongest horse—as well as a stout coil of rope and a lantern. I then rode out to this field.

I should say here that my grandfather owned many fields, owns even more now I should say. It was his way to creep across the land like a slow flood as his neighbors died off or fell upon hard times. He often said our purpose here is to subdue the savage wilderness. This particular field had been subdued and worn out when my grandfather was a boy living in town. Now it was my grandfather's, and he saw fit to subdue it again.

When I rode up, Douglas was so absorbed in his labors that he took no heed of my approach, and only realized I was there when I called out his name.

He stuck his shovel in the ground and turned to me. It was then I saw the bloody stripes criss-crossing his chest—the result of my lying abed like some swooning princess, while Douglas—no more free to go than I to fly—paid for each hour he spent in my company with a dozen lashes under Winthrop's arm.

It was Winthrop's practice to tie the slaves to a post, hands behind their back, whipping their stomachs and chests, even the women. It was his theory that this technique was more efficient since most slaves had grown immune to having their backs whipped.

Douglas could not curse me as I deserved, or even upbraid me for my thoughtless behavior, as he would certainly have done to any friend who had used him so. He was a slave. Instead, he nodded to me most courteously, and said, "Miss Pearl, I have to work now. I be working most all night," and returned to his labors.

I dismounted and told him I intended to work the night through myself and had brought along Bucephalus and a rope to help us both, as well as food and a lantern. He had but a pick and a shovel and a long metal shaft for prying—I don't recall what it is called.

I don't believe I shall ever see again the likes of the look he gave me then. His voice took on a tone I'd never heard before even when we played as children or when, more recently, we had talked in my room. It was the voice of a friend, I realized. Once again he was brave. He said, "Nancy done told me that you was going to grow up into trouble, but she never told me the trouble was going to be me. You can leave the food and lantern—and I would be much obliged—but you can't be working in Mr. James's field. You get us both killed."

I was prepared for this and said, "No one need know I am here. Three slaves saw me leave—they will tell no one. My mother and grandfather, I am sure, are quite content to leave me to my room and my Bible. And finally—judging from the stumps I can see from where I'm standing—you will receive upwards of twenty lashes in the morning without the aid of Bucephalus and myself, and I will not allow that to happen!"

Douglas laughed and said, "You could outtalk a preacher, Miss Pearl."

"I would prefer that you address me as 'Pearl,'" I said, for I had been wanting to say that for some time and had hesitated without knowing quite why.

"All right," he said, "but old ways die slow and hard, and you still be 'Miss Pearl' when anyone else around."

"Say it, Douglas, please."

"Say what, Miss Pearl?" He shook his head. "See there? I done already forgot."

"Please say my name, that's all. Just that. You don't have to say anything else."

He was silent for so long I thought I would have to repeat my request, when he said, "Pearl," in quite the kindest, gentlest way I had heard it spoken since my father went away.

I rolled up my sleeves and asked him where I should begin, but he was still not persuaded, saying, "Leave the rope and the horse, then. I can finish easily in no time."

"But I would have to walk back to the house," I objected.

"You mean," he said, "that you would work out here in the cold and dark all night, but you can't walk five miles back to the house?"

"That's precisely what I mean," I said, and that seemed to settle the matter. Over his manly objections, I bandaged his wounds, and he was forced to confess that he felt better. I have never understood the male aversion to any act intended to alleviate their pain!

When we set out to work, I soon upbraided myself for failing to bring a harness. Douglas reassured me, however, that we could "make do" and fashioned a quite serviceable harness with a length of the rope. His knot tying was a wonder to behold. He informed me that an old slave around the place named Sam, a cabin boy in his youth, had taught him all the knots that sailors use.

With Bucephalus rigged as handsomely as any three-masted schooner, we sailed back and forth across that field, uprooting everything in our wake. Bucephalus—raised a gentleman's horse—was not used to hard work at first and refused to understand what was expected of him until I jumped upon his back and informed him that I wished to sail on—in spite of the fact that he was harnessed to a stump! In the end, I think he rather enjoyed the opportunity to show off his sure-footed strength. When I was not astride Bucephalus, I manned the shovel and was quite adept, though I confess, dear husband, that wielding a pick proved too much for me. If you ever fancy to take up prospecting again, I will only be able to help with the shoveling!

At about four o'clock in the morning, we were done. We built a fire and settled down to eat our dinner, warming strips of ham and pieces of bread over the fire.

I am sorry. I must set this aside. I have uprooted a field of memories too painful for the light of day.

Later the same night

I'd not intended to write in this book again when I left off this afternoon, but when I saw it in the moonlight, I lit a lamp and sat down. I have almost pitched this book into the sea a dozen times over today. I suppose I will be tempted to do so every day of this journey, until I deliver it into your hands, where once read it can't be taken back.

Why am I telling you all this? I awoke with that

question on my lips this very morning. Lies are much easier than they are reputed to be, and silence tells no lies. I am sure there are episodes in your past you have no intention of ever telling your wife. This is more than that. This is more than a time that is gone.

I had thought that I would tell you the story slowly and carefully, but no fine storytelling will blunt the pain of what I must say, so I will say it straight out.

Douglas and I became lovers that morning by the fire. We fell asleep, and at dawn were awakened by the sound of Winthrop galloping out to claim his victim. At first he was delighted that he had Douglas in such a deadly snare, in the arms of his master's granddaughter. I pointed out, however, that his own conduct over the past few days could easily make him appear to be an accomplice in the crime. A tearful, penitent girl, I said, could make the case quite convincing. He considered this and vowed silence to my grandfather. But a few weeks later he told my mother what was transpiring between Douglas and myself, knowing that my mother would never put any stock in anything I had to say—truth or lies, tears or no.

My mother had Douglas hung from an oak outside my bedroom window. I was forced to watch until I fainted. I was unconscious for three days. I do not even know where he is buried.

Not too long afterwards, I discovered I was pregnant. I have a son—a mulatto son. He will be six years old this December. He is why I am writing this book. I hope to persuade you to take him in. I could not hope to lie about his origins, for he is nearly as dark as his father. He is also as brave and true.

In desperation—facing whoredom or marriage—I have abandoned my child to marry you, a man I've never met, on the other side of the continent. Perhaps—in spite of your instructions to the odious Mr. Tarrington that your wife have no children—you might make such a foolish gamble yourself for the sake of a child.

There, I have confessed my great secret, and feel better

for it. I wish no deceit. You must be thunderstruck with what I have told you. I am sorry. Enough revelations for one day. Good night. I sleep.

Thursday, July 11, 1850

I pick up this book again after a lapse of several days as one might pick up a dead snake—knowing it can inflict no real harm but flinching still from the imagined venomous strike. On two separate occasions, I carried it onto the deck with the intention of tossing it into the brown waters of the Mississippi where we lay anchored these last four days. Both times, however, I returned to my cabin and discussed the matter with the Devil, who—as you might imagine—thought the whole enterprise foolish from the outset.

"Why must you tell him all this?" he asked me, as he had asked me many times before.

"For my son," I replied.

"How will he benefit? He is safe and sound with his rich great-grandfather instead of being a whore's son—isn't that enough? You now wish to uproot him from a life of luxury for one of hardship in the wilderness?"

"My husband must know the truth," I insisted.

At this he laughed. "Truth is a much overvalued commodity. Husbands can only hope to know the truth of the moment they are wed and each moment thereafter. Most of them desire a good deal less of the truth than that! Toss the book into the water and visit New Orleans with the other passengers. It is a lovely place, or so I hear."

I finally settled this argument by announcing that I shall decide what to do with this book when I meet you. Until that time, how shall I know if I wish you to read it? Until you read it, it is nothing more than my chatter to myself. Unread, it creates the comforting fantasy that I am grappling with the mysteries of my future, bringing them to heel under the harsh lash of the truth—when, in truth, I know it will most likely create a muddle of its own!

But I wish to fire off the first salvo, husband! Victory is dear to me when the spoils are my son. Truth is, I would return to him immediately if such were possible. I could—through a feigned illness and a dose of feminine charm—easily book passage on the next vessel back to Charleston, and from there I could persuade some gentleman to take me to my grandfather's door. But what then? I could not carry my son away, for I would have no place to take him or even the funds to obtain lodgings for more than a week or two. My attempts to support my son and me have persuaded me that the only means to that end open to me is whoredom—and that only so long as I am young and pretty. No, I will continue on the course I have set.

Enough of this fretting. I can choose to hand you this book when I set eyes on you, weeks later—or never, as I see fit. I trust I will know what to do. At such moments I usually do. I shall not brood on it any further. Knowing I have this freedom makes the truth come easier—for you must admit I have great temptations to lie!

We are now steaming toward the Isthmus, but I wish to tell you of our last day in New Orleans, for it is this day that has given me new hope for the future and a resolve to tell my tale to the end.

As I have said, I had stayed aboard the Ohio during our sojourn in New Orleans, and I had a bad case of "cabin fever." Mr. and Mrs. Banes came back on board, bidding me join them on an outing to visit the cemetery! Owing to the swampy land hereabouts, the dead are all housed above ground in crypts often quite marvelous to behold. Mr. and Mrs. Banes, having exhausted the sights of the city, intended an outing to admire these houses of the dead.

What an odd thing to do, I thought, but by this time I was so eager to leave the boat and my morbid thoughts that I soon agreed to accompany two people I do not like on a tour of graves. The things that loneliness will drive us to do!

Fortunately, it was Mr. Morgan who elected to take us ashore, and when he heard of our plans, he said he too planned to visit the cemetery to pay respects to his mother.

You can imagine my shame—that we set out to gawk where his mother was laid to rest—but he seemed not at all offended by our plans, and even advised the inquisitive Kitty as to where the finest mausoleums might be found.

Once in the city, I wished to wander among the old French dwellings that still stand below Canal Street, but Kitty had already viewed them all, it seemed, and wished to make her way to the graves as quickly as possible, as if they were a carnival awaiting her just over the horizon. Mr. Morgan hired two carriages—one for Mr. and Mrs. Banes and her dog, the other for Mr. Morgan and myself.

We soon found ourselves driving down a road made of shells! The rain of recent days had left everything glistening in the sun, but this road, white as bleached bones, shone with such intensity that I could not look at it for long without my eyes squinted near shut. I contented myself with examining the willow and cypress growing along the roadside, shrouded with gray moss hanging down in long streamers. I fancied shapes in the moss—ghosts and serpents and fantastic beasts—and was thankful we were making our journey by the light of day!

When we reached the cemetery, Kitty's dog scurried about in a frenzy, yipping—I feared—loud enough to wake the dead! I amused myself with the image of a great hellhound swallowing this barking mop with a bite!

Soon, however, the wonders of the place made me quite forget Kitty's dog. I have visited cemeteries before back home in Virginia—walked under the trees on the lush grass—read the quaint inscriptions as if from a book. This was altogether different—for here we were greeted by a City of the Dead! Here were the dead marshaled before us! Each structure, large and small—and there were myriads of them—housed a life that was gone. They were fantastic dwellings of alabaster, marble, and other stones whose names I do not know. All shades of white—I hadn't known there were so many—glowed all around us. Moving among the angels and saints and high towering crosses, I thought I could hear the dead whispering among themselves—heard God saying to Ezekiel: "Can these bones live?" It was easy to imagine the doors of these vaults opening and their inhabitants stepping forth into the light of day to tell their stories.

In the midst of this reverie, Mr. Morgan asked if I would accompany him to his mother's resting place. This request startled me, not only because of the fantastic flight my thoughts had taken, but also because I had assumed he would wish to commune with his departed mother alone. But he said the most marvelous thing—"I wish for her to meet you"—as if my fancy were true and his mother might entertain us for tea before her crypt!

As we made our way down narrow avenues to his mother's resting place, I surmised that his mother must have died in humble circumstances, for we left behind the elegant palaces of this city to come among the rows of modest hovels—row upon row of them—that made up the neighborhood of the humble dead.

His mother's tomb was one of the smallest, a plain stone sarcophagus. Inscribed upon it was the following—

Isabel Gutierrez Morgan
1798–1837
Her sins which are many are forgiven
for she loved much:
but to whom little is forgiven
the same loveth little.
Luke 7:47

If you should read this, and if you be the one, dear

husband, to lay me to rest years hence, kindly inscribe my grave with precisely these words. They are spoken, as you no doubt recall, of Mary Magdalene, with whom—of all the many persons who inhabit the pages of the Bible—I feel the greatest affinity.

I told Mr. Morgan my feelings, and he told me that he had chosen the inscription himself when his mother died, suiting as they did his mother's sad fate. With little prompting from me, he told me her tale, which I shall share with you.

Isabel was the beautiful daughter of a Spanish merchant whose family had come to the city of New Orleans when it became a Spanish colony. At first they prospered, but as the city passed into the hands of the French and then to the Americans, each change in government seemed to mark a reduction of their circumstances until they lived a hard life on the fringes of poverty. In 1816, the cholera took both parents, and Isabel, after much difficulty, turned to a life of prostitution to survive.

Mr. Morgan's father, he said, was never married to his mother, but she wished his name on her tomb just the same. Mr. Morgan never knew his father except by his mother's accounts of him. He was a sea captain, she said, from Boston—a fine and gentle man with a boisterous sense of humor, who had died at sea when Mr. Morgan was but a babe in arms. There had been some talk, apparently, that his father would claim them as wife and son, in spite of the life Isabel had led, but his death, of course, canceled such hopes.

Mr. Morgan spoke little of his raising up as the bastard son of a prostitute, but it was clear to me in his voice and manner and in the lines etched deep in his face, that it had been a harsh and troubled time that only served to strengthen his devotion to his mother—whose sufferings were much greater than his own. To the world, she might have seemed a sinner of the worst stripe, but to him she was a kind and loving woman who put her son above all else.

When Mr, Morgan was scarcely grown, with dreams of going out into the world to make his fortune and release his mother from the bondage of whoredom, she died at the hands of a man who falsely accused her of stealing from his purse as he slept. Mr. Morgan heard the argument in the next room but paid it no mind—for he was hardened to such crudities—until he heard his mother scream—a piercing, incoherent cry of pain. He burst into the room to see her killer fleeing through the window and his mother dead on the floor, a knife in her chest.

As Mr. Morgan, a great strong man, spoke—with tears streaming down his face—I realized why he had brought me to this place. He had wished to try our friendship with the truth—forging stronger bonds between us, or sundering them altogether. As you may well imagine, his sad story and the ready comparison to my own circumstances prompted me to burst into tears and profess the greatest sympathy for Isabel's sufferings and his own. After we had consoled each other a little, I told him all I have told you in these pages—and more besides—prompted by him to continue my tale to the end.

I was much uplifted by this pouring forth of the truth and by Mr. Morgan's sympathetic attendance to all I said. While he has no intentions to marry me, he is a man nonetheless, and I fancied that his kind attention to my words forecast your own reading of the truth weeks hence. He said that no man—unless he had a heart as hard as the marble tombs around us—could fail to be moved by the particulars of my story. Far from demonstrating my wickedness, he said, they showed my honesty and loyalty and capacity for love—qualities that any man should welcome in a wife!

This was like a stone rolled away from the tomb of my heart so that hope might come forth again. I thanked him so vigorously that he soon grew embarrassed, and I spared him further womanly effusions. Bidding farewell to his mother, we made our way back to Kitty, who was complaining to her husband that she wished there were more angels—she especially fancied the angels—as if her entreaties might prompt him to call up a legion of the heavenly host for her inspection. Her dog scurried about tirelessly, ready to yap at them should they arrive.

On our journey back to the Ohio, I resolved to tell you the rest of my story, having now rehearsed it with such good results to Mr. Morgan. And thus I have taken up my pen once more. But alas, I grow drowsy as we steam on through the night. The expanse of rolling waves seems like a great hand rocking this ship—its cradle—and I the babe within it sailing on to the land of dreams.

And so, good night.

Friday, July 12, 1850

Good morning! It is a beautiful day. The breezes are warm and gentle, and the sky is clear. I have set myself up on the deck once more with a determination to tell my tale. I can almost hear you saying (what is the sound of your voice I wonder!) "Get on with it! Tell me what happened next!"

Well, as you may imagine, I could not long conceal my pregnancy from my mother, who now took me up as her especial calling—a proven sinner of her own to bring to repentance through regular doses of insult and the Bible. She hovered about me from dawn till dusk. Her sole and constant subject?—my whoredom.

Nothing is more galling, I suppose, to a Savior (as my mother fancied herself to be) than one who does not believe herself in need of salvation. I would have readily married Douglas, if the law would have allowed, and if he had not been cruelly murdered at her order—a crime more horrible than any I had committed. She was a whirlwind of chapter and verse which I bore with hostile indifference, only venturing to speak to correct her misquoted texts and garbled renditions of the holy word. Our interviews, therefore, concluded most often with a blow or two to my head which I'm sure my mother saw as coming from the arm of the Lord.

One day, when she was thus demonstrating the love and mercy of God, she directed her fist at my stomach—my head being effectively shielded by my arms. Without hesitation, I diverted her blow and knocked her to the ground, for I feared for the child within me. She sat on the floor dumbfounded, looking into my fiery eyes and then to my swollen belly until a look of comprehension stole slowly over her features.

"You are carrying that demon's child!" she hissed. "You are pregnant by that nigger!"

I beseeched her to be silent or else I would be forced to knock her down again. Whether it was the fear of my force or of my rage I cannot say, but she scurried out the door on her hands and knees as if the Devil himself were hard upon her!

As I stood in that room, my fists still balled up with rage, I knew I had reached a crossroads in my life. I knew that I would not be left alone for long, that my mother would return in force with half the household to bring me low. I asked the Devil what I should do, and he said it was clear I should flee, for I would most certainly be ill-used if I stayed.

I argued against his advice—foolish arguments I cannot and wish not to recall—and failed to take his wise counsel. Much woe to me!

In about a half an hour, my grandfather appeared in the room and sat down, bidding me sit across from him, for he had something to say. This was a most singular occurrence and unsettled me more than a whole legion of his minions descending upon me. My grandfather and I had never sat thus, face to face, to converse on any subject whatsoever. My heart froze to contemplate what might have prompted him now to deal with me thus.

He asked me if I intended to have the child—meaning did I wish to murder it before it saw the light of day?

I flared up like a bonfire at the very suggestion and told him I would die before I would kill the child within me.

Still, he remained calm and listened to my onslaught with greater indifference than he would have shown a crazed woman in a play. "Very well," he said. "You may remain here, and be provided for, but be advised, he is mine." With that, he quit the room without another word.

This was a puzzlement indeed, and it was days before I understood its import. I read the answer in my mother's eyes. She no longer berated me with tirades of salvation, but rather she watched me seated by the fire or moving through a room with the burning looks of jealousy and hatred. It was then I recalled my grandfather's "he." My child was to be the male Grier my grandmother had failed to give him, his compensation for the curse of a daughter and then a granddaughter. Little matter he was fathered by a slave, little matter he would most likely bear in his features the signs of his origins. So long as my child was a son, my grandfather intended to have him.

Once again, I pondered the Devil's advice—but where could I go? As my time approached, I had no choice but to stay where I could be brought to bed with a midwife to attend me. With this resolve in mind, I asked my grandfather if I might have a different room, for I did not wish to have my child in the room where I had witnessed his father's murder. He said I might have the garret apartment, and with Caroline's help I moved all my belongings that very night.

I spent the remainder of my time in that apartment, seldom venturing into the rest of the house. I would look out the tiny window at my grandfather's great plantation and try to imagine the life my son and I would lead. Oh yes, by this time I too was convinced by means unknown to me that the life I carried within me was a boy. I was sure my grandfather did not mean to make a slave of him, that he might even educate him and raise him up to be a gentleman. It was all I could hope for, and I comforted myself with fond visions of a young man, my son, living the life his father deserved but had been denied.

I will spare you the details of my long and difficult labor except to say I was almost taken from this world giving birth to my son. He was placed in my arms and I looked up to see my grandfather peering down at me. "What will you name him?" he asked.

I had long pondered Nancy's words on her deathbed and rehearsed the story of my great grandmother in my mind. From Nancy I knew she'd had a husband who died before she married my great grandfather—a husband who had loved her dearly—named Miles. It was this name I had chosen for my son. When I announced it, my grandfather scowled as if I had turned over a stone to reveal a nest of spiders.

"It will do," he said, and left me.

I wish I could communicate to you the joy that comes from holding a child in your arms who has sprung from your loins—who seems, nay is, a part of you come to life. Miles, while not quite so dark as his father, was the very image of him—a fact which caused everyone distress but me. He had the same dark intelligent eyes, the same strong cheekbones and chin. His ears—tiny crescents—were like mine. He cried not at all and listened most intently to all the goings on around him. In those early days, I fear, there was much unpleasantness for him to take in, as the two of us were a scandal whose proportions grew apace with him.

When Miles was scarcely six months old, my grandfather left the plantation on business in Norfolk. In the past, I had always looked forward to these absences of the Master of us all. But since the birth of my child, my mother's looks had grown increasingly distracted, and I had begun to grow fearful of her.

The night before, as I had lain in my bed asleep, she burst into my room holding the massive family Bible aloft as if it weighed nothing at all. Her eyes were ablaze, her hair flying in all directions, her free hand pointing a finger like a drawn arrow at my heart. In a wild and terrific voice she shouted these words from Revelations and quit my room in an instant:

"Thrust in thy sharp sickle, and gather the clusters of the vine of the earth; for her grapes are fully ripe! And the angel thrust in his sickle into the earth, and gathered the vine of the earth, and cast it into the great winepress of the wrath of God! And the winepress was trodden without the city, and blood came out of the winepress, even unto the horse bridles, by the space of a thousand and six hundred furlongs!"

As the Devil and I have noted, blood up to a horse's bridle—even a small horse's—spread over two hundred miles is a good deal of blood for the wrath of a benevolent deity. But I knew my mother had not thus visited me to discuss theology but to communicate her crazed desire to kill me—and perhaps Miles as well. I shivered with fear all the rest of the night and watched with trepidation my grandfather's carriage disappearing down the lane at dawn.

I paced my room, Miles in my arms, until once again I resorted to the only ally at my disposal and summoned Caroline to my room. I bid her, in as matter-of-fact a tone as I could muster, to keep me advised of my mother's doings.

"She been acting most peculiar, Miss Pearl" she said. "Put Sam to work whetting a scythe since first light this morning. Say she want it sharp enough to cut stone."

I let out a shriek and Caroline beseeched me to tell her what was the matter. Amid sobs of fear I related what had passed between my mother and me the night before, and she offered to stand guard and prevent my mother's mounting the stairs to my room. She said, "Don't you worry child"—though she was younger than me—"I'll stand in her way like some dumb cow in the road, too stupid to move. I'll wear her out for sure."

I had little confidence in this plan but had none of my own that wouldn't expose Miles and myself to even greater danger. I sat on my bed, my child in my arms, but he grew restless and I laid him down on a pillow where soon he was asleep, unaware of the danger.

After a time, I cannot say how long, I heard a terrible row downstairs, and then footsteps mounting the stairs, accompanied by the thump of what sounded like a heavy staff. I sprang to my feet and blocked the door with a chair. The sound of my mother's approach thundered in the narrow stairwell beneath my room. She pushed at the door, and finding it blocked, threw herself against it with all the force of her madness and burst into my room.

Her eyes were not my mother's eyes, but those of a demon! They fixed on me as I imagine a serpent eyes its prey, freezing it with terror before it strikes. I watched in a trance as she hoisted the scythe into the air and swung it in a vicious arc. I came to my senses just in time to avoid the blade as it passed behind my head, but the shaft struck my face with a jarring blow and knocked me to the floor. She ran past me, and I looked up to see this demon who had been my mother standing over my bed, one arm wrapped around Miles, the other still brandishing the scythe!

The posts on my bed were stout spindles of oak topped with heavy knobs. The one closest to where I lay had long been loose, and I had used the space beneath it as a hiding place for trinkets since I was a child. I sprang to my feet and seized this post in my hands. It was at least four feet long—an unwieldy weapon at best—but I swung it at her head with all my might.

Her knees instantly buckled. I threw aside the post and plucked the screaming Miles from her arms. She pitched onto her knees and fell face first upon the scythe. Its bloody tip protruded from the middle of her spine.

It occurs to me as a great revelation, the obvious truth that you have a mother as well. What must you think of me—having just read the words above? "The woman has slain her own mother!"

I suppose that you love your mother, as most are reported to do. I wish I could tell you that I loved my mother deeply and mourned her passage. I cannot. I hate my mother, hate her still though she is dead at my hands. She would have killed me and rejoiced in it, killed my son as well—as she had killed his father before him! I wish I could believe in Hell, so that my mother might dwell there, but the Devil I know would never conceive of such a place—so that I can only hope that the spirit dies with the flesh and she no longer haunts the world.

It is a terrible thing to hate one's mother—quite the most painful emotion I have ever felt—a pain that never seems to diminish as grief and sorrow do. I cannot wish such sufferings on my son. I could not bear his hatred. I would rather die now on this wretched boat.

But perhaps he will not hate me because he will not remember me. He is only a child. No one will tell kind stories about me like Nancy told about my father. He will know I murdered my mother, his grandmother, and spirited him off to Richmond. He will know that four years later I brought him back to his great-grandfather. He will know I abandoned him. He will know me only by those facts. Me, his mother, he will know not at all.

I have seen in my grandfather how such stories take power over the heart and mind. His mother left him when he was too young to recall her in later years, but his father tirelessly instructed him in the proper loathing of the woman who had abandoned them and fled with an odious man, taking William—her son from her marriage to Miles—but leaving young James behind.

Very well. Perhaps he must hate me, though I have

begged my grandfather not to poison his mind against me. At least this way he will not have to see his mother fail him. He will not have to see his mother humiliated and beaten at every turn. He will not have to witness his mother turn whore.

The day I picked up your newspaper advertisement in that hotel lobby, I was waiting for a Mr. Pirketsen—a traveling drummer and a guest at the hotel. I was to follow him up to his room at a discreet distance. I had never done such a thing before and was amazed at the ease with which the whole business had been arranged. It saddened me, really, that it should be so simple.

But as I have told you, I saw your advertisement. It promised a home, and Mr. Tarrington confirmed that I should have 320 acres *in my own name* by the terms of the laws of that territory. It is to this home that I have fled.

Wednesday, July 17, 1850

We arrive at the Isthmus tomorrow. I have been advised by Mr. Morgan that writing in a journal will not be a luxury possible in the jungles we shall traverse. I shall, therefore, stow it away in my trunk for safe passage.

Saturday, August 17, 1850

You have been up to now a stranger to me. As much as I have struggled to imagine you, you remain as yet an image in a daguerreotype, a name on a contract. Frank Strickland. In my mind's eye, I can see my own name, Pearl Withers, there beneath it. I will meet you tomorrow after a long and difficult journey.

As we lie off the coast of the vast Oregon Territory I can see that it is a wild and savage region, perhaps no place for children. But Miles has lived a life full of danger and want and hardship with more strength and courage than I have ever shown. He has lived his life with me, and for that, thus far, he has suffered greatly. Perhaps I am wrong to want him with me in so wild a place. But I can't help but feel that if he had a home—even if, outside, Hell itself were boiling over—he would finally, at long last, be safe.

I give this book to you, dear husband. May you read it with charity and a good heart. Your wife come tomorrow,

—Pearl

I STOPPED READING, TEARS STREAMING DOWN MY FACE. I WAS clutching the wooden lioness in my hands. I set her back on the desk and dug around in my pockets for a tissue. I looked on the shelves, in the desk drawer, but there weren't any. At least he doesn't think of everything, I said to myself, slamming the drawer shut, wiping away the tears with my hands.

I used to have nightmares that Cathy would show up—rehabilitated and wanting her children back. I'd stand before a judge and argue desperately, hopelessly, to keep my kids. The judge would listen. He'd even smile benevolently, encouraging me to tell him everything, to lay out my pain in great detail. But I'd always lose. I'd wake up screaming as they were being led away by the judge himself.

I ran my fingers over the page before me, touching Pearl's signature as if it were her face. The tears on my hands soaked into the paper, but the ink didn't blur. Pearl was going to lose, had already lost. I knew it in my bones. Frank Strickland, whoever he was, didn't give a damn about her son.

Sniffling like a kid, I wiped my face on my sleeve. Stop it, I told myself. No one's going to take your kids away. Whatever happened to Pearl was over and done with a hundred years ago. It was just a sad story now.

But I kept seeing Douglas, hung before Pearl's eyes. Her mother, so that she might witness the suffering she was offering up to the Lord, didn't even glance at the dead man hanging outside the open window, but watched her daughter's anguished face, searching for some sign of her redemption. I clenched my fists and imagined the bedpost in my hands. It had the heft and feel of a weighted baseball bat. I felt the jolt of smashing her skull, watched her crumple to the floor.

I stared at the floor of the office as if she lay there, impaled on a scythe, dead by her own malice. I knew Pearl at that moment, her child in her arms, wondering where on earth she was going to go.

I laid my head back and took a few deep breaths, staring at the ceiling like a blank sheet of paper, moments of Pearl's story flashing through my mind like film clips. What incredible material, I said to myself.

I sat upright and started typing notes into my computer—lists of images: The City of the Dead. Nancy on her deathbed. Bucephalus with Pearl on his back pulling stumps from the ground. Pearl's tiny cabin on board the *Ohio*. The book still open on the desk beside me, Pearl writing desperately, charmingly, hoping to enchant some stranger into rescuing the son she herself had already abandoned for a few hundred acres of wilderness and a man in a daguerreotype.

I typed furiously. I couldn't believe my good fortune. When I ran out of images, I opened a file naming everyone mentioned in the journal, with a sentence or two about each one so I could begin to keep them straight.

I paused, as an image of Miles formed in my mind—a long thin face, thick hair and brows. He looked at me accusingly with large, angry eyes. I felt like a jackal preying on the dead, even though he was—they all were—long dead before I was even born. My favorite writing teacher used to say, *only trouble is interesting,* and here was trouble in abundance. I hadn't made it happen. I couldn't make it not happen. All I could do was tell their story. I made a note to look up Anubis, the Egyptian god of the dead, a jackal if I remembered correctly.

As I typed in *Miles,* I froze, my hands hovering over the keys. I opened up the name file for the Grier novel and scanned it, looking for matches with Pearl's journal. Three of them—Nancy, James, and Miles—were names and characters I'd made up entirely as I wrote, and yet they were in Pearl's journal. Though her Miles was Susanna's great great grandson, he was named after my invented Miles— Susanna's dead husband.

They were complete fabrications, they never existed, but here they were in a journal written over a hundred years ago. Not that it mattered *when* it was written. Here were my characters, from my novel-in-progress, in someone else's story.

I thought back to that night when I found Robert's letter on the microfilm. I'd made up all three characters on the spot before I'd done any research at all. I still had the notes I wrote that night on the backs of discarded Xeroxes. I'd looked at them so many times I practically had them memorized.

She even names William, I realized. I'd thought about him as William for so long, I'd almost forgotten that the only name history had left him was "her son." But Pearl knew his name, the name I'd given him. I struggled to make sense of it, but nothing worked. I turned back through the pages of Pearl's journal, ran my hands over the paper. For the third time in a single morning, I was afraid, deeply and inexplicably afraid.

"Squirmy worms, squirmy worms," I heard behind me, and I jumped. Lorena's tiny fingers wriggled beneath the door. This was a game she'd invented when she was four. I based Jess's chant of "Worms, worms" in Chapter One on Lorena's.

"Hi Lorena," I said through the door, though my part of the game would've been to grab the squirmy worms so she could squeal and giggle just as she'd done when she was four.

The worms withdrew, and I leaned out from my chair and opened the door. Sunlight streamed through skylights around the perimeter of the ceiling, flooding the library with a warm, rich light. Lorena stood before me, still in her nightshirt, Heather under one arm, the other reaching for me. "I'm hungry," she said, and climbed onto me, squirming to arrange her long, bony limbs on a lap that'd grown too small.

I hugged and kissed her. "Good morning, Lorena."

"Good morning," she said, kissing my cheek, hugging me hard around the neck. "Why're you crying?"

"I *was* crying," I said. "But I'm not crying anymore." I offered a big smile as proof.

"But what *were* you crying about?"

"I was reading a sad story about somebody who lived a long, long time ago. I'm okay now." I wrapped my arms around her, hugging her and shaking her, so that she started to giggle. "I'm okay now," I said, "except I've got this bony giggly kid in my lap." She laughed some more.

Then I held her close, her head on my chest, my chin resting on top of her head, and rocked her slowly back and forth.

"I wish I could remember Daddy like you and Kareth do. It's not fair," she said. "Kareth remembers all sorts of stuff." This was a complaint Lorena had voiced before. I wished I could help, but there was nothing I could do but hold her more tightly.

"It's not fair, is it?" I said. "Your daddy loved you very much." I sat her up and looked her in the face. "You look just like him, you know. He used to call you his little goober."

"He called me *goober?*"

"He did indeed."

She laughed. "That's funny."

"Your father was a very funny man. And you know what else?"

"What?"

"He always woke up hungry, just like you—*I'm hungry, I'm hungry.*" I made Tom sound like a storybook bear and bounced her on my knee to signify the earthshaking tread of an enormous bear.

Lorena laughed and called out, "I'm hungry too, Daddy."

"Then let's go eat," I rumbled, kissing her and setting her back on her feet.

We walked out onto the balcony hand in hand. The compass rose beneath us was bathed in sunlight. The chandelier cast rainbows all about the room. "This is very pretty," Lorena said.

"Is anyone else up?" I asked.

"The lady who gave us dinner is in the kitchen. She told me where to find you."

"Her name is Rachel. Is Raymond up?"

"I don't know. Kareth says you like Raymond."

"Don't you?"

"Yes. I like his horses, too."

"Is Kareth up yet?"

"She's watching TV. She sent me to find you. Who is that lady?" We were passing the stained-glass window. She pointed at the Magdalene.

"That's Mary Magdalene and Jesus from the Bible."

She walked right up to it. The figures towered over her. She pointed to the nearly opaque black glass that formed the open tomb. "Did he come out of the ground over there?"

"Yes, he did."

"Did he use that shovel?"

I laughed. "I don't know, darling. He might have."

We'd both stopped as if in a museum. Lorena was studying the Magdalene. "She is very pretty," she announced. "She looks like you."

"I don't have long, golden hair," I objected.

Lorena looked up at me and made a face. "I *know* that," she said. "Her *face* looks like you."

I started to contradict her, but she was right. The Magdalene looked younger than me, but the nose, the eyes, the mouth—she could've been my younger sister. I looked at the Jesus. His angular features were obscured by his hair and beard, but the eyes—I knew the eyes. I stepped back and bumped into the rail, reached back and held it tight. I'd met him a week ago, and yet here were the two of us enshrined in his house.

"Are you okay, Marion?"

I turned away from the window to Lorena's upturned face. "I'm fine, dear," I lied.

I led Lorena to the girls' room, steadying myself on the rail, trying to look perfectly normal. I'd told Lorena I was fine, and now I had to pretend I was. The room was a mess, the contents of their backpacks scattered to all corners. I set Lorena to getting dressed and started gathering up clothes and books and hair paraphernalia. Happy TV music came from the next room. "Kareth, turn off the TV," I called through the door. "And get dressed."

"I'm already dressed," Kareth called back, and soon after the TV fell silent.

Kareth and Raymond came through the door. I straightened up, tossing a handful of clothes on the bed. He was dressed for riding—those skintight pants, high boots, a thick hooded sweatshirt. He looked very nice indeed.

"Good morning," I said. "I didn't realize you were in there."

He kissed my cheek, put his arm comfortably around my shoulders. "Good morning. Kareth and I were watching a little *Rocky and Bullwinkle*—Mr. Peabody and the Wayback machine. It's one of my favorites." He was quite jovial.

As I looked up into his smiling face, names in an old book, painted faces—nothing more than a few lines on the glass—didn't seem to matter. This, right now, was real. "Do you always go for such intellectual fare?" I teased.

He drew himself up in mock dignity. "Mr. Peabody is one of the great historians of the twentieth century—every bit as accurate an any Ph.D. and vastly more entertaining."

Kareth gave me the universal look of knowing adolescence. "Stepmo—it's satire."

"Stepmo?" I groaned. "Don't you guys have enough nicknames for me?"

"But it's cool."

Argument was pointless. Besides, I didn't feel like arguing with anyone or anything. I rested my head on Raymond's shoulder and put my arms around his waist.

Lorena had finished dressing and was standing before us, Heather in hand. "Are we going to have breakfast now?" Heather asked.

"Once again, Miss Heather sets us right," I said.

Raymond bent over to speak to Heather face-to-face. "Do you like strawberries and whipped cream?" he asked her.

Heather, Lorena, and Kareth bounced up and down, nodding furiously, squealing.

"Just tell Rachel you're ready for breakfast," he said. He laughed out loud as they shot through the door and clattered down the back stairs like coal down a chute.

"You're really good with my kids."

He smiled. "They're good kids."

I laid my palms on his chest and spoke without looking up. "Thank you for my lioness. She's the most wonderful gift anyone's ever given me."

He kissed the top of my head. "Timothy used to tell me that if I made each animal with great care and devotion to the gods, then I would become the animal and know its power and wisdom."

"Did you become my lioness?" I asked quietly, my heart pounding.

"I certainly did."

I looked up at him. "And what did you learn from her?"

"What I already knew," he said softly. "That I love you."

A tightness gripped my chest, terror and exhilaration

hopelessly entangled, for I knew his words were true, that he meant them, that now, no matter what else happened, my life had already changed. I wanted to say, *I love you too,* believed it was true, but I stopped myself and whispered, "I know."

I touched his lips with my fingertips, kissed him on the mouth. He held me close, lifting me from the floor, twirling me around slowly as if in a dream. I burrowed my face into his neck. Don't be afraid, I said to myself. Not this time. Please, please, don't be afraid.

He set me back on my feet. "Am I still moving too fast?" he asked.

I kissed his neck. "We both are," I said.

As we went down the back stairs to breakfast, he took my hair in his hands. "I like your hair down," he said. I reached over my shoulders and clasped his hands in my hair and squeezed them hard.

IN THE DINING ROOM, THE GIRLS WERE ALREADY DEEP INTO strawberries, sweet rolls, and hot chocolate. They didn't even look up when we came in. Coffee was waiting for me. A small pitcher of cream beside it.

"How far did you get with the journal?" Raymond asked me as we sat down at the table.

"About two thirds of the way through. She's off the coast of Oregon. She's just made her plea for Miles and signed off. I stopped to take some notes." I started to reach for the sweet rolls, but Raymond held up his hand.

"I've ordered something special for you," he said. "It should be here shortly."

"You're being too nice to me."

"Impossible."

I laughed. "Oh, you don't know me very well if you say that."

"What did you think of Pearl's friend, the Devil?" he asked.

Kareth glanced up quickly at that but didn't say anything. She looked back down at her plate, listening. "Isn't that great?" I said. "I loved him."

"I was rather fond of him myself. Do you think she actually talked to the Devil—or was he a hallucination?"

I poured cream into my coffee and watched it diffuse. I hadn't wanted to answer that question in my own mind. It was a story, material. It didn't matter if it was real. Sometimes reality just got in the way and had to be changed anyway.

"I'm not so sure those are the only choices," I said. "She might be speaking figuratively, an elaborate way of talking to herself."

Neither one of us was convinced. "I don't know," he said. "She seems to think he's real."

I laughed. "I know. But I don't want her to be crazy. I like her too much. She doesn't seem crazy to me."

"Would conversing with the Devil necessarily make her crazy?"

"It'd certainly be a good start."

Kareth looked up from her bowl of strawberries and whipped cream. "Who's crazy?" she asked.

"I was saying she's *not* crazy. The woman who wrote the journal I told you about that I came here to read—her name's Pearl."

Rachel came in from the kitchen, a big smile on her face, and set eggs Florentine in front of me. "I don't believe this," I said.

Raymond beamed. "The heroine in your novel made herself eggs Florentine as a treat. I was hoping that detail was autobiographical."

"You've hoped correctly. This is my absolute favorite breakfast. I never make it—the girls hate it. Thank you, Rachel. Thank you both."

Rachel bowed and smiled her way back into the kitchen. Raymond gestured for me to eat and enjoy.

Kareth's curiosity still wasn't satisfied. She chewed

oughtfully on a strawberry. "But why did you think this
oman was crazy—or didn't—or whatever—in the first
lace?"

"According to her journal," Raymond said, "she talked to
he Devil, just as you and I are talking, and apparently
elieved it was actually the Devil."

"Cool," Kareth said.

"Is that real or make believe?" Lorena asked, looking up
rom her strawberries, her mouth smeared with red.

"That's the question," Raymond said. "If she really was
alking to the Devil, then she *wasn't* crazy. If she only
elieved she was talking to him, when she really wasn't at all,
hen she *was* crazy. Understand?"

"I don't get it," said Lorena.

I reluctantly abandoned my eggs Florentine and pointed
t Heather on the seat beside her. "Is Heather a real
unny?" I asked her.

"No," she said.

"You only pretend she's real, right?"

"Right. Real bunnies can't talk."

"What Raymond is saying is that if you *really* thought
Heather was real, and she wasn't, then that would be crazy."

"But if I *thought* she was real," Lorena asserted, "then she
robably would be."

Kareth rolled her eyes. "God Lorena, it's just a stupid
tuffed bunny no matter what you think."

"Would too!" Lorena howled.

"Enough," I snapped. Lorena glared at her sister, who
ave her a thin, superior smile. "Have you two finished
ating yet?"

"Yes," Kareth said for them both. "Can we go riding?"

"It's fine with me," I said. "You'll have to ask our host."

"Certainly," said Raymond. "I was hoping we could all go
or a ride after breakfast."

"Even Marion?" Kareth asked in amazement.

"No," I said at the same time Raymond said, "Yes."

The girls exploded with laughter. "Oh come on, Steppie, —

it's fun!" The transformation into excited pups was instantaneous. They pounced, one on each arm, beaming a Raymond, knowing in him they had an invincible ally. A last they would get me on horseback.

"I have to work," I said.

"I promise you the entire afternoon without interruption," he said.

Amid the racket of the girls chanting, "Please! Please Please!" Raymond added in a kind, reasonable voice, " have a horse named Angie who's as gentle as a grandmother." He smiled. "In fact, she *is* a grandmother."

I looked from face to expectant face. Who was I to argue'

He even had riding gear for me, so before I knew it I was walking down the path to the stables in riding pants and boots, a helmet on my head, Raymond at my side. It was a beautiful day, crisp and clear, with no sign of the snow forecast for that night. The girls had already fled to the stable, laden with carrots and apples, to spend as much time as possible with the horses.

I felt like an idiot. I'd taken the girls to lessons for years now because they'd begged and pleaded, but I'd been afraid to get on a horse my whole life. It wasn't the horses that scared me—I liked them. It was riding, being up high. I was afraid of falling.

"Are the pants supposed to be this tight?" I asked. I felt as if my lower body were bound by a giant Ace bandage.

"Yes. You grip the horse with your legs. Loose pants will slip and diminish your control."

"I'm just dying to control a thousand-pound animal."

He laughed and gave me an affectionate hug. "Don't worry. I'll be right there. And besides, you look great in those pants."

I shook my head. "Just when I start to believe you, you have to reveal your basic dishonesty."

"I'm never dishonest," he said, quite serious.

I looked down the path, tried to make my voice casual and offhand. "I got a good look at the Magdalene this morning.

162

It's very unusual. I've never seen such an erotic depiction. Is it another reproduction?"

He slowed the pace. "Yes. The original was made in Flanders in 1555. It was commissioned for a church there. It was nearly completed when the artist was disgraced, so it was never installed."

"You have the original sketches?"

"I have seen them."

We'd come to a stop in the middle of the path. I could hear the children laughing and shouting in the distance. "Do you know how the artist was disgraced?"

He looked off at the horizon as he narrated the story. "The model for the Magdalene was the artist's younger sister. He placed her beside a mirror so that he might pose for Christ. They worked in a shed behind the church. One day the priest discovered them in an incestuous embrace."

"What became of them?"

He smiled grimly. "She was placed in a convent to become a bride of Christ. He was castrated and hanged."

"Good Lord." I shuddered, wrapped my arms across my chest. "Lorena says I look like the Magdalene," I said.

He turned and looked into my eyes. "You do," he said. I stepped up to him and put my hands to his face, molding them to the semblance of a beard. He looked at me steadily. He seemed to know exactly what I was doing.

"You look like the artist," I said.

He nodded and took my hands into his.

"Raymond, I don't understand."

"Faces mean nothing," he said. "It was a very long time ago."

"Why would they look like us?"

"I don't know," he whispered. "Don't be afraid."

I pulled his face to mine and kissed him. I wanted to devour him, to be rooted to this place and this moment. We clung to each other, and I refused to be afraid. Gradually, we loosened our grasp on one another, and became two lovers holding each other in the morning sun. I heard again the sound of the girls' laughter, and I broke our embrace and took his hand, giving it a tug. "Come on," I said quietly. "My kids are waiting."

AS WE WALKED INTO THE STABLEYARD, LORENA CALLED, "HI Sweetie Pie!" from atop a chunky brown pony. Kareth, mounted on a tall gray, stared off toward the river, not wanting to be embarrassed any further by the spectacle of her idiotic sister blurting worn-out pet names at the top of her lungs.

Thomas stood with three other horses, all tacked up and ready to go. I'd expected to have thirty minutes of grooming and tacking to work up my courage or back out. Now it looked like I had five. "Good morning, Thomas," I called out a little too loudly in my nervous chirp.

"Good morning, ma'am."

I knew immediately which horse was Angie. I recognized her as the horse the girls had petted the day before. She was white and drooped in the middle like the roof line of an old house. She was also enormous. I pointed at her. "Is that Angie?" I asked Thomas.

"Don't worry," he said. "She's as sweet as she is big."

She stared at me with huge, tired eyes. She didn't look like she wanted to go riding any more than I did. At least she wouldn't run away with me. The worst that could happen was she'd fall asleep on the trail and I'd have to walk back.

Raymond started checking her saddle, adjusting the stirrups, looking back and forth at my legs. I was rapidly approaching the point of no return.

"Talk to me," I said to Raymond. "Take my mind off the bones I'm going to break when I fall off this twelve-story grandmother I've agreed to climb."

"You'll do fine. You've always been brave."

I laughed nervously. "How do you know what I've always been?"

He yanked on the girth. Angie hardly seemed to notice. "You're brave enough to raise somebody else's children, brave enough to spend the weekend with a crazy recluse who's in love with you." He yanked the girth again, harder this time. Angie bobbed her head up and down, lifted a huge hoof and let it drop with a thud. "You've always been brave," he said with conviction. Raymond straightened up and turned to me. He clasped his hands together and held them palms up, so that I might step into them and mount Angie. "If we don't mount up soon," he said quietly, "your girls will be worried about you. They're afraid you're going to back out."

I looked over at them. Their eyes were trained on me. *Don't blow this one, Marion,* they seemed to be saying. *We like this one.*

I stepped into his palms and he lifted me onto Angie as if I were weightless. I swung my right leg over her broad, sloping back. She did a shuffling sidestep as I put my feet in the stirrups, and I clutched the reins in a death grip.

I know how to do this, I told myself. I'd hauled my kids to countless riding lessons. I'd quizzed the girls' riding teacher so that I could make Susanna a more convincing rider. But this was a real horse underneath me. She felt steadier than I'd thought she would—like straddling a huge, breathing boulder. When I was a little girl, in spite of my fear of heights, I'd loved to climb the huge tree in our backyard, because I could hug the trunk and feel secure. Angie reminded me of that tree. I took a few deep breaths in sync with her and settled into the saddle.

Raymond stepped onto a milk crate at Angie's left side, so that he seemed about eight feet tall. He took my hands, gently prying them apart and laying the reins in them so that they entered each hand between my third and fourth fingers, and emerged between thumb and forefinger. He folded my hands into fists, placing them side by side, thumbs up. "You'll have more control this way," he said.

Still holding both my hands in his left, he laid his right hand on my sternum and pushed. "Straighten up a bit—you won't fall off." When I was sitting up high and straight, he took my leg, one hand on my knee, the other on my thigh, and pressed it against the saddle. "Like that. Don't let any sunlight show between your thighs and the horse." I tightened my thighs around Angie, and Raymond studied me, nodding his approval. He took my ankle in his left hand and pushed my heel down, rubbing his right hand up and down my calf. "Stretch that muscle. Good. Keep your heels down like this. How does that feel?" He still held my leg in his hands, looking up at me, the faintest naughty smile on his face.

"It feels fine. Would you do the other leg?"

"Gladly."

"Maybe we should ride first," I said. I nodded at Angie. "How do I make her go?"

"Give her a kick and say 'Walk.'"

"How about 'Whoa'—does she know that one, too?"

"It's her favorite word. That's why I chose her for you. Just pull back evenly on the reins, and she'll stop. Even thinking about stopping will usually make her stop."

I looked down at him, trying to seem cool and collected though my heart was racing. I reached out and touched his cheek. "I'm not afraid of you, Raymond. You're not crazy— you're one of the sweetest men I've ever met." He winced with the pain I'd seen before, only this time he didn't try to conceal it. He took my hand, kissed my palm, then placed it once again on the reins.

"Remember," he said. "Thumbs up. Heels down."

He mounted his tall, black mare. One by one, the other horses walked toward the trail. "I'll follow you," he said.

"Walk," I said calmly but forcefully, and gave Angie a kick I hoped was only a wake-up call. She lurched into a rhythmic motion, now an ambulatory boulder. I thought of the old jungle movies where Sabu rode an elephant, and smiled to myself. This isn't so bad, I thought. Why've I been afraid to do this?

We rode single file down a narrow path, the girls and Thomas quite a bit ahead of us, Raymond behind me. I wasn't so brave as to attempt turning around in the saddle, but if I listened closely I could hear his horse a few yards back. Bits and pieces of Thomas's tales of the racetrack drifted back to me, but not enough to make a continuous narrative. I just let myself bounce slowly along on Angie's back, thumbs up and heels down, trying to figure out this man who was in love with me. What was it he'd said before? *Happiness is fragile.* He seemed afraid of losing me, and we'd only just met. I figured there was something in his past that scared him. I could certainly understand that. But if I can overcome my fears, I thought, moving down the path like Sabu, certainly he can overcome his.

I REACHED A BROAD, FLAT FIELD WHERE THOMAS AND THE GIRLS were cantering around the perimeter. Kareth stopped in front of me. "That was a canter, Marion."

"I know, dear. I've only seen you do it once a week for five years. Just because I can't do it doesn't mean I can't identify it."

"Sure you can do it. You want to try? You just tighten your legs, lean forward, and—"

"No," I said. Angie, to demonstrate our solidarity, stood firm, as if she'd become a feature of the landscape. Kareth shook her head and rode to Thomas and Lorena on the other side of the clearing as Raymond rode up beside me.

"Let's go down by the river," he said, and pointed toward a path into the woods.

I looked at the dark line of trees and felt a twinge of fear. "I don't know if I'm quite ready for that," I said, though I wasn't sure what I meant.

"There's a pleasant place to talk," he said.

The kids and Thomas were now jumping back and forth over a fallen tree—so obviously not in need of me, I couldn't use them as an excuse. "Okay," I said in my nervous register. "That sounds nice."

He headed toward the path and Angie took it upon herself to follow at a leisurely pace. I caught up with him just as the path entered the woods, and we were shrouded in trees, leafless now. A flock of crows called back and forth around us. A screech owl peered out from the hollow of a tree. "Did you read my second chapter last night?" I said to Raymond's back.

"I did indeed."

"Well, what did you think?"

"It's very good. I'm particularly impressed with your depiction of Anthony."

"He's a terrible bastard," I said.

He looked at me over his shoulder. "How exactly—what makes him a bastard to you?"

I thought about it a moment. "He's a chameleon, appearing to each person in the guise of what they want him to be. He treats everyone as a thing, a pawn. I'd say that makes him a bastard."

He nodded his head. "I quite agree."

The path wound through a stand of pines close on either side. The smell filled the air. The ground was thick with pine needles. I could hear the rush of the river ahead of us. He dismounted and tied his horse to a tree limb. He walked up to Angie's side and held his arms up to me. "Let me help you down," he said.

It seemed a very long way to the ground. "Couldn't I stay up here?"

He just stood there smiling, his arms up in the air waiting for me, as if he would gladly spend his whole life waiting for me.

"How should I do this?" I asked, pointing at Angie.

"Take the reins in your left hand and take hold of her mane, swing your right leg over and take hold of the back of the saddle with your right hand. Then take your left foot out of the stirrup and slide down. I'll catch you."

I took a deep breath and did as he said. He caught me by the waist and set me on the ground. I looked up at him, my hands on his chest. "Thanks for my riding lesson."

"I told you you were brave."

He led me to a rock at water's edge that looked like a stone Volkswagen mired in the current. He spread a blanket over its mossy surface. I wondered who else he'd brought to this spot. The trees shrouded it from view, and the sound of the water seemed to seal it off from everything.

Raymond picked up a piece of wood about four inches in diameter and ten inches long and began stripping the bark from it with a pocketknife. Long curls of wood fell into the water and spun away into the current. "Tell me about the boy," he said.

I took off my riding helmet and shook out my hair. "William?"

"Yes, William. I liked William a great deal." He had a wistful tone to his voice, as if he were speaking of someone he'd once known and lost.

"I based him on myself as an adolescent—mooning about, longing for adventure." Raymond's right hand moved over the wood in a quick rocking motion. I couldn't yet tell what it was going to be. "What did you like about him?"

He stopped whittling and looked into the water rushing by us. "His devotion, I guess." His blade started moving again. "It's rare."

"I noticed something very odd as I was reading Pearl's journal this morning," I said.

"What is that?"

"Several characters in my novel show up in Pearl's journal."

He didn't look up from his whittling. "How is that odd?"

"How is that odd? You've got to be kidding. Raymond, I made these people up out of whole cloth—James, for example. He's not mentioned in Grier's letter. I've found no evidence of any kind that Robert and Susanna had a second son, and yet there he is, Pearl's grandfather. Nancy's my novel's Nancy grown old. Pearl's little boy is named after the Miles I invented for Susanna. William is the name I gave Susanna's son. One character, I'd say it was a coincidence, maybe even two or three, but four? No way."

I could see now he was whittling a boat, canoe-shaped but fatter in the middle. He was hollowing it out with the point of the blade with a twisting motion, as if he were tightening a screw. "Perhaps somehow you know what really happened," he said. "So that your novel and Pearl's journal are based on a common history." He shook the shavings from the boat into the water. The current sucked them under.

"But what 'somehow'? How on earth would I know what really happened?"

He shrugged. "Clairvoyance? Reincarnation?"

I made a face. "Don't be ridiculous." I watched him work, watched another boatload of shavings hit the water and wash downstream. "The journal could be a fake," I suggested.

"That doesn't solve the problem, does it? A shared fantasy, a shared reality—they are equally impossible, are they not?"

"I guess so." I turned it over in my mind. There was no way to make sense of it. "How did you come by this journal in the first place?"

He stopped whittling and turned to me. "Pearl's husband-to-be, Frank Strickland, is the architect who designed Greenville," he said. "I've tracked down every artifact from his life that I could."

"Good Lord. Pearl marries a slave smuggler?"

"Not exactly a marriage made in Heaven."

"Is it awful?"

"I'll let Pearl tell you."

"But you still haven't told me how you got your hands on her journal."

He looked down the river, touched his forehead with the tip of his blade, ran the blade lightly down his scar. He obviously didn't want to tell me. Finally, he shook his head and sighed. "It was buried in a strongbox with Frank's body. I had it exhumed."

I shuddered at this. "But how did you manage that? The law . . ."

He abruptly turned back to me, looked me full in the face. "I broke it," he said. "I broke the law. I paid someone a great deal of money to dig up Pearl's journal for me, no questions asked."

"But how did you know it was there?"

"I couldn't know for sure. It was next to impossible to track down the gravesite—the earthquake changed the face of things. But I was able to locate the undertaker's records, and he made note of a strongbox placed in the coffin alongside the body. I had to get my hands on that box. I've become somewhat obsessed with the life of Frank Strickland."

I drew my legs up to my chest and wrapped my arms around them. "Well, he's starting to give me the creeps, and I haven't even met him yet."

"Do you think I'm horrible for desecrating a grave?"

I thought about this. "No. I'm afraid it's the sort of obsession I understand. If there were a strongbox out there somewhere in Susanna Grier's grave, I'd be there with a pick and shovel. Besides, I'm benefiting too much from the crime." I shook my head. "But let's talk about something else."

"Anything you like."

"How about Raymond's past."

He smiled. "I guess I envy Mr. Peabody. If the past is not to his liking, he simply changes it."

"Okay," I said, moving up next to him, leaning against him. "We'll start there. You like cartoons. Did you watch them all the time when you were little?"

"Actually, I watched my first cartoon when I was fourteen. I snuck into my parents' bedroom and watched *Felix the Cat* on their little black-and-white TV. My parents didn't approve of talking animals. They were blasphemous —the talking animals, that is, not my parents."

"This was in Africa?"

"No, we returned to the States when I was twelve. My father took up radio preaching for a while, then TV evangelism. That's why they had a set in the house—so that my mother could watch him late at night."

"Are they still alive?"

"Yes. But I've been on my own since I was eighteen. I haven't had any contact with my parents in twenty-four years. At first, I wrote my mother, but she never answered. I'd joined the realm of the blasphemous."

"It sounds like religion was the big issue between you and your parents."

He gave a bitter laugh. "You might say that. Everything was an issue, but for my father everything was religion. He intended me to be his heir, the Little Preacher, but I failed to show the proper respect." He'd started whittling again, drawing the blade in long, quick strokes down the length of the hull.

"He gave me Bible verses to memorize, and at first he was quite impressed with my abilities. But one day when I was eight I was a little too eager to go with Timothy to pick up the mail and recited my verses perfectly before I'd barely had time to read them, much less commit them to memory.

"From then on, he knew something was different about me, and as I got older, I enjoyed the fact that I frightened him, that he feared I was possessed by demons." He stripped the wood from the prow with quick, arcing strokes. They leapt from the blade into the water. The prow narrowed to a sharp curving line. "My father is quite a believer in demons."

"I should've thought he'd credit your abilities to miracle, divine grace, something like that."

Raymond shook his head. "For my father, grace was simply a Perfect Judge's begrudging stay of execution for a bunch of totally worthless criminals. It certainly wouldn't act through his son, his disrespectful son. He began to beat me—not sparing the rod being biblical—but it was more of an annoyance than anything else. He was too afraid of me to put any real muscle in it. I made a great weeping wail of it though. To keep my mother on my side."

"Tell me about her."

"She was young, desperately trying to do the right thing. It was my father who originally 'brought her to the Lord,' as they used to say—a pun they seemed completely unaware of. My father was the absolute authority in all things. She'd sneak me food when I was sent to bed without supper—that sort of thing—and she was always merry whenever there was a lull in our hostilities and she was allowed to be openly nice to me.

"But she'd put herself on the sidelines. There was nothing she could do. It was between me and him."

He held up the boat, examining the hull, sighting down the length of it, and went back to work. "I was pretty miserable. But when I was ten, some well-intentioned Christian willed his library to the mission school. There were boxes and boxes of books—Homer, Shakespeare, Milton, Chaucer, Wordsworth—the library of a well-read man. As I watched my father digging through the boxes, I felt like a starving man at a banquet. My father had no use for such books. He taught the savages to read with Dick and Jane. Grown men and women were made to see Spot run so that they might graduate to the only book that mattered— the Bible.

"He stuck the boxes of godless books in a shed and forgot about them. I managed to steal the key and snuck out to read whenever I got the chance. I devoured them, filled my life up with them, reading them all, box after box. I'd read about half of them, when one night he followed me and discovered my secret. I pleaded with him, but he commanded me to be silent and watch as he doused the books with gasoline and burned the shed and its contents to the ground.

"After that, I began to plan ways to kill him, spent hours devising one plot after another. When he announced his plans to return to the States, I decided to kill him in transit, figuring that a long boat trip would provide several opportunities to push him overboard.

"Anyway, it was the week before we were to leave when Timothy and I managed to get away to camp in the bush. We wouldn't have been allowed to do it for pleasure, of course, so Timothy made up some task or other that would take us away overnight, and my father was more than glad to have me out of his sight.

"I knew this would be one of the last times I'd see

Timothy, and I told him, as we were sitting around the campfire in the evening, about my memory, about all the books I knew by heart." Raymond stopped, smiled to himself. "He was very nonchalant, unimpressed. So I began to tell him more and more, quoting all the wisdom I had at my command, getting more and more angry that he didn't seem to appreciate the extraordinary creature that I was. I finally told him—to let him know just who he was dealing with—that I was going to murder my father, because I knew him to be a complete, narrow-minded fool." Raymond paused a moment, staring downstream, shaking his head. He folded his knife and put it in his pocket, laid the boat in his lap.

"Timothy stood up from the fire and stretched—tousling my hair in this way he had, as if he still thought I was just a little boy—and walked into the darkness. At first I thought he'd gone to relieve himself, but then he didn't come back. I called out to him, but there was no reply. I was all alone in the bush at night. The rifle, which Timothy had leaned against a tree, had apparently gone with him. I began to be frightened, remembering all the stories I'd heard about the bush at night. I thought I heard the sounds of big cats prowling in the dark. I sat up all night by the fire, burned up most everything flammable I could find except the tents and the bedding.

"Finally it started getting light, and when I could barely make out one tree from another, I saw Timothy, sitting cross-legged on the ground, the rifle in his lap, watching me.

"I flew into a rage. Didn't he know he'd frightened me? Hadn't he heard the big cats?

"He stood up and dusted himself off and said calmly, 'I figured, if they come too close, you would tell them one of the stories you recall from the great huge past and frighten them all away.'

"I didn't say much on the way home, but I decided not to kill my father."

He picked up some of the shavings from his lap and

fashioned two figures from them by tying slender pieces around larger ones to make arms, legs, and torso. When he was done, he set them in his boat. Leaning out so far I was afraid he was going to pitch over into the water, he set the boat on the current and it shot away, disappearing beneath the low branches that hung over the water downriver.

When he straightened up, I slid my arm under his and locked arms with him. We sat in silence for a moment, swaying slightly, both still looking downriver. He seemed indeed like a little boy recalling a "great huge past."

"What became of Timothy?" I asked.

"He died two years ago. I wrote him once a week, confided everything to him, asked his advice. He had a friend who read my letters to him and wrote his replies. The friend wrote to tell me that Timothy had died. He didn't say how, except to say, *Timothy very, very old.*"

Raymond looked into my eyes. "I could use his advice now."

"And what would you ask him?"

"What I should do now that I've found you."

"And what do you suppose he would say?"

"What he told me when I first asked him that question— that when I found the right woman, she would know what to do."

I smiled. "And what's wrong with that advice?"

His face clouded over, and he looked away. "You don't know me. You don't really know who I am."

"I could say the same to you."

He turned back to me, took my hand in his. "No, Marion," he said, his voice full of conviction. "I would know you anywhere, anytime."

And I believed he would.

AT NOON WE ROUNDED UP THE KIDS AND WENT BACK TO THE HOUSE for lunch. After lunch, Raymond insisted on honoring his promise to leave me the afternoon to work. He said he wanted to read the rest of my book. I went up to my room, peeled myself out of my riding clothes, and took a long, hot shower.

"Felix the Cat," I muttered to myself. I imagined the young Raymond in his parents' bedroom, the only light the glow of black and white, seated on the floor to leave no sign on the neatly made bed that he'd ever been there, watching the antics of blasphemous animals, his heart burning with rage. I wanted to sit down on the floor beside him and hold him in my arms.

Instead I retrieved my computer from the office and stretched out on the bed to reread the last chapter I'd been able to write of Susanna's story, knowing he was reading it himself. I hoped he liked it. I hoped he could help me figure out how to end it.

Susanna's Story

Chapter Three

When Susanna entered the parlor, Robert was pouring their brandy; Anthony was admiring Robert's collection of pipe tampers on the mantelpiece. "This one is splendid," he said, and smiled at Susanna. Robert had yet to notice her.

"You have an eye for quality, Anthony. That's the pride of my collection. The design is called the endless knot. Silversmith in London made it for me just before I set sail for Virginia." They both looked at the silver tamper in Anthony's hands. It was slender and delicate, no more than three inches long. "Smoke a pipe, Anthony, if you like."

"Good evening," Susanna said. "May I join you?"

"Where in the devil were you?" Robert said.

"I was in the kitchen."

He turned to Anthony. "She spends more time with the niggers than she does with me."

"Have some brandy," Susanna said. "You're ever more pleasant when you're drunk."

"I believe I will." He handed Anthony his drink and sat down, taking a large gulp of brandy.

She smiled at Anthony. "Anthony, before you sit down, would you please pour me a glass?"

"Certainly, ma'am."

He poured her a brandy and handed it to her, waiting for her to sit down before he took his chair. Robert was not so eager to have Susanna present tonight. He had the vague sense he'd embarrassed himself the night before beyond the fact of his drunkenness, but couldn't remember how. Whatever it was, Susanna would remember. She remembered all his failings. "I was about to sound Anthony here on the subject of Newton, a subject, I believe, you have found tedious in the past."

Anthony had settled into his chair, one of Robert's long clay pipes in his hands. As he listened, he packed the tobacco into the bowl with the tamper. Susanna couldn't take her eyes off his hands, the strong sinuous movement. "Newton is tedious," she said. "But I would be most interested in hearing Anthony's views on him."

Or about anything, she added to herself. Anthony looked up from the pipe and smiled at her. In the two years Anthony had been with them, she'd scarcely taken notice of him. He was a nice-looking fellow, pleasant enough, charming even. But she'd had no notion she would so readily take him into her bed. She realized only now, thinking back on it, that he'd been preparing for months—one sly, testing glance after another—for the bold look he'd given her the night before. She'd come to expect his glances, look for them—she realized with a blush—wait for them.

Just as his influence over Robert had grown until he was virtually doing Robert's job for him without Robert's seeming to be aware of it, he had taken possession of her, it seemed, without even touching her. Now I can't stand to be away from him, she thought. My life has taken an odd and dangerous turn just when I'd thought it would never move, as if I were tied to a stake.

"Susanna, I was speaking to you," Robert said.

Both men were looking at her, one glowering, the other smiling.

"What did you say?"

"I was suggesting that you might prefer one of your novels to a discussion of natural philosophy."

"No. This is much more diverting. Men discussing matters of great moment, the winds of thought puffing up their sails, are endlessly amusing. Don't you agree, Anthony?"

"Most certainly. That is why Plato entertains—transcripts of foolish men arguing, with Socrates the greatest fool of all."

"What? You believe Socrates a fool as well?" Robert exclaimed.

Anthony laughed. "But a most entertaining fool, sir: he talks so splendidly."

Robert poured himself some more brandy. "Very well, there is something in what you say. Plato is merely speculating, but Newton—why, the man has seen into the very mind of God and told us His thoughts."

" 'To every action there is always opposed an equal reaction'—begging your pardon, sir, but that strikes me as not quite worthy of the Deity."

"You disappoint me, Anthony. It is its very simplicity that shows its divinity. Newton has done nothing less than show us the simple and elegant principles which govern the universe."

"Which govern planets and pendula and projectiles perhaps, but if I may say so, sir, he understood persons not at all. As Master of the Royal Mint in his dotage, he seemed to think a disk of metal with the king's face on it worth more than the life of my grandfather—had him burned at the stake, he did, and many others who practiced his trade."

"Trade? I take it you mean the treasonous usurpation of the rights of the crown—counterfeiting. This has been a family business for you, I gather?"

"Most definitely, sir. I learned it at my father's knee. It does less harm than many a landlord. I fashion a coin from metal extracted from the earth only a few feet from the 'precious' metals the mint uses. It is quite as attractive as the genuine article—the king looks quite as fat and happy as on the real coin. For this I should be burned alive? Hardly an 'equal reaction' to my action."

Robert smiled. "Is this the argument you put forth during your trial?"

"Oh no sir, I purchased mercy at the going rate from a judge who was excessively fond of the king's coinage."

"Ah, there you have your 'equal reaction'—a scoundrel pardons a scoundrel."

"Begging your pardon, sir, but he is in England, a fat lord, and I am here, a slave. Inequality is the order of things, I fear. Take your own case, sir—the victim of a thief. It's not my place, sir, to take notice of such things, but if we are unable to apprehend the criminal who's been perpetrating these thefts, I would imagine you will be in dire financial straits, will you not?"

"You know damn well I will. You keep the books. You keep your eye on every coin that clinks for miles around. I daresay you know how much young William has pilfered and stowed away under his mattress."

Susanna bristled. "Whatever money my son has in his possession, he has earned."

Anthony smiled. "The boy has only a shilling or two." He snapped a twig from a log and stuck it in the flames, drew it out and lit Robert's pipe with it. "I confess I've always had a fascination with money. I have made it my profession. I understand that it is all an illusion—counterfeit or true—but quite the most powerful illusion going."

Robert laughed too loud, slapping his palms down on his thighs. Susanna had never seen him like this. So gay, and so frightened. She had no idea what he was afraid of—his ruin or his savior.

"As you might imagine," Anthony said after Robert's laughter had died down, "I was not entirely a pauper when I came here. I most recently came into a small portion of the earnings which my transportation has made inaccessible, and I wish to purchase my freedom."

Robert was brought up short. "You're joking," he said.

There were tears in Anthony's eyes. It had happened abruptly as he stumbled over the word "freedom." One moment he was the wit, the next he was the tortured man. "Not at all, sir. I would have every intention of remaining in your employ, but I must be a free man whatever else I am. I must be able to hold my head up, sir."

Susanna had learned long ago that tears only annoyed Robert, but here he was leaning forward in his chair, taking all this in, his face etched with concern, believing it completely.

"How long have you entertained such feelings?"

"If I may be so bold, sir, from the moment I was loaded onto the *Justitia* as part of the cargo, a bit of goods to be sold. I have often thought that burning would've been better, but alas, I'd proved a coward in the face of death and bought my slavery to avoid it."

Robert rose and took a pipe from the mantel, staring into the fire as he filled it. Anthony cut Susanna a glance, grinning like a schoolboy making a fool of the schoolmaster.

Still turned toward the hearth, Robert said, "What are you proposing?"

"I regret to say, sir, that I lack sufficient funds to entirely make up for your recent loss, but I have half that amount, and would gladly tender it to you in exchange for my freedom—staying on, of course, at whatever wage you might deem appropriate."

Robert rocked back and forth on his heels, turned, and smiled. "You are worth considerably more than twenty-five pounds, but I believe your resourcefulness has earned your freedom. Very well, consider it done."

Anthony drew a rolled-up document from his coat and handed it to Robert, along with a bag of coins. Susanna was sure Robert would balk then—suspect the papers so ready to hand. But Anthony said in a quiet, confessional tone, "Forgive me, sir, but my longing for freedom has so long weighed upon me that some time ago I drew up the necessary document and have carried it with me, looking at it time and again, as a solace you might say, as a comforting illusion of my own."

"Perfectly understandable," Robert said, and spread it upon the table. Scarcely reading it, he signed with a flourish. He stood ridiculously tall, the benevolent despot, and handed it to Anthony, a superior smile upon his face.

Susanna hated him. It was the only sort of kindness he knew—the mercy of the monarch who delivers his subjects from his own evil. The bag of coins remained on the table.

"Thank you, sir," said Anthony. "I am really quite overcome. With your permission, sir, and yours, madam"—he turned and bowed slightly—"I must beg your leave to be alone at a time such as this." He left the room with Robert's pipe tamp in his pocket.

"I had no idea," Robert said to her when Anthony had gone, "that he was so earnest after his freedom."

James's room had been fashioned from a portion of the attic. The ceiling sloped at a steep angle. At its highest point, Susanna could just barely stand erect. James was playing with wooden soldiers and horses upon the floor. On one side were arrayed the soldiers; on the other, the horses—as if they meant to do battle with one another.

He looked up at her. "What is 'wealthy'?" he asked her.

One of the soldiers marched across the rug and knocked over a horse with its head. "Why do you ask?" she said.

"Father says I will be wealthy."

"Wealthy means having a lot of money."

"Will William be wealthy?"

"No dear, I don't think he will. William, I hope, will be a scholar."

"What's a scholar?"

"Someone who learns many things, who always wants to learn new things."

"Will we live in Scotland soon?"

"Did your father tell you we were going to Scotland?"

"He told me before."

"I'm sure your father will tell us when we're to go to Scotland."

"Have you been to Scotland?"

"I was born there."

"Is it grand?"

"It is grand enough, I suppose. I prefer it here."

"Why?"

"I was happy here."

James seemed to consider this for a moment. He picked up the fallen horse and examined it.

"Who is Miles?"

"He was my first husband."

"Father says you love Miles and not us."

"Sometimes your father says things he doesn't mean."

"Is Miles dead?"

"Yes dear, he has been dead for many years."

"Do dead people love?"

"I really don't know, James. There are those who believe they do little else, forever and ever."

He picked up a soldier in his other hand and banged the two of them together. "Nancy called me a name."

"What did she call you?"

"Snakebit."

She pulled back his bedclothes, and he climbed into bed still clutching the soldier. "What is 'snakebit'?" he asked.

"It's Nancy's way of telling you you were being mean. Were you being mean?"

He gave her the identical look Robert would give her whenever she implied any criticism of him. "No, Mother. Nancy is mean to *me.*"

She kissed his cheek. "Good night, dear."

"Does Nancy sometimes say things she doesn't mean?"

Susanna looked down at him, her head nearly brushing the ceiling. "No dear, I don't believe she does."

He stood the soldier on his chest. "Nancy is a slave, isn't she?"

"Yes, she is."

A faint smile spread across his face. "Good night, Mother," he said.

She made her way to her room and lay on her bed. She closed her eyes and tried to see Miles's face. Recently she had to begin with William's face and add the touches of age and the subtle differences between them. Miles had been happier than William would ever be. She remembered a time walking through a meadow, William perched upon his father's shoulders, arms wrapped round his head so he wouldn't fall. Miles laughing, William anxiously looking down, beseeching his mother to set him back on the earth.

When Miles died, she'd never expected to marry another man she loved. It would be too much to ask.

Husbands and wives needn't love each other. But when she married Robert, she hadn't known she would hate him. With each day she spent with him, she saw some new feature of his character she found loathsome. She'd often wondered whether she would have hated anyone who wasn't Miles, but didn't believe that to be true. Robert was not a bad man, but his weaknesses and failings—even the things he fancied to be his strengths—constituted a species of man she could not abide.

So formal, even businesslike, had been their courtship (since she had no expectations of love, and Robert seemed only shy and reverent) that she'd taken little notice of him before their marriage except in those particulars by which anyone might judge a match. She'd known his prospects and his ambitions. The man, she'd known not at all.

Almost since he was born, James had been exactly like Robert in every way. Everyone commented upon it. "Little Robert," Gordon called him. James, naturally enough, lived to be like his father, sought to please him as if he were Zeus on Olympus. He emulated his stride, his gestures, his vision of the world as best he could comprehend it. And sadly, to Susanna at least, he seemed to comprehend it quite well. He became more his father every day. How could she love him? She didn't hate him. She couldn't hate a child. But she did not love him. And for that, she hated herself, for only an awful woman could not love her own son, and it was only natural that he should not love her.

William heard his mother passing his door without stopping. He knew this to mean she was upset about something. She tried to hide from him any pain she felt. She felt guilty, he thought, for the burden of grief she had laid upon him when his father died. She rarely talked about that time, but when she did, she called herself thoughtless and selfish. He knew she had married Robert partly out of some sense that William should have a father. William wished she would lay her burdens on him rather than always seeking to take on his. And if she would not ask for his aid, then he must be vigilant for every opportunity to offer it unbidden.

In all the tales of love affairs William had ever read, trouble was hard upon the heels of passion. Would Anthony now kill Robert, or Robert kill Anthony? He couldn't imagine the latter, but he knew that it was certainly possible, for Robert could have them both arrested if he got wind of what was going on. Would Anthony and his mother run away—sailing away to who knows where? Would they take him with them?

He imagined the three of them on the deck of a great sailing vessel, plowing through the waves. Mister Jack was there, his arm and his life somehow miraculously restored, and a huge bird perched upon the bowsprit. Would his mother take him on such a journey? Where would they go? Anthony had been all over the world. He imagined some distant island, natives dancing on the shore.

He watched this scene for a while, then shook it out of his mind. This was no time to be childish. He must watch and wait and keep a clear head, for his mother might need him in whatever came to pass—might need him as she had never done before.

He cleared his writing desk, took out his poem, and tried to put everything else out of his mind. If he could finish it and get it right, he wanted to present it to his mother as a gift.

The Progress of the Moon

Star-decked Diana hangs her bow up in the sky
Come home from hunting all the day in
*   shadowed wood nearby*

*She wraps herself in sable against the evening
    cold
As Philomel entertains her Queen with dark
    tales of old;
She sings of Daphne fleeing the sun to become
    his laurel crown
She sings of*

But this was dreadful. He took a fresh sheet of paper
and began over again. He wasn't happy with the
metrics—he never was—but the idea, he thought,
might work yet.

The Progress of the Moon

*Bright Diana hangs her bow high in
    star-decked sky,
Home from her silent groves, unseen by mortal
    eye;
She dons a sable cloak against the ev'ning cold,
Bids Philomel sing to her of dark tales of old.
She sings of fair Daphne become a laurel
    crown;
She sings of false Medea weaving a mortal
    gown;
She sings of sad Io lowing among the stars;
She sings of Aphrodite—snared—embracing
    Mars.*

*She sings the Queen's progress across her black
    domain.
Fields glisten with fresh tears to hear such woes
    again.
Her subjects come to greet her, loudly they
    complain
That mortals ape the gods, eclipsing joy with
    pain.
Diana makes no answer, the sky grows pale
    and wan,*

*The brightening grove receives her, once more
      she is gone.
Aurora and her lover from their slumbers rise,
And in a blaze of crimson, fair Diana dies.*

William wiped a tear from his eye and looked over what he'd written, then out the window at the moon, a crescent hanging in the sky. He pictured his mother as Diana, perfectly beautiful, sitting on a throne, alone and infinitely sad. He would show the poem to Anthony. He showed Anthony most everything he wrote. Perhaps he would understand its inspiration and treat his mother with kindness and love.

He heard his mother quietly passing his room again, heard her making her way to Anthony's room beneath the stairs. He held his breath and listened.

Susanna waited until Robert had fallen asleep, then stole down the stairs to Anthony's room. It was small, little more than a closet. His bed filled half of it. The rest was a battered armoire and a writing desk. He lay on the bed reading.

"You frightened me half to death in the orchard."

He smiled. "I thought you rather enjoyed it."

"Robert almost saw us."

"And what if he had? Would you really mind so much?"

"He might kill you. He has a violent temper."

Anthony laughed aloud. "Robert? Better men than he have tried that. A violent temper doesn't bestow a talent for violence."

"Have you killed a man?"

"Yes, on occasion."

Robert's pipe tamp lay on the desk. She picked it up, turning it over in her hands. "I don't love you," she said.

"Are you quite sure?"

"Yes."

"Then why are you here?"

"I don't know. You asked me to come."

"So I did."

"You tricked Robert into giving you your freedom."

"So I did."

"How do I fit in? What do you want from me?"

"There is nothing dishonest in my feelings for you. They are quite passionate, I assure you."

"So I am your whore."

"One buys a whore. One steals a wife. It is altogether different."

"Both are then cast aside."

"You misjudge me. I intend to take you with me, to Norfolk, then home to England."

"That's impossible. Robert would have us both hanged."

Anthony grinned. "We have money," he said. "Anything is possible with money."

"How much money?"

"Twenty-five pounds in ready cash for our immediate expenses."

"The stolen tobacco."

"Not only beautiful, but clever."

"There was never any tobacco stolen."

"Quite true."

"And Robert sold you your freedom in exchange for half the money you stole from him."

"True again."

She didn't know what to say.

He grinned again and arched his brows. "Ain't I a rascal though?"

She laughed. She couldn't help herself. Robert standing before the hearth, granting Anthony his freedom—what a bloody fool.

"Come here," he said.

She set the pipe tamp back on his desk as if it belonged there, and went to him.

* * *

When Susanna awoke, Anthony was fully dressed, sitting at his desk, writing by lamplight. In Anthony's windowless room, she had no idea of the time. A strip of light shone under the door, so it must be morning. She listened for the sounds of Jesse's heavy tread as he hauled in firewood and set the fires, for Nancy's broom upon the floors, but everything was silent. It must be quite early or quite late.

She watched Anthony in profile bent over the page, his dark eyes flickering back and forth as he formed each letter with care like a draftsman. She admired his large eyes, his long, angular face, his black hair pulled back, the sensuous curve of his mouth. She watched his hands. The left held the page steady as the right one held the quill. She had never seen such powerful hands. They frightened her a little, but she found his touch exciting—strong and powerful, but not brutal. At least not yet.

Why should I go with this man? she asked herself. He is dangerous. He has killed men before. And perhaps women.

He turned to her and smiled. "Good morning, Susanna. You are awake."

She gave a start. "Only just now. What time is it?"

He pulled out a watch and flipped it open. "You needn't worry. Even if Robert is up and about, would he think to look for you here? I think not."

She began to gather together her clothing. Anthony had insisted she disrobe completely. She pulled on her stockings in quick, angry movements. "I still wish to know the time," she said.

He smiled at her, watching her dress. "Having second thoughts? You've had your little adventure and now it's back to Mistress of the House?"

"No. I simply wish to know the time. It's a simple question. Why must you torment me like this?"

"Torment? You misjudge me. Here, see for yourself." He unhooked the watch, snapped it shut, and tossed it to her.

The gold case was engraved with *RG*. "This is Robert's watch."

"So it is."

"You stole it from him."

"Right again. As he was so generously granting my freedom, I was freeing his watch. It was a whim. I haven't done much in that line since I was a boy. I wanted to see if I could still do it."

"Perhaps you are still a boy."

"I should say you know better."

"Don't be vulgar."

"Very well. Now that you have poor Robert's watch, aren't you going to observe the precious time?"

She opened the watch. It was a quarter past six. "I must go."

"Do you still intend to come away with me to England?"

She shook her head. "It's a mad idea."

"That is not what you said last night."

Her cheeks began to burn. His gaze was so steady, so frank in its intent. "I was . . . carried away."

"Is it so terrible to be carried away?"

She looked down at the watch in her hand, snapped it shut. "No. It is quite wonderful actually, but it's impossible. I have a son."

"You have two sons."

She couldn't say anything. She couldn't look at him. It was as if he could see into her. She wanted more than anything in the world to leave this place forever with William, to leave Robert and James behind. What a monster I must be, she thought.

Anthony rose from the desk and walked over to her, lifted her chin with his fingertips and smiled down at her. "You wish to take William with us? I have no objections. I am fond of the boy."

She closed her eyes, and he brushed away her tears. She seized his hand and pressed it to her cheek. "How can I leave my son?"

"If we take James with us, Robert will hunt us to the ends of the earth. If we take William, he will say good riddance."

"But Robert's not going to sit idly by while we sail away to England."

He sat down beside her and turned her face toward him. "Look at me," he said. She opened her eyes. He was smiling. "Robert will rejoice in your absence as much as you will rejoice in his, and he cannot pursue me without undue embarrassment to himself."

"I don't understand."

"It is unfortunate for a manager to mismanage his family, but unforgivable to mismanage his company's concerns. He has embraced disaster, allowed a known criminal to take over his duties and conduct matters for his own criminal ends. If he sounds an alarm at my flight, he will be caught himself."

"But how will we manage it?"

"The doing of it is all arranged. It only wants your consent."

"I must speak with William."

"Of course."

He looked at her quite sweetly. With the slightest pressure of his fingertips on her chin, he pulled her face to his, kissing her cheek, her eyes. "Come away with me?" he whispered.

"Very well," she whispered.

"We leave tomorrow at dawn."

"But . . ."

He pressed his hand to her lips. "It is all arranged, as I have said. Now you really must quit my room before anyone is up and about. I will make everything clear to you this evening. I suggest that you absent yourself from the place today—call on some gossipy acquaintance." He kissed her cheek and led her to the door.

She hesitated, her hand on the knob. "You don't intend to harm him, do you?"

"Robert? Certainly not. That would only ensure pursuit. No, Robert will be quite occupied with other matters when we depart." He held out his hand and smiled. "The watch?" he said. She gave it to him and left.

A few hours later, Anthony entered the kitchen. Jess and Rachel were on the floor playing a game with pebbles. Nancy sat by the fire sewing. "If you looking for Jesse," she said, "he down at the carriage house fixing up a wagon so you can drive him to Hell."

Anthony held up his hands. "Nancy, you misjudge me. We merely intend to escape bondage."

She scowled. "Once he 'escape bondage,' what's going to get him loose from you?"

Jess scooped up a handful of pebbles and let them rain down on the floor. Rachel howled in protest. "Jess!" She drew back her arm to strike, but stopped when she saw Nancy was watching her.

"Hit your brother, child. Go ahead. I want you to."

Rachel glared and slumped. "But Mama, he don't play right. He's stupid."

"He ain't stupid, child. He's three years old. Now y'all get out of here. Beautiful day out—ain't too many warm days like this one coming up. Now get."

Jess and Rachel trudged toward the door as if exiled from Eden. Rachel risked a small shove to Jess's back as they cleared the door.

"They call you mother?" Anthony asked.

"You got some objection?"

"Not at all. I think it quite fitting. You clearly

possess a mother's concern for their well-being." He sat down in the chair Jesse usually occupied.

"I told you, Jesse down at the carriage house."

"I came to talk with you."

"I got nothing to say to you."

"Then you can listen for a time. As you know, I intend to make my escape. Miss Susanna and William will be accompanying me, and Jesse as well, I believe."

"Miss Susanna taking off with you?"

"Yes. Which brings me to my next point. It is her urgent desire to take Jess and Rachel with us to England to raise them up free. Unfortunately, booking passage for so many will quite exhaust my funds— with the necessary bribes and so forth—so that I am forced to withdraw my offer of passage for you as well."

"I ain't going nowhere with you."

"Then the matter is resolved. Everyone gets their desire."

She studied him. "Miss Susanna say she want to take Jess and Rachel to freedom?"

"Correct."

She pondered the fire. Anthony couldn't be trusted. But Susanna, she would do what she said. Jess and Rachel, with Susanna's help, could have a better life than they would ever have here, or wherever they were sold. And what could she do to stop them anyway, without getting Jesse killed or sold? "What you want out of me?"

"I haven't yet told Jesse that you must remain behind. I am aware of his strong attachment to you, and I fear he might refuse to leave without you."

"Don't be worrying about that. I already told him I wouldn't go and he be going anyway."

"Then you have no objections to leaving things as they stand?"

"My objections don't make no difference. I keep them to myself."

"Then we are agreed. I will come for the children before dawn tomorrow."

Robert sat in his study and tried to interest himself in Newton's *Opticks*. He wondered where Susanna had taken off to. Here he was, his last day of freedom before Jamieson came to plague his days for who knows how long, and everyone seemed to have packed off somewhere. They must plan a meal for the man, of course. Anthony had already seen to his lodgings, so at least that was out of the way.

Anthony rapped on the open door and stood slightly bowed, waiting for Robert's permission to enter. Robert beckoned him in. "Anthony, Anthony, and how fares your first day of freedom?"

"Quite splendidly, thank you, sir, but I must confess it is not quite real to me as yet."

"I would suppose not. You wouldn't have any notion where my wife's gone off to, would you?"

"I believe she took young William to call upon the Pattersons."

Robert nodded. "No doubt she and Gordon will have a splendid time dis ussing my faults." He motioned for Anthony to sit down. "Anthony, does it strike you that my wife has been acting rather oddly of late? Have you noticed anything of that sort?"

Anthony took his seat, perched on the edge, his back straight. "If I may say so, sir, she does strike me as being somewhat wistful these past few days."

"Wistful?"

"Yes sir."

"I suppose that's as fair a term as any."

"Perhaps she needs to visit relatives, sir. I understand that women are much improved by such visits on occasion."

"As luck would have it, unfortunately, all her family is dead."

"Perhaps that is the source of her unrest."

Robert shook his head. "It is most precisely, I'm afraid. It's that bloody Miles."

"Miles, sir?"

"Her first husband. William's beloved father. Saint Miles I call him."

"I take it Miss Susanna is overly attached to his memory."

"It's a sickness, it is. The man had been dead and buried for four years when we were married. She had no right to marry me or anyone else until she'd laid up his memory as well."

"I quite agree, sir. This must be quite painful for you, a devoted husband such as yourself."

Robert snorted. " 'Devoted husband' indeed. Save your charm for Jamieson tomorrow. I'm no more devoted husband than you are a deacon. I'm no husband at all. She has no use for me."

"You provide her with a very fine home, sir."

"What is that? Bricks and lumber." He waved his hand in the air. "But you didn't come in here to discuss my matrimonial woes. Not business, I hope, on your first day of freedom?"

"I am afraid so, sir. I have come into some information which I felt I must communicate to you immediately. I interviewed a Mr. Hubert who has a small dwelling near the warehouse."

"He is a drunkard, I believe."

"Most definitely, sir, but like many of his persuasion, a most keen observer of unusual goings-on in the middle of the night. I am fairly certain that the thefts were performed on the last three consecutive Sundays."

"Why would a thief choose Sundays?"

"If it is slaves performing these thefts, as you suspect, many are given leave to roam about the countryside on Sundays."

"Yes, I hadn't thought of that. So you think there might be another attempt tonight?"

"Precisely, sir."

"What course of action do you suggest?"

"I'm afraid I am at a loss, sir."

Robert struck his fist on the desk. "We will simply have to notify the authorities."

"Begging your pardon, sir, but they will wish you to rehearse the basis for your suspicions, and you can hardly do so without revealing the prior thefts you have paid so dearly to conceal."

"But if there's another theft tonight, we can't possibly rectify the loss before Jamieson arrives."

"That is our dilemma, sir."

"We must simply ensure that this robbery is not successful."

"What do you intend to do?"

The solution came to him in a flash. "I will apprehend the criminal myself. I know he is coming. He will not know, however, that I will be waiting for him. I've simply to hide and wait."

"But sir, if he is overzealous in his confession, it could prove embarrassing for you."

"Then, dammit, he won't confess. I am a superb shot. If a nigger is stealing from me, I can have him hanged, can I not? I don't see that shooting him in the act will make much difference one way or the other."

"I am most inclined to agree with you, sir. I believe your plan has every chance of success. I have determined which door the thief has been using. It will be easy to determine an effective hiding place for your ambush."

Robert laughed. "Rather like hunting from a blind."

Elizabeth Patterson offered her husband, Gordon, some more tea. He declined, made a face, then said, "Oh damn it all, I can't converse without tea, and would there be any of those little cakes left about?" He winked at Susanna, who could not help laughing in spite of all that weighed on her mind.

She looked over at William, who looked to be in another world—sailing the seas with Anthony, no doubt. She'd only just told him of their plans on the carriage ride to the Pattersons. He had been so transported with joy, she was left feeling unsettled. He expects so much more from our flight than I do, she thought. I am doomed to disappoint him. He caught her gaze and smiled at her, a gay conspirator's smile, and she forced herself to smile back.

Dora, a tall, pale girl with sad eyes, appeared with more of the little cakes and blushed as Gordon heaped her with compliments, as he heaped his plate with cakes. She had been Gordon's patient since the death of her husband, a carpenter even younger than she. Susanna recognized her ailment as grief. Gordon employed Dora as his only servant.

Gordon owned no slaves and was notorious in the town for his strong antislavery views. He was tolerated because he was one of the few physicians for miles around, as well as a constant source of entertainment to his slaveholding friends. "Human beings," he often declared in the taverns, "were never meant to be cattle. It kills the spirit! And how does one doctor the spirit? With freedom, I tell you!" He would bang down his fist and his companions would bait him, regaling themselves with his comical opinions. He was rumored also to harbor revolutionary sentiments, but he was not so foolish as to voice them among his Loyalist neighbors, who would not find those quite so amusing.

After gobbling down several little cakes, Gordon asked Susanna how Robert and little Robert fared.

"I wish to apologize for his rude behavior last Friday," Susanna said.

"Rude? He was just being Robert. It bothered me not in the least. You're too hard on him, Susanna.

Robert has his flaws, I grant you, but he's a good man."

"Perhaps I know his flaws better than you do, Gordon."

"And perhaps I know some you do not."

"If you are referring to the ancestry of his slave children, I am quite well informed."

Elizabeth Patterson was seized with a fit of coughing. "Pardon me! Pardon me! The crumbs, you know! It's nothing! I'm fine! Really quite fine!" No one seemed alarmed save herself, but she reassured them quite forcefully in any event, then smiled on William, who seemed least alarmed of all. "And how are your studies progressing, William?" she asked with the greatest interest.

"Quite well thank you, Mrs. Patterson. I am in the midst of the *Aeneid* at the moment. It is really quite splendid."

Gordon said, "I take it you are quite fond of your tutor, Anthony."

"Oh yes sir, he has been all over the world."

"No doubt he has. Does he ever recount his exploits to you?"

"Oh yes. Just yesterday he told me of a mate of his who had his arm bitten off by a shark!"

Once again Mrs. Patterson commenced coughing. Gordon rolled his eyes and slumped back in his chair, waiting for her protests of well-being to subside. When her eyes alighted on Susanna, he said, "I believe young William was telling us a story about a shark, Mrs. Patterson. We should let him continue, if you have recovered from your cough."

She gave him a thin smile. "Certainly, Mr. Patterson. I was forgetting your taste for gruesome tales."

"Unlike my views, Mrs. Patterson, my tastes are shared by many, wouldn't you agree, Susanna?"

"I read *The Castle of Otranto* with great amusement."

"There? You see? Tell on, William."

William found his thoughts in a jumble, as he often did in the presence of Mr. Patterson. "Tell on, sir?" he said.

"You were telling us about a shark, I believe."

"Oh yes sir. I'd forgot. It took off his arm, and he'd only just repented his sins!"

Gordon smiled. "The shark?"

"Don't pay him any mind, dear," said Mrs. Patterson. "My husband finds it amusing to mock the young on occasion by feigning ignorance. If you will simply tell us who repented his sins, I believe Mr. Patterson will allow you to continue with your story uninterrupted."

"Mister Jack, the mate of Anthony's. He'd just told Anthony he was repenting his sins when the stupid captain makes several of the convicts jump into the ocean to get him a bird he'd shot for no reason at all."

"The captain sounds like a dreadful man. Do you recall his name? I know most of the captains in the convict trade."

William pondered for some moments. "Carter," he said. "Captain Carter."

"I knew Carter. Hanged himself a few years back. Somervell told me about it. He did it at sea, if you can imagine. His first mate went to rouse him, for they were coming upon high seas. When Carter didn't answer their calls, several lads charged the door and stumbled right into him, swinging this way and that as the waves pounded the ship!"

"Why did he kill himself?" William asked, his eyes wide as saucers.

"The note he'd pinned to his chest said 'I *cannot* face the grief.' When they reached port, the first mate went to notify the family of Carter's death, only to find they'd all been slain—three fine sons and a wife—by a robber who was never apprehended!"

"A lovely story, Mr. Patterson," said Mrs. Patterson. "Now would anyone care for more tea? Susanna? William?"

Susanna handed Elizabeth her cup and spoke out, "I would be interested to hear any stories either one of our storytellers might have to tell of Anthony, living as he does under my own roof."

Gordon beamed at this permission to hold forth. "Somervell has a word or two to say about your Mr. Anthony. He remembers him quite well, he does."

Susanna waited for Gordon to go on. She sensed he was testing to see how eager she was to hear his tale. She hoped that William would goad him on, but William seemed to be off again in his own thoughts. "And just why," she said after she could bear it no longer, "does Mr. Somervell remember Anthony with such clarity?"

"Colin claims that each consignment of convicts—like a pack of wild dogs—selects its despots and followers in a matter of days. Usually two or three die in this process, and the rulers maintain their power by the most ruthless means imaginable. He has a collection of weapons taken from convicts that would make your hair stand on end. As you may imagine, such a throne is typically an uneasy one, with numerous challenges from below. Your Anthony, however, was the undisputed potentate of his voyage across. Colin said he'd never seen anything like it. Men who could have snapped him like a twig withdrew in fear at his approach, while others constantly fawned upon him seeking his favor. He strode about the ship as if he were a passenger on a pleasure voyage."

"Anthony possesses a commanding presence," Susanna said quietly.

"A rather unfortunate possession in a servant, I should think."

"I thought you did not approve of human bondage, Gordon."

"I do not. But in the case of a man who has

murdered his fellow creatures, it seems a mercy in the face of the alternative."

"His crime was counterfeiting."

"Look in his eyes, Susanna, and tell me his crimes stopped there."

Suddenly William, who everyone had assumed was not listening to the conversation, jumped to his feet. "Anthony is my friend! He is smart and brave— smarter and braver than anyone here!"

Susanna spoke in a calm, low voice. "Sit down, William."

His face fell, and he stared at the floor. Then, slowly, he slumped into his chair. "I am sorry, Mother," he said. "I am sorry, everyone."

"William," Gordon said. "Look at me." The boy reluctantly raised his eyes. "Before I accept your apology, I wish to take exception with half of your assessment of Mr. Richards. That he is smarter than us all thrown together, I have no doubt, but as to bravery, he has none." He held his finger in the air. William's eyes were fixed upon it. "He has no fears, I'll grant you. But is that bravery? Certainly not. Bravery is some poor human creature filled with fears pressing on in the face of it." He waved one arm in the air and his voice grew louder. "You want the bravest of us all? It's Dora! Dora who lives on with a heart and mind torn apart by the cruelest fortune! All her joys and hopes dashed into ruin. Anthony brave? No. He has no fears to overcome! He is afraid of nothing! He simply acts as he pleases, without fear, without humility, and, I'll wager, without the slightest trace of human kindness!"

The room fell silent. From the yard, they could hear the steady thump of Dora beating a rug. Each blow seemed to shake the anger from Gordon's features, until he was a sad old man whose passions had run away with him again. He got to his feet and spoke in a small, formal voice. "I apologize if I have spoken my mind too forcefully, but I could not in good conscience keep my counsel. I dearly hope, Susanna, that I will see you and William again very soon. I thank you, Mrs. Patterson, for the cakes and tea. With your permission." He turned and left.

Elizabeth stared after him, her eyes glistening. "He frets about you two," she said. "He only means to be a true friend, and to Gordon that means taking on others' woes." She shook her head. "I often think on the injustice—that his good heart brings him so little joy." She smiled. "Though I am grateful that it has always brought much joy to me."

After leaving the Pattersons, Susanna and William called on everyone she knew in the town, and returned home just before twilight. Jesse was loading up a wagon full of furniture, and Robert was nowhere to be seen. Anthony stood in the yard in shirt and breeches as if he owned the place, and greeted them with a jaunty wave. William's face shone like the setting sun.

Anthony took her aside and said, "Nancy's begged us to take Jess and Rachel with us so that they can be free. It might prove a hardship, but I could not say no."

"Certainly not," Susanna said.

I SHUT OFF MY COMPUTER AND CURSED TO MYSELF. EVERY TIME I reread this chapter it was like hitting a brick wall. That was it. As far as I'd been able to write. I'd exhausted the givens—that Susanna goes with him, that William, or whatever his name was, and Jess and Rachel go as well. As Anthony said, *The doing of it is all arranged. It only wants your consent.* But now it was time for them to take off—and I couldn't write it. Up to this point the story had flown out of me. But every time I tried to write the next chapter, I'd type and delete, type and delete, until finally I just saved myself the trouble and quit typing.

The problem, it seemed to me, was Susanna.

I didn't want her to go with Anthony, even though I knew she had to, even though I knew that if I were her (which was precisely the way I "made up" Susanna—by pretending to be her moment to moment), I'd go. I felt by this time as if I actually had. I'd imagined it often enough.

Maybe that was why I couldn't write it. Susanna had become too real to me, the identification too complete, so that I felt like I'd already done it—that I'd carried three children off in a wagon to almost certain disaster just because I had the hots for a sociopath—and I wasn't eager to do it again.

I thought again about my characters showing up in Pearl's journal as if they were real. *Perhaps somehow you know what really happened,* Raymond had said. But the idea was absurd. I didn't believe in the supernatural in any form, from God and His angels on down to tarot cards and lucky rabbit's feet. But I couldn't explain what my creations were doing in that journal without some magic or trickery.

When I read Pearl's journal, it was as if I were her. Sometimes I felt as if I knew what her next sentence would be. But when I was a girl I'd gone around days on end believing I was Anna Karenina, David Copperfield, and Jane Eyre—as I was reading their books. I was a novelist. Pretending to be other people was what I did. It came easily, sometimes too easily.

I looked around the room I was in now. Beside the window was a small cherry armoire. Yesterday, when we'd first arrived, it'd been locked. Now, I noticed, there was a fat iron key in the lock. I got up off the bed, crossed the room, and turned the key. The inside of the armoire looked and smelled new. In the top drawer was the card of a furniture maker from Lovingston. The other drawers were empty. The only thing in the armoire was a cotton shift hanging from a peg. I took it out and held it up before the window. It was bright white and freshly laundered. I held it to my face and burrowed in its softness.

I spread it out on the bed, noting the gussets under the arms, the slender cuffs. It was Susanna's, only it wasn't old and yellowed as a two-hundred-year-old garment would be. It was another reproduction. Raymond must've had it made after he'd read the first chapter of my book. It was exactly as I'd envisioned it.

Exactly.

It was more like the shift I'd seen in my head than the drawing in the history of costume book at work had been, more like my imagined one than what I'd written on the pages Raymond had read. I laughed at myself. How did I know what the imagined garment looked like anymore? It was months since it'd flashed through my mind for a second. This shift, apparently fashioned from my words, only seemed real—like the words themselves.

But why had Raymond had it made and placed it here for me to find? I stepped back from the bed, looking around the room. And then I realized why this room had seemed so familiar. This was supposed to be Susanna's room. And now it was mine. Like a stage set. He'd even given me my costume. I looked out the back window and saw the old kitchen below me, the stable beyond, but there was no apple grove, no children in the yard, no husband snoring in his bed.

"Why are you doing all this?" I said aloud.

I imagined myself inside the chemise, standing before Raymond, imagined him lifting it off of me, gesturing toward the bed. I imagined myself, spread out on the bed, waiting for him. "Stop it!" I said. "You're being ridiculous."

I plopped down unromantically beside the chemise and picked up my lioness for comfort, tracing her contours with my fingertips. I held her up, studied her face, my face. *She is very pretty,* Lorena had said of the Magdalene. *She looks like you.* I set the lioness back down on the bedside table and got to my feet. I needed a drink.

I cut through the adjoining bath and across the girls' room to the back stairs. I could hear the girls whooping it up in the next room. I hoped Raymond's pool table survived. When I stepped into the kitchen, Thomas was standing at the counter with a plate of cold chicken and a beer, a *Star Trek* novel facedown on the counter. "Hi Thomas," I said. "Is there another one of those beers?"

He pointed at the fridge with a drumstick. "Plenty in there. If I was you I'd have me one of Mr. Lord's special brews. They mighty good—least that's what I hear."

I got a beer out of the refrigerator. It was from some tiny brewery near Charlottesville and had Thomas Jefferson's picture on it. I wondered if Anthony Richards had ever known Thomas Jefferson. Somehow I doubted it. "I really appreciate your riding with my girls," I told Thomas. "They had a great time."

He shrugged. "Enjoyed it myself. Don't usually get much chance to ride for fun. They good girls, no problem at all. The oldest, she be something on a horse if she stay with it."

"She really loves it." I took a deep swallow of my beer. "Thomas, I don't want to put you on the spot, but to tell you the truth, I don't know Mr. Lord very well, and I'm kind of curious about him. Have you known him long?"

Thomas straightened up, looking past me at the stairs and then the kitchen doors. "Going on five years," he said.

"Then you must know him pretty well."

He studied me a moment. "I work for him. We ain't friends, you understand. He keep to himself."

"I'm sorry. I know I'm out of line here, but I thought you might be able to tell me a little about him. Does he have many visitors?"

He shook his head emphatically. "People buying horses is all. Few years back, there was a bunch of Spanish folks, but they weren't company. Stayed a couple of days, and they was gone. Came in the middle of the night and left the same."

"What were they doing here?"

"I don't ask no questions, Ms. Mead."

"Call me Marion, please."

Thomas sighed, bounced up and down on his toes, and turned to me. "I tell you one thing—you're the only woman I ever see him take any interest in. When those Spanish folks was here, there was this little fox took a real shine to Mr. Lord. Any fool could've seen it. He don't even care. Tell you the truth, I figured the man didn't take to women till you come along."

"How did he make his money, do you know?"

He shrugged. "Man's rich is all I know. Crazy rich."

"How rich is he?"

He leaned toward me, quiet, confidential. "When I was working at that racetrack, I was nineteen years old. Got into trouble all the time. It was that kind of place. But I didn't mean anybody any harm. I wasn't mean, you understand. I was just a stupid kid, carrying knives and shit, talking tough. But then one night somebody mix me up with some other skinny black kid done screwed him over some way or other and comes for me, and I kill him. I didn't mean to. But the man dead anyway, right? And I was what they call a 'chronic offender' 'cause I had me a little shoplifting problem before I started working at the track.

"But what the hell does my story matter? I didn't have to kill the man. I could've just cut him a little, sent him home to his mama." He took a swig of his beer, the first he'd had since I walked into the kitchen. "But I killed him, and I went to jail. I'd been there two years, looking at five years till we even talking about parole, when Mr. Lord, he write me and ask me real nice if I want a job training his horses. I figure the man's crazy, but I give the letter to my lawyer. Next thing you know, I walk."

"How did you know him before that?"

"That's what I'm saying—I never laid eyes on the man till I got out of prison. Told me once I reminded him of somebody he knew a long time ago—but how's somebody like him gonna know somebody like me? Don't make any sense."

"How did he find you?"

"He never told me. I never ask." He shrugged. "He probably asked some judge friend of his to keep a eye out for a trainer."

"Just like that? I want a trainer who's in jail?"

"That's right. Took him one week to get me out." He held up seven fingers. "Seven days." He wrapped up the plate of chicken and put it in the refrigerator, washed his hands at the sink, and stuck his book in the back pocket of his jeans. "I got to be going. I got work to do." He started backing toward the door.

"What's it been like to work for Mr. Lord? It couldn't be too bad if you've stayed this long."

Thomas shook his head, laughing. "You just don't get it, do you? Anybody rich enough to get you out in a week can put your nigger ass back inside 'fore you can say, 'Officer, I didn't do it.'" He opened the door behind him. "He got a *whole* lot of money, Ms. Mead. No telling how much. And he like you special. If I was you, I wouldn't worry none about me and him."

"What about Rachel?"

He stiffened slightly. "Rachel decide things for herself," he said, and ducked out quickly, closing the door behind him.

I LEANED BACK ON THE STAINLESS STEEL COUNTER AND TOOK A deep swallow from my beer. Thomas's story left me unsettled. It struck me how little I knew about Raymond. I'd come chasing after him, after a journal I wasn't even sure was real. How did he know so much about Frank Strickland? I'd done enough historical research to know that the kind of information he seemed to have about him was almost impossible to come by. Maybe he was making it all up. Maybe he was insane, a criminal for all I knew.

There was a phone in the kitchen, but I figured the sitting room would give me more privacy. Raymond was two floors above me. If he came down the stairs, I'd hear him. Of course, he might pick up the extension, but if he was really in love with me, he wouldn't begrudge me a phone call to a girlfriend.

The sitting room was dark, the fireplace cold. I turned on a bronze lamp with a fringed shade. The light cast elongated shadows from the weapons over the mantel. At first, I didn't think there was a phone, but I spotted the wall jack and followed the wire to a cabinet beside the chair Raymond had sat in when we were in there before. Inside was a Mickey Mouse phone of the sort Kareth and Lorena had campaigned for unsuccessfully after our trip to Disney World.

I took the receiver from Mickey's hand and dialed. It rang seven times. She must be busy, I told myself as she answered in a rush. "Virginia Historical Society, Andrea speaking. How may I help you?"

"Hi Andrea. It's Marion. You busy?"

"You wouldn't believe. Every jerk in Richmond is trying to figure out who their great-great-aunt was. I hope you're having a good time with my Saturday."

"I'm having a wonderful time."

"Don't give me this 'wonderful time' stuff—tell me, tell me everything, tell me the details."

"I haven't slept with him yet."

"You haven't slept with him yet! Why not?"

I heard a muffled male voice saying, "Excuse me, miss," apparently a patron trying to get Andrea's attention. "Hang on," she said to me.

"Sir," she said, the phone against her voice box, "I'm on the phone long-distance to a Virginia Historic Landmark. Whatever you're looking for has already been sitting around for at least a hundred years and can wait for another five minutes. The card catalogue's over there if you want to get started. I'll help you when I've concluded my important phone call."

There were a few beats while, apparently, the patron sulked away. "So why haven't you slept with him yet?"

"I've only been here twenty-four hours."

"Marion, I thought he was hot for you."

"He is. He's in love with me."

She shrieked in my ear. "No kidding!"

"Andrea, control yourself. It's not that simple. There are complications."

"Jesus, Marion. What could complicate a rich guy in love who wants to fuck you?"

"There's just been some weird things going on. I can't explain. I'm beginning to wonder if this journal is for real."

There was a long silence.

"Andrea?"

"You're going to let some bullshit question of literary scholarship stand in the way of my fantasies? What is it with you, Marion? Do you just not like sex?"

"I'm probably going to sleep with him, okay?"

"Promise?"

"Come on, Andrea."

"Promise."

"Okay, I promise."

"So is that what you called me for, to promise to sleep with him?"

"No, I want you to find out a few things. I want to verify some things he's told me, find out more about him. He's very rich. He must've shown up in the news one time or another."

"Let me get this straight. You're calling me to do a background check on this guy before you fuck him? Is that what you're saying?"

"I wouldn't put it that way."

"Marion, you are too much."

"Will you do it?"

"Just a second." She put the phone against her voice box again. "Lady, can't you see I'm on the phone?"

I couldn't make out the woman's reply, but Andrea muttered, "Bitch," as she came back on the phone. "Okay, what is it you want me to do?"

"Have you got a pen?"

"How much you want me to find out? Hang on."

The phone clunked as she laid it on her desk. I could hear her pushing things around in hopes of unearthing a pen. "I already told you," she said in the midst of her search, "I'm on the phone." After the open and slam of a couple of drawers, she picked up the receiver. "Shoot," she said.

"Find out whatever you can about Greenville, the plantation he lives in—especially any hard evidence as to who designed it. See what you can find out about these people, all mid-nineteenth-century Virginia—Frank Strickland, Philip Pendleton Nalle, Pearl Withers, Gerald Withers, Faith Withers. And could you see what you could find out about Raymond Lord—his family, where his money comes from."

"I'm not a news service here."

"Call up Mary Louise at the *Times-Dispatch*. She'll do it for you."

"Why don't you call her?"

"Andrea, I'm making this call on the sly. He could pick up the extension any minute."

"And hear what? That you want me to get the scoop on a bunch of people who've been dead for a hundred years?"

"I'll call you at home later—early this evening if I can."

"And what are you going to be doing?"

"Right now I'm going to finish reading that journal I told you about."

"Marion, I'm afraid you're losing your sense of purpose here."

"I'm doing fine, Andrea. You'll love it, I promise. Now I've really got to go. Thanks for everything." I put the receiver back in Mickey's three-finger gloved hand and crept silently up the stairs to read the rest of Pearl's journal.

Frank has gone into Oregon City with Joshua, his old
slave. Slavery is illegal in the Oregon Territory, but that
means nothing to Frank Strickland. He means to have
slaves—the law be damned!

Who am I writing to? What is the point of this?
Damned book! It makes me laugh just to look on you. He
can't read! He looked as if I were offering him a basket of
snakes and pushed it back. "Don't read," he said. "Don't
care nothin' 'bout it."

"I could teach you," I said.

And he laughed, as if I'd offered to teach him how to
have a baby. How the gods must be laughing! I have
grown mad in a single week!

But perhaps that is why I should write down my
thoughts, so that I won't go mad. I need my wits about
me in my present circumstances. Circumstances I
marched into armed only with stupidity: From the boat to

the judge, from the judge to the land office, from the land office to the lawyer—marriage, land title, and will—three signatures—one Pearl Withers, then two Pearl Withers Strickland—and I had signed my life away, bouncing into the wilderness on Frank's damned wagon, a complete and utter fool!

Why did I do this? What made me think that a cheap whore deserved more than this? That a pretty story would set everything right? Telling him the drummer that day was to be my first—the Princess of Virtue.

But what man would believe that I wanted that drummer to be the last—or better, that he could wait his lifetime and I would still not have mounted those stairs and knocked on his door?

Once I held that newspaper in my hands, with its promise of home and land that was mine, nothing would have stopped me. Nothing did stop me—not my good sense, not my son. What will you make of all this, Miles? Years hence, when you can read, if you could take up this book, what would it mean to you? Even now you would see some of the lies. But you would see the truth as well. There are few lies. I loved your father. I didn't have to tell Frank Strickland that. I didn't have to tell him of your existence. But I thought I could persuade him. I thought he would understand. You must believe that is true.

It doesn't matter now anyway. If you were here, you would only be a slave. I have told him nothing, will tell him nothing. I matter not at all to him. I am three signatures—320 acres of fine farmland—his land when I die.

And I will die soon, I should think. Frank is not a patient man.

Miles, you knew I was wrong to leave you. I knelt down, but you wouldn't look me in the eye. "I have to leave you," I said, and you wouldn't say a word. "I love you," I said, and you tucked your chin hard against your chest.

TIME AND TIME AGAIN

So I kissed the top of your head and climbed into the carriage. What else was I to do? When the carriage lurched into motion, I went mad with grief. I leaned out the window, calling out to you, waving my arms in the air, knowing that if you once looked up, I would not be able to leave, that I would fling myself from the carriage before I could leave you. But you never looked up, not once, and soon you were just a speck on the face of my grandfather's house, and I was bound for Charleston—bound for this horrible place.

I know now that I should have leapt from that carriage—knew it then as well. Then, you would have looked up, and I never would have left you. When I sat in the back of the wagon as Frank drove me here, I thought of that long carriage ride away from you. There was no fine carriage this time, but as we bounced along, I thought I had made this journey before. Joshua was sprawled out asleep at my feet, his white hair shining in the moonlight. I closed my eyes and tried to remember why this wagon seemed so familiar. I felt you nearby, only a few feet away, and another child in my arms, huddled in fear, and I knew I was riding to my death, that I should dive into the wilderness and run for my life. I opened my eyes. There was no place to go. There was only Joshua, old and feeble-minded, ready to die, slave to a madman, and Frank himself, lashing at the mules. At least you are safe, on the other side of the continent. That thought gave me joy, darling boy, and I was able to gather my wits and wait to see what would happen and wait for my chance to escape.

This is foolish nonsense.

Wednesday, August 28, 1850

There are certain advantages in being the wife of a drunkard. There is always whiskey, and he sleeps a good deal of the time. Join me in a drink, sweet Devil. I have a tale for you. Only you will appreciate its delicious ironies.

I was sitting by the fire reading over this very book, when he demanded to know "what in blazin' Hell" I was doing.

I answered, as sweetly as I could, that I was reading.

"Read it to me," he demanded in that Lord and Master tone he employs just before he lapses into the slurred mumbling that constitutes his late evening conversation. "You writing about me, woman?"

He calls me "woman." He addresses Joshua as "nigger." He refers to everyone else in the human race, except for someone named Billy whom I have yet to meet, as "them." His is a small world.

As you may imagine, a few pages of this book would most likely prompt him to smash my head with a shovel. So I told him I composed stories, expecting him to lose interest immediately. But no indeed, he was transformed into a boy at bedtime, demanding to hear a story.

I told him the story of Daniel and the lion's den, pretending I read it from these pages. He liked that fine, especially the part about Nebuchadnezzar being turned into a cow, and demanded I read him another.

Quite foolishly, I chose the story of David and Bathsheba.

"Once upon a time," I said, "there was a great king named David who had fought his way to the throne after a life of poverty and hardship."

"What was his game?" Frank asked.

"A shepherd."

"Shit. No wonder he couldn't make no money. Sheep." He spat in the fire, shaking his head, then looked up at me. "Well, get on with it."

"As I was saying, David was a great king, but he was lonely. There was no woman in his life."

"Wait a damn minute. He's king and he can't get no women?"

"None that pleased him."

He laughed—a snorting, hooting laugh rather like pigs

squealing—and said, "They all please me that ain't snotty bitches." He laughed again. "And ain't no bitch gonna be snotty to no king!"

"Right you are, I'm sure," I said. "Who would want her head chopped off? And David was a man who knew this, as you will see if I may finish my story."

He scowled, and I went on: "One day he was walking on the castle walls, when he spied the most beautiful woman he had ever seen, stretched out naked in the sun on the roof of a house below him."

"Naked!" Frank blurted out.

"That's right."

"Right out there in the open!"

"Exactly."

"Goddamn."

"Yes. Well, you can imagine what he did, he summoned her to his private chamber."

"You ever do that?"

"What?"

"Lie around naked outside?"

"No."

"Well goddamn, we got 640 acres here. Give it a try."

"Perhaps when the weather is warmer."

"It's August, woman, it ain't gonna get no warmer than this. I think you oughta do it tomorrow." He spat into the fire—one of his favorite modes of communication. This time it meant that his thought—if such it may be called—was actually an order.

"Very well," I said, knowing he would forget by tomorrow, for the liquor absolutely stews his brains.

"So what happened to this bitch?" he said.

I wished I had the resolve to smash his head with a shovel, but knew I didn't, not yet. "Bathsheba came to his chambers," I said, and his eyes lit up. "He made love to her and was determined to have her for his own, even though she was married to a soldier in the king's army."

"Goddamn," Frank muttered, but I ignored him.

"The next battle to be fought, David ordered that Bathsheba's husband was to be placed in the front of the fighting and be abandoned by his fellow soldiers in the thick of battle so that he would be sure to die.

"And that is exactly what happened, and Bathsheba married the king."

"Goddamn. Did she know what he'd done?"

"I think so."

"You think so? Whose story is this, anyway?"

"Yes, she knew."

"What a bitch. How'd she know?"

"A woman could tell such a thing of her husband."

He spat in the fire. "Maybe she just liked being queen. Bet you'd jump at the chance to be queen. You're here, ain't you? Married to a man what got 640 acres of land. Course she wanted to be queen. Why else would she marry him?"

"She was pregnant."

He laughed his braying laugh again. "Ain't they always?" he said.

"Don't you wish to hear what became of the child?"

He stopped laughing and looked at me oddly, as if I were someone he couldn't quite place. "Tell me. What happened to the kid?"

"He died a week after he was born and when David was told of it he said, 'I shall go to him, but he shall not return to me.'" There were tears in my eyes, but he did not seem to notice.

"Goddamn, what a story." He tossed off his whiskey and stood up.

"There's more."

"I've heard enough," he said. "That David was one smart son of a bitch."

He walked across the room and started removing my clothes as if they were on fire. They aren't much but they are all I am likely to have, so I told him I'd take them off before he made rags out of them. Then he gave me a lascivious smile and watched me undress while he removed his own clothes—hopping around on one foot trying to get his boot off, getting all tangled up in his shirt as if he had to fight it to get it off of him.

As usual, he was rough, as if he wanted to sunder me in half, but blessedly quick. I've had worse, and soon he was asleep on top of me. I rolled him off of me but couldn't sleep, dreaming of Miles. So I lit a lamp, and to the sound of Frank's snoring, I have told a tale to you, old friend, and shared a glass of whiskey. If he asks for a story again I'll tell him of Samson and Delilah and give him something to worry his dreams.

Monday, September 2, 1850

I have decided to deliver this book into your hands, John Morgan, by whatever means I may hope to do that. Whether I will be in its company, I cannot say, but it is my fervent wish that it be so. I must tell you what I have discovered of my husband and his plans, so that perhaps you may stop him, and if I am slain, know that Frank Strickland was my murderer.

You must think it odd indeed that I should deliver this book to you, after cruelly abandoning you in San Francisco. If you only knew how I have missed you, how I have cursed myself for leaving you, how much I love you, John Morgan.

You read most of this book as we lay on my bed in the Hotel Americano, and the truths glossed over in its pages I laid bare to you. And still, you did not scorn me but loved me so sweetly it broke my heart. I tried to tell you everything, but I have held back two incidents I must confess to you now.

First, I must tell you I lied about not being able to book passage on the Oregon. I exchanged my ticket for one on the Falcon, so that I might remain with you those few weeks longer in Panama City and on the voyage to San Francisco. It was I, not fate, who kept me in Panama.

When I returned to the Hotel Americano to tell you I couldn't leave, the joy in your face was the warmth of the sun to me. I wanted you to kiss me. It must have shone in my face like a bonfire, but you wouldn't kiss me, I knew, because I was engaged to be married. So I did a thing I am not ashamed of, I put my hands to your face and pulled you to my lips. You hadn't honor enough for both of us.

I have often thought of that moment and rejoiced that I didn't let it pass, for then we would not have made love, and we would not have spent together the happiest time of my life.

I have slept with many men, as you know. I was a whore. I'd watched the only man I'd ever loved except my father hung before my very eyes. His crime? Loving me. I had a son to feed and possessed no skills. I was a whore, but am one no longer. It was a choice I made. It is a choice I renounced when I kissed you.

When I was a whore, no one but Miles loved me in all the world, and he was as yet too young to know what his mother was. He only knew that I was his mother. My whoredom harmed no one save myself.

I knew you loved me. Once I returned your love—entreated you to love me—I could be a whore no longer, and not be a monster in my own eyes. I was a fool to think that coming here was anything more than whoredom on a grander scale.

But before I speak of my present circumstances, I must tell you of the strange events that occurred, as we made our way across the Isthmus, during our stay in Gorgona. As you will recall, we had danced with the aristocracy before the Alcalde's house—waltzing with a slow grace to the music of violins and guitars—while the peasants held their fandango on lower ground.

As we danced, your hand on my waist betrayed a more than common shyness in your touch, and when I sought your eyes, you looked away to the hills beyond the circle of light, as if the huge black shadows would be bathed in light if only you stared at them long enough. But throughout the evening I caught you gazing on my countenance with the kindest, most tender affection. Such a sweet crime. Who would prosecute you? Certainly not I. All the guilt—if guilt we need feel—is mine. Of all I have done, I would only change leaving you to honor a vow to a madman.

At the conclusion of the dancing, Ambrosio, our delightful guide, announced a concert for "los amigos Americanos"—"our American chums" was his own charming translation. I laughed in anticipation of his performance. Ambrosio, always smiling, would surely sing a witty song. I didn't know he would be calling me forth to stand trial for my love. And love you, I did. I had known that for days, borne it with me like some airy dream I wished to prolong late into the day. Ambrosio awakened me.

I know you must remember the song Ambrosio sang—

"Ten piedad, piedad de mis peñas!
Ten piedad, piedad de mi amor!"

I looked up at you and asked what the words meant. You spoke softly, your voice full of emotion—"Have pity, pity on my heartaches! Have pity, pity on my love!" You did not look away for the longest time, and I knew the sentiments of the song were your own. I thought you might kiss me and hoped that you would—regardless of contracts or husbands or conscience. But you didn't. It was then I realized you would never make overtures to a married woman, for such you regarded me to be. It wasn't that I'd been a whore—for I was fairly certain you had guessed that secret days before—but that I was a wife. I realized I would have to decide, once for all, just what I was—if I were to love you.

You escorted me to my hut, which I shared with Kitty and her dog, and then you disappeared into the night, your heart and mind no doubt in as great a turmoil as mine.

Inside the hut, the dog would not leave off yapping whenever anyone or anything made a noise within a hundred yards. I told Kitty that she should keep it quiet, for I had heard that the natives hereabout considered dogs a delicacy—especially the little ones who were said to possess the tenderest, sweetest meat. Even now, I smile to think of Kitty huddled in her hammock, an umbrella clutched in her hand, her dog held fast as she vainly tried to stifle its incessant squeals, yaps, and whines with a childish babble of her own. I had begun to entertain the notion that perhaps the dog loathed Kitty quite as much as I did, and this accounted for his generally odious behavior.

I lay in my cot and amused myself with this notion, but there was no hiding from the feelings stirring within my breast. After an hour's vain search for the forgetfulness of sleep, I rose from my hammock and followed the sound of the wooden drums to the peasants' fandango, still the scene of the greatest jollity.

I spied Ambrosio, seated among a semicircle of men, passing a jug of what I took to be spirits. I approached him and told him his song had been lovely.

The other men clamored to know what I'd said to him, and when he told them, they burst into laughter and poked each other in the ribs as men will do. Is there some special organ there, which only men possess?

I plucked the jug from an old man in the middle who was waving the jug in the air and laughing the loudest. I raised it to my lips and took a swallow. It was rich and strong and smelled of the jungle. "Tell him," I said to Ambrosio, "that his village is lovely."

Once again they all laughed, but there was no punching of the ribs. The old man, whose name was René, invited me to be seated to watch "the woman dance" which was about to begin.

I took my place inside the circle and looked toward the
fire where all the women were gathered. No sooner had
my eyes fallen upon them than the drums began and they
began to dance. The only music was the chattering drums
and the women chanting "Nya nya nya" in a nasal
monotone. The dance was everything. They moved with
such beauty and passion I was quite taken away. I have
never seen women looking so beautiful—young—
old—all of them possessed by a voluptuous spirit, like
Eve in the Garden or Mary Magdalene at Jesus' feet. It is,
I imagine, how a woman must look to a man in love—
perhaps, I thought as I was sitting there—how I look to
you.

At the conclusion of the dance the men rushed forward
and piled their hats upon the head of their favorite—their
joyous laughter filled the night.

René and Ambrosio and two other men returned to me.
All the others had gone off with wives and sweethearts. I
took these four to be the only true bachelors in
attendance. They were perhaps a little puzzled what to do
with me, their guest, so Ambrosio began to tell me the
wonders of the area, as we passed the jug. He said there
was a mountain close by with a single palm atop it where
one could stand and see both oceans. I asked him to take
me there—a request he repeated to his companions in
Spanish—and they burst into laughter.

I took this to mean that this mountain was either far
away or a fabulous tale for gullible women and asked
Ambrosio which it was. Ambrosio posed the question to
his companions, and René smiled and stretched his hands
toward the shadows, then pointed to his eyes. "Es la
noche," he said.

I blushed with embarrassment for my stupidity, and
René told me, through Ambrosio, that if I wished to see a
great distance through the darkness, I should visit Itsa
and she would show me my future.

Imagine. A trip to a fortune teller's hut deep in the

jungle. I could hardly contain my excitement. A neighbor of mine in Richmond had put people in touch with the dead for a few dollars—though all the dead sounded just like my neighbor, and her customers were practically ghosts themselves. But these men were not speaking of a charlatan. In their minds at least, she was a true seer.

"Take me!" I demanded, and with yet another laugh they led me into the jungle. It was a frightening journey, and many times I thought of turning back. Ambrosio instructed me to follow the path, but I confess I could not see it! It was like being in the belly of a leviathan, so complete was the darkness.

Finally we came into a clearing where Itsa sat in front of her hut, feeding a small fire with twigs and branches. She was incredibly old. Her long white hair hung loose down her back. She smiled at us, and the men all bowed a little, as if she were the great-grandmother of them all. René asked if she might tell my fortune, and she bid us all sit down with a sweep of her arm.

"Your name is like jewel," she said to me.

"It is Pearl," I said.

She tapped her chest. "My name, Itsa." She looked into the fire, then up into the rising smoke. "You love a man," she said. "He is boatman?"

"Yes."

"There is other man?"

"Yes, I am bound by contract to marry a man in Oregon. I am on my way there."

"This man, you know him."

"No, I have never met him."

"Is not question. Is what I am saying. This man, you know him. You can see him if you look. He is very bad man. His heart is false. He not remember what love is. Stay with boatman. Bad way you going. Look. You see." She pressed her fingertips to her temples and squinted her eyes. "Look. Look. You understand?"

I did not have to speak for her to know I did not.

"Your head. Is full of thoughts. All the time, thoughts.

Your head break soon. So full." She put her hands into the air as if holding her own head, swollen to the size of an enormous pumpkin. "No thoughts," she said, throwing out her arms into the air. "No thoughts." She hugged herself and smiled. "Corazon," she said. "Heart."

I knew then she was speaking the truth. I knew it long enough to arrange passage on the Falcon, long enough to sail all the way to San Francisco as your lover.

But then I was haunted by the thoughts I must rehearse to you now, for they visit me still: My love has murdered one man and abandoned his son. I have been four years a whore and most recently a fool. I have mad visions and talk to myself. Why should you love me? Are you mad as well?

I sailed for Oregon—to honor my vow, I told you—but that was another lie. I had decided that I deserved my fate and you did not deserve the fate of me. With that mad logic I betrayed you.

Now, I cannot help myself—I hope you are mad. I fervently, selfishly hope so! For I love you, John Morgan! I love you with all my heart whether I deserve your love or not. I had thought that when Douglas died, I would never love another. For five years, I did not.

I will find you, John Morgan, and we will celebrate our reunion, and you will read these pages in my arms!

Wednesday, September 4, 1850

As I read over what last I have written, I am filled with doubts. My danger is real, and my chances of reaching you are small. I may be dead when you read these pages. I cannot speak only of love.

Yesterday, Billy came to visit Frank and to inspect me, Frank's latest acquisition. Billy is an odious little man. He's no bigger than I am, his teeth are rotten, and he smells like a raccoon. It is through him—my husband's accomplice and audience—that I have seen what sort of man I have married and why he has married me.

Billy sat down by the fire which Frank insists always be

blazing. Joshua's chief duty consists of chopping firewood to feed this flame, even though Joshua is so feeble I fear he will hurt himself with the ax. When Frank is not around, I've started busting up kindling. It was something I'd never done. But I'd sat as a child and watched and listened as Sam taught Douglas how to do it, and I remembered everything he said. Later, when busting kindling was part of Douglas's morning duties, I'd sit on the steps and talk to him as he worked.

But I stray from my subject. This page is like talking to you, John. I'm so glad of that. I will always remember our long hours of conversation, moving from one subject to another like children playing tag and all the world was "it." I have no such luxury now. I leave at first light, only a few hours away. I must press on with my story.

Billy, as I have said, is my husband's accomplice. He sat by the fire grinning at me, and said to Frank. "She's a pretty one, Frank. I never thought we'd get no pretty one." He leaned forward and winked at me. "You was my idea," he said in a confidential tone.

Frank spat into the fire. "Ain't never had an idea in your life."

Billy looked wounded. "Didn't I write that fella Tarrington? Didn't I write that thing for the newspaper?" He turned to me for support. "I says to Frank, I'll get you a woman. I'll be damned if I won't. And when you gets your plantation, you can treat me to your prettiest darkie wench!"

My blood froze at this, and they both looked at me, smirking. I tried to manage a neutral tone. "Plantation?" I asked.

Billy grew as excited as a boy with his first gun. "Frank knows all about plantations from Virginia. With his 640 acres and my 320 up next to it, we got damn near 1,000 acres! Get us some niggers and we'll be planters!"

"Shut up!" Frank barked at him, and Billy shrunk back into his chair like a whipped dog.

"Sorry, Frank. I didn't mean no harm. I was just talking."

"Well, you talk too goddamn much. Now shut up!" He scowled at both of us, daring us to speak. It was a dare I feared I must take, for I knew my only purpose had been to secure for Frank an additional 320 acres, though as far as I could tell he had done nothing with the 320 he had possessed already except to build this ramshackle house upon it, and I am sure Joshua did most of the work.

I screwed up my courage and smiled at Frank. I felt rather as if I were courting the favor of a coiled snake set to strike. "Tell me about your plantation, Frank. I grew up on a plantation. Perhaps I might know something useful to you."

From what I had been able to determine through my own observations, Frank's skills consisted of brutality, drunkenness, and cunning of the sort one finds in certain mean-spirited dogs. From clandestine talks with Joshua, I had discovered that Frank had not been a miner in California but a gambler, most likely a dishonest one. I showed Joshua the daguerreotype, and he pointed to the man standing behind Frank. "That's Massuh Charles," he said. "Massuh Frank done won me off'n him in a card game. Massuh Frank, he somethin' with a deck of cards!"

I asked him whose pick Frank had slung over his shoulder, and he said, "That be Massuh Charles's pick. He give it to him for the picture."

"Did he win that off him as well?"

He laughed. "Oh no ma'am. Massuh Charles try to bet that pick in the game and Massuh Frank, he say 'What hell I want with any goddamn pick!'" He laughed again and shook his head. "Massuh Frank, he don't like work none."

I asked Joshua where he was from, and he could not remember. It broke my heart to see him wrestle with his memory, slump in failure, then smile at me sadly. "Don't recollect," he told me. Imagine: This old man must spend his last days working for Frank, when it should be Frank and I who are busting up kindling to keep Joshua warm!

I am sorry. I stray from my story again. But surely you know by now it is a failing of mine, a failing (I remember you once said) you found charming.

In any event, I had reasoned that Frank knew precious little about plantations, and that I might persuade him I was a potentially useful ally. He squinted his eyes at me and leaned back in his chair like he does so that he looks as if he's going to tumble into the fire any minute, and said, "You grew up on a plantation? Then what the hell you doing here?"

"I had a disagreement with my mother, and she bid me leave."

"What'd you do, get your petticoats muddy?" He spat in the fire.

"Something like that. This was four years ago. I fled to Richmond. I was penniless, with few skills. I was not brought up to work." I hung my head in mock shame.

"Took to whorin', did you?"

"That's right."

Billy and Frank were too far apart to engage in rib poking, but they exchanged glances with much the same effect, for they both fell to laughing and snorting. Frank slapped his knee and said, "Well, Billy and I can't hold that against you, now can we, Billy?"

Billy, his body bobbing up and down like a marionette, said between wheezing laughter, "No Frank, we sure can't!"

I saw that one of Billy's chief roles was to give Frank the illusion that he was amusing. "I am glad to hear it," I said. "And what line of work did you pursue, Frank?— before becoming a planter, that is."

The laughter stopped. He set his chair back on the ground and took another look at me. "You a smart bitch, ain't you?"

"I have been told so, yes."

"All right, then. I was a gambler. Cards." He pulled a battered pack out of his coat and shuffled them on his lap, whistling "Oh Susanna!" the whole time. He beckoned us to draw our chairs in closer and dealt a hand for the three of us. "What you got?" he asked Billy.

Billy fanned his cards on his lap. "Two pair, Frank, deuces and jacks."

Frank turned to me. "He starts it off with a pretty good bet. Let's see yours."

I spread my cards on my lap. I had a full house, three kings and two fives. Frank continued his lecture: "Now you bump it up real good. This is your hand. You're sure of it. It comes to me, and I ain't got that much money left since I've lost the last three hands, but goddamn, I feel lucky, and what the hell, so I'm in it. Now Billy, he knows not to drop out, and you two commences to bet and raise like there's no tomorrow, and me, I'm just in it for no good reason. The pot gets bigger than a pile of shit in a bull's pen 'til nobody's got nothing left. Then we show our cards."

Frank fanned his cards for Billy and me to see. He had four fours. Billy wheezed with delight—"Ain't he something though?"

"He certainly is," I said. "Why did you give it up, Frank?"

He scowled. "Some goddamn fool's always trying to shoot you. Got to shoot them first. Hell, might as well just hire out to shoot people to begin with! Gambling plays out. Got to move around too much." He threw the cards in the fire and spat at them. "Got to stay too sober."

He leaned back in his chair and took a long swallow from his whiskey jug. His face took on a wistful expression I would not have expected ever to cross his mean-spirited features. "Being the master of a plantation," he said. "Now that's just about the best goddamn life there is. I seen that back in Virginia. Men with so much goddamn money—slaves wiping their noses for them—they wouldn't have nothing to do with somebody like me." He took another deep swallow. "That suits me just fine. Let them come round here, and it'll be me not having nothing to do with them. Soon as I get me some niggers, this'll be the biggest goddamn plantation ever was anywheres." He turned on Billy, his eyes blazing. "You get me any goddamn niggers yet?"

Billy cowered in his chair. "No Frank. Nobody's got any. Fella told me there wasn't going to be any more slaves in Oregon, said they was even going to get rid of all the niggers was already here! I been trying, Frank."

"Did you try that fellow over yonder got a whole family of them?"

"He said he can't sell them, Frank, said he's promised them their freedom and they're going back to Ohio."

"Shit, how much did you offer him?"

"He said it don't matter, Frank, that they'd just run off anyways if he try to sell them."

"I got the goddamn money," Frank said, drinking again. "I got the goddamn money! What the hell he mean, no more slaves?" He lurched to his feet, staggered to the door, and flung it open, leaning his head out and calling to Joshua to "get the hell in here."

Joshua stood before him in the middle of the room, Frank towering over him. "Whose nigger are you?" he demanded of Joshua.

"Yours, Massuh Frank."

"Goddamn right!" He looked at Billy and me through bleary eyes to make sure we were paying attention. "And where you live, nigger?"

"On your plantation, Massuh Frank."

"You want to go back home, nigger?"

"No Massuh. Don't recollect home. I 'spect one place pretty much like another."

"Goddamn right. Except in this place, I'm the boss. Ain't that right?"

"Yes Massuh."

"Well, get back to work then." He gave Joshua a shove toward the door that almost knocked the old man from his feet. "See there. Nigger's so goddamn stupid he don't even know where home is!" He went to a cabinet and pulled out a rolled-up paper and spread it on the table, pounding his fist on it. It was a plan for a magnificent house. "Now there's a goddamn home!" he said. "My home!" he shouted, and stumbled to his bed, falling into it in a great stinking heap. He lies there still.

Billy stood as if to take his leave, and I had to act quickly. "I know someone who can help you find niggers," I said. "A ship's captain. I could send a letter to him."

Billy's face lit with hope, and he sank back into his chair. I tore a sheet from this journal, scrawled out a message, and sealed it with wax. I handed it to him and asked him to mail it.

He studied the letter. "This John Morgan's a captain?" he asked.

"Yes, and he has friends in the slave trade—Africans, young and strong."

He glanced over at the snoring Frank. "We better tell Frank about this, ain't we?"

"What if it doesn't work out?" I said. "Then he'll be twice as mad."

He accepted the wisdom of that observation and rose to his feet a messenger with a purpose—to put my letter on the next boat out of Astoria.

Will it reach you? I don't know. But I can't risk remaining here, dependent on Billy's silence, for Frank would quickly see through my ruse. I have come to realize that he takes a dram of something other than spirits—a relentless purpose that drives him on, and what I suspect is a great, if inebriated, cunning.

After a long search, I have found his precious money and taken enough to travel to San Francisco if I can make it to Oregon City on one of his mules. I leave at first light in the morning. He won't wake up before noon. I pray my letter has reached you, and I will find you waiting for me when I arrive.

I READ THE LAST PAGE OF PEARL'S JOURNAL AND TURNED IT OVER to see if there was anything written on the back. There wasn't. I'd never really know what happened to her, though it was hard to imagine anything other than death at Frank's hands. I started to close her book, when I noticed that things weren't quite right. I held the book open to the light and ran my fingers down the frayed edges of ten or fifteen pages that'd been torn out at the binding. There'd been more, apparently, and now it was gone.

I had journals at home with blank pages torn out for shopping lists or quick notes to the girls. Pearl says she tore out a page for a letter to Morgan, but that was an emergency. Somehow I didn't think Pearl would casually tear pages from her treasured book. Which meant someone else had torn them out. Whoever had possession of the journal after her.

Frank, I would guess. Or Raymond.

He'd wanted me to read this journal, knowing the whole time that the ending had been torn out of it. Why hadn't he told me? What the hell was going on?

All my fears caught up with me. I stood up and closed the book and placed it in the center of the desk as I'd found it waiting for me. Bait for a trap. This is ridiculous, I said to myself. I've read the journal—or what he let me see of it. Now I should get my girls and go home.

I went directly to the girls' room. They were laughing and shrieking as I rapped at the door. "It's me," I said, my hand on the knob.

"Don't open the door!" they shouted at me. "We're getting dressed up for dinner. It's a surprise."

"I'm not so sure we're staying for dinner," I said.

They let out an anguished groan. "Why not?" they wailed.

"Never mind. Do you know where Raymond is?" What was I supposed to tell them—pack your things, your stepmother's running from ghosts?

"He's taking a nap in his room," Kareth said.

"Thanks," I mumbled. Of course he was asleep. He'd been up all night carving a gift for me. I imagined stealing away as he slept, I imagined waking him from a sound sleep to tell him I was running away. I couldn't do either one.

"Are we staying for dinner?"

"I guess so," I said. I drifted back into my room, kicked off my shoes, digging my toes into the plush carpet. I picked up the shift from the bed and held it up to me, posing before an imaginary mirror, then laid it back on the bed.

I went to the window and leaned my forehead against the glass. The weather had turned. I stared out at a dome of thick clouds, bare frozen fields. The glass was cold and vibrated with the gusting wind. I wrapped my arms around myself, remembering Raymond's arms around me, desperately wanting to feel them again.

I didn't want to run away. I'd waited too long to feel this way.

And what would I be fleeing? A series of spooky coincidences, or a man who was in love with me? Maybe that's what truly frightened me. That's what had always frightened me before. That's what "didn't feel right"—that look of love in their eyes that I couldn't give back to them—so I'd take off. I'd been willing to steal Tom's love because I could give it back to his daughters, if not to him. I remembered Raymond's eyes, full of love, as if he'd been waiting his whole life for me, and I wanted to love him. He needed something from me. Of that, I was sure. I wanted to give it to him. I hoped, when the time came, that Timothy was right, and I would know what to do.

I SAT THINKING FOR A GOOD LONG WHILE. BUT WHEN THE LIGHT began to fade, I thought to check my watch. It was five-twenty. Andrea lived on Kensington, a five-minute walk from work. I might be able to catch her before Victor got home.

I tiptoed down the spiral stair and stepped into the darkened sitting room. I didn't bother with a light. Mickey's buttons glowed in the dark.

Andrea picked up on the fourth ring.

"Jesus, Marion, I just walked in the back door. I've still got my coat on."

"Did you find out anything?"

"I don't suppose I could call you back in five minutes."

"Andrea, I'm downstairs in the sitting room, sitting in the dark. He could walk in on me any minute."

"Well, I'm standing in my standing room—my kitchen—we don't have any rooms for sitting—and it's as well lit a mess as you could ask for. Care to trade?"

"Andrea, can you just tell me what you found out—pretty please?"

"Okay but I want a fucking cherry on top of it, Marion."

"You'll get it. I've promised already. So tell me about the house."

"Okay, the guy Nalle you wanted me to check on built the house. He started it about 1851, finished it in '54. There's some Civil War stuff, you want that?"

"No. How'd Nalle pay for it?"

"A sudden, unexplained upturn in his fortunes."

"Unexplained?"

"That's what it says."

"Any speculation?"

"This is Virginia, Marion. That wouldn't be polite. If this was Jersey, I'd say it was something illegal, but he never got caught."

"Who designed the house?"

"A guy named Jeremiah Morton, according to one of the reputable sources on historic landmarks—but I called a friend down at the Department of Historic Resources and had him check the file on the place. There's *nothing* in the file on Morton. I called the guy who wrote the reputable source to find out the basis for the attribution, and he told me ever so politely to fuck off." She lapsed into a parody of a Virginia blueblood—"I fear he found me rather crude. Or maybe the attribution's shaky and he didn't want to get caught with his pants down."

"So what are you saying—did Morton design the house or not?"

"I'm saying I wouldn't bet the farm on it, but I can't say he didn't. There's no hard evidence either way. It could just be some family story with nothing to back it up. Hell, if you listen to Virginians' family stories, Thomas Jefferson designed half the buildings in the state. Who did you think was the architect?"

"Frank Strickland."

"There's not a word on him anywhere."

"What about the others?"

"Only Pearl and Faith Withers showed up. Pearl went nuts and knocked off Faith—her mother—with a scythe. And also a slave."

"That's not how it happened."

"Come again? You want the reference on that?"

"No, I don't doubt that's what it says."

"It's in a monograph on women and violence in the plantation system. Some Ph.D. plowed through all the antebellum crime records she could get her hands on. She gives Pearl several pages."

"What else does it say about her?"

"Hang on." The phone hit the counter with a resounding crack and Andrea's briefcase slammed down beside it. Paper rattled, and I could hear Andrea cursing to herself. "Here goes," she said, still shuffling through pages. "What do you want to know?"

"Anything about her."

"There's not much here, really. The girl and her mother were abandoned by the father when she was young. Then the girl killed the mom and the slave and ran off."

"Anything about a child in there?"

"Nothing."

"What does it say her motive was?"

"Let me see. Here we go: *As we have seen in several other cases thus far, violence erupts in these women when they are abandoned by their fathers, either literally, as is Pearl's case, or figuratively, when the role of patriarch subsumes the role of nurturing parent; this violence, however, is misdirected at fellow victims of patriarchy—other women—rather than its rightful target—the absent father.*"

"Who wrote that?"

"Miriam Seawalter, Cornell University."

"Does she give Absent Father a name?"

"No. Seen one, I guess you've seen them all."

"Did you find out anything about Raymond?"

"Ooh, I loved the way you said that—*Raymond*—with that little quiver you get in your voice when you're excited."

"Are you going to tell me, or are we going to analyze my voice?"

"Okay, okay. You've got Mary Louise to thank for all this. I told her you'd buy her lunch."

"Fine, anything."

"Let's see. To start off with, Raymond Lord is actually Raymond Lord, Jr., Senior being the well-known TV preacher."

"I never heard of him."

"Oh yeah. He's on after the guy who dresses up like he's a sheriff in a Western with bad sets."

"You watch this stuff?"

"Victor does. It's funny actually. One night—"

"Andrea, could we stay on task here?"

"Don't give me that parent talk, Marion. I hate that shit. 'Stay on task, Andrea.' Jesus."

"Okay, but could I hear about Cowboys for God some other time? What did you find out about Raymond Lord, Jr.?"

"His father says his son's in the hands of Satan. He talks about it all the time on his show, cries and gets down on his knees. He's a real ham bone."

"What else? How did this start?"

"You're so damn impatient. I'm getting there. During a live Easter broadcast in '67, Junior, who was sixteen at the time, denounced his father as, and I'm quoting here, 'a vulture preying on the sins of others.' He had more to say, some of it pretty wacked out apparently, but they got him off the air and hauled him away to the family retreat in the Smokies. He pretty much disappears from the face of the earth after that until the late eighties, when he's under investigation for possibly smuggling in illegal aliens, mostly Central Americans. No convictions, however. Mary Louise says it sounds like some sort of political deal to her.

"Most recently, he purchased Greenville and everything around it for an exorbitant amount of money and succeeded in pissing off every historic group in Virginia when he restored it. Would you describe his house as 'an architectural nightmare'?"

"It's odd, but I rather like it."

There was the sound of a door opening and closing in Andrea's kitchen. "Victor's home," Andrea said. "Hi Victor. It's Marion on the phone. She's calling from Tara."

"Did you find out anything else?" I asked.

"Do you want hamburger or fish?" Andrea asked Victor. I couldn't make out his reply.

"What do you mean, you don't care?" Andrea snapped. "Why should I make dinner if you don't fucking care?"

"Cook the fish," I practically shouted into the phone, "but would you *please* tell me what you found out?"

I heard a door open and close again. "It's okay," she said. "He went out in the yard. He'll putz around out in the cold. He can cook his own fucking dinner. If he wants to go ahead and die while he's still walking around, that's his business. But he's fucking not taking me down with him."

"Andrea."

"I know. 'Stay on task.'"

"No. I wanted to say I'm sorry."

"Don't worry about it. I'm just making a deal. We've been through shit before, right? Anyway, your Raymond is apparently richer than God, but nobody knows where the money came from. He could buy and sell his old man ten times over, and *he's* not exactly in the poorhouse."

I heard someone on the back stairs, voices in the kitchen —Rachel's small voice, and then a baritone. Raymond.

"I've got to get off the phone immediately," I said. "He's coming."

"Wait! This is the best thing—get this: His own father's trying to have him declared mentally incompetent. The hearing's set for the middle of next week. He says his son suffers from 'bizarre delusions possibly dangerous to himself and others.' He's got a dozen shrinks lined up to testify."

"And what does Raymond say?"

"He won't talk to reporters. Mary Louise said if you could get his story, she'd buy *you* lunch."

Someone's feet blocked out the light at the bottom of the kitchen door. "Gotta go, bye," I said, and practically threw Mickey into his box, flinging the little door shut so hard it bounced back open.

The kitchen door swung open; Raymond's shadow filled the doorway. "Here you are," he said. "I've come to ask if you'd like a cocktail before dinner." He let the door swing closed behind him, plunging us in darkness except for Mickey's buttons.

"I'm sorry," I said, standing up. "It wasn't so dark when I came in here. I lost track of the time."

"That's quite all right. Sometimes I enjoy sitting in the dark myself. It's peaceful."

"I'm glad you found me," I said as cheerily as I could manage. "A drink is just what I need." I couldn't see his face, but he had to suspect what I'd been doing. Why didn't he just call me on it? Why didn't he get pissed off?

Raymond crossed the room and opened the door to the foyer. "There's a nice fire in the library," he said.

I went to his side without looking at him, following the fan of light on the floor. He led me to the overstuffed chairs in the library where we'd had coffee in front of the fire the night we met. There was a deco cart with liquor, ice, and glasses parked beside his chair.

"Scotch?" he asked, picking up a glass.

I nodded and sat down. He remembered, of course, but asked anyway. He made my drink, poured himself a cognac. Rachel stuck her head through the door to the dining room. She and Raymond exchanged a few words in her language, and she shook her head at him and left.

"What did you say?" I asked.

He settled into his chair. "I told her she was working too hard. She doesn't like to hear that."

I couldn't relax. I sat perched on the edge of my chair. "How did Rachel come to work for you?"

"She worked in my father's organization. She wished to come to America. From time to time he employs young Asian women to work for him, offers his influence to help them become citizens.

"Anyway, I got a phone call from her former employer, who was under the mistaken impression that he'd contacted my father. Our names are the same. I let him believe I was my father, and arranged for Rachel to come work here."

"Why?"

"Not to put too fine a point on it, I suspect my father's paternal interest in young Asian women isn't motivated by his fine sense of Christian love." He ran his fingertip along his scar, down his nose.

"Does she like it here?"

Raymond smiled. "Oh yes. She likes Thomas. He and Rachel have been lovers for some time now. There's no connecting door between their apartments, so they've worn a path between the two doors. They think I don't know."

"And would you object?"

"I'm delighted for them, but it's clear they wish to conceal it from me. I suspect Rachel has religious scruples concerning such matters. They can't get much privacy out here, I'm afraid, and they can't really get away. Neither one of them has a driver's license. Rachel can't read enough English to take the test, and Thomas had his driver's license permanently suspended by the time he was eighteen."

"He told me how you came to hire him, a letter out of the blue while he was in prison."

"Hardly out of the blue. It was quite an elaborate procedure actually. You know government programs."

"Government programs?"

"Thomas didn't explain this to you?" He shook his head. "I hired Thomas under an early-release program for young men who seem destined to one prison term after another. The idea is to employ them young in some skilled position, wiping the slate clean so to speak."

"So he could quit working for you anytime he liked?"

Raymond shook his head and looked into the fire. "Sadly, no. I'm not saying it's impossible, but his criminal record is really quite foreboding. He was first arrested when he was nine. The fact that he's worked out splendidly here, relatively free from temptation, probably wouldn't weigh too heavily with a potential employer."

I took a drink from my Scotch, studied his profile, the firelight playing off his features. He made everything sound so perfectly reasonable. He seemed genuinely concerned for the young man who only figured he was *crazy rich*. But I had a hard time believing he was crazy. In my youth, I'd dated crazy men for sport. Raymond wasn't like them. Or maybe it was me that was different this time. This time I didn't want him to be crazy. This time I wanted to love him.

"I called my friend Andrea at work and had her check up on you," I said.

He didn't seem particularly surprised or even angry.

"She told me your own father is taking you to court."

He nodded. "That's right."

"You told me you had no contact with your parents since you were eighteen."

"I haven't. My father's lawyers have met with my lawyers. He wants to destroy me."

"For your money?"

"There's that, I suppose, but more because he believes I'm possessed by demons."

"Are you?"

He smiled ironically. "Sometimes I think so." He took a sip of his brandy. "Your feelings toward me have changed. You're more distant, cautious. Something Andrea has told you has upset you. Do you fear I'm insane?"

I shook my head. "No, it's not that. Your father's the one who sounds crazy. It's something else." I looked down at my drink, ran my fingers around the rim of the glass. "I finished Pearl's journal. The last several pages have been torn out." I looked up at him. "Why didn't you tell me? Did you tear them out?"

He looked back at me steadily. "No. Frank did. He burned them. I've made a transcript of them I'd intended to give you tomorrow."

I didn't say anything for a long time, and neither did he, as we looked into each other's eyes, though he knew what I was thinking.

Finally I said, "Raymond, that's impossible. If Frank burned these pages over a century ago, you can't make a transcript of them now. What's going on, Raymond? How do you know anything about Frank Strickland outside the pages of Pearl's journal?"

He turned away, shaking his head. "I can't tell you."

"Why not?"

He looked back to me, his face sad and defeated. "If I do, you'll think I'm mad, and you'll leave, and I'll never see you again. I would just like this weekend with you and your daughters. It's no small thing to me." He looked down at his hands, which lay in his lap, palms up, like two dead things. "I mean you no harm."

I reached out and took his hands. He clung to mine, but wouldn't look at me. "Listen to me, Raymond. It's no small thing to me, either. I've never felt this way before, not with Tom, not with anyone. Whatever you think happened to some old drunk a hundred years ago isn't going to change that. I'm not going to leave."

He kept looking at our hands, shaking his head. "Look at me," I said. He raised his head and I looked into his eyes and repeated, "I'm not going to leave."

He looked at me, startled and grateful beyond reason. "Thank you," he said.

"So tell me," I insisted. "How do you know so much about Frank Strickland?"

He searched my eyes. They looked back at him unflinchingly, ready for anything he might reveal to me.

"I would prefer to tell you his story," he said, "and then you'll know how I know."

"Very well," I said, releasing his hands and settling back into my chair. "Tell it to me."

He stared into the fire, the flames playing off his face, apparently ordering the story in his mind. He began without looking at me, telling Frank's story to the flames.

"Frank Linwood Strickland was born in North Carolina, on the edge of Dismal Swamp. His father made illegal whiskey. His mother helped drink it. Frank was their only child, born with a blood alcohol level the envy of any wino on the street. He was slow, stupid. Thinking for him was like wading through deep mud. He'd never been to school, never seen anybody but his father's customers—and, after his father died when he was ten or eleven, his mother's customers.

"After his father died, he tended the still. Most of the time he sat around and drank, listening to the men's talk when they'd 'sample the wares,' as they called it. What little he knew about the goings-on in the world beyond the swamp he picked up from customers' stories.

"Mostly, they talked about ways to make money, which to hear them tell it was an endless battle between themselves and the law. The law, Frank's parents had impressed upon him, was the chief enemy of a good life. There were a few of the men who worked on this side of the law—tracking runaway slaves for rich planters. They were the worst of the lot, though he liked to hear their stories of plantation scandals—like tales of the gods.

"But he was especially drawn to the smugglers. In his mind they were one notch below the unattainable status of planter. One of them, Ezekiel, was quite a storyteller. His favorite scene was himself and his contraband making his way through the swamps on a moonless night, triumphing over more law enforcement personnel than the whole state of North Carolina then contained.

"Lies, he learned listening to Ezekiel, made the world more exciting. Frank had little confidence in the truth. He suffered from a bizarre madness: He remembered things that'd never happened—never could've happened. He remembered being rich, but he'd always been poor. He remembered being real smart, with everyone laughing at his jokes, but he was a slow lout, the butt of jokes, never the teller. He remembered a beautiful woman—like none he'd ever seen—who ran off with him, but the few women he'd seen when he went to town wouldn't give him the time of day. He'd tried to tell some of his memories to his mother and a few of the men. They just laughed at him, told him he was crazy. One of them, nicer than the rest, took him aside and explained that his brains were stewed, that drinking since birth had made him think things that weren't true. This made sense to him. He took a certain comfort in being crazy. He didn't have to bother with what went on in his head. None of it meant anything.

"Anyway, his mother despised Ezekiel, who was short and ugly and had a high raspy voice, so it was often just the two of them drinking together by the still while his mother was back at the house with some other fellow.

" 'I don't just smuggle,' he tells Frank one night. 'Smuggling comes and goes. You spend a lot of time waiting around for this boat or that. So I plays a little cards.' He took out his deck and started doing his shuffling tricks, showed Frank a few simple cheats. He was spellbound.

"Ezekiel left him the deck, and he found that if he could stay this side of drunkenness, before all his memories turned into a mass of words and faces, he could remember the cards in every hand—if he knew the order they started out. And all he had to do was look at them for a second to know that. He practiced over and over, alone by the still in the afternoon, tending the fire. He dealt the cards on the ground in a circle, pointing to each imagined sucker and telling him exactly what he had. They were so impressed, they gave him all their money—each fat cat one of them.

" 'I been practicing with the cards you give me,' he told Ezekiel the next time he saw him.

" 'That so?' he said. 'Well, let's see what you can do there, Frankie. Them cards look like you been using 'em to start fires with.'

"So Frank dealt out the cards fast as he could and rattled off each hand, grinning like a fool.

" 'Not bad,' Ezekiel said. 'Gather 'em up and take another long look.'

"Frank did so.

" 'Now give 'em here,' Ezekiel said.

"Frank handed them over, still grinning like a fool.

" 'You sure you took all the time you needed?' Ezekiel asked. 'You didn't have 'em no time at all.'

" 'No,' Frank said proudly. 'It don't take me no time at all.'

"Ezekiel promptly shuffled the cards seven times and dealt them out. 'Show me which'n's which, now,' he said.

" 'I can't,' Frank objected. 'You mixed 'em all up.'

Raymond laughed softly to himself. " 'You mixed 'em all up.' Ezekiel had a good laugh over that one. 'Ain't enough,' he told Frank, 'to remember everything. You got to arrange things the way you want 'em from the get go.' He pointed at one of the five hands he'd dealt out facedown. 'That fellow over there won big,' he said. Frank turned over the cards and it was four jacks and a queen. The other hands were good enough to keep everybody in, building the pot. 'That winning fellow could be me,' Ezekiel told Frank, 'splitting everything with you right down the middle, and you could be the dealer—the dumb kid fooling everybody, dealing your old friend Ezekiel into the easy life. How about it? I'll teach you everything I know.' He looked at the swamp all around them. 'You don't want to spend your whole god-damn life out here in the woods with your mama, do you?'

"Frank left with him that night. He was about sixteen. They worked their way up and down the coast, from North Carolina to Florida, playing cards and smuggling now and again, though Frank soon discovered that Ezekiel was pretty small-time in the smuggling trade. But that was all right with Frank. He was out of the swamp, had lots of money to spend, and better liquor than he'd ever made.

"But one night in Nags Head, Ezekiel was hauling in his winnings, close to five hundred dollars, when one of the other players—not even the one who'd lost big—stood up and shot him through the head.

"Frank didn't take time to wonder whether the guy with the gun knew he was in on it or not. He jumped out the window and ran hard as he could till he could hear nothing at all behind him.

"He was walking along the road that night, trudging north with no particular destination in mind, the sky full of stars like you never see it anymore, when one of his memories started nagging him. It was a sugar plantation. He often drew pictures of grand houses, remembered great lands, dozens of slaves. But in this particular recollection, a beautiful mulatto slave brought him a rum punch in the evening as the sun was setting and called him 'massuh,' bowing deep. 'I'll be a planter,' he told himself.

"So when he got to Norfolk, he found work in the slave

business. By this time he was big and strong and fierce-looking, perfectly suited for herding people. He laid off cards for a good long while. All he could think of every time he picked them up was Ezekiel's head exploding not six feet away from him."

We'd both been looking into the fire as he spoke. Now, he turned to me. I kept my eyes fixed on the flames. "You know a good deal of the rest of it from Pearl's journal. He worked his way up in the slave-smuggling trade, until he fell in with a partner who figured out the more he played on this dolt's plantation fantasy, the less Frank noticed he was being set up to hang for both of them so the partner could have the plantation and slaves to himself. He even encouraged him to draw the plans for this house.

"When things fell apart, Frank got a boat going to the gold rush and went back to cards for a while, though he almost ended up like Ezekiel several times. Then he heard about the land deal they had in the Oregon Territory—twice as sweet if a fellow could find himself a wife. Men were marrying eighty-year-old widows to get that extra three hundred and twenty acres. He thought he might just get that plantation he remembered, after all."

Raymond stood up and turned the logs with a poker so that a shower of sparks flew up the chimney. "All he needed to do was find him a wife and a partner dumber than him." He tossed a log on the fire, shoving it into place with the poker, and sat back down. "Neither one proved to be easy, but he had enough money from the goldfields to buy slaves, if he could get the land for free. When Pearl answered that ad in Richmond, he figured he was all set.

"He got word from Tarrington that Pearl was coming when she was apparently in the Hotel Americano with Captain Morgan. He had several weeks to set things up and gloat about what a smart son of a bitch he'd turned out to be. He walked around the place looking for likely accidents to befall his new bride, counting the days.

"He was practically beside himself when the *Oregon* docked in Astoria. When Pearl wasn't on it, he cursed his fate and went on a binge, trying to wipe it all out once and for all—every last vision of pasts that'd never been and futures that'd never be.

"One memory, though, just wouldn't leave—this woman he'd known, seemed like forever. She'd come to him most nights in his dreams. She talked to him, she made love to him. Sometimes she cursed him, but she was always there.

"He'd tried to imagine her in the whores he hired from time to time, but it wouldn't do. She was herself, just like those whores were themselves, whoever he might pay them to be. In his dreams, she was all different ages, had different names, her hair might be red one time and gray the next—but it was always the same woman—just at different parts of her life. Many nights he woke up clawing the air, crying and screaming, knowing that what he'd thought was real was just a dream. No such woman had ever existed—and even if she had, she wouldn't have anything to do with him.

"About two weeks into his binge, he was lying on his back, gagging on his vomit, the stars blazing at him like that chandelier, cold hard ground at his back—when she came to him for the last time. She was all around him, everywhere he looked—standing at the edge of the clearing, the dark woods at her back, calling to him: *Get up off your drunk ass, Frank, and follow me!* He'd never seen her looking so beautiful. He wanted to go with her. He'd never wanted anything so much. He concentrated every bit of sense he had left on rolling over, getting to his feet, and walking into the woods. But all he could do was roll his head from side to side, seeing her everywhere. She laughed and laughed. He tried again, reaching down for whatever he could find inside himself that gave a damn, until he was sure if he didn't move, he was just going to die right there on that cold ground. He screamed, but he couldn't hear himself. He closed his eyes, and the stars exploded inside his head. And all the time, he could still hear her laughing.

"When he woke up, his eyes were pooled with rain and the

sky was gray, a cold, misty rain dripping off everything. He was stiff in every joint, but he could move, and he got to his feet. She was gone, of course. The woods were empty. Somehow he knew she'd never be back, that he'd missed his chance."

Raymond stared into space as if this dream woman were before him. He took a deep breath, and finished off his brandy.

"He said good riddance, told himself it was stupid to snivel over somebody he'd never known, somebody he was never going to know, somebody that was just too much liquor poured over too little brains.

"Later on that day, he got word his new bride was coming after all. *Who needs you?* he said to his dream woman, figuring he'd finally arranged things just the way he wanted them. He'd be a planter with lots of slaves and have no need of anything from anybody, real or imaginary. He bathed in the stream and boiled his best clothes for the occasion. He whistled to himself while Joshua drove him to Astoria to meet his bride.

"When Pearl stepped off that boat in Astoria, he recognized her immediately as the woman in his dreams made flesh, beautiful and desirable, like Bathsheba to David. All of a sudden he didn't feel so damn smart anymore.

"She looked at him in horror. He figured somehow she remembered him too—from her nightmares, by the look of it. She offered him her book, her eyes on the ground, forcing herself to go through with whatever had brought her halfway around the world. Whatever it was, it sure as hell wasn't him. His head was already crammed to overflowing with books he could recite but not understand. They scared him, the whole endless store of them, and he didn't want more. He'd never been taught to read—his parents didn't know how to read—but he'd been able to read on sight whatever words crossed his path. He regarded this ability, like much else in his life, as an inexplicable curse, further evidence of his madness. He turned the book down flat.

"This is a hell of a trick, he said to himself. My dream woman comes to life, but she hates my guts. All the time they were going through the wedding and the land office and the signing and the swearing, he kept watching her, trying to figure out what he was supposed to do with her. He remembered being handsome and smart and charming—but he wasn't any of those things now, didn't know how to be them if he tried.

"By the time they got back to his place, and he'd drunk a few, he figured he was just going to have to kill her like he'd planned, dreams or no. It felt like all the anger in his whole life had come home to roost, and his memories made a swarm in his head that only drink would quiet."

Raymond was staring into the fire, his face lit with firelight. A chill passed through me watching his profile, his eyes squinting, watching, as if Frank and Pearl were in the flames doing everything he said.

"The very first morning, he marched her out on this ridge he'd found—to do a little berry picking, he said—knowing the very bush he would set her to picking so he could push her to the rocks below. He sat under a tree a few yards off watching her hand go back and forth from bush to basket, her fingertips turning red from the berries. He could kill her, he told himself. There wasn't anything to it. Just give her a shove when her back was turned. He'd killed people before, even a woman one time. But they were all going for him 'cause he'd cheated them. Pearl hadn't done anything to him. She hadn't done anything except show up in his dreams laughing at him, he reminded himself.

"He got up and came up behind her. She'd sailed halfway round the world to make a fool out of him. He took a drink and tapped her on the shoulder, offering her the bottle. She turned him down, saying it was too early. But he told her he was her husband and he said to have a goddamn drink. They were standing right by the edge. The rocks were fifty feet straight down. She reached out and took the bottle from his hand, wiped it off, and took a swallow.

"She might've laughed at him once, he told himself, but

now she was his wife, and she had to do what he said. He planned to keep it that way, whether she liked it or not.

"He didn't like it that she hated him, but he figured she'd change her opinion of him once he was a planter. But when he let her in on his plans, she hated him even more. Sooner or later, though, he thought she'd see the handwriting on the wall and treat him nice. He didn't see that she had much choice.

"Then he woke up one morning, and she'd run off with a mule and a good deal of cash—quite a bit more than Pearl's journal makes it sound. He flew apart with rage. He'd deliberately been made a fool of once again, his love, as he supposed it to be, cruelly scorned.

"He tracked her down to her hotel and told the desk clerk she was his wife, trying to run off, and the clerk laughed at him—as if to say what'd he expect, stupid and ugly as he was? He slid a pistol across the counter and stuck it in the clerk's fat gut. The clerk quit laughing and gave him a key. Pearl's room was on the top floor, and as he was climbing the stairs, wheezing and feeling awful, he realized he must be sober, for he hadn't had a drink in at least two days. Memories were exploding in his head. He remembered being enveloped in flames, his own flesh on fire, until he thought he was going to scream. He fell down on his knees, but soon that high-and-mighty desk clerk would have the law all over him and he didn't have time for any of his crazy nonsense. He picked himself up and went on.

"He listened at the door and heard Pearl pacing inside. When she was close, he flung it open. She stood before him—the most beautiful woman he'd ever seen, her eyes blazing with hatred and anger. His hands hung at his sides like stones—the key in one, a pistol in the other—and he bowed his head in shame.

"In that instant, Pearl turned heel and dashed across the room, snatching up her book. She flung open the window and leapt out into space before he could even take a step. As simple as that, and she was gone, the curtains blowing in the breeze as if she'd never been there. He hurried to the window and saw her dead body sprawled on the street in an impossible shape, her arms still wrapped around her book.

"He climbed out the window and scurried down the drainpipe. He took her in his arms and wailed like a wounded animal. He looked up and saw a ring of people around him, all looking concerned. None of them, as yet, appeared to be the law. He pulled her book from her arms and held it to his chest, then laid her body down on the road and plunged through the crowd between two old men. He took to the alleys, running back to his hotel fast as he could, hoping the fat desk clerk didn't remember him any too well.

"He decided to burn her book without reading it. He figured it might be incriminating, and he wasn't so sure he wanted to know what it said. He sat before the fire and tore out the last few pages from the back, but when he saw her handwriting he remembered her sitting up late at night, the scratching sound of her pen as she wrote and wrote, and he let himself read just a little. When he realized she was writing to some other man, he burned with jealousy and read the fistful of pages through. He flung them into the fire and flew into a mad rage, got himself thrown in jail for the racket he made.

"All through the night Pearl's words ran through his head, accusing him, calling him to account as he lay in that jail, stone sober for the first time in his life, remembering everything, half scared to death. In the morning, he'd quieted down and was set free. He ran back to the hotel and found Pearl's book in the trash bin. He sat down in the alley and read it straight through, discovering, among other things, that it had, after all, been written for him.

"When he'd done, he found a blacksmith to make him a waterproof box and sealed up Pearl's book in it. Then he took it to an undertaker and gave him the rest of his money for a plot and a casket and the promise that the box would be buried with him.

"He now was sure that his madness was real, that his reality had all been a lie, that he'd been a complete and utter fool. He just wanted to start all over again. He sat down on the undertaker's front steps, just about noon, and shot himself through the head."

Raymond stopped talking. The only sound was the fire and the gusty wind outside.

After a long time, I whispered, "You're saying you were Frank—that you remember his life."

"And many more before that. And you were the woman who haunted his dreams, my dreams, life after life."

He'd turned to face me, his confession done. I kept my eyes on the flames. I felt dizzy, as if I were falling. His story made sense of everything. I sat there numb, my own thoughts unreal to me. His story made sense of everything, and it was completely mad.

I looked into his eyes, the firelight reflected in them, and saw that he believed it. He believed all of it. "How does Susanna's story end?" I asked quietly.

"You can remember. You've remembered most all of it."

I shook my head. "I've been trying to write it for months."

"Don't write it. Just remember it." He reached out and caressed my cheek. "Remember me."

I pressed his hand to my face and closed my eyes. "I'm not sure I want to," I said.

"You must."

There was a quiet rap on the dining room door. Rachel opened the door and peeked in. "Is supper now," she said. I let myself be led into dinner.

THE DINING TABLE WAS SPREAD WITH A WHITE TABLECLOTH, PER-fectly centered, the corners precisely draped. The table was a forest of plates and glasses and silverware and napkins folded into swans. Silver candlesticks rose from a center-piece of creeping cedar woven around long-stemmed white roses laid across one another like crossed lances in a fan.

I looked down at myself and realized I was still wearing jeans and a sweatshirt with a picture of a wolf on it, a coffee stain at his feet. My hair hung like a horse's mane.

The girls were already seated, wearing the Laura Ashley

dresses Tom's mother had given them at Christmas, their hair twisted into shapes only Kareth and a can of mousse could imagine, their nails a metallic red I'd last seen on fifties hot rods. They beamed at me, enchanted with their own prettiness, the Groucho and Harpo of glamour. As Raymond seated me, I caught a strong whiff of perfume, as if someone had soaked a rag in it and clamped it over my mouth.

My girls. They looked at me expectantly, apparently unaware that I was in a fog.

"You both look lovely," I managed, and asked automatically, "Did you remember to take a shower?"

"Yes Steppie dear," Kareth said in her mock-obedient-daughter voice—showing off for Raymond.

"Raymond let us use his shower," Lorena said. She gave a sideways glance at her sister, hoping she'd learned what to say next. "It was way cool." She nodded at her own considered opinion.

Rachel came in bearing a tureen of soup. She was dressed in a French maid's uniform. She even wore the little cap, her hair in a tight bun. She served us with careful formality, as if this were a religious ritual and she must strive to obliterate her personality.

Raymond told us, "As a girl Rachel cooked for a French clergyman who was something of a fussy gourmand. He also must've weighed half a ton." A smile played at the corners of her mouth as Rachel passed through the swinging door to the kitchen.

Raymond had taken the clergyman's place by pretending to be someone else, just as Anthony would've done. Did that make him Anthony? I imagined my hands on his face, touching his eyes, his mouth, wanting him to close his eyes and be silent, just be Raymond, there, in my hands. But it was too late for that. He'd told me too much already. I felt like Frank surrounded by his dream woman, unable to touch her, listening to her laughter.

At some point, he must've become obsessed with Anthony

Richards and the Griers, tracked down Pearl's journal—
and then I'd come along with my ad in the *Times*. He would
have to find a place for me in his madness, paint our faces on
the Magdalene. That would explain everything but didn't
tell me what to do.

What would it do to him if I were to leave him now after
I'd promised I wouldn't, abandoning him to his father, like
his mother had done? But how could I stay here with my
children with someone I knew to be mad? I sat there being
pulled this way and that, immobile, waiting for a sign.

I watched him with Kareth and Lorena. Their three faces
were vivid and precise, as if everything else in the room were
dissolving and they were the only solid objects. I listened to
their voices, the rise and fall, the intonations. I didn't listen
to the words. They didn't mean anything. Unburdened of
Frank's story—the story he believed he'd been waiting 143
years to tell me—Raymond's face glowed. The girls chat-
tered at him adoringly. His great, dark eyes went from one
to the other. When he spoke, they attended each word with
silent reverence.

As the main course was set before me—a stuffed fish,
whose eye stared up at me—I heard Anthony: *I ask you
who's free, Marion, Mister Jack or the shark?*

Maybe I'm the albatross, I thought—shot dead to see
what sort of thing it was, flown about like a kite, turned into
a symbol. He loved some idea he'd conceived of me before
we even met. But when he looked at me, when he touched
me, I had to admit, it was as if he already knew me. But what
did that mean—that he was what he seemed or that I
wanted him to be? Maybe I just wanted him. I remembered
the night I'd written Susanna and Anthony's bedroom
scene. I'd wanted Anthony then.

A shriek from the girls brought me back to the dining
room.

They were laughing at Raymond. He'd tied his napkin
into the shape of a rabbit who talked with Bugs Bunny's
voice—perfectly done. There was only the slightest move-

ment of Raymond's lips. I wasn't surprised to add mimicry and ventriloquism to his talents.

The girls were chatting with Raymond's napkin—or Bugs Bunny, depending on your point of view—and seemed not to mind at all that I hadn't said a word for at least half an hour.

But suddenly Bugs hopped up to Lorena and said, out of the blue, "Eh Lorena, whaddya remember about your daddy?"

There was a stunned silence, and then Kareth said in a small, earnest voice, "She was just a little kid when Daddy died. She doesn't remember anything."

I started to intervene, to stop what must be an awful moment for Lorena, but Bugs said, "Dat ain't so, is it, Lorena? Three's not so little. I bet you spent lots of time with your daddy."

"I guess so," Lorena said quietly.

Bugs turned to me. "Ain't dat right, Doc?"

"He loved to give you your bath," I said to Lorena. "The two of you made a fine mess of the bathroom."

"See dere?" Bugs said. "All you got to do is close your eyes, like dis, see?" Bugs, of course, had no eyes to close, but Raymond clamped his shut, and Lorena promptly closed her own.

"Now pretend you're splashing away in da tub, three years old. See how everything's bigger?"

She nodded.

"It's real bright in dis bathroom, ain't it?"

She nodded.

"So you can see everything real good, I bet."

She nodded again. I could see her eyes moving behind her lids as if she were dreaming.

"So, eh, whaddya see in da water?"

"A boat," she said.

"Oh goody, I love boats. So, eh Lorena, dis boat got a name?"

She smiled wide. "Red Boat!" she exclaimed.

"Whose hand is dat making Red Boat go? Look right on up his arm and take a look."

Her face lit up, and she reached into the air. "Daddy!" she said. "Daddy!" Her eyes came open wide and she beamed at us all, our eyes glistening with tears, even Kareth's. "I saw Daddy!" she shouted. "I saw him for real!"

Raymond's napkin was now a napkin again, lying on the table with his hands folded over it. "See there," he said in his own voice. "Three's not so little."

Lorena looked at Kareth, perhaps expecting her to contradict this absurd notion, but instead Kareth looked like she might start bawling any minute. "I remember Red Boat," she said.

Raymond called toward the kitchen door, in Rachel's language.

"What did you say?" I asked.

He smiled. "I suggested to Rachel that it was time for dessert."

AFTER DESSERT, I TOLD THE GIRLS TO GO UPSTAIRS AND GET READY for bed. Kareth came to my side and spoke so quietly I almost couldn't hear her. "Would you and Raymond come up and put us to bed like you and Daddy used to do?"

I hugged her so tightly I'm sure I must've frightened her. "Certainly, darling," I said. "We'll be up in a few minutes." Lorena scurried over and claimed a quick hug, then followed her sister up the stairs.

When they'd gone, Raymond said, "I suppose you'll wish to leave in the morning. I don't really expect you to stay now."

"I'm not going anywhere," I said. "That was very sweet, what you did for Lorena."

"It was a small thing."

"You know better."

"I just helped her remember. Red Boat was a stroke of luck. What sort of boat was it, anyway?"

"A little tug." I took his hand. "Why is it you're so intent on helping everyone remember?"

"The past shapes us. If we forget, we forget who we are."

"Sometimes it's best to forget." I touched his face, and he closed his eyes. "If I think of you as Anthony or Frank, I want to run away. If I think of you as Raymond, I want to stay."

He opened his eyes. "And how is it you think of me?"

I kissed him on the mouth. He took me in his arms and pulled me onto his lap, holding me close. He kissed my face and neck, slid his hands under my shirt, caressing my bare back.

"We have to put the kids to bed first," I whispered.

We went upstairs, and after my goodnights, he kissed and hugged the girls and wished them sweet dreams. They hung round his neck, and he closed his eyes and held them for a moment before he laid them on the bed and tucked them in.

I whispered to him at the foot of the back stairs that I'd come to his room as soon as the girls were asleep, and he ascended with a chorus of farewells behind him.

I STRIPPED AND GOT INTO THE SHOWER, SCRUBBED SLOWLY FROM head to toe, held my face in the pulsing water. I toweled myself and put on perfume and dried my hair, brushing it out while it was still damp. Before I left the bathroom, I peeked into the girls' room. They were already sound asleep. I put on the shift and went up the spiral stair to Raymond's room barefoot, my hair hanging down my back.

When he opened his door, I stepped into his arms. "Don't say anything," I said. He kissed me tenderly and lifted the chemise over my head. We lay on the bed, and he made love to me with a passion and intensity and reverence for my body I'd never felt from anyone before, as if we'd only have this once, and it would have to count for everything.

When we lay still in each other's arms, I couldn't hold him close enough. "I love you," I whispered, and he drew in his breath. I felt his tears on my neck and hoped he was crying for joy.

MY EYES CAME OPEN IN THE DARKNESS. I WAS WIDE AWAKE. THE only light in the room came from the sea-green numerals of the clock radio: 3:43. Raymond lay sleeping in the shadows beside me, his breathing deep and regular.

I'd been dreaming. I'd seen Robert sitting in a rocking chair in the darkness, a pistol in his lap. It was vivid and precise. I could smell the bales of tobacco piled around him, could still smell them now that I was awake.

I knew what he was doing there. I watched him, waiting for what would happen next, letting each moment pass by, until I saw the doors burst open, and I was Susanna in a wagon, the road receding behind me in the morning sunlight. I wouldn't let the image go, clung to it like the sheets balled up in my fists, until I had it, each scene of it, the end of Susanna's story, like a line of beads laid out waiting to be strung.

I swung my legs over the side of the bed and hurried out into the hall, naked beneath the laughing angels, scrambling down the stairs to the second floor in a controlled fall. I shoved the library doors aside like swinging doors in a hash house and ran full tilt down the balcony, my feet slapping on the wood floor. I burst into my bedroom, stumbling over the jeans I'd left lying on the floor, and turned on my computer.

Susanna's Story

Chapter Four

Robert rocked back and forth in the glow of a smoky lamp. He had no idea of the time. Somehow he'd mislaid his watch. The rocking chair had been Anthony's idea. It was part of a shipment of furniture for Mr. Rutherglen, who would not be needing it this night. It was a lovely thing—willow with inlaid roses of cherry wood.

He had a small table beside him with a pot of tea, now grown cold; Horace's *Odes*, which he hadn't glanced at for well over an hour; and his pistols, cleaned and loaded well before the slit of light beneath the door had faded into black. He held a pipe in his hand, but had run out of tobacco about the time the tea had grown cold.

He had wanted to come before night fell, "to be safe," he'd told Anthony. He couldn't very well tell the man he was afraid to be outside after dark. He had not expected to be so frightened inside the warehouse, but its cavernous darkness was unfamiliar and seemed to stretch away forever like a moonless night. Outside the sphere of the lantern's light was utter blackness. He was surrounded by tobacco—hogsheads of it stacked everywhere—but he didn't dare venture out of the light.

The door, he knew, was ten feet directly in front of him. His plan was to extinguish his lamp the moment he heard anyone at the door. He reasoned that anyone entering this place would bear a lamp—for how else would they see past the ends of their noses? His target would be illuminated, directly in front of him. He couldn't miss.

Anthony had warned him he might have to wait until dawn, but how would he know when that was? He stared intently once again, straining to see a light beneath the door, but he could see nothing. Damned eyes. Once, he'd followed Jesse into the stable, and thought he'd fallen into a black pit. He'd told Jesse to lead him out of the place at once. Damned humiliating being led about by a slave—"Watch your step here, Master. There's a barrel right in front of you."

At least he could still read, if there was sufficient light, though sometimes the words turned to squiggly shapes like microscopic creatures and swam about the page. Thank God for Anthony, he thought, or I would probably be blind by now.

Susanna knew. He was sure of it. She never said anything, of course. She never did. He never knew silence could be so powerful until he'd married that woman. She hated him. But what had he ever done to deserve her hatred except to be alive while her blessed Miles was dead? Perhaps if I were to die, he thought, I might be sainted as well. Even blindness might do. *Susanna, bring me my brandy. Yes, my dear, dear husband.*

The lamp began to smoke. Reluctantly, he turned down the wick. The smoking stopped, but the light shrank. He poured himself a cup of cold tea and drank it down. He had already fallen asleep twice. He didn't want to sleep through this rare opportunity for bravery.

"I killed a man breaking into the warehouse," he could hear himself saying over breakfast in the bright morning sun. Susanna's eyes would glow with admiration. "I sat in the dark all night," he would tell her casually, and her eyes would fill with tears.

There was a scratching sound behind him and to the left, then a bump and scurry. Rats. They were everywhere. Gordon had suggested a cat, but Robert hated cats, low sleek creatures creeping about in the dark. The rats didn't bother him. It was the darkness itself.

He rocked back and forth trying to light the ashes in his pipe. The sooner we return to Scotland, he thought, the better. James can get a proper education. Susanna, with her beauty and intelligence, will be the talk of Glasgow. Even William can enter University. Why not? Many a stupid boy took a law degree. But all this wanted money. He never seemed to accumulate any money. The business seemed to prosper, but his own wealth remained modest, lost to him in a maze of figures.

But things would turn around. He was sure of it. Anthony had told him that once these thefts were stopped, profits would soar. Back in Scotland, Susanna would forget Saint Miles and become a proper wife. So beautiful she was, so very, very beautiful.

He was startled from his reverie by the sound of a wagon driving into the yard. He took the pistols in his hands and blew out his lamp. The blackness was absolute. He stared ahead, hoping his eyes were still on the door. The darkness solidified as if he were encased in obsidian. His heart began to race, and he couldn't breathe. A key slid into the lock, and the rats all around him scurried for cover. He raised his pistols. The door heaved open, the groan of the hinges echoing from the rafters. A man's shape appeared in the faint gray square of the doorway; his upraised arm was tipped with a point of light.

Robert fired when the shadow filled the doorway, but it kept growing larger. The light arced toward the floor and there was the shattering of glass. Out of the darkness, a huge weight struck him the length of his body. The chair splintered beneath him and collapsed. His head struck the floor with a jarring blow, and he passed out for a moment.

He awoke in utter blackness. A body lay on top of him, the chest against his face. He grabbed hold of it to push it off and discovered the stomach was blown away. He squirmed his way free in a panic, crawled on all fours to the faint light of the doorway, lurched to his feet, and emerged into the morning. The sun shone clear of the horizon. The morning breeze chilled him. He looked down, saw his clothes soaked in blood, and fell to his knees.

Jesse was dead. Susanna had no doubt of it. That was the freedom this adventure had bought him.

"Mighty convenient," Jesse'd said to Anthony as they'd driven to the warehouse early in the morning. "Master Robert say fix this wagon just when we be needing one."

"Nothing convenient about it. Mr. Jamieson is coming tomorrow—an event I have known of for two weeks and have used as the basis of my plans."

The wagon was the property of Glasford & Sons. It had sat idle for some months since Robert had ordered Jesse to overload it and two wheels had collapsed. With Mr. Jamieson's imminent arrival, Robert had ordered the wagon's repair.

"What if he don't show?" Jesse said.

"It's enough that Robert believes he is coming. His actual arrival will have certain advantages, but is not absolutely necessary. We need only a day's advantage, and surely we can trust Robert to be a coward for a day."

When they pulled up to the warehouse, Jesse said, "What we need to be coming here for, anyway?"

"Mr. Rutherglen's rocker. You'll find it right inside the door. It's a special favor for the captain who will carry us to freedom."

Jesse'd climbed down from the wagon and walked to his death.

Late in the afternoon, at Anthony's direction, William had turned the wagon down a narrow road to the river. "We make camp here," Anthony had said. A stone building, the roof caved in, stood beside a dilapidated pier.

Now it was dusk, and Susanna, Jess, and Rachel waited in an overgrown clearing at water's edge. Anthony and William had gone off to gather firewood.

Susanna pulled Jess up into her lap and gave him a piece of bread. Rachel was gathering flowers and lacing them through the wheels of the wagon, which stood a few yards away. Jess stood in Susanna's lap, his stout little legs wobbling slightly. "This bread is good," he said.

Anthony was really quite clever, she thought, letting William drive. When the shots rang out, he'd shouted, "Get us out of here, boy! For all they're worth!"

And of course, William had lashed the team into headlong flight without a moment's hesitation.

It'd been all she could do to gather the children into her arms so that they wouldn't fly out onto the road. She'd looked back to the warehouse to see a tiny figure emerging from the doorway, then they'd topped the hill, and it was gone.

"What was that sound?" she'd shouted to Anthony over the racket of the team and wagon.

Anthony, his eyes on the road ahead, shouted back, "Pistol fire."

"Are you sure?"

"I am most familiar with the sound, I assure you."

"But what has happened?"

"Jesse is shot, I expect, most likely slain."

"We must go back."

He'd then looked at her, said not a word, had no intention of speaking, sitting on a keg of Robert's brandy, a pistol stuck in his breeches like a pirate in a novel.

She was booty. She had no voice.

Now Jess bounced up and down on her lap. "Zanna, give me ride!"

"Zanna's tired," she told Jess. "Let's take a look at Rachel's flowers, shall we?" She stood up and set him on his feet. His hand in hers was a tiny thing, no bigger than a sparrow.

When they'd arrived, Jess had been crying, and she'd run about the clearing with him atop her shoulders as Miles used to do with William when he was a child. Rachel had remained quiet and watchful and had needed no comforting.

Now she looked up at Susanna. "Do you like my flowers?"

"They are very pretty."

Jess broke free from her hand and raced around the clearing. Susanna sat back down upon the grass.

"Is Mr. Anthony coming back?" Rachel asked.

"Yes, he's gone with William to gather firewood."

Rachel pulled a spindly red flower with a long stem from the ground and carefully wound it through the spokes. "Is Jesse with Nancy?"

Nancy had said to her as they were leaving, "I hope you know what you doing with these children, Miss Susanna."

She'd said, "Don't you worry, Nancy. I'll do right by them." But what would that be now?

"Yes," she told Rachel. "Jesse is with Nancy."

Rachel plucked another flower and continued to weave.

Jess was still racing around the clearing. He was now flapping his arms and squawking, apparently pretending to be a turkey. There was a loud explosion from the woods, and he sprawled on the ground.

For a second she thought he too had been shot, but he sat up and looked around, his eyes wide with terror. He had only stumbled in fear. She searched the line of trees where Anthony and William had disappeared, the direction of the explosion that still echoed in the clearing, though it'd come from some distance.

Nothing stirred in the wood. Jess ran across the clearing as fast as he could and fell into her arms. He curled into a ball in her lap and clamped his eyes shut as Susanna watched the gathering darkness of the wood.

"That be another pistol shot, don't it, Miss Susanna, just like Mr. Anthony say before."

"Yes Rachel, I think you're right."

"See my wheel?" she said, and pointed to the wagon wheel, its spokes laced with yellow and purple and red and green.

"It's quite lovely," Susanna said.

Rachel tilted her head to one side and tried to smile, but couldn't manage it. "I make it for Jesse," she said, and suddenly a sob broke from her.

Susanna held her arms open, and Rachel stumbled across the small patch of ground between them.

William staggered under a load of sticks, while Anthony strolled on ahead of him empty-handed, a dead rabbit he'd shot dangling from his belt. "It's the way of the sea," Anthony had explained to him. "I'm the captain. You're the mate. I find the supplies; you carry them."

William had wanted to say, "This is not the sea,"

but chose the camouflage of worshipful obedience instead. He didn't quite trust Anthony anymore. Nor his mother either, for that matter. He feared that perhaps she'd gone mad. Whatever Anthony was up to, however, William was sure Anthony knew precisely what he was doing.

William had wondered why Anthony chose him to drive the team when clearly Jesse would've been the superior choice. Then Jesse was shot, and William, reins and whip in hand, drove them away as fast as he could, Anthony shouting in his ear so that he couldn't think that it was wrong, that Jesse was dying because Anthony had sent him in there, and Anthony wasn't doing anything at all to help. Then he remembered Mister Jack. Now I'm Mister Jack, he'd thought to himself, but wasn't sure exactly what he meant.

"Let's rest a while, shall we?" Anthony said as they came upon a lightning-blasted tree, so huge at the base it would've taken three Williams to reach around it. This was an old wood, and there were several trees larger still that they had passed underneath.

William dumped the sticks on the ground and sat on the moss-covered log. Anthony had one of Robert's pipes and was filling it with tobacco, tamping it with one of Robert's silver tampers. If I am Mister Jack, William thought, then who is my mother?"

He said, "Anthony, do you love my mother?"

Anthony smiled, puffed on his pipe. "That depends upon what you'll be meaning by that word 'love,' now doesn't it? Now what might your meaning be?"

William refused to trade question for question. "You know all about meaning, Anthony. It's what you've taught me—that meaning is everything. I think you know what I mean by love."

"You are indeed a marvelous pupil, and you are right. I know precisely what you mean, and the answer is no. But let me ask you this—does your mother love me?"

It'd never occurred to William that she did not. Why would she do such a thing if she didn't love him? But he knew immediately that Anthony was right, that his mother didn't love Anthony, had never loved him.

"Why did you bring Jess and Rachel?"

"I intend to sell them to the captain of the vessel that will take me to Barbados."

"Does my mother know that?"

"Of course not."

"You're going to kill Mother, aren't you?"

"You're a good lad," Anthony said, and pointed his pistol at William's chest. "The brightest pupil I have ever had. So I am sure you will understand why"—the muzzle flashed and jumped, and William flew backward into space and landed like a rag doll on the pile of sticks he'd dropped on the ground—"I must kill you as well."

Anthony rolled him off and picked up an armload, enough for a small fire to take the chill off. In a few hours he would be snug in his cabin, bound for Barbados.

Shortly after a second shot had rung out, Susanna saw Anthony walking out of the woods, a load of sticks in one arm, the other high in a jaunty wave. She cried out, "William!" and he dropped the sticks on the ground beside her, jarring the children from their torpor, sending echoes out over the waves.

"I showed him how to set a snare. We shot at a plump hare but blew most of him away, I'm afraid." He dropped a bloody carcass on the ground. "I told him to be back before nightfall."

He rummaged in the wagon, came back with a bucket, and set it on the ground beside her. "Fetch some water and I'll make us a stew, the likes of which you've never tasted."

The woods were dark. Even out in the open, the

light was almost gone, the sky gray and heavy. "William is in there?" she said.

"Cluck, cluck," he said, laughing. "Give the boy some freedom, let him have his little adventures. He'll be fine."

Jess and Rachel were both clinging to Susanna, both half asleep, half afraid. She spread her wrap upon the ground and laid them down upon it. She stood and gazed at the river. It was wide here, a hundred yards or more. She took the bucket in her hands. "I love my son."

"And he loves you. If he is quite lucky he will burst with pride to return home from the hunt and set a fat hare at your feet." Anthony was already building a fire, shaving kindling from one of the sticks with a long, thin knife she'd never seen before. He must keep it in his boot, she thought.

He struck a spark and caught the kindling. The dry sticks popped and flamed. The heat and smoke struck her in the face. Rising to his feet, he put a finger under her chin and tilted her head back, kissing her gently, his lips barely brushing hers. "Now would you get the bloody water before my fire burns up?" he said with a smile.

She trudged toward the river, looking back at the woods, now through a line of smoke. Then she turned to the water, some eight feet below her, down a steep bank.

He's dead, she thought. He's killed him.

Then she felt his arms slip around her waist and pull her back against him. She felt his breath upon her neck; then he kissed her and whispered in her ear, "It has been wonderful, again."

She spun round in his arms, planted her forearms against his chest, pushing hard, knowing he wouldn't move. He whispered her name, and she looked up at him. He had a look she'd never seen on his face, a wistful sadness.

He bent and kissed her neck, pressed his right fist between her shoulder blades. He swelled his forearm, releasing a small catch, a thin bow of beaten metal. She jolted in his arms as a seven-inch shaft pierced her spine. He pushed her off the blade into the water and dove in after her, pulling her by the hair to a narrow strip of beach downstream. He beached her half in the water, half out, staring up, her eyes still alive. With his knife, he cut a lock of her hair and laid it on the beach, then dislodged a large stone—about twenty or twenty-five pounds—from the mud. He held it above his head and dropped it onto her face until he was sure she was unrecognizable. He removed her rings, pulled her back into the water, pushed her into the current, and rinsed himself off. He stood in the shallows, letting the wind dry him, watching the sun set upstream. He stepped onto the beach and picked up the lock of Susanna's hair. He tied it in a knot and slipped it into his coat pocket, along with the rings.

I QUIT WORKING ON THE LAST SCENE AND SAVED IT, PUT MY computer to sleep, and set it on the bedside table. The lioness started sliding from my lap, but I grabbed her before she went over the edge of the bed and set her on top of the computer.

I lay back on the bed, still naked, numb, staring at the ceiling, feeling like everything I'd just written had actually happened to me. I have to get out of here, I told myself. I rolled out of bed and looked out the window.

The world had turned white. Snow came down in thick, heavy flakes. There were eight or nine inches already on the ground. Thomas was in one of the far paddocks, a tiny dark figure, leading a pair of horses toward the barn. Nothing else moved but the snow. I felt the cold air on my bare skin. My van wouldn't get a hundred yards in this snow, and it was still coming down. We were trapped.

I went into the bathroom and put on my robe, listening at the girls' door, but I couldn't hear them. I went in without knocking. Their bed was empty. Clothes were scattered everywhere. I started down the back stairs and heard their excited babble, mingled with Rachel's laughter, coming up from the kitchen. They'd apparently set themselves to entertaining Rachel as she prepared their breakfast. I listened a moment longer. No Raymond.

I thought about calling the police, but what would I say to them? They'd be in no mood for crank calls. They were probably hauling people out of ditches up and down the interstate.

I went back to the bathroom and turned on the tap, splashing my face with cold water, toweling it dry. My eyes were red and puffy. I looked like somebody who hadn't slept, who'd written three deaths in four hours—one of them, according to Raymond, my own—crying most of the time.

I also looked like I'd had my "screaming good fuck." My hair was in a wild tangle, my skin was splotched with red. I looked into my eyes. Had I just slept with a man who'd murdered me, who'd murdered my son, a man who wanted me to remember it all? What in the hell had I been thinking coming up here in the first place? Dragging my kids along. I closed my eyes. I had to get a grip. I could berate myself later. Right now I had to keep things calm. Right now I had to find Raymond and pretend that everything was all right.

I thought I heard the sound of footsteps in the library, Raymond's heavy tread echoing through his cavern of books.

I threw on some clothes, and went out into the library. The skylights, buried in snow, were dark. Snow had built up along the seams of the Magdalene so that it was obscured by shadows, the scene merely patches of color and light. The chandelier hovered overhead, glistening with yellow flames in the darkness. A low fire burned in the fireplace. Raymond, dressed in a dark heavy coat and knee-high boots, stirred the coals and hurled a log onto the fire with an angry grunt, returned the poker to its rack with a loud clank.

He sat down heavily, staring into the fire. His boots were muddy and the bottom of his coat was caked with snow. I closed the door quietly behind me. He gave no sign that he knew I was there.

I took a deep breath and gripped the rail to steady myself, mounting my smile before I spoke. "Good morning," I called down to him, trying not to chirp but failing.

He slowly turned from the fire. He looked at me as if he couldn't imagine what I was doing there. "Good morning," he said in a small, flat voice.

I felt his eyes upon me as I came down the stairs and walked to the fireplace, making a great show of warming myself by the fire so that my hands hovered inches away from the poker. They shook, and I tried to disguise it by rubbing them together. "This fire feels great," I said too cheerily. I wouldn't have fooled Lorena. I looked into his eyes, and quickly looked away. All the passion was gone. Instead there was a distracted sadness, the dazed absence of depression or madness.

"The snow is lovely," I said brightly.

"I woke up and you were gone," he said.

"I was writing. The ending came to me, and I had to get it down. I often write early in the morning." I tried to seem casual and relaxed, all in a day's work. I watched him out of the corner of my eye.

"I listened at your door. I heard the click of your keys. I was hoping you wouldn't finish it—at least for a while longer." He tried to smile but couldn't manage it. "You must hate me now," he said.

"Who says I must?" I said, turning a smiling face to him, trying to control the quaver in my voice. "Not me, Raymond."

"But I murdered you and your son . . ."

I shook my head. "Anthony did. Not you."

"But I *was* Anthony!" he shouted, bringing his fist down on the arm of his chair. "Don't you understand?"

I'd jumped backward, knocking the fireplace tools over.

He sprang to his feet. "I'm so sorry," he said.

I knelt, gathering up the poker and the tongs.

He started toward me. "Let me help you," he said.

I scrambled to my feet, crouching slightly, the poker in my right hand, poised to strike. "I've got it," I snapped. "I'm fine."

He froze. We stood there a moment, neither one of us moving, our eyes fixed on one another. The clatter still seemed to echo all around us. The tongs and shovel still lay at my feet.

Finally, he drew himself up, looking about the library as if he'd been a guest and he was now about to take his leave. "I see," he said quietly. "I see." He pointed to a small stack of pages on the floor beside his chair. "I've brought you a transcript of the close of Pearl's journal. I'll be in my office. You can have the library to yourself." He maintained his distance as he walked to his office. He hesitated, his hand on the door, staring at it. He closed his eyes and swallowed hard. I thought he might break down, but he looked back at me. "I want to apologize for last night. I should never have given in to my feelings. I was being selfish, thoughtless."

I couldn't speak. I just stood there, frozen.

He rested his forehead against the door. "Anthony was much worse—I was much worse—than you could possibly conceive."

"What does it matter?" I said, my voice shaking. I gripped the poker more tightly in my hand.

He dropped his hand from the door. "Would you like to know why I murdered you?"

A chill passed through me and I felt dizzy, as if I might faint. I shook my head, unable to speak.

He came around in front of his chair. "Sit down, and I'll tell you."

"I'll stand."

"Then I shall make it as brief as possible."

He sat down in his chair. His eyes were burning. He leaned back, crossed his legs, the storyteller in the parlor, but there was a quickness to his movements, a tautness in his face that revealed a great anger. His voice was full of venom and loathing. It was as if the Anthony from my pages had come to life and sat before me.

"When I—when Anthony—turned twenty-five, I went out carousing to celebrate my birthday—a delicious irony for me. I smoked a good deal of opium and entertained myself by recalling all my twenty-fifth birthdays as something of a reunion of fools, regaling my companions with the story of one fool after another.

"I ended up in a sleeping prostitute's rooms, quite alone, staring through a tiny window into the empty street. I had yet to meet you, of course, though I was certain that I would. You were the one constant, life after life. No one else returned. No one else haunted me. We failed each other with amazing thoroughness, life after life.

"I hated you. I hated your colossal ignorance of thousands of days I could recall in precise detail. I hated your inevitability, your necessity, it seemed. What good were you, I wanted to know, except as a sort of infinite forgetfulness of every life I'd ever lived? You made my memory of those lives, as the Buddhists say, the sound of one hand clapping—a loathsome sound, I assure you.

"But still, there I was, staring out some whore's window wishing you'd step out of the shadows so that I could stop my bloody waiting, and we could do the whole damn thing over again.

"When it came to me how I might change things."

Raymond studied me for a moment, a pathetic woman shivering before the fire. "I reasoned thus: If I were to die at that very moment, in the chair I sat in—if I were to plant a pistol against my head and fire without hesitation—then I would've cheated the game for one life at least, having died without ever meeting you." Raymond pantomimed his words, holding an imagined gun to his temple for a moment, then dismissed it with a wave of his hand.

"'Very well,' I said to the Fates. 'I'm tired of waiting. I'm tired of waiting on her pleasure like some child with no will of my own. I will arrange when I am to meet her. I will select the time, the place, the precise circumstances of our rendez-vous, and if she isn't there, I'll kill myself. But if she is, I vow, I'll kill her straightaway—and live out the balance of my life in perfect contentment, quite free of her forgetful-ness.'

"That night I wove a plot out of thin air, deciding each detail on the basis of whim, as if I were planning a revel. I even woke the whore up and told her my plans, as I smoked yet more opium and downed a bottle of wine.

"I decided I should like to go to America, for it was one of the few places I'd never been. I'd discover you there and proceed to ruin your life. I'd steal everything you had, destroy everything you cared about, and murder you. I thought it would be a great irony to meet you as a slave as I asserted my freedom, a nice touch to let the crown bear the expense of my passage by transporting me as a sentenced criminal.

"I selected counterfeiting as my offense for it was my father's line, and I knew I could count on him to betray me to the authorities when the time came, if I made it seem to his advantage. I wanted the risk of being burned at the stake, you see, for I entertained the superstition that death by that means would destroy my soul once and for all. Twice before, I'd narrowly escaped such an execution and found it quite the closest thing to a terror of death I'd ever felt—though I had every confidence I could avoid such a fate once more with a well-placed bribe.

"I selected Barbados for my final destination because I'd been there in my younger days with Captain Carter and thought it a pleasant place to live out my life—free of you for a lifetime of wealth and leisure.

"I demanded writing materials and frightened the poor whore half to death, waving pistols in the air, spewing wild stories. She sent her young son out to fetch paper and quill and ink in the middle of the night. By the time he returned, the story was rich with embellishment, and I wrote it all down in a rush.

"I signed it with a grand flourish and commanded the

whore and her son to witness it with their marks. Then I hung out the window, vomiting for upwards of an hour and a half, and passed out.

"Next morning, I gathered up the pages that lay on the floor by the window and rolled them up into a tube, tied them with a strip of cloth from the whore's bedding. I kept them close at hand for the rest of my life.

"Of course, I realized in the morning light that you might show up at any moment as my story unfolded, but I was convinced you wouldn't, that I could make you come on my terms.

"And so it was. You stood there on the deck of the *Justitia,* literally the first woman I'd laid eyes on in America, Robert pacing up and down before me, waiting, nay, begging to be gulled. So I stepped forward, and sold myself to Robert. I looked you in the eye, saying in my mind, 'Remember me, and I shall spare you,' but of course you didn't. You never did. But I saw enough lust smoldering there to know my plan would work—that the Fates had accepted my bargain, and I was to kill you.

"I gained control of Robert's affairs in no time at all, formed the necessary alliances. Within a year, I'd acquired a plantation in Barbados with Glasford and Sons money— the one Frank was later to recall with such fondness. Jamieson's visit and Jesse's longing for freedom gave me the tools I needed to destroy you and everything you cared about, to obliterate you." He leaned forward, his voice a whisper. "To *forget* you."

He rose to his feet. "But nothing is ever so simple. Like a fool, I hadn't bartered Jess and Rachel for my passage as I'd planned but took them to Barbados with me as my own, giving the captain your rings instead. They hated me, of course, particularly Rachel, and soon she became your chorus: *Master Anthony,* she would say, *wouldn't Miss Susanna enjoy this lovely sunset? Master Anthony, isn't it terribly lonely here, never seeing anyone? Shall I bring you another drink, Master Anthony? Master Anthony, have you been having those awful nightmares again? I heard you screaming all the way to my rooms. What is it, Master Anthony, that haunts you?"*

As he spoke Rachel's words his voice grew louder, until he was almost screaming, his hands cutting through the air. He walked back and forth, getting closer and closer with each pass. He stopped, an arm's length away from me, and closed his eyes.

When he opened them, his voice was calmer, almost matter-of-fact, his hands in his pockets. He moved back and forth with small shuffling steps, his eyes everywhere but on me. "After twelve years in Barbados, I journeyed to London and arranged for the disposition of my property on whatever wretch I was to become, though as it turned out, Frank was too stewed to know a fortune awaited him, and it remained unclaimed until I turned eighteen in this life and wrote my barrister.

"I returned to Barbados and instructed Rachel to have the slaves build a bonfire on the beach with a stake in the middle of it. I'd read in the literature of the Inquisition that the witches were often wrapped in wet rags before they were burned, so that they might feel the actual flames of Hell as they died, and thus be prompted to repent. I walked into the surf dressed in several layers of clothes, a tablecloth wrapped around me. When I came out of the sea, I instructed Jess to tie me securely to the stake, and asked that Rachel light the fire with the pages I'd written in that whore's room before Rachel was born.

"And so she did, stuffing them into my mouth after the fire'd caught. As the flames leapt up around me, I prayed for my soul's death, for the end of me. But my prayers were not answered, and in the last moments of my life as Anthony, I begged for forgetfulness. Begged to be a fool. It took nearly fifteen minutes for me to die. I'd had my fifteen minutes in Hell, but still my soul wouldn't die."

He was standing inches from me. He peered into my eyes, looking as if he had indeed journeyed to Hell and back. I thought I might scream. If he came any closer I resolved to hit him with the poker, but he didn't. He walked back to his chair, pointed toward the stack of pages on the floor. "Read them," he said bitterly. "Take heed of what Pearl says. She knew me for what I was." He took something out of his shirt pocket, knelt, and laid it on the pages. "I stole this from you," he said in a quiet voice, his rage seemingly spent. "I return it to you." He straightened up, turned on his heel, and went into his office, closing the door behind him with a loud click.

My knees were weak, and I was having trouble catching my breath. I stumbled over to his chair and gripped the back of it to steady myself as I looked at the stack of pages at my feet, the thing nestled on top of them. At first I couldn't tell what it was in the flickering light, but then I saw it all too clearly. It was a lock of red hair tied in a knot.

My hands shook, and I felt a wave of nausea as I stabbed at the thing with the poker, until I finally caught a few strands of it and flung it into the fire. I sat down heavily, the poker on my lap. I stared at the carved faces on his door, listened but couldn't hear a sound. I had to stay there. I had to know precisely where he was. I didn't dare turn my back on him for a moment. Somewhere behind me, completely unaware of any danger, my children were laughing and joking. I swore that if he took a step toward them, I'd kill him.

I'm not sure how long I sat there, my hands wrapped tightly around the poker, glaring at the door, before I looked down at the stack of pages he'd left for me. He'd typed them into a computer, printed them out on a laser printer, so that they looked like pages in a book, a document for someone like Professor Seawater. *Read them*, he'd said, and, as if in a dream, I could not resist them. I took them up, tilting the pages toward the firelight, and read Pearl's last words.

Monday, September 9, 1850

I have reached San Francisco too weary to write a word. Tomorrow I will inquire after the Falcon. For tonight, I sleep.

Wednesday, September 11, 1850

How maddening! No one can tell me with certainty when the Falcon will arrive! "She has run into some difficulty, ma'am." That is all anyone could say! I hope you are in no danger, sweet John. Hurry to me, I beg you, for I fear I have only a short time before Frank finds me here—his money will draw him like a magnet!

Friday, September 13, 1850

I have lost all hope—this morning I saw Joshua in the street! Frank must be here as well. The Devil bids me fly, save myself, set out for Sacramento, or connive passage on some ship bound for anywhere. I am done with such stratagems.

I have money enough for two more nights' lodging. I will stay here, for surely the Falcon will steam into the harbor with you at the helm. I can almost see you there, gaily waving to me!

Sunday, September 15, 1850

I awoke early from a dream of my death—vivid and brutal—and I realize that you will not come, dear John—that I have thrown away my chance for happiness, and I will never see you again. You will never read these words, but I set them down anyway: I love you!

Good bye. Please forgive me.

It is you, Frank, I wish to address. I have readied myself for the task, for I have drained my brandy dry, and I fancy I am quite as drunk as you are—so that what I say might prove intelligible to you.

Oh, I know you don't read, that you are quite impervious to anything I might say in these pages, but perhaps your hands might burn as you lay them on these words, searing the truth into your flesh!

It is a pleasant fantasy in any case. I must entertain myself somehow as I wait for death.

Today I have been thinking on what Itsa told me about you that night in the jungle—that I knew you. The notion was absurd, of course, and I drove it from my mind. But I admit to you that I have known it to be true for some weeks now. One night you took me, as was your custom, in a brutal rush of passion. You stank. So drunk, it was a wonder you could move at all. I endured you. But when you were spent, and I laid you on the bed like a dead man, I studied your sleeping form. Your features, purged of the emotions which usually animated them, were actually quite fine, fit for any purpose, good or ill. I recalled my mother's face in death—free of hatred, sundered from her precious God, and I realized who you are. I told no one, not even the Devil. But now I will tell you.

You are an angel sent by God to destroy me—the same God who tested Job, the same God who told Abraham to murder Isaac, the same God who filled my mother with the passion to murder her only child.

Oh, you are too deceived to know what you are. Perhaps you actually fancy you will become a great planter someday—your seed as numerous as the stars in the sky! Perhaps you actually believe the land my death will purchase will save you. Perhaps you believe you serve only your own clever schemes. But I know you serve Him who enslaves us, then demands our blessing.

But you should know—I would warn you if I could, my husband—that God murders all His darlings when He's done with them. And they love Him for it, even Jesus, who turned his back on his own mother and left Magdalene weeping at the tomb, but would not deny God and followed Him to death. All so that God might forsake him and rejoice, and bid us all rejoice at the glorious deed He had done!

I will not! I cannot!

You come for me like Samson, my husband, animated by the will of God, slaying everything in your path. But someday soon—be warned—you will stand chastened and blind and bring your temple crashing down around your head and know you've been a fool!

But I waste my words on you, Frank. Even if you could read these words, even if they did indeed burn into your flesh, you would not heed them. A silly woman talking to herself, telling stories to no one. No one will pay them any mind—save God perhaps.

God! The thought makes me laugh!

Are You laughing, God? Are You reading these words, knowing each one before I know it myself, bursting out of Your trousers—for surely You must wear trousers! Black, creased, girding up Your belly full of bile—laughing Your manly laugh, Your superior laugh, too good for the weak.

It was You who punished me for loving Douglas, conceiving a child, and loving him. It was You who took him from me in hopes of making him just like You—a ravenous maw hungry only for power!

I fled into this wilderness only to find You waiting with Your rich bounty! Are You still reading, God? God, who will soon or late find me here and sacrifice me on Your Glorious Altar?

Let me tell You a story, God. Hear *my* sermon. Hear *my* prayer—

When I was a child in the kitchen, begging Nancy for stories of my own father, my own past, I selfishly never thought to ask *her* story, until one day I was prattling on about the Bible (for I'd just met the Devil and was full of excitement over what I thought of as his book), when she allowed she'd never read the book herself, since she could not read.

I knew this, of course—my grandfather allowed no reading among his slaves—but it had never struck me just what that meant before. She'd heard the stories on Sunday morning when Grandfather rounded up the slaves in the yard, rain or shine, and read to them from the Bible. You must've relished the delicious irony from Your throne—one of Your slaves preaching to his slaves!

But back then I was still a child, the Devil only a newfound friend, so I whispered to her in the hushed tones of Adam and Eve in the Garden—"Nancy, do you believe in God?"

She set aside her bowl and paring knife, and looked me up and down. "How old you be, child?" she asked me, and I replied that I lacked a few scant days of being fifteen.

"'Less you're a preacher"—she instructed me with a sharp edge to her voice I'd never heard before—"don't go asking folks that question."

I never wished to give offense to Nancy, for she had always been my dearest friend, and so I hung my head and asked her forgiveness, fighting back tears, for Nancy had never spoken to me in such a tone before.

"I'm sorry, child," she said. "You didn't mean no harm. Truth is, I turn to the Lord only once, but I did it fierce, with all my heart, and He knock me down, lower

than the pit I was in, and I don't call on the Lord no
more after that. But that ain't no story for a child."

I howled in protest that I was not a child, that I was
now a woman, as she should know, for what my mother
called Your Curse had come upon me, and Nancy had
seen to me and washed my soiled bedclothes and let me
stay by her all the day! I grabbed her hands and knelt
before her, begging that she tell me her tale. And so she
relented and told me it was when her husband died, her
Jesse, and her children had been stolen from her, that
she'd prayed and wept, prayed and wept for week upon
week. For she'd been taught that God was Love.

"And just when it come to be a comfort to me," she
said, "Mr. Robert sit down to breakfast one morning, and
he got a letter with him. He say, 'You know what this
letter is? It is my humiliation!' And I said nothing, figured
it had something to do with his wife running off with that
convict, and all the trouble he was in. I felt sorry for him.
I suppose that's what I done wrong—a slave girl feeling
sorry for the master.

"He struck me down to the floor, bound my limbs, and
forced himself on me. All the time I'm praying he'll kill
me, set me free out of this world. I begged God to kill
me, but He weren't through with me yet.

"I was lying on the floor, still bound. I don't know how
long I been there, when I see James, your grandfather,
just a little boy, sitting on the stairs looking at me, and I
ask him to help me. He walk over to me, no bigger than
that butter churn over yonder, and he say, 'You are a
slave,' and smiles at me like a little angel. 'You are a slave
and a liar,' he say to me, and leave me lying on that floor.

"I ain't had no use for the Lord after that."

After Nancy told me this story, as You no doubt recall,
I went out into the woods and screamed into the great
empty sky that I would hate You always with all the
strength I could muster. Then I lay in the creeping cedar
alongside the stream like a soft bed and waited, listening
to the waters rushing by.

TIME AND TIME AGAIN

I lay there for a long time, and when You didn't strike me dead on the spot, I laughed like one possessed, rolling about like a child—forgetting how patient You can be.

But he's coming now, isn't he?—Your Avenging Angel! Drunk and loathsome and rapacious! Your own Darling! Your Precious Seed!

Let him come. I am ready to die. I know You now. You can't frighten me anymore. He will come. I am sure of it. But he shan't have me, for I have put myself upon these pages, and my life is my own.

It is said You attend to the fall of a sparrow, and I should imagine You do—its fall, its pain, its death and putrefaction. So it should not surprise me that I find myself in such straits—a whore bartered for land and slaves, my son sacrificed on Your Altar. I should imagine You take great pleasure in my tale.

I wish I might wrestle with You like Jacob, wrench a new name from You, extract my own covenant from You. For You know nothing of Love—only mindless obedience and heartless sacrifice. You deserve to be judged by Your own Law.

And how would I judge You, God? Surely You already know. But let me say it, let me write it bold upon the page like Your Own Commandments—

I pray that You would die!

Sting Yourself with Your own Venom and leave this wretched world!

Lord God of Hosts, I loathe You with all my heart and soul!

As I read Pearl's last words, my hands shook. The thin membrane between Pearl and myself broke, and I felt her words in my mouth, felt the rage and hatred and agony that had wrenched them out of her, out of me. Knew my own life as a headlong flight from an avenging angel, frightened of love, flirting with danger.

I could hear Pearl screaming in my head—*Lord God of Hosts, I loathe you with all my heart and soul!* I'd never said such a thing out loud, but I knew it was there, deep inside me, under all the layers of fragile reasonableness—Pearl's madness—like a diamond inside a lump of coal.

I rose to my feet, and the poker in my lap clattered to the floor with a terrible racket.

I froze, staring at Raymond's office door. He must've heard that. I bent down and picked up the poker in my left hand. The pages of Pearl's journal were still clutched in my right. I rolled them into a tube and stuck them in my back pocket.

What was he doing in there, so silent in that tiny room? How long was I to sit and wait in fear? I walked quietly up to his door and listened, but heard nothing. Was he even in there? "Raymond," I called, knocking on the doorframe. The library echoed with the sound, but there was no answer. I studied the door, looking for the latch to open it. The man with the donkey in the foreground held a staff in his right hand. When I looked closely, I could see it was a separate piece of wood from the rest. I reached out with trembling hands and pulled it, and the door swung open.

I jumped back, but there was no one there. The office was empty and dark. The secretary was bare, the drawer open and empty. The animals were gone from the shelf. I cursed myself for a fool—standing guard over an empty room, while my children were alone and unprotected. The door I'd thought was a closet stood ajar. I opened it and discovered a dark, narrow hall running behind the bookcases, across the front of the house, a small door at the end.

I ran the length of it and burst through the door into the foyer. I looked up the stairs, but I would've heard him if he'd gone that way. I crossed into the sitting room and was momentarily blinded. The front curtains were open, and the glare from the snow filled the room, throwing long shadows across the floor and walls.

Above the mantel, on the wall covered with weapons, was a blank space, two empty pegs. A silhouette of what had been there was faintly visible as a discoloration of the wallpaper. I held my arm to the place and shuddered. It would've been too big on me, but I knew what it was—a spring-loaded shaft, two leather straps to bind it to the forearm.

I heard voices from the kitchen and burst through the door. Rachel was washing dishes. Thomas stood beside her, drying a wineglass with a dish towel.

"Rachel, where are my girls?"

She smiled at me as if she didn't notice the poker or my strident tone. "They outside," she said, pointing out the window. "Make snow woman. Very happy. Excited about snow."

I ran past her out the back door. The girls were in the near paddock, pushing a huge ball of snow toward the center.

I screamed at them, "Kareth, Lorena, come in the house *immediately!*"

Their heads came up simultaneously, like startled deer. "Now!" I shouted, and they broke into a stumbling run through the snow.

"What's wrong?" Kareth asked as they reached the house.

"Just get inside," I said, herding them into the kitchen, helping them out of their coats and boots.

"But I want to know—"

"Not now!" I snapped. I turned to Rachel and Thomas. "Where is Mr. Lord?"

Thomas was studying me. "He's down at the stable."

"You're positive."

"Course I'm positive. Come through here maybe twenty minutes ago. What's happening here, anyway? You look like you seen a ghost or something."

My mind was racing. I had to get us out of there. I'd call the police and get them there on some pretext or other. I was a writer. Surely I could come up with a convincing lie. "Kareth, Lorena, go up to the room and pack as quick as you can. Do not screw around, you got it? I'll be right up. I'm going to make a few phone calls."

"Not on this phone," Thomas said. "Been out all morning. Some wire's down somewhere. Happens all the time."

"Shit!" I struck my fist on the counter and started pacing like a caged animal.

"Mr. Lord hurt you?" Rachel asked me timidly.

The girls were still standing at the foot of the stairs, gaping at me as if I'd gone mad. "Go on upstairs!" I shouted at them. "Pack, now!" They ran up the stairs.

I turned to Rachel. "I believe he means to kill me and my girls."

Rachel gasped and turned to Thomas. "I told you is bad man," she said. "I told you evil coming for sure. I told you!" She started crying and Thomas took her in his arms.

288

"Why you think something like that?" Thomas asked me.

I took a deep breath, steadied myself on the counter. "He believes he killed me and my son in a former life. The weapon he supposedly used is missing from his collection on the wall in there. What does it sound like to you?"

Thomas shrugged. "The man's plenty weird all right, but murder—I don't know."

"Have you got a gun?" I asked him.

His eyes narrowed. "I'm a convicted murderer, Ms. Mead."

Rachel turned to me, drying her eyes. "He has gun," she said.

Thomas shook his head. "Rachel, goddammit!"

Rachel glared at him. "Thomas!"

He held up his hands. "I'm sorry. I'm sorry." He turned to me. "Rachel's hell on cursing. So now that you know I'm in illegal possession of a firearm, you want to tell me what I'm supposed to do with it if I'm fool enough to go get it?"

"I don't know. Maybe nothing. I just know Raymond has gone to an awful lot of trouble to tell me he's an evil and dangerous man, and maybe we should listen to him."

"The man's crazy is all."

"Most likely. That's exactly what I've been saying."

He looked back and forth from me to Rachel. Neither of us said a word. "I give up." Thomas sighed. "Have it your way, but I want to know what's going down when I get back." He kissed Rachel on the cheek. "You just stay put here," he said, and went out the back door.

Rachel wrung her hands and watched Thomas through the back-door window. "I know bad come to us. I not supposed to work for this man. I supposed to work for *good* man. *Christian* man. Instead, I work for Devil man. Pray all my life come to America. Make fine dishes for Reverend Lord. Not come here for rich man and his horses."

"You prayed to work for Raymond's father?"

She turned to me and nodded vigorously. "Very great man. Christian man. His son trick me—say Reverend Lord want me here, but I write him, and he tell me his son Devil man." She put her hand on her chest. "Always tease me. Making the joke. Not always funny. Say crazy things. More crazy since he find you in newspaper. Run up and down stairs. Up and down, up and down."

I could see him in my mind's eye, listening to the sound of his own footsteps, completely mad, completely alone. "What crazy things did he say?"

She thought a moment. "Tell me he wait all his life for you. Act like little boy. He say when you come he give farm to me and Thomas for wedding present!"

"He said he was giving you the farm!"

She mistook my shock for disbelief. "I am telling truth. He say crazy things all the time."

She'd said "wedding present" as if that in itself were offensive. "Do you and Thomas plan to marry?" I asked gently.

She rocked her head from side to side and turned back to the door. I'd touched the nerve at the heart of all her troubles. "Don't know. Don't know. Thomas not a Christian. Been to prison. Is great sin what we do. God punish us for sure." She began to cry again.

I put down the poker and took Rachel by the shoulders, turned her to face me. "When did Raymond tell you this—that he was giving you the farm?"

"Night you come first time. Tell me that night."

Thomas came through the back door with a small black pistol and a box of shells. "Now, you want to tell me what's going on?"

"Did he say *why?*" I asked Rachel.

"He say he want to 'mend.' Something like that. I don't know what he talking about. He laughing at me, I am sure. Always laughing."

"Make amends?"

She nodded. "That's what he say—'make amends.'"

I turned to Thomas. "Do you know anything about Raymond giving you Greenville?"

Thomas laughed. "Rachel told me about it. It don't mean nothing. You got any idea what this place is worth? One of these horses worth more than I make in a year. He's gonna give that to me and Rachel? That's a good one."

I'd started pacing up and down. Why would Raymond want to give his home to Rachel and Thomas just because I'd showed up in his life again? Why would he give up his treasured home at all? Where would he live? Then it hit me.

"He'd have to put it in a will," I said aloud. "He'd have to write it down. Just saying it wouldn't mean a thing." This wasn't something he could just keep tucked away in his memory. He'd have to set it down in good legal prose for all to read. This was something I could lay my hands on. Something I could know was real or not. I'd been wringing the pages of Pearl's journal in my hands like a washcloth. I stopped and unrolled them across the stainless steel counter —Pearl's words in crisp, ten-point sans serif.

"Where is Raymond's computer?" I asked.

Thomas said, "It's in the office."

"No, it's not. There's nothing in there."

"Not in the house. Out at the barn. Got all the horses' papers and such out there. It's in the back, next to the garage."

"Girls," I called out, but they were already sitting side by side at the bottom of the stairs with their backpacks at their feet.

"What?" Kareth said quietly. They were huddled together, both terrified. Lorena clutched Heather in her arms.

I remembered how Raymond had held them in his arms the night before, as if he were leaving them, telling them goodbye. I knelt down, hugged and kissed them both. "Stay here with Thomas and Rachel. Do exactly as they say." I turned to Thomas. "You take care of my girls. I'm going down to the stable."

"No," said Rachel, stepping in front of the door.

"Please. I may have this all wrong. He may be intending to kill himself."

Her head snapped back, her eyes wide. "Kill *himself?*" Her hand dropped from the door. She looked into my eyes. "Why?"

"To make amends."

She stepped back from the door, hugging herself in fear that the Devil man might kill himself. "Run, you catch him."

"Just 'cause a man kill himself," Thomas said, "don't mean he won't take a few folks out with him." He'd dumped some of the shells on the counter and was loading a clip.

I picked up the poker. Thomas was right, but I couldn't stand around waiting to see whether Raymond was a psychotic killer or a ram caught in a thicket of his own devising. I had to find out the truth. I went out the back door and started down the path, skidding in the snow. It was still coming down. I wished I'd been wearing more than jeans and a sweatshirt, but I couldn't turn back now.

As I ran into the barn, the horses shifted and stamped in their stalls from one end to the other. "Raymond," I called out, but there was no one.

Halfway down the aisle, a cross-aisle led to the office. Through the glass door, even in the darkness, I could see a computer sitting on a large desk. There was a row of file cabinets on the far wall beneath a window into the garage, where the Hudson gleamed in the shadows like a big blue whale. A battered sofa was beside the doorway. I tried the knob, but it was locked. I smashed the glass with the poker, turned on the lights, and opened the door.

The computer had been shoved to the back of the desk. Newspapers were spread out on the desktop. A tugboat carved out of wood, painted red with white trim, sat on the paint-smeared newspapers. There was a card propped against the bow. *For Lorena,* it said. The paint on the tug was still wet, and the trash can was full of wood shavings. The jar of paint was open. The brush lay on the newspapers, still wet. In a daze, I picked up the brush and smeared the paint across the newspaper in bright red *X*'s, capped the paint, and wiped my hands on a rag. He must've come directly from the library, made Lorena her boat, and left.

The file cabinets were all locked. I pushed the boat aside and turned on the computer, laid the poker on the desktop. My hands raced across the keys. There were dozens of directories, hundreds of files, none of them named "legal documents" or "will." I tried several searches but came up with nothing. He seemed to sort his correspondence into directories of people's names. Each letter was named after the date it was written.

I opened a directory named "Hastings." Lists of files scrolled by. I stared at the screen. One of these might be the file I was looking for—the scrap of evidence I thought I needed. It could be anywhere. It might not be in there at all. A bit of paint on my index finger smeared the *H* with red. I tried to wipe it off with my shirtsleeve, but that only made it worse. "Dammit!" I shouted.

There was a directory named "Timothy" with dozens of files, week after week. They stopped a couple of years ago. I stared at the column of dates, each one a letter to a dead man. Timothy had told him I'd know what to do. I imagined Raymond sitting at this desk, carving a boat for a little girl, all for a memory that wasn't even his own. I remembered my arms around him. *I love you,* I'd said. I remembered how I'd felt, remembered what, in that moment, I knew.

Take heed of what Pearl says, he'd told me.

I knew what he meant—"Hate me as I hate myself." But goddammit, I wasn't going to do it. Anthony and Susanna, Frank and Pearl, God Himself, could all go fuck themselves. I wasn't going to let Raymond kill himself. I reached out and turned off the computer, and the screen went blank. I wasn't going to let him go.

I ran back out into the barn. There was one empty stall at the far end. The nameplate read, *Camilla.* Of course, I said to myself, that *would* be the black mare's name. Every other goddamn thing in the place was made out of some memory or other. I stepped outside into the snow. The hoofprints of a single horse went off toward the river, out of sight. The snow was a good ten or twelve inches. There was no way I could catch him on foot.

Angie was in the last stall, lazily munching on her feed. I slipped a bridle on her, trying to remember how to do something I'd seen done a hundred times, but had never actually done. I fumbled with it until I thought it wouldn't fall off, and led her to a bench on the side of the barn. I climbed on top of her and took the reins as Raymond had taught me. I kicked her hard and said, "Canter." Immediately I wished I'd put a saddle on her, but I hadn't wanted to take the time, and I wasn't sure I knew how to do it anyway.

We moved down the path like a stone rolling downhill, gaining momentum, and I felt myself rolling from side to side, losing control. *Keep your eyes on where you're going,* the girls' riding teacher always said. I stared at the line of trees ahead of me, a thin dark line in a field of white, and tightened my legs, leaning forward, resisting the urge to pull back on the reins. He was in those woods somewhere, I was sure of it, about to sacrifice himself. Because now he finally loved me.

Angie picked up speed, and her gait smoothed out. The snow-covered ground flew by me. But he couldn't believe I loved him. How could he? I saw myself as I must've looked, poised to strike him down. All of a sudden, Angie lurched to one side to avoid something in our path, and I flew through the air, landing in a heap, half buried in the snow at the edge of the wood. Angie stared at me sorrowfully. I couldn't get back on her without something to stand on.

I staggered to my feet and ran as best I could in the direction of Camilla's hoofprints. I lost track of the number of times I stumbled and sprawled face first in the snow. My face and hands were numb. My feet ached with cold. I stopped, trying to catch my breath, and heard the river just ahead.

A stand of pines, bowed with the snow, hung over the path. They showered me with snow as I pushed through them. It clung to my hair and went down my back. I emerged from the woods and saw Camilla standing idle, looking toward the river. Raymond stood in the current, the water near the tops of his boots, his back to me, looking downriver. I broke into a run, calling out his name. I slipped on the icy shore, scraping my hands on the rocks as I plunged into the bone-chilling water. He spun around, startled by the sound. I sprang out of the water into his arms and clung to him as we staggered back and forth in the current. I felt as if I might shatter from the cold, but I locked my arms tight around his waist.

"What are you doing?" he shouted.

"I won't let you kill yourself!" I shouted back.

"Let me go!" As he tried to struggle free I felt something hard, like an iron bar, brush across my back. I closed my eyes and braced myself, but he quickly pulled his right arm away from me. "Please let go," he said. "I beg you."

"So you can kill yourself? No way."

"But you don't understand. I've pledged my life to you since I was sixteen, pledged that when you came to me I would sacrifice my life, everything I had, to atone for what I've done. To treat myself as I'd treated you—merely a means to an end—to murder myself as I'd murdered you."

I was shaking violently. "What *you* don't understand," I screamed at him, "is that I'm not letting go of you until you shoot your fucking toy into the river, or I freeze to death." It felt as if my legs had been sheared off by the current. My hands felt brittle. I didn't know how much longer I could hang on. I beat my head against his chest like a child beating her head against a wall. "Raymond! Stop it! You're too old for this Lord Byron bullshit!"

"Lord Byron *bullshit?*"

"You know exactly what I mean."

I buried my face in his chest, breathed in the wet wool of his coat. I could feel his heart beating beneath my forehead. He let out a sigh, and there was a terrific jolt from his arm. I turned my head to see a metal shaft arc into the air and fall into the water without a splash, maybe thirty yards downstream. I slumped into his arms, and he carried me ashore.

He wrapped me in his coat and put me on Camilla's back, mounting up behind me, and we rode to the barn.

He stripped off my wet clothes and laid me on the sofa in his office, wrapping me in several blankets, rubbing my hands and feet. He hadn't said a word. I watched him as he worked over me, his brow creased with worry. When I'd quit shivering and was sitting up, wrapped in a blanket, he offered to go to the house to get me some dry clothes.

"That might not be such a good idea," I said. "Thomas and Rachel are with the girls. He has a gun."

"You thought I meant to murder you."

"Yes."

"Did you do this?" He pointed at his office door, the shattered glass on the floor.

"I wanted to look at your computer files. I wanted to see your will."

"My will?"

"Rachel said you told her you were giving Greenville to her and Thomas. She thought it was a cruel joke. I wasn't so sure."

"Did you find the document you were looking for?"

"No."

"Then why did you come after me?" He sounded almost angry. I'd ruined his plans.

"I found Red Boat."

"I see."

"No you don't. Otherwise you wouldn't be trying to kill yourself. I love you, Raymond."

"You thought I was going to kill you."

"And you let me think it. You wanted me to think it. You deliberately frightened me half to death, so you could go off and have your grand male gesture. What were the girls and I supposed to do then, celebrate our good fortune?"

"But I'm not who you think I am. You have no idea of the monsters that live in my memory."

I'd heard enough of his memories. "How much do we get, Raymond?"

He pretended not to know what I was talking about.

"The will, Raymond. What do we get?"

His voice was quiet and sad. "I've left Greenville to Rachel and Thomas. I've left everything else to you."

I shook my head. "You son of a bitch. And you expected me to live with that? Anthony wanted to obliterate me. Frank wanted to own me. But you, you want to break my heart for some fucking ideal and a pot of money. Thanks, but no thanks."

He'd turned away. I wouldn't understand. "You should return to the house," he said. "Your children will be worried."

"I guess you should've thought of that before inviting them to witness a suicide. But I'm not leaving you alone, and I'm not going back to that house without some answers. There're still things I want to know, that I deserve to know. What became of Miles?"

"Miles?"

"Miles, Pearl's son. My son."

He shook his head. "I don't know."

"You don't know?" I reached out and turned his face to me, but still he wouldn't look at me. "You don't know? I thought you knew everything, Raymond."

"I don't know everything."

"Then quit acting as if you do. You're human like the rest of us no matter how much you remember. We all remember enough to be found guilty. I don't remember it like you do, but in my bones I'm sure I abandoned my son. Should I kill myself for that now? Or should I love the children I've got? You're still trying to frighten away the big cats, Raymond. Why don't you just invite us to join you by the fire?"

He looked into my eyes, his face lined with pain. Finally, he shook his head and rose to his feet. "I can't. It's not that simple. I've given my word."

"Your word! To whom? To what? Give it to me, Raymond!" I pounded my chest. "I'm the one who needs it!"

He didn't say anything, just ran his finger up and down his scar.

"What happened when you were sixteen?" I asked him. "You denounced your father, pledged yourself to suicide. What is it, Raymond? What happened to you?"

"I changed," he said quietly. "I finally changed."

"Tell me what happened—you owe me that much. Then you can do whatever you want."

He sat on the edge of his desk, staring at the floor. "Very well. I do owe you that.

"It was Easter Sunday, live television. When my father finished his sermon, I was to recite the Crucifixion from Luke into the camera. The telephone number would be flashed across my chest, and buckets, already seeded with tens and twenties, would be passed through the crowd.

"It was the same pitch he used every Easter." Raymond drew himself up. His voice took on a brittle edge. " 'Remember the wounds in His hands!' he'd shout. 'A carpenter's hands, now broken and useless! Remember the wounds in His feet so horrible that even if they took Him down from the cross, He'd never walk again! Remember the lance thrust into His heart to make sure that He was dead!' " Raymond leaned over me, the imagined congregation. " 'Do you remember?' "

He gave me no chance to answer. " 'Yes!' you'd shout back."

He straightened up, shouting now, raising his hands to the heavens. " 'Remember the jeers! Remember the curses! Remember the crown of thorns digging into your flesh, the blood in your eyes! Remember the tomb, black and cold and stinking of death!' "

He whirled around, pointed his finger at me. " 'Do you remember?'

" 'Yes!' you'd shout even louder than before."

"And then he'd strut around the stage with a self-satisfied smirk, as if the congregation were a bright class, and he their doting master." Raymond acted out his father as he spoke. "And then he'd stop in midstride, as if something terrible had just occurred to him, and look around slowly at the huge crowd as if he'd just seen them for the first time, and they'd fall dead silent. 'But do you remember,' he'd say quietly now, so they'd all have to strain to listen, 'do you remember who it was who drove the nails through our Lord's hands and feet? Do you remember who it was who pierced His heart with a bloody lance? Who cursed Him, reviled Him, bargained for His clothes, and murdered Him—who only came to save us?'

"His voice would drop to a near whisper. His eyes would burn into one sinner after another cowering in their seats. 'Do you remember who it was who betrayed Him for thirty pieces of silver?' Then he'd point them out: 'It was you with your beautiful diamond ring. And you with your fine coat. And you looking to buy some fancy new car to drive yourself to Hell in! And every day you drive the nails in deeper with your lust, pour the gall into His wounds with your greed, deny Him in your hearts!' He'd hang his head in shame, cry real tears for all their sins.

"Then he'd fall on his knees and spread out his arms and tell them, 'But the Lord will forgive all of you, each and every one of you. All He asks you to do is remember who you are, remember what you did to Him, and beg His forgiveness, show Him with a free faith offering that you want to make amends!'"

Raymond rose to his feet and stood before me. "The organ started playing, and the buckets went out, my father still crying on his knees. I got my cue. I could see myself on the monitor. I began, 'And when they were come to the place, which is called Calvary, there they crucified Him . . .' and I couldn't go on. I couldn't take my eyes off all these people digging into their pockets, giving everything they had to my father because he'd just told them how awful they were when he was a hundred times worse than any of them. The cameraman started waving at me, the guy in the sound booth was jumping up and down, the women in the front row had lowered the handkerchiefs from their eyes. My father got up off his knees and came toward me, pretending to be the concerned parent.

"'Stop,' I said, and took out my knife. 'Don't touch me.'

"Everyone was staring at us. I leaned into the microphone and launched into a tirade against my father. I wanted to tell everyone the truth about him, but as I watched their faces looking at him with anguish and concern, looking at me with a knife in my hand, I knew the truth about him didn't matter one way or the other. I was more evil than all of them, more evil than their wildest imaginings.

"I told them that I remembered more than Bible verses, more than the dreary little sins my father used to extort money from them. I told them about my lives. I told them about you and what I'd done to you in graphic, brutal detail. They let me tell it all to the stunned congregation—though they'd cut off the TV feed by then." He gave a sad, ironic smile. "I found out later, the station showed cartoons."

Raymond closed his eyes and sighed, swallowing hard. His voice began to shake. "I threw down my knife, and my father and a dozen of his men took me to a room in the basement and tied me to a chair. My father told me he knew who you were. He said you were a devil come to claim my soul for Lucifer and that he was going to cast you out once and for all. I think he really believed it. All of them prayed to God as he beat me with his belt. My father commanded me to beg God's forgiveness, and He would drive this Jezebel from my heart.

" 'Say it!' he screamed at me." Raymond's voice broke, tears streamed down his face. " 'Say it! Say it! Say it!' " Raymond slashed his right hand back and forth, swinging an imaginary belt. " 'Beg God's forgiveness! Give your life to God!'

" 'No!' I screamed at him. 'No. I beg *her* forgiveness! I give my life to *her!*'

"Then he went for me with the knife. It took six of them to pull him off of me." Raymond bowed his head and began to sob, fell to his knees before me.

I took his head in my hands and kissed his forehead. His scar was a tiny ridge beneath my lips, wet with my tears. "I forgive you," I whispered. "I forgive you."

He shook his head, pulling away from me. "You can't," he said. "No one can."

He wouldn't listen to me. It was mere words. "Give me your knife," I said, and he raised his eyes to me. I held out my hand. "Give it to me."

Silently, he reached into his pocket and drew it out, placed it in my upturned palm, still bleeding from my fall on the rocks. As he watched, I opened the blade, long and sharpened to a fine edge. I could see in his eyes, as he knelt there before me, that if I were to plunge the blade into his heart, he would not resist, that he would accept it as his due. I took a handful of my hair and passed the blade through it, throwing the knife to the floor. I tied the hair in a knot and placed it in his hands, wrapping them around it, holding them tight. "A gift," I said, looking him in the eye. "I love you. Here and now. Don't be a fool. Love me."

He closed his eyes, tears still streaming down his face, and nodded.

"Don't ever leave me again," I said. "Promise me."

"I promise," he whispered.

IT'S BEEN HARD FOR HIM, I SUPPOSE, TO FIT HIS VAST LIFE INTO THE narrow compass of a life with me and the girls, but he doesn't complain. In fact, he seems quite content. We have a small place not too far from Greenville with a few horses and a big garden. Raymond gave most everything else away.

I've just finished my novel and have started another. Raymond too has started taking notes for a book, but he says he's not ready to show me anything yet. He says it will be an autobiography of sorts, though he'll call it fiction.

My favorite thing to do these summer days is take the kids for a ride in the Hudson, around dusk, watch the moon rise over the fields. Raymond always lets me drive. All four of us play the radio-button game my dad and I used to play. Or sometimes the girls ride quietly in the back seat and listen to their stepmother and their stepfather telling stories. Sometimes by the time we get home, they're both asleep and Raymond insists on carrying them into the house, though I tell him they're too old for such nonsense.

Later on, lying in bed, I tell him, "This life we die of old age, together. Next life you can end it however you want."

He laughs and takes me in his arms. "I'll remember that," he says.

Acknowledgments

I'D LIKE TO THANK LIZ DARHANSOFF AND ANN PATTY, WHO have always been a joy to work with; Laurie Bernstein, who, while she came to this project late, provided me with the enthusiasm and guidance to see it through to the end; Katia Brock and Betsy Daniel for information on horses; Bob Renjilian for information on Hudsons; Doug Harnsberger for architectural information; and Rebecca Herald and Bobbe Kriz for information about past-life experiences.

I'd also like to thank the staffs of the following institutions, who (unlike my fictional Historical Society employees) were always most helpful and courteous—the Virginia Historical Society, the Virginia Department of Historic Resources, Colonial Williamsburg, and the Virginia State Library.

I'd especially like to thank my wife, Really, who first showed me that ad in the *Virginia Gazette,* helped me sketch out this book on an envelope, and has been with me every step of the way.